UNRAVELING EMBER

UNRAVELING EMBER

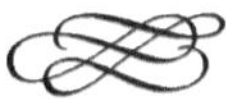

YETSIRA KATSION

ISBN 979-8-9919953-0-6 (ebook)

ISBN 979-8-9919953-1-3 (paperback)

ISBN 979-8-9919953-2-0 (hardcover)

NOTE TO THE READER

WHEN readers hear "romantasy" they don't always think about the possible elements that might accompany such a genre. *Unraveling Ember* is a romantic fantasy, yes, with an emphasis on *romance*. Still, before you start to read, I'd like to warn you about some possible triggers.

Physical abuse, sexual assault, eating disorder, general depression, anxiety, violence, murder, cursing, and explicit sex scenes are all incorporated into this book. Mental health is extremely important and therefore I urge you to consider the content ahead of you before turning the page.

However, if you've ever found yourself stuck between choosing *two* book boyfriends, well then, I encourage you to flip the page and continue reading.

Choices are left to be made.

Or are they?

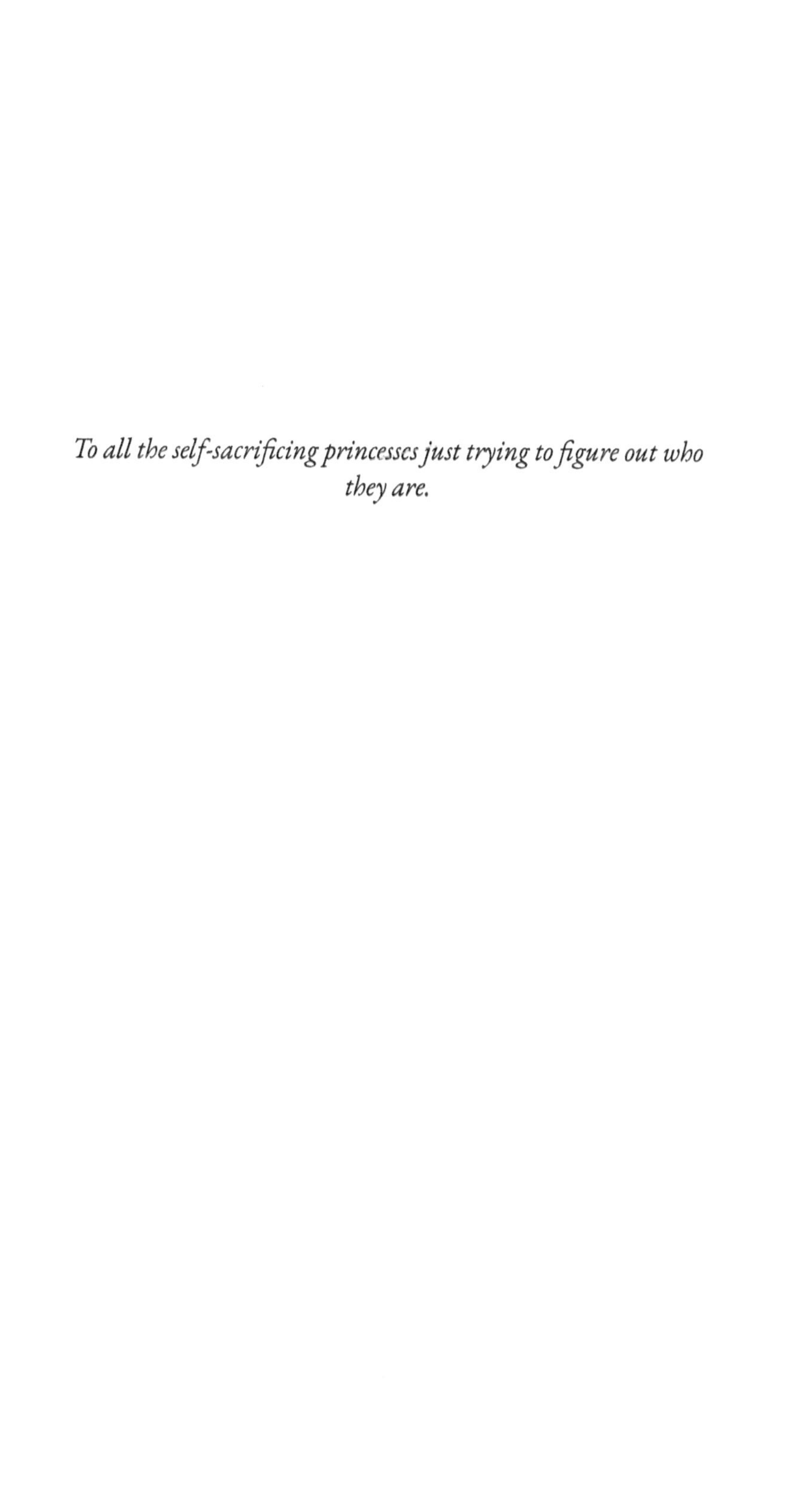

To all the self-sacrificing princesses just trying to figure out who they are.

THE SONGS THAT INSPIRED IT ALL

Klyeria
Linel
Kora
Atravelien
Balle
Agatharea
Wellin
Jeran
N
W
E
S
Lea Sea

PROLOGUE

"You are the Fated Daughter, Ember." No choices. No self-inflicted destiny. Just fate. A life where the duration has already been pre-selected.

"You will be Queen."

"You will reign over the Kingdom."

"You will give your life for this if it comes to it, Ember."

"You will."

You can get used to this type of life, or you can find other ways to make it your own. When the very way you want to live has been stolen away from you, you learn how to make hidden choices that give you a sense of control. Hidden choices that could make you fall in love. Hidden choices that could get you killed.

My story is meant to be my own, not theirs. They aren't the ones holding the quill and ink, I am. Little do they know their "perfect" little Ember won't be so perfect one day. I won't hold my chin so high, I won't comb my hair how they want it, and I certainly won't speak the way they want me to speak. I won't be this broken down princess they hold so high on a pedestal. I'm going to be free. I'm taking my fate back into my own hands.

At least, that's what I tell myself at night before I go to sleep. That's what I murmur to myself to keep going during my lessons.

That's what I let myself so hopelessly believe. That glimmer of hope, that glimmer of me that peeks through is a dangerous notion of the possibility of a different life. A notion that won't exist no matter how many nights I tell myself tomorrow will be different. Tomorrow will *never* be different. Fate has made sure of that.

CHAPTER 1

I'd always wondered what kind of life lived beyond this earth. Was there anyone looking back at me from the stars? Was there anyone also wishing for a different life? Wishing with all their might that they had been born to a different family or even to be born a different species?

Because right now I wish I'd been born a bear or maybe a squirrel. Something that didn't require royal etiquette.

Gods, my back aches.

"Sit up straight, Ember!" Professor Soren doesn't call me by my title. According to her, I haven't earned it. Her scratchy and irritating voice echoes against the stone walls as my back straightens instinctively, my neck muscles tensing as she stalks closer.

Her pasty white skin is so thin I swear it would pierce through if I were to poke it with the quill in my hand. Professor Soren has been teaching us all since we were children and she has always looked like she was on the brink of death. If the wind blew too hard, she'd fly away with it.

"Let that be the last time I have to remind you." She looks over my shoulder and scoffs in disgust. "What kind of penmanship is that?" I bow my chin slightly, murmur an apology in the submissive manner she wants, and continue through the math exercise we're working on. *Fucking bitch.*

I wonder what type of math will be required when I become queen. It could be the middle of the war and I doubt someone would barge into my office asking if I knew how to solve calculus problems.

The sound of quills on parchment fills the silence as she stalks away and I finish the equations with haste. The room is much too grand now for the small group of us. The walls are gray cobblestone cracking from age. The windows stretch from the floor and arch just before they reach the tall ceilings, letting in rays and rays of sunlight. A chalkboard lines the entire front of the room, already donned with the coursework we've gone over.

There are rows and rows of desks, but only a few are full. There used to be bigger classes full of royal sons and daughters, but now there's only eight of us. My court is small, the smallest in generations.

All of us are twenty turning twenty-one soon. Our birthdays are spread across the year. All of our mothers and fathers planned their pregnancies so that we all would be a brand-new lineage of royalty for the Agatharean kingdom. Agatharea once thrived, but since the war with the Klyerian kingdom, our numbers have dwindled significantly. Entire provinces have been wiped by Klyerian soldiers who've sacked the cities and burnt them to ashes. Since there's only us to rule for the foreseeable future, the teaching wing will be empty until we have a new set of heirs.

Throughout the day we have a set schedule of studying. The morning hours are dedicated to everything academic. Math, reading, comprehension skills, our kingdom's history, etc. Then we get an hour break to change and prepare for the second half of the day, which is then dedicated to the arts. We must be extremely knowledgeable, be quick minded, talented, and desirable. The royal sons and daughters are nothing short of perfection once we emerge.

We're in our last year of studying. In fact, we're in the last weeks of it now and the anticipation is unbearable. The thought of never having to look at a textbook again just seems too good to be true. My outer mold is almost complete: proper, innocent, and intelligent Crown Princess Ember. *Little do they know.*

Like magnets, my eyes find Jasper, who's back is to me, placed several rows ahead because Professor Soren knows we would talk too much if he were near. He's wearing a white tunic that hugs tightly to his back and when he shifts, the muscles of his back ripple. *He's your best friend, when did you start noticing his back muscles?*

Jasper's messy head of curly brown hair shakes a bit as he gets stuck on a problem. You can always tell what Jasper is feeling; he has a hard time hiding it. As if he senses my stare, he turns over his shoulder and flashes a crooked smile at me, his dimples making their usual appearance. I scrunch my nose at him in return.

Jasper's eyes are a leafy shade of green and hold thousands of thoughts in them at all times. He shakes his head again and turns back to his paper before Professor Soren says anything. But I could tell in the look he gave me that he's seconds away from giving up and making up some excuse to get out of here like he always does. *You and I both.*

He and I have been best friends since I could walk. Jasper is the safe place I run to when things get too hard. He's always been a breath of fresh air that pulls me out from under the pressure of who I'm supposed to be. Brownies under the willow tree and that silly boy are all I need to escape. My attention is snapped away again when Professor Bitch, I mean Soren, starts speaking.

"Go ahead and place your papers on my desk as you leave. You are all dismissed. Ember, please stay behind once the room empties." She doesn't look up from the papers she's holding as everyone gets up to leave. Jasper throws me an apologetic look before placing his papers on the desk and slipping out the door in a haste to escape the dragon sitting at the desk. A tug in my gut has me glancing at the hall, and for a brief moment I see River, my personal royal guard, standing outside. But I can't stop and stare. *As much as I'd like to.*

She does this all the time, intentionally singles me out in front of everyone and I'd like to kick her teeth in for it. I hate being at the center of her attention or anyone's attention for that matter, but that's what my life is isn't it? Being the heir to the throne?

She doesn't trust me to be the best I can be when she's not watching me. She needs to mold me into something that goes beyond perfection. All of my professors do, courtesy of my parents. But I swear, where there are seemingly no flaws in my performance, she somehow finds some. One hair out of place and I'm done for. There's never been an acknowledgment that I'm doing *something* right. I could get the answers completely correct, and the only feedback I would get is that I didn't do it fast enough.

I stand up slowly, keeping myself steady by holding onto the desk as I rise. *Replace that anger with submission, tilt your shoulders back, and unclench your fists.*

"Yes, Professor Soren?" My voice is even until I see what she's holding and then it falters. My speech. I was told by the queen I would need to have one written and ready for the upcoming Winter Solstice ball. I worked all night on that thing. *I swear to the gods if she—*

"Did you really think any of this would be appropriate to say at the ball?" She doesn't even look at me. Her tone says everything I need to know.

"I really—"

"No. Do not try to excuse this poor example of a speech. You were asked to speak as if you were the queen. Is this how you plan to rule?" She takes the parchment and crumples it into a ball, placing it into the trash bin beside her desk. "Write another tonight and I expect it on my desk in the morning. Do not disappoint me again, Ember. It is all you've done as of recent and neither I, nor the king or queen will stand for it. There's so much at stake and we won't have you messing any of it up. You may leave now." She finally looks at me, her eyes dripping with distaste. *For fucks sake.*

I should've expected that. This is the first time I've ever written something that I actually believe in and of course it's everything she hates. I lower my chin as I walk out of the door, giving her the show she wishes to see. I can't even look at River, I'm too embarrassed by the fact that yet again, he's witnessed my supposed incompetence.

"Keep your back straight and chin up, Ember," the wretch calls, adding to my mortification. As always, River doesn't say anything nor does he glance my way as we fall into step together heading toward the kitchen. So I mimic his unaffected appearance, even if it's much harder for me to keep up the guise.

I take a deep breath as his scent fills my nose with mint and earth. *Gods and goddesses.* There's no scent on earth that could rival the heavenly aroma he wraps me in every time he is near. Professionality be thrown to the hells, I could breathe him in as my last breath and not have any regrets except that I hadn't inhaled him more. But he is my guard, and I am the princess. These are the roles we've been given and the roles we must keep up. *Yet in a heartbeat...*

River is exceptionally tall, and the broadness of his shoulders only adds to the sheer size of him. His guard uniform consists of a sword, brown pants, and a black tunic that leaves nothing to the imagination. The royal crest is sewn into the breast of his tunic, shimmering red against the black. Black leather straps criss-cross across his chest full of throwing knives I've seen him play with for fun when we're in the garden. That's the most he'll let loose of himself. It's quite impressive.

The pommel of the sword is woven in solid gold and red rubies are encrusted into it, looking much too fancy to kill someone with. The light catches on the rubies, shining patterns onto the wall as we walk. I've never seen him without it. I'd love to see him wield it, but he doesn't let me watch him train.

River's midnight hair is a perfect mess of waves that curl over his ears and fall over his forehead, brimming his eyebrows but never covering his eyes, so it doesn't block his view. Though it's rare if I ever get to look into his eyes. He won't look at me. And I'm not sure why that bothers me so much, but it does. I'd never yearned for a man's eyes to sear my skin the way I do for his.

I do know they're an incredible shade of ocean blue. The kind of deep blue that seems impossible, almost like a night sky but when the light hits them, they're as bright as can be. He has facial hair that's trimmed short and neat, and he never lets it get too long. But he never shaves it completely off either and thank the heavens for that. The ruggedness it adds to his appearance is toe-curling. The man is a walking god.

And that's all I know of River—what he looks like and that his duty is to keep me safe, even if that means giving up his life. And for someone who may one day lay his life down in the line of duty, he makes it extremely apparent he wants absolutely nothing to do with me. *Add his name to the bottom of the ever growing list.*

The smell of warm bread fills my nose, and I'm immediately broken from my thoughts. I stop before we get to the lunch hall and River comes to a halt alongside me. With a smile, I peek my head into the kitchen and find Chef Jean.

He is my favorite person besides Jasper. Chef Jean became a second sort of protector to me very early on. Without him, I'm not entirely sure I would have made it to this point.

I watch him fondly for a moment as he loads bread into a basket to be taken to the lunch hall for us. He's swaying side to side along to a song only playing in his head when he notices me watching.

"Primabella! I've made your favorite today!" His soft accent shines through, warming me up. He always says that. He thinks everything he makes for me is my absolute favorite. He's not wrong; Chef truly has a gift for cooking.

"And what might that be?" I walk toward him, reaching for a piece of bread when he slaps my hand away.

"Uh uh uh, you have to wait, but it's your favorite soup.

There's quite a chill today so eat up." He looks me up and down, making a tsk sound. "You're looking too thin; that cold breeze will blow you right away. Go, go sit down, the food will be out in a moment." He shoos me away and I chuckle softly.

I can't count the number of shooting stars I've wished upon to make him my father instead. He's everything a father should be: compassionate, loving, and kind. But alas, the gods have a different plan for me.

I touch his shoulder softly before walking away with River close by. He's always just under a foot away, if not closer, and no one else dares to get too close when he's with me. His proximity is intense, something I keep thinking I'll get used to, but the goose-bumps on my arm and the tug in my core tells me otherwise. *You'd make this much easier on yourself if you didn't think about how close he is.*

River has been my guard for a little less than a year now, getting used to his overwhelming presence isn't any easier than the first time I met him.

I wish things were more comfortable between us. I spend every waking second with him; he's glued to my side no matter where I go. River eats, sleeps, and breathes for my protection, but that's as far as it goes. I've had other guards who I eventually deemed friends. They got to know me, and I got to know them. It added a layer of trust to our arrangement, knowing *who* exactly would be saving my life.

And here I am, almost a year later, and there are only small things I know about River, things that could consider me obsessed. Which I'm not. But I do notice things about him. *Details.* Why wouldn't I? How could I not see the way his jaw ticks when Jasper puts his hands on my shoulders and shakes them—something Jasper's always done. Or the way he clenches his fists so tight that his knuckles turn bone white when I disappear into the office with my father.

There's no way River knows what happens inside. My father is nothing but discreet. The bruise on my back is purposefully placed for that matter. I think it's that River doesn't like me out of his sight. River is diligent, that I'll give him. He takes this job seriously, maybe too seriously.

And despite the fact that he's made his stance on our professional relationship very clear, I can't help the pull I feel toward him. There's a burning just under my skin whenever I'm near him. And that scent? Addicting. But, like everything else, I tuck all of that away into a little box deep, deep down, where it can gather dust and be forgotten. Or at least I try. *Princess and guard.*

We enter the lunch hall, and River sits near the entrance, scanning the room. Tall windows allow the sunlight to pool into the space, illuminating the long tables that fill the room. Only one table is needed to seat the eight of us, but at one point all of the tables were filled with students. The design of our castle, alongside our kingdom, is simple. It's always been about keeping things clean and elegant. It's bland if you ask me, but no one does.

I keep my head forward as I walk toward the table full of all my peers. There's a spot open next to Jasper, reserved at the end of the table. Jasper immediately smiles once I get close.

"There she is. What did Soren say?" he asks, already munching on a piece of bread as I sit.

"Oh you know, the usual," I mimic her accent and sneer, "*You are an abomination, Ember. Truly a rat could've written a better speech than you.*" I laugh softly at the end, not entirely offended by Professor Soren's words; they're not new and nothing compared to what I've heard before.

Jasper chuckles before responding, "No one gets her accent like you do. I'm sorry, Em." He offers me a sad smile before taking another bite, crumbs dropping onto the table.

"She wants me to rewrite the whole thing," I mumble as I glance up at the servants placing a bowl in front of each person. The delectable smell of vegetables and chicken broth wafts up to my nose through the steam. My stomach rumbles silently at the sight and smell. But there's a soft voice in the back of my head telling me I shouldn't finish this meal today. *I'll never be thin if I keep eating the way I want to.*

"I read the speech, Ember, it's perfect. I doubt she even read it. You know, she does that sometimes." He grabs a spoon, and I watch as he brings a spoonful of broth to his lips. *His lips now, Ember? Who are you?*

"I don't know, Jasper. She was staring right at it." I break the bread, dipping a piece into the broth before taking a bite. An array of flavors hit my tongue, and I'm overcome with satisfaction. My body sags, a soft groan escaping my lips. "My gods, Chef is magical." I could be having a horrible day, but Chef's cooking can always make it better. My back straightens before anyone has a reason to say anything about my lack of composure. Jasper glances at me before clearing his throat and looking back at his bowl.

"Well, do you still have the second copy?" He turns to face me again. I had written the speech twice just in case anything were to happen to the first one. Sometimes my papers or homework have a weird habit of disappearing right before I'm supposed to turn them in. Robert, one of my peskier court members, has very sticky fingers.

"Yes, of course I do." I take another bite, a bit of broth dripping down my chin. Jasper dabs at it with a cloth before it spills onto my dress. The action is thoughtless, like he was naturally meant to do it. My lips part slightly as I watch him. These moments have begun to feel timeless—just two people who have been around each other for way too long and know to expect each other's mishaps. He pulls away quickly before anyone can see the interaction.

I'm not supposed to have close relationships with anyone. Obviously, I do. But the Crown Princess is supposed to be elegant and responsible, and she can't do that if she's goofing around with her peers. That's why, very early on, I was isolated from them. I was raised much differently from the life my court knows.

If anyone were to go back and report these types of interactions, it would be my head on a stick. Everyone knows Jasper and

I are close, though, and no one really notices moments like these since everyone else at the table is too engrossed in the food or themselves. I lick the rest of the broth off my lips, keeping myself from smiling before going back for more.

I find myself glancing at River, who's staring straight over my head. His shoulders are taut, and there's an emotion etched into his features that I can't quite decipher from here. He dips his head and resumes eating. I must be imagining things.

"Then just hand that one in, and we'll see if she actually read it. And if she did," Jasper pauses, having pulled me back to the conversation, "well, then you can call it a mistake and have another one handy."

"Is this a wager I hear?" I cock an eyebrow at him, setting my spoon down.

"I suppose it is. I truly don't believe she read the speech. Do you?" I nod. There's no way Professor Soren didn't. Cocky dimples make their appearance. "Then we have a wager, if I win, you're doing my homework."

"And if I win, you're helping me sneak out this weekend." He chokes at that. I pat his back softly as he recovers, gaining the attention of a few of our classmates. *Oops.*

There's a little more than a quarter left in my bowl and I decide to stop there. That's enough for today. Hopefully, the queen will notice a few pounds difference and be satisfied with what she sees. I know I'm not as thin as the other girls. Where they might be naturally petite, I have natural curves in my hips and chest. And though my waist is small, it's not enough. I'm a normal girl, but normal for my mother is too fat and not perfect enough. *I'm never enough.*

"No, Ember." He gives me a stern look, setting his spoon down, pushing his now empty bowl forward.

"Yes, Jasper." I look up at him through my lashes, hoping and pleading with my eyes.

"Bloody hell, woman, you're going to get me kicked out, or

killed, or both." But he's smiling, so I know he'll do it, even if I am wrong about Professor Soren.

"Thank you." The servants come around to gather the bowls and utensils. A servant I've come to know as Jane, a girl somewhere around our age, perhaps a few years younger, hesitates when she sees my bowl still slightly full.

"Princess, would you like a few more moments?" She doesn't quite meet my eyes as she looks up.

"No love, thank you though." I smile warmly at her, hoping it eases the tension I can see in her shoulders. She gathers my bowl and rushes out. Jasper has an odd look on his face, but it's quickly erased when he notices me looking.

"Ready for the fun stuff?" he says as he stands, offering his hand to help me up. I take it softly, ignoring the warmth that spreads from his hand to mine. *Seriously? Warmth?*

"Oh boy, am I." My voice is flat, unamused. The second half of the day can be hit or miss. Some days, I relish in the dancing and playing my cello. Other days, I find myself so utterly and completely exhausted that I can't seem to put the same energy day in and day out to play the role we're expected to.

As royal sons and daughters, we are expected to be perfect in every way possible. We must be smart, talented, beautiful, and flawless. We must be able to dance, sing, and play instruments with ease and grace. We must be prodigies. Why else would we be allowed to have such royal standings if we weren't the best of the best?

Jasper grabs my shoulders, shaking them, and I can't help but chuckle. Whenever he does this it always manages to make me feel a little better.

"There we go, that's the spirit." He gives me another one of those crooked smiles. It's that smile, and the shake of my shoulders, that I'll forever be grateful for. *My sweet, silly boy.*

Once we reach River, I steal another glance up at him and swear I see a flicker of movement in his jaw. Sometimes I feel like I imagine it, because then his face is back to its brutally beautiful, stoic state, like emotion doesn't exist in him.

"I'll see you in a bit, Em. Get out of that terrible dress." Jasper winks and walks away with the rest of our classmates to their dorming quarters, which are in the same building of the castle that holds the teaching wing, simply referred to as the Main Quarter. My room resides in a separate building, off to the east side of the Main Quarter, referred to as the East Quarter. I was put there to ensure "no distractions would come" at any time of day or night. *To keep me a virgin is more like it.*

River and I walk in silence, and I wish I could say it was comfortable. He opens the door for me, and I brush past him, my shoulder faintly rubbing against his lower chest. My skin and his are completely covered in cloth, but I swear I can feel the heat from his as if it was my own. I move quickly away from him, hoping that he didn't notice. The door shuts behind us, and I'm met with air much colder than I expected. I welcome it at first, thankful for the cold cooling down my heated cheeks.

The East Quarter is meant to be strictly used for meetings and holds a couple of offices, so no one is ever really in there. It's bittersweet in ways. I love the privacy it provides, but the isolation is lonely. River's room is stationed across from mine, and that temptation alone is an entirely different dilemma.

We reach my building quickly, and to avoid having to walk past River again, I open the door myself. River grabs hold of it from behind me, and I'm all too aware of how he makes sure not to touch me again. Just like I'm aware of how he never looks at me or speaks to me. He stays right behind me as we walk up several flights of stairs. I shove all of it to the back of my mind and enter my room without looking back at him. *Guard and princess—act like it.*

The door shuts behind me, and I let out the harsh breath I had been holding. How could someone so intimidating and cold be so beautiful and magnetic? It doesn't seem like anything fazes him. It's as if nothing can penetrate the titanium wall he's put up to keep people out, and all I want is to break it down. *Just to get a glimpse.* I immediately sit on my bed and lay back, pure exhaustion taking over. I have a little while yet before I need to be back in the Main Quarter. *A little nap wouldn't hurt...*

"Ember." A low, rich voice sounds in my ear. I must be dreaming because voices that delectable don't exist. I hum softly, rolling onto my side, eyes still shut, drifting off again.

"Ember Lauraine." That same voice says my name again, and my body absorbs it all over. But when I realize that it didn't come from a dream, my eyes fly open, and I'm met with an icy gaze. *Fuck.* I rise up, immediately brushing my hands over my hair, which I'm sure is standing up in all different directions. The clock above the fireplace tells me I'm probably going to be late.

"You have ten minutes before we need to be back." River's voice hums in my chest. I don't have time to register the fact that River actually just talked to me. *He's in my room.* With that, he walks back out and shuts the door behind him.

Bloody hell. I race over to my closet, stripping from the awfully itchy dress I'm ordered to wear all day, quickly dressing into a loose white tunic I'm allowed to wear for our dance lessons, and a pair of old, well-worn leggings. They allow me to move freely from the confines of a dress. There's a small hole forming in the knee, but so far no one has said anything. I slip on a pair of my dancing shoes and rush into the bathroom. My hair is as crazy as I thought. *Lovely.*

Long, wavy black hair tumbles down my shoulders, resting at the bottom of my back. I quickly comb through it with my fingers and re-wrap it in a low bun again. A few curls frame my face, but I don't have the time to tame my hair anymore. I rush to the door, throw it open, and start running, knowing that River will be right behind.

Jasper and the rest of our classmates are already waiting in the dancing hall, and thankfully Professor Kryle isn't in the room when I arrive. Otherwise, I'm sure I would've heard something about how being on time is actually being late and blah, blah, blah. I take a deep breath, settle next to Jasper on the floor, and begin stretching.

"What happened to you?" Jasper sounds like he's trying not to laugh. I shoot him a look that could kill.

"I fell asleep." I sigh and lean over my right leg, resting my head on my shin as I stretch each side out as deeply as I can. The muscles in my back stretch, and I have to grit my teeth to bite through the pain radiating from the bruise on my upper back.

"Ember? Sleeping? Who's ever heard of that?" Jasper chuckles, leaning back on his hands. I can feel his gaze on me as I switch to my left leg.

"Ha. Ha. Very funny. Thankfully River woke me up; otherwise, I would've slept through supper. Last night was rough." Jasper's eyes go wide at the mention of River.

"He actually spoke?" he whispers. I laugh softly; his astonishment is *very* warranted.

"Yeah, he did, my *name*. Actually, my first *and* middle name. He gave me ten minutes to change and get here on time." I sit back up and bring both feet inward into a butterfly stretch. "I think that's the second time he's ever spoken to me. The first being when he was introduced to me." *He likes to communicate in nods and blank stares.*

"Wow. What a guy." Jasper's voice is flat, and I glance over at River, who is, of course, still scanning the room. What he's looking for, I have no clue. My stomach does a little flip when I think about the way he said my name, but I ignore it. *Be professional.*

"Well, I'm not dead, so he's doing a good job so far." Jasper gives me an incredulous look as we stand.

I look around again, wondering where Professor Kryle is. He's never late, and with the Winter Solstice ball coming soon, I'm sure he wants us all to be perfect for the dance he's been teaching us. As if reading my thoughts, Jasper turns and says,

"You're extra lucky today; Kryle isn't on time to yell at you about your timely untimeliness." I laugh at that and stretch out my upper body. "But I'm sure he'll say something about that hole in your knee; how dare you show off that much skin?" We both look at the hole that looks bigger now than it did a second ago.

"Oh, how sorry I am! Forgive me if my skin makes it difficult to contain your lust! We both know how charming the kneecaps can be." We both fall into a fit of laughter that is soon cut short when Professor Kryle finally walks into the hall a couple minutes late.

"Forgive me, lords, ladies, and princess; the king needed to have a word with me. Have you all stretched?" Professor Kryle is a shorter man, with a stomach that hangs over his pants. He's balding a bit in the back of his head, but appearances aside, he's a brilliant dance instructor. We all nod and go to get into our positions.

I'm paired with Jasper to begin, but throughout the dance I will end up with the other three boys as well. All of us interchanging our partners with such grace and such fluidity that the audience may not even catch that we have switched at all.

"Let's begin then, shall we?"

CHAPTER 2

Professor Kryle is quiet for a moment, studying us all until he is content to have the pianist begin. Jasper's hand is fitted into my waist while the other holds mine tightly. There was a me before this that never noticed Jasper and how he touched me. Now it's like my body is eagerly awaiting some type of physical attention. *He's your best friend; get a grip.*

I tighten my hand on his shoulder and take a deep breath as we begin to move. Everything turns into a blur as our movements become one. The melody seeps into my veins, and just like that, I'm lost in it. It awakens something in me. The concoction between the harmonious movement and the music electrifies my nerve endings, making me feel more alive than I have in days.

"Excellent job, Ember!" Professor Kryle's gruff voice pulls me out of my trance, and I offer a small smile of gratitude toward him. He's the only professor that compliments any of my work.

Soon I'll be shifted to Robert. Robert isn't always easy, and I can't fault him for that when he's been raised by pompous, self-indulgent parents. Of course, he was going to come out a bit of an ass. He has short, cropped brown hair and plain, dark brown eyes, but Robert has a certain swagger that only he can get away with. *Wait, is that a booger?*

I falter for a moment, too caught up with the bat hanging in his cave, and nearly step on his foot. He shoots me a look of disdain as we quickly recover.

"Watch it, I just bought these; they're suede!" he whispers harshly. I roll my eyes before peeking back up at him. *Yup, that's a booger.*

"You might want to blow your nose after this," I suggest, trying not to laugh because now Professor Kryle is throwing visual daggers our way. Robert scoffs before sniffling, shaking his head at me.

It's not long before I'm being swept into the arms of Easton. Easton has beautiful, dark brown skin and kind honey brown eyes that match his equally stunning sister, Viola. They're twins with identical, kind hearts. He's often reserved, but also has quick wit and a strong sense of leadership that will be good at the core of our court.

"Gods help his province," Easton mutters, watching as Robert continues to sniffle with Daisy now dancing with him. Easton's arm stretches as we separate from each other, shortly before returning to one another in a spin.

"It's the goddesses he needs—a woman's touch." I pause, looking up at Easton while we move in sync. "And her intelligence." We both laugh quietly, dipping our heads to smother the sound. Robert means well, but he needs work. I glance at Professor Kryle, who raises an eyebrow at us. I smile at him before being guided into another pair of arms—Cameron's.

Cameron is a fiery, ginger-headed fellow who shadows everyone—almost like a little duckling. He hasn't quite figured himself out yet, and I'm not sure what that says about him as a leader, but I know he'll get there. Cameron is quite the skilled dancer, as we push each other to be our best when we dance together. I dare say he's better than Jasper, but I would never tell Jasper that. *I'd probably be murdered on the spot.*

Cameron doesn't say anything as we dance—he doesn't have to; his body says enough. Cameron skillfully lifts me off the ground, spinning me before slowly lowering me with my hands on his shoulders. Then I'm finally being shifted back to Jasper, who turns me before my back collides softly with his chest. I'm spun back around once more before the piano softens, and every single girl is being dipped, toes pointed, with our partner leaning over us carefully.

My eyes collide with his green ones, and I notice he's breathing a little hard, but not from exertion. I become fiercely aware of Jasper's hand on the outside of my thigh, keeping my leg up. I try to still my own breathing with little success. *Stupid lungs, stupid body, stupid hormones.*

After several seconds, Professor Kryle claps his hands, finally releasing us from our position. Jasper's hand briefly drags up the side of my thigh before disappearing from my leg. *Gods have a little mercy on me.*

"Absolutely excellent everyone! There are a couple things I must go over, but with specific people. Go ahead and take a quick water break, and we'll return shortly." Professor Kryle walks over to Easton and Daisy. Daisy is as dainty as the flower she's named after—petite, with short blonde hair; she's beauty and sweetness wrapped into a human body.

Parched, I walk to the pitchers of water and help myself to a glass, and then another. I lick the water off of my lips when my eyes wander to River on their own accord, like they normally do. He stands beside the door, staring straight ahead, away from me. But the need to talk to him is much too great, so I saunter over, mustering the courage I hardly have to do this.

"Thank you, River." Quickly, I add, "For waking me, that is. You could've let me sleep, and then I would've missed this and gotten in trouble. Which would've been fine; you're not my babysitter. I mean, actually, you kind of are, seeing as you make sure I don't do anything dangerous and all." *Shut the* fuck *up, Ember.*

My voice cracks slightly at the end, and I don't look at him as embarrassment floods my cheeks again. I still can't believe he came in to wake me. How did I not hear him? Or the door? I look forward, and for the faintest second, I meet his eyes in the reflection before he looks away.

"No thanks necessary, Ember." There it is again—my name rolling off of his tongue. It takes every bit of my will not to close my eyes and lean my head back to commit it to memory. The deep timbre of his voice, the slight rasp—gods what I'd do just to make him talk more. *Walk away, now.*

One foot in front of the other, I find my way back to reality and Jasper, who happens to be talking to Professor Kryle.

"Oh good, Ember. Please, I want you and Jasper to demonstrate the beginning for the class. Show them how it's meant to be natural, how you're meant to show that you're one organism moving together. Each time you trade to another partner, you have to demonstrate the becoming of one. You two do it best." Professor Kryle is excited; he's practically vibrating as he talks about his choreography. Jasper flashes me a cocky look, and I scrunch my nose at him.

"Of course, Professor Kryle," Jasper and I say at the same time. Professor Kryle smiles knowingly and moves to the piano. He says something undistinguishable to the pianist, and she nods. We take our normal spots, assuming our position.

"No, move to the center," Professor Kryle demands, then turns to the class to address them as we move to the center and look at each other. "This dance is about unity between all of you. You will all rule different parts of this kingdom one day, and you need to show that you can do it in such a way that it doesn't feel like eight different rulers—but one." He turns to the pianist and nods.

Jasper and I breathe as one, exhaling on the same breath. I catch sight of Sierra in the mirror for a moment, and she gives me a single nod. Sierra is the woman my mother wishes I was. The woman I've been compared to my entire life. She is light where I am dark. She has long, silky blonde curls, bright twinkling blue eyes, and porcelain skin a goddess would be jealous of. Her body is composed of perfect ratios, and anything she wears fits her like a glove.

It wasn't any easier for her being compared to the Crown Princess growing up. Things weren't always good between us, but I think we're coming to an understanding lately that it's behind us. I don't blame her, and she doesn't blame me.

I close my eyes, letting my mind melt away again. The piano starts, and we move with it. Soon, all I can hear is the music, and instinctively, I let my body match the rhythm.

Jasper moves right along with me, our movements feeling as though they're one with the melody. When it comes to the part where we normally separate, we don't. I half expect the professor to stop us once the beginning is over, but when he doesn't, we just continue.

I lose myself in Jasper, and for reasons I don't understand, I become hyper-aware of him this time around. Every move, every touch, every press against each other is something it wasn't before. Something it shouldn't be. But I don't deny myself this. *It's wrong, but I'll let it feel right.*

Everything rushing through me starts to pour into Jasper, and I hear his breath hitch in my ear at the intensity at which this dance has taken. The well within me that I usually keep so tightly locked peeks open, relishing in the dizzying adrenaline that's awakened the power deep inside. Any thoughts of Cameron being better than Jasper have been swallowed up by what's happening to us right now. *Keep it together. Push it back down.*

By the end, his green eyes are staring down at me intensely, and I can't look away. When did Jasper and I get like this? When did things change? He used to be the boy who would wipe his boogers on the bottom of my dresses, and now here we are, breathless and full of tension that *never* existed before. I glance down at his lips. *When did those get so full?*

I flicker back up to his eyes as we begin to straighten out. The silence in the room is thick, and I really can't breathe properly anymore. Gods, and all our peers witnessed that? Has someone poisoned my food to make me a horny bastard?

I take three big steps away from Jasper, putting desperately needed space between us. He turns away, and I can't see the expression on his face anymore, but I see the tension in his neck and shoulders. At least I'm not the only one stressing here. Best friends don't act like this.

"Exactly. EXACTLY. That!" The professor turns to the rest of our peers. "Take yourself out of it; let the music work its way into you. Stop thinking so much! You all have grown up together. Look around. These are the people who know you, who you can trust. Stop letting differences and little things affect your work of art." Some are nodding; some are staring at me or Jasper.

I look down at the ground, suddenly finding it *so* interesting. What I would do for some cold air on my heated face right now. Maybe River will...

Where is he?

I look around the room and find that he's not in here. Normally, River doesn't ever let me out of his sight. Or, well, I mean, he doesn't *look* at me, but he's always within feet of me, always ready at a moment's notice. But then I notice he's standing outside the door instead, his back leaning against the frame. *He never does that.*

"Alright, let's run that a couple more times before you're all split up elsewhere." Professor Kryle's voice pulls me back, and I shake my head. I'm sure there's an explanation. We run the dance several more times, and by the end, whatever I had been feeling earlier completely dissipates, and my breathing feels better. *See, he's just your sweet, silly best friend, nothing more, nothing less.*

Needing an excuse to go to the kitchen, I grab the empty pitcher and some glasses before wordlessly slipping into the hall. It's empty, which makes me even more confused as to why he was out here. River seems more wound up than he normally is. There's a tightness in his shoulders that makes me want to reach out and touch them to release whatever tension is there. But I don't do that. I can't do that. *Stop thinking about your guard. Stop thinking about your best friend.*

We begin to walk together, and I have to refrain from gripping the glass so hard it'd break. Jane, the servant from earlier, moves to take it from me as I enter.

"Don't worry about it, Jane. Thank you, though." She nods quickly and goes back to rolling out more dough for dinner tonight. I place the glasses in the sink and grip the counter for a moment.

That can't happen again. Things between Jasper and I *can't* change. No matter how much I might crave being wanted, I can't sacrifice the one thing in my life that has always made sense. The one person in my life who's constant. *Not even to just feel something.*

But here I am thinking about going there. Wanting something I shouldn't just because my body hungers for it. *But your heart isn't in it.*

I busy myself washing whatever's in the wash bin, letting the sting of the hot water pull me from the swarm of thoughts starting to rage through me.

"Jane, will you or anyone pack my dinner up for me, please? Once I'm done, I plan to take it to my room." I keep my voice calm and steady as I face her, drying my hands on a rag.

She's wearing a long gray maid's gown that's just a bit too long. It's soiled at the bottom from dragging on the ground. Her hair is short; it just barely brushes the tops of her shoulders, and the lines of stress and exhaustion are already apparent under her eyes. I hate asking any of our servants to do anything for me; they're terribly overworked—something I hope to change when I take the throne.

"I can just bring it to your room, Princess." She smiles quickly at me, an attempt to let me know that it's no issue for her.

"No, no that won't be necessary. I'll come by and pick it up, thank you. Take a moment to rest once you're done with the dough while you're at it. Just take a moment to breathe." I lay my hand softly on her shoulder, squeezing it. She visibly relaxes under my touch and offers me a tired smile. She'll try.

Fuck, I need to get going. I try not to look at River as I pass him on the way out. I fail. Miserably.

I should care that I'm late, but at this point there's a familiar numbness spreading through me, and I can't find a reason to care.

The last thing set in my schedule for the day is playing the cello while everyone else meets for singing lessons with Professor Karlen, a bright, spunky woman who produces the most incredible-sounding lords and ladies. Except for me.

Typically, everyone who comes from a royal family can sing to some capacity; the talent just happens to run in each separate family line. *If you have a voice that yearns to be listened to, then you have a voice that can reign over the lands.* Or so the archaic tradition goes. Except, from a young age, when I would attempt to sing, no one could hear me. I could hear myself clear as day, and I *swear* I was singing.

There's nothing more frustrating than begging to be heard, and no one being able to listen. No matter how loud I belted, no one could hear a single note.

No one could figure out why. Every doctor in the Agatharean kingdom was called to solve the mystery that was my voice. How could she speak but not sing? Was she lying to the entire kingdom? She had to be faking it. I heard it all.

Eventually, to lay down the growing rumors, one doctor chalked it up to some weird phenomenon with the vocal cords, and they chose something else for me to do. Another musical talent, so that everyone could be distracted with that instead of my failure.

They put me in a room with various musical instruments. Piano, violins, violas, cellos, brass instruments, woodwind— everything you could think of was there. They let me *choose*. It has been one of the only choices I've ever made in this life. I walked around the entire room, touching each and every instrument, waiting for one to jump out at me, to speak to me, and tell me it was the right one. Once I got to the cello, I was completely taken over with the sense of déjà vu. I knew. Somehow I knew this was my instrument; this was meant to be the voice I apparently didn't have.

But I do have a voice—a singing one. I've since learned that there are some things better left unsaid. Keeping secrets is the only type of control I have.

The door to the office we use for my lessons is slightly ajar when I arrive. My cello sits in the corner beside a chair that overlooks the gardens. I murmur a quick apology to Professor Endapyn as I take my seat. He is a frail, older man with skin as wrinkled as old leather. He's as cruel as Professor Soren, and the next two hours are going to go by painfully.

I stopped trying to achieve perfection a long time ago. It doesn't exist. But as harsh as Endapyn can be, he is equally brilliant. He's cultivated me into something I never thought I'd be with this cello.

River closes the door, and the sound draws my eyes to where he stands beside the entrance. *He must be so tired from standing all day. He should sit.*

But I brush the thought away as soon as I see the look on Professor Endapyn's face. He looks angry, and impatience is rolling off of him in waves. I quickly take hold of the cello; the dark cherry wood glistens in the setting sun. Lamps and candles have been lit in preparation for the sun's disappearance, illuminating the room in a warm glow.

Find the balance in the bow. Take a deep breath. Adjust your posture. Close your eyes. Slip into tranquility.

Before I start, the professor lets out his first reprimand of the night.

"You're holding the bow wrong, Ember." He bites out my name, as if my name somehow scalds his tongue like tea that's too hot. I look Professor Endapyn in the eyes as I adjust my hold ever so slightly. He nods curtly, and I resume my starting position once again. My eyes flutter close as I begin the piece.

Sometimes when I play, all I can feel is the cello; all I can hear is the melody. It feels like my veins are soaking up the notes straight into my blood. I wonder if I can get there today. I need to get there today.

"Stop." I let out an exasperated sigh and look at him. "You're getting sloppy. Focus, Ember. Stop thinking too much. If you keep thinking about what note you're playing next, then you're always going to be behind. You're not a child anymore, so stop playing like one. You know better than to be late to class; don't test my patience by being late to your entrances in the music."

Professor Endapyn leans back in his velvet-green armchair once again and gestures for me to start from the beginning.

I look at River, who's staring straight ahead, once again over my head, outside the window. I look out the window, trying to see what he sees, but fail to see anything other than the dusk sky.

It takes everything in me not to growl at the frustration that's grown into a dull roar within me. Gods, I have no idea what's gotten into me today. But I hone in on it instead. I slam my eyes shut and let go finally.

The melody soon fills the air, and with it, my anguish. I pour myself into the cello, and the cello pours me out in a concoction of sadness and harmonies. Thoughts of my future, my secrets, River, Jasper, my parents, my professors, and everything that weighs so heavily on my conscience disappear as I finally lose myself in the strings. Time becomes irrelevant, and once I finish the song, I'm not entirely sure how much time has passed.

"Again," he says, and that's how the night goes. Numerous times, I'm stopped mid-song and asked to change the smallest details. I try my best to keep myself in that harmonious sweet spot, but the more I'm interrupted, the harder it is to let go so easily. After a long and grueling two hours, I'm finally released.

My fingers are throbbing from the consistent attack on the strings of the cello. The hairs hanging off of the bow are just as much of a representation of how I feel. The cello is well-loved and taken care of by the staff, so it'll be brand new and tuned when I return tomorrow. Sometimes, I come in to play her on my breaks or at night when I can't sleep.

I roll my neck, stretching the muscles there. But when I stand, an involuntary groan escapes at the tenderness in my back. Between the dancing and now keeping it so straight, it aches more than it did earlier. *Gods, I'm lucky he didn't break a rib back there.* River bristles at the sound, and my head snaps to him at the movement.

"Are you okay?" he asks, but almost apathetically, as if this is a question he's required to ask. Which, I suppose, in a way, he is. Still, the sound of his voice is enough to make me forget the pain. *Three times in one day. This day must be a dream.*

"I'm fine, just a long two hours sitting in the same position." I flash a smile at him, fixing my tunic as I walk past him out the door. "You know, you don't have to stand during that lesson. It's okay to rest, River." But no answer comes—just a stiff nod, and that's it. *Ugh.*

We grab my dinner, which has been graciously packed into a sack, and make our way hastily out of the Main Quarter toward my room. I walk as fast as my feet will carry me, eager to put space between me and that damn building. Once we reach my room, I stop, and with my back to him, I murmur,

"Goodnight, River." And with that, I close my door, not waiting for a response I know won't come.

CHAPTER 3

Do I always make good decisions? In my eyes? Yes. To my guards? Probably not. But what they don't know won't hurt them. So, once I'm sure River's asleep—or at least I hope he is—and I know Eli thinks I'm asleep, I begin my escape for the night.

Eli is my night guard. He's been assigned after one of the servants slipped into my room one night when I was around twelve years old. I'll never forget the glint of the knife in the moonlight. My regular guard at the time, Myka, came running from his room at my screams and tackled the servant down. The servant kept screaming that he wanted to take something the king and queen loved, the way they had from him. I still don't know what they took from him. I've always tried to find out.

There was no way for him to know that my parents didn't love me like that. That loss wouldn't have avenged him in the way that would've made him feel better. And when the king wanted to sentence him to death, I asked him not to. Since it wasn't public news yet, they instead had him sent to a prison in our southern province, Wellin. Wellin is located near the Lea Sea which is named after the Goddess of the waters, Leana. The marks I received for defending him were...extensive.

Eli is the tallest and strongest man I've ever met. A beast of a man. He has to duck a little to enter any door, and his tunics are always barely hanging on by the seams. But he also happens to be extremely gentle and smart—not that brawn negates intelligence.

He and I have shared many late-night talks when I can't sleep. I've learned that Eli sometimes meets male suitors when he's released from duty in the mornings. Vicariously, I live through him and his quest for love.

He lives with his parents because they've gotten too old to properly take care of themselves. He has three sisters, though only two are living. That's something he doesn't talk about much. He loves a good fight. He swears he never starts them but will "always properly finish them." Eli is caring where it counts, but he can also be very serious when he has to be. Tonight, I'm probably going to piss him off if he figures out what I'm doing. *So, don't let him figure it out.*

This isn't my first escapade. I started doing this several years ago after meeting a woman named Olga in the closest village to us, Balle. Though I've offered to pay for housing, for food, for anything—she refuses. So we compromise, and I bring her food whenever I can slip out without being noticed. She's often offered guidance in ways I hadn't known I needed.

After quietly wrapping myself in a midnight-blue cloak, so dark it matches the night sky, I let the well within me open, and the rush of power fills me eagerly. There's always a certain ache that I carry in my core, at the center of my very being, from keeping my magic locked up. But it's necessary to my survival. No one can know what I possess.

However, I have learned that small uses of magic every once in a while are helpful to keeping that well locked up. So, with little effort, and simply just glancing, the wicks of every single candle in my room go out. The small release practically has me purring in delight.

I walk over to the window and listen for Eli. The shadows of his boots remain unmoving, even as I silently open the window. If the gods can just stay on my side a little longer, that would be wonderful. It's not often they side with me.

Laying my hand against the cold, gray stone of the castle, I beckon the vines into an organized ladder, which lies flush against the wall, ready to hold me as I quickly climb down. When I land, my boots make a soft thud on the gravel. But no other footsteps come rushing toward me.

"Not too bad," I murmur to myself, flicking my hand to make sure the vines go back to how they were so no one notices a thing. Getting out of my room isn't the hardest part—leaving the castle grounds without being spotted by another guard is.

All I have to do is make it to the outer wall that leads to the edge of Atravelien, the forest. Once I make it there, I'll be safe to begin my trek to town. There's a door covered in overgrown plants, vines, and weeds that's been forgotten about. This is how I get in and out. I just coax the overgrowth out of the way to get through.

The magic is coursing through me in full waves now, and once that lid is opened, it's hard to close. But after practicing control for almost sixteen years, I've got it down fairly well. And it's all thanks to Chef Jean.

When I was a young girl—right around five, when my powers first kicked in—I remember walking into the kitchen, hungry for a snack. There was a large basket of apples sitting on top of the long prep table. The kitchen was empty, and I was much too short to climb up.

At the time, I didn't really understand my power. I just knew if I thought of something, it would happen. But I had no control, and I was lucky that, up until that point, no one had noticed the random candles flickering on and off—or now, the apple floating through the air toward me because I was hungry.

But I wasn't alone. Had it been anyone else, the course of my life might've gone very differently. I'd probably be used in ways unimaginable for the king and queen. But Chef Jean was there, watching me with curious, somehow understanding eyes. He knelt down beside me as I took an innocent bite of that sweet apple.

"I can help you," he said. "But it has to be a secret. Just between you and I. No one else can know, Primabella." I remember nodding eagerly. *A secret! How exciting!* This is where my love for secrets began. Only I knew about them; only I could control who knew and who didn't.

He taught me to imagine my magic as a box with a lid and a lock, and every time I felt the power rising, I had to stomp it down. Shove it. Push it into that box and keep it there, where no one would ever know. He's never told me how he knows how to do it, and I stopped trying to ask.

It was hard. As a little girl, all I wanted was to use it to my advantage, but even then, the wrath my father showed toward me was enough to scare me into keeping it hidden.

I open the door as quietly as possible, but the old hinges creak. *Oh, for fucks sake.*

But no footsteps sound, so I scramble out and into the freedom of the large forest that looms above me. Atravelien is named after our Goddess of nature, Atravel, who's beautiful, strong, and unmerciful. It stretches on for an eternity from east to west, with seemingly no beginning and no end.

Slinking into the shadow of the trees, I become enveloped in Atravelien's signature scent—sweet, yet sickening. Somewhere between floral and rotten. And despite having wrapped myself in layers, the chill of the forest seeps into my bones. It's not long before my teeth begin to chatter, something Jasper teases me about relentlessly whenever I get cold.

Balle is a village of merchants. Merchants of any and all kinds, even the underground black market types they think we don't know about. But if there's something special you want to find, you come to Balle to find it. If you want to make quick money, you come to Balle. It's why there's an influx of homeless people here trying to make a living. With the war, so many have been displaced, and my parents have refused to do anything to aid them in rebuilding their lives.

I try to think twice before I complain about my life when I think about theirs. I can endure my suffering a bit longer until I reach the throne. Every bruise. Every mark. I remind myself it's for them one day.

Whispers through the leaves weave their way into my ears, making chills that have nothing to do with the cold crawl up my spine. Atravelien is rumored to have unspeakable creatures dwelling within its shadows. We've lost so many soldiers here without any knowledge of who or *what* has taken them. Some bodies have never been found, no trace of their belongings, and no tracks to follow. They go in and never come back out.

Atravelien surrounds our castle from the north and partially encircles us from the east and west. North of our castle stretches the forest until you reach the kingdom of Klyeria—the kingdom we're currently at war with.

My father, King Nicholas Canmore of Agatharea, and King Bleren Blackwood of Klyeria, are at odds over that patch of Atravelien between their two kingdoms and who should be able to control it. Their fathers started the war, and they've continued it. The reason for the war? Heavens if I or anyone know. At this point, it's all been lost in translation.

The most common consensus is simply for more land. For control. To conquer.

I don't believe that.

Atravelien provides some safety from each other—but not enough. Soldiers still penetrate the other's land, and we attempt to take what's not ours. We've forbidden any villagers from crossing through the forest to Klyeria, and Klyeria has done the same. Only our soldiers make the crossing on missions to scout the forest for Klyerian soldiers who dare to sack our villages, leaving them in ash if we don't find them in time. This war has been raging for four decades now, and no white flag has dared to wave. I plan to stop it as soon as I take the throne.

A branch snaps, echoing through a suddenly silent Atravelien. *Not. Good.*

Self-preservation eludes me as I stop and peer into the darkness. Suddenly, a large stag steps into a small patch of moonlight, and I freeze. His antlers form a perfect "U", the smaller branches spreading in a beautiful array of symmetry. He turns his head toward me, and I hold my breath, soaking in the stunning grandeur of the animal.

I'm lost for a moment.

I swear it takes a step toward me, but then another branch breaks in the distance, and just like that, the stag is gone, disappearing into the inky blackness of the forest.

The longer I spend here, the more dangerous this quick trip becomes. I've let too much time pass as it is. Once I see street lamps, I step away from the edge of Atravelien and back into the comfort of civilization.

I take this moment to begin pulling all the magic coursing through me back down. The pull and stretch of it against my skin aches as I shove it way, way down. It feels like it protests, as if it's almost sentient on its own. But once I'm able to wrangle it all in and close the lid, I relax a little, knowing that it's put away—out of mind, out of sight.

The further I get away from the castle, the further I get away from the Ember I pretend to be. The sweet, innocent princess I've been raised to act like. The girl who submits, who talks softly. She doesn't curse or want for things she shouldn't. At least, they don't know that she does.

I slip a little into me—or what might be me. I don't know who that is anymore. I just know what I'm not. And it's not the girl confined in those gray walls.

An array of smells hits my nose—spices, garbage, warm bread from somewhere nearby, probably baking for the next day, and something sweet that fills the air.

Olga usually sits on a bench at the edge of the town square, overlooking the courtyard. Whenever I come to find her, she's always there. The same place, day in and day out. As I round the corner that leads to our spot, I'm met with emptiness. She's not here.

My first instinct is to panic, so I jump straight to the worst conclusions. She was murdered. Mauled by a bear because she strayed too close to the forest. She's fallen ill somewhere. *Relax.*

I sit on the bench and wait. Maybe she'll show up.

There's a pond in the middle of the square, with fish and various birds that use it as a home before they migrate. Just beyond it are a couple of men outside the town's most famous tavern, Marb's. The glow of their cigar butts illuminates their rugged faces, worn from hard labor and a long day. I keep my hood up, covering my face and my identity. No one needs to know who I am or that I'm out here so late and alone.

Several minutes pass, and as I watch the men, my knee begins to bounce up and down rapidly. I'm so caught up in the whirlwind of terrible things that could've happened to her, I don't notice the footsteps approaching on the cobblestone road. A soft hand touches my shoulder and instead of jerking with fear, I'm overcome with a sudden sense of peace. I already know then—Olga is here.

She's covered in a dark cloak, dirty and in tatters. Her skin is tanned and wrinkled, but in a soft and comforting way. Age has been kind to her, though I don't truly know how old she is. Her hair looks like it was midnight black at some point, but now it has been taken over by stunning silver streaks.

"Child, what are you doing here so late?" Her voice is soothing, with an aging rasp at the end of her words, and a chastisement that belongs to a grandmother.

"I wanted to see you. I brought you some food." I rummage through my sack and pull out the pouch, handing it to her. She holds it in her lap, peering inside.

"Ember, did you eat *anything*?" My head snaps over to her. Swallowing silently, I nod.

"I had them pack me extra food on purpose."

"You're a terrible liar." She puts the pouch back in my hands, but I refuse to take it.

"It's a waste with me; with you it'll be nourishment." I place it gently back in her lap, placing her hand over the cloth and holding it there. "Please take it," I beg.

She stares at me a long while before nodding in defeat. This is often how our meetings begin.

"So stubborn." She sets the sack beside her, shaking her head. I laugh softly.

"I prefer the term headstrong; it sounds better." She smiles again at that. It falls silent between us, but it isn't uncomfortable. Sometimes when I come here, we just sit. We sit and watch the town square until it's empty, and I have to go again. And somehow, I leave feeling better than I did before—*healed*, in a way, without having released a word.

The street lamps glow softly on every corner, keeping the courtyard well lit. Every so often, a breeze comes through, causing them to dim for a split second before roaring back to its original flame.

"What's going on in that head of yours?" Her voice is barely above a whisper. She always has a way of pulling the truth out of me.

"I..." I don't know where to start, or where to stop. "I'm losing myself. I can feel it. Little by little, day by day, there's this numbness taking over. Then there's this rivaling part of me, aching to live. Aching to *feel*. But the road has been made clear. This is what my life is supposed to be. And I will endure it until I can set my people free. But is it wrong to wish there was another way?" I turn and look at her, studying the planes of her face. A small voice in me wants to hear her tell me I'm wrong about my life. But when she hesitates, something in me hardens.

"It is never wrong to wish to escape the confines of abuse, my dear. It won't always be like this. Make it to the Winter Solstice ball. After the ball, things will change." She looks away from me, her gaze drifting up toward the night sky.

"Fate doesn't change," I say simply. I stand, and she looks at me like I've just wounded her.

"Ember..." She says my name with a throat full of emotion I can't quite detect.

"I'm sorry, Olga. It's not your fault my life is like this. I shouldn't expect you to have answers that could change my life or unseal the decisions already made for me by those blasted gods above us." I retie the belt of my cloak.

"That's it right there, Ember. Only you have the power to unseal it. Only you can let yourself out of the tiny box. Only you can take your life into your own hands. It's always been you who must make the change, Ember." She stands as well, taking my shaking hands in hers. I don't look at her as a single tear falls down my cheek. *Fuck, where did the tears come from?* Gingerly, she lifts her hand and wipes it away. My body calms at her touch, and I lean my head into her palm, closing my eyes, relishing the moment.

"You're just the bud of a flower right now, but you're about to blossom in ways you didn't think possible. I just know it." But before I can even think about what that means, the sound of horses trotting into the square interrupts us. *Godsdamn it, can't I just get a break?*

The castle guards come to a halt in front of Marb's and begin questioning the men first, who begin to point at us. *Fuck.* Olga turns to me, her face frantic. "Go now. I don't know when I'll see you next, but look inside you to remind yourself of who you are." She kisses my hand, then walks behind me toward the guards.

I don't look back as much as I want to. Instead, I walk nonchalantly, stuffing my hands in my pocket as I round the corner of one of the brick buildings. There, I pause to listen.

"Who was that you were just with?" a guard demands.

"That was my granddaughter; we were just chatting, and time got away from us. I don't get to see her often, and she was just visiting. Even brought me a cooked meal." Her voice is so calm, even I believe her for a second.

"Where did she go?" The same guard pushes further.

"Home. You gave us a bit of a scare." Then something shifts in her tone. "Who are you looking for?"

"The princess. She's snuck out of her room," a different guard responds in a monotone voice. My jaw drops. The guards usually never release such information. If people knew I was out, it could put me in even more danger. They're trained to keep their missions a secret. *Some fucking guards.*

"She's not here. Check her room again; perhaps you missed her." There's almost a sing-songy tone to her voice as she suggests to them what to do. It's an odd way to talk, but somehow it works. Which is unlucky for me.

Their horses take off a moment later. *Damn me to the hells; I'm going to be in so much shit.* Now I need to double back before the guards make it to my room. If I even can.

I run as fast as my feet can carry me, but I'm no runner. And I certainly do not train for this. I don't train at all. But it's peril I get there, so I ignore the terrible burning and gasping in my lungs as I push on through the forest.

Like a blast through me, I let the magic work on intuition, moving the vinery to the side to enter the door. It squeaks again, and I want to scream so many un-princess-like curses at the gods and goddesses. But I swallow my anger and wave my hand to place the plants back as they were.

There's nowhere to hide as I walk through the gardens. I can't even pray to the gods to not be spotted because, well, they're obviously not on my side right now. A guard rounds the corner. Of course he does.

I throw myself behind a bush, leaves falling into my hair, and gods knows what else. *Please, please let there be no bugs in here.* I hold my breath as the guard walks through, checking the wall where I presume he heard the squeak. Once he doesn't find anything, he turns and walks back to where he came from.

One, two, three, okay, run.

I book it to my wall, waving a hand to make that ladder again, and the vines quickly assemble into my path to safety. *Hopefully.*

I begin to ascend, making it to my window sill. Without removing my hands from where they're holding me, I ease the window open. It's beginning to feel almost too good to be true when I make it inside and no one's waiting for me. My mistake happens when I wave my hand to let the vines go back to normal, and shut the window at the same time. The magic is rushing so much that I don't control how much I give into it, and the window shuts a little too loudly. *Great.*

There's some shuffling in the hallway, and I waste no time throwing myself into my closet. I strip out of everything, getting myself back into a long-sleeve nightgown that drapes down to my shins. There. I never left. I was always here. In my...closet. *I'm fucked.*

I'm walking out when my door busts open and in spills Eli and River. I smooth out my nightgown before looking up at them, acting startled. But I'm also still breathless, and I can hardly cover that up or the flush in my cheeks.

"What are you both doing?" I say at the same time that Eli says, "Where the hell have you been?" Slowly, I let the proper, innocent Ember slide back into place. I let the softness seep back into my voice, and just like that, the princess is back here in the castle.

"I was just in my closet. Why are you in my room?" I look only at Eli, refusing to look at River.

"Right, and I'm the King of Agatharea," Eli deadpans. "I was in here looking for you. I knocked to see if you needed anything, and there was no answer. When I came in, you were nowhere to be found. And I checked the closet." He doesn't raise his voice, but I have properly pissed him off, and I'm not making this any better by trying to lie.

I have no answers. None that won't give away my only means of escape. The thought of losing even a fraction of freedom is killing me. Eli must see it on my face—the slight panic starting to build. But before he can respond, River steps forward.

My entire body goes still. Suddenly, my lack of oxygen has nothing to do with my run.

My efforts to keep my eyes off of him become futile as they slowly drag up to his face, which seems even more devastatingly beautiful in the moonlight.

He's still clad in his nightwear, and technically, he doesn't have to be here, so I'm confused as to why he's up. Eli's on duty; so he could handle this. Handle me. River's hair is messy—the good kind of messy, the kind that means he whipped himself out of bed for me. But *why?*

As he stops in front of me, he reaches up, and I flinch away from him. But the hit doesn't come. I don't know why it ever would. River would never, and has never, laid his hands on me. His hand pauses as he searches my face, searching my eyes for an answer to my reaction. Then I watch as he softens, but only for a moment, before he gingerly reaches up and takes something from my hair. A leaf. Then the cold River returns.

"Stop acting like a child and tell us where you were. Now." *Like a child.* My heart constricts in my chest, but I lift my chin, trying to act unaffected. River flicks the leaf down to the ground and takes his place at Eli's side again. I let out a harsh breath.

"I was in the garden." I look River in the eyes this time, challenging him.

"Try again. We had guards down there, and they didn't see you." This time, Eli speaks. It looks like River has reached his word count for the day. My gaze shifts to Eli.

"I was. That leaf is from the Weary bushes that only reside in our garden. I was down there because I needed some fresh air. I hid when they came around." Eli looks down at the leaf resting in front of my bare feet.

"How did you get down there? You didn't come past me." Eli is confused now, because I'm making sense. Those bushes are sacred to our garden. Every Summer Solstice, they blossom with the most beautiful flowers, which last only a short period of time —flowers that glow with bioluminescence in the moonlight.

"I climbed down." I don't offer any more explanation than that. Behind my back, I wave my fingers in one short motion so River and Eli can't see. I can feel my magic bring the vines back up to my window, but not in the same organized fashion I usually do —just enough so that it's believable.

"Impossible." Eli moves past me to the window. River stays where he is, watching Eli and not me. I turn and stand beside Eli as I open the window.

"I climb down the vines and then climb back up when I'm done. That's it." Eli leans over, looking at the vines and then me. He shakes his head at me.

"Why would you do that, Ember? You could seriously injure yourself. You and I have been to the garden many times. Why would you go on your own?" Eli's anger has been replaced with true worry. It softens me for a moment, rendering me silent as I look between him and out at the freedom I know I'll never have again.

"I just needed fresh air. On my own. That's all." I tell them softly, bowing my head in defeat.

"Do that in your room. Crack the window open. Don't climb down it." Eli sighs in frustration. "You can't be out there alone."

I say nothing.

What is there to say?

There's no use in trying to explain the freedom I yearn to have. So, I nod and murmur an apology. River is the first to leave, slamming his bedroom door shut. I look at Eli, who pauses in my doorway.

"We just want to keep you alive, Ember." And with that, he shuts the door behind him.

That numbness seeps further into my chest, taking root a little bit more than it did before.

How do you keep someone alive when they're already barely living?

CHAPTER 4

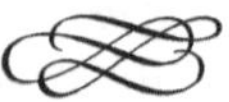

Over and over again, I've replayed Olga's words, and still, they make no sense to me. *It's always been you who must make the change, Ember. You're about to blossom in ways you didn't think possible.*

What does that *mean*?

I tried to sleep, but it kept echoing in my head, pestering me awake relentlessly.

And then there's River. *Stop acting like a child.* The rage those five words ignited in me makes me want to pound on his door and let him have an ear full.

I'm not a fucking child. He doesn't talk to me or look at me. He barely acknowledges my existence, and then has the audacity to talk to me like that? He's the child. *Learn how to use your words, River, then we can talk. Asshole.*

My feet pad silently on the cold floor as I pace back and forth. The sun is starting to peek up from the horizon, slowly and lazily rising. The light begins to pour into my room through the windows, shining onto the walls in a blazing glory.

With my inability to sleep, I rewrote another speech—one that sounded like the king and queen. One that talked of conquering, of power, and all of the self-righteous things my parents indulge in as the royalty of Agatharea. One that would please them.

Beside it is the spare copy of the one I wrote from my heart. One that speaks of ending the war. One that speaks of building the people back up. One that promises personal involvement in bettering their lives.

Gods, I actually hope Jasper is right.

My legs carry me into my closet, where I turn on a lamp to illuminate the space. Gowns of all different types line the walls. The queen makes me wear gowns two sizes too big to hide the curves of my body. She hates to see them. So many of the dresses don't fit right, making me look not much like a princess and very much like a sack of potatoes laying in Chef's kitchen.

I drag my hand along the forest green gown that just arrived a few days ago for the Winter Solstice ball. This is a huge celebration for us, the next line of royal lineage. So, the most talented seamstress, Melana, was ordered to the castle to make specially ordered gowns and suits for us all. I was the last to sit with her.

"I have a special dress I made just for you." That's when Melana flipped to a whole new page in her well-loved sketchbook. Princess etiquette says you shouldn't leave your mouth hanging wide open. But, how could I not when I saw her design?

Somehow, she'd captured the deep forest green of Atravelien that seemed impossible to mimic in real life, but I had no doubt she'd be able to find the right fabric to do it. The arms were covered in lace vines and floral that carried over onto the chest and bodice, which dipped into a low V that I'm sure would never be allowed. But how could I say no?

The dress tapered off to the floor in silk, not billowing out like some of the other dresses I'd seen. No, this one went straight to the floor from my hips, pooling in the back in a small train. The back was exposed, scooping just at the bottom. And one of the best parts? There was a double slit drawn—one for each leg. *My parents would kill me for wearing it.*

Which is precisely why I nodded immediately. She took my

measurements there and said she'd return with all the dresses soon enough. And when she did, I wasn't allowed to try it on. I even asked her how she'd know it would fit, and she told me,

"Trust me, darling, I know it will. But the reveal is the best part. Just wait." So I have.

Instinctively, I reach for a plain black dress, much too big for me. One that swallows me whole and leaves everything to the imagination. But when my hand touches the dress, I freeze.

It is so often that I obey without hesitation—so often that I play my part as the submissive princess. Wear the things they want me to wear. Do my hair how they want it done. Talk how they want me to talk.

But there's something *restless* inside of me. And it's becoming harder and harder to ignore as it battles with the numbness that usually hijacks my body and pushes me through the mindless acts of playing Princess Ember.

That restlessness is dangerous, and it's pushing me to do things I normally wouldn't otherwise.

But godsdamn, does it feel good—even if it's just for a brief moment.

So, I turn and grab a different black dress. Still plain, but it's the right size. It's one I wear when and if I'm in the public eye with my parents. Which is rare, but when that happens, they at least want me to look somewhat put together.

The gown hugs me everywhere it should before falling to the floor from my waist. There's a sense of confidence that fills me, and it awakens something else in me—something I can't quite put my finger on yet. With some flats on, I slip out of my closet and head over to my bathroom to deal with my hair.

The air is still a little steamy from the bath I took, but the mirror has started to clear from the fog. Normally, I'd have to pull my hair up. But the freedom I feel just from leaving it down feels too good to tamper with. I look at myself, and a small smile forms on my lips.

I think I actually like who I see today.

Her eyes are the color of auburn leaves during the heart of the fall season, as molten as the embers of a fire floating into the night sky, glowing almost as bright as the sunrise climbing over the horizon. They're the reason she got her name.

Her hair falls to her waist in soft, midnight waves. There are layers and layers of them, some tendrils framing her face, which is laden with freckles and a pert nose that she constantly scrunches.

Her skin appears stark against the dark fabric, pale from spending so much of her time confined in these walls. But as a little girl, when all her time was spent outdoors as much as she could muster, she was as tan as could be. As if she were made to be in the sun, absorbing all the rays the sun was willing to give her.

With wide hips, round breasts, and a small waist, she still stands apart. Thick thighs and a round bum aren't the standards here. But today, she hides none of that. An hourglass figure is nothing to be ashamed of. The healthy weight in her arms and at the bottom of her stomach, which isn't as flat as the others, is okay because it's *normal*.

At least, that's what I try to tell myself when the thoughts get too loud, too dark, or too much. I try to be careful. I try not to skip too many meals. But the queen's words are loud above all else.

I use some of my favorite perfume before finding myself content with what I see. There will be consequences. I was already expecting them for last night, so I might as well make them worth it.

Once my things are gathered into my satchel for the day, I approach my door, grabbing the handle. But it's *his* voice that halts me in my spot.

"Did you check on her this morning?" And I hate myself for it, but I step closer, putting my ear to the door to hear River better.

"No, I didn't. Back off, River. I'm sure she's fine," Eli says quietly, not wanting me to hear.

"Did you check on her at all to make sure she didn't leave

again?" He sounds... worried? No. That can't be right. Maybe annoyed that I interrupted his beauty sleep last night, sure. *But not worried.*

"I trust her." Guilt pierces my heart for last night. I make a mental note to offer him a more authentic apology later before walking over to my desk. The chair makes a loud noise against the floor as I push it inwards—loud enough they'd know I'm in here and awake.

I wait until I hear Eli leave before walking back to the door to open it. *I will not look at him. I will not talk to him. I will treat him as he does me.*

River follows behind me silently, but the air is thick with tension. He's still upset with me. I don't know why he can't let it go. I'm fine. Everyone's fine. I open the door that leads through the garden I said I was in but don't hold it open for him. Maybe I'm being petty, but I'm pissed too. I hear him catch the door with his hand, a small sigh escaping his lips. *Don't laugh.*

When we reach the Main Quarter, I may or may not try to do it again, but of course, he's ready this time. He takes the door, and the shiver that racks through my body has nothing to do with the cold draft and everything to do with his proximity. *Keep it together. Be a tough bitch.*

I'm so focused on being Miss Unaffected that when we round a corner, I don't notice the servants bustling through with carts. River, who of course *is* paying attention, immediately grabs hold of my arms, pulling me back into his very hard chest. He yanks us out of the way of the oncoming traffic, saving me from sure injury.

His hands aren't on my bare skin, but they're scorching me as if they were. I can feel the rise and fall of his chest as he breathes almost as rapidly as I am. And for a moment, we don't move. We stay there, stuck. Frozen.

Say something, Ember. Tell him you're mad. Tell him to talk to you. Tell him you're not a child. Tell him to treat you like a person.

His fingers tighten on my arms for a moment, and all of the

words in my head empty as I hone in on them. But then reality hits and time resumes. What seems like minutes was probably seconds, and he releases me all too quickly.

"Keep walking." And I obey. Not because I'm the submissive princess everyone knows me to be, the one who does as she's told.

No.

I listen to River for an entirely different list of reasons.

With a renewed haste, I find myself in the kitchen in no time.

"Good morning, everyone." My voice comes out surprisingly even. Servants look up, and a few smile; a few say good morning back, and a few just nod and return to work. I snatch an apple from the basket and hop up on a bench off to the side.

"Primabella! Good morning! Why aren't you in the dining room?" He glances at the apple I'm eating while he starts to chop some of the other apples to put into the oatmeal they're making.

"Just wanted to see you, and it's warm in here."

"Ah yes, winter is so close, I think the first snowfall will be tonight. Do you want me to serve you here, then?" He's already pouring oatmeal into the bowl, not waiting for my answer. Cinnamon fills my nose when he brings it over, and my stomach growls loudly.

He takes the apple from my hand, looking at it with a shake of his head before replacing it with the bowl he just made.

"Bon appétit, Primabella. Please finish your meal this time." He sits beside me. "Jane tells me you haven't been eating." I glance at Jane, who looks at me apologetically but also with concern.

"It's nothing to be worried about."

"Is it my cooking?" Chef fiddles with his apron.

I take a quick bite of the oatmeal, and I don't refrain from groaning with pleasure. Who knew something so foul-looking could be so delectable?

"Heavens no, you know you're the best we have. You know..." I look over to where River stands just outside the door, well within earshot. "It's nothing, Chef, I promise."

"If you say so, sweetness. Enjoy! Let me get back to work

before the rest of those scoundrels come crawling in here." He laughs as he stands up.

He returns to the other servants and helps them take everything out to the dining room. The room goes quiet for a moment.

I relish the silence while I eat. It's not easy finishing, but I do my best to push past the dark clouds that shroud my vision as I near the end. When I'm done, I move to the sink and do the dishes like I did yesterday to pass time. My thoughts consume me as I scrub the bowls in hot, soapy water.

"Ember!" I jump, startled at the sudden noise. The bowl drops back into the water, and I turn around with my sleeves lifted past my elbows, hands wet.

And there stands my mother, Queen Eloise Canmore. "Ember, what are you doing?! Washing dishes?! You shouldn't be in here. Leave the dishes for *them*, that's what they're paid for. And what are you *wearing*?" Her voice comes out in a rush of disgust.

"A dress?" The words come out dripping with an attitude I didn't intend to have and immediately regret. I begin to dry my hands, averting my eyes.

"Do not speak to me with that tone," she hisses through her teeth.

Make yourself small. Bow your chin. You are below her.
But I'm not. And I'm sick of acting like it.

"All I am doing is helping. A queen is a woman of her people. Who am I if I'm not to be in the same places, doing the same things as them? I cannot, and simply will not, rule this kingdom from the throne and have everyone else do all of my dirty work." My tone is calm, collected, and strong. There's no bite, no attitude. Just grace.

She's taken aback by my words. This is not the Ember she raised. Her throat rises and falls as she swallows.

"Very well then." She brushes something imaginary off the front of her modest white gown. My mother is a very beautiful woman. Her skin is still smooth despite her age, and her hair is a beautiful shade of blonde, almost gold. Her eyes are a pretty hazel. I'm told my eyes come from generations before them in her lineage. Otherwise, I don't resemble my mother in the slightest. I've been told I look much more like my father. She clears her throat. "You're to be in your father's office after you're done for the day. Do not be late. Lose this attitude before you arrive. You don't want to upset him." With that, she leaves.

I half expected her to smack me like she has plenty of times before, but when I look around, I realize there are several servants still in here. Can't have them know what they're really like, now can we?

I'm about to turn and take my leave when a small figure blocks my exit.

"That was amazing, Princess. Thank you for your help." Jane gestures to the dishes as I pick up my bag from the ground by the bench and sling it onto my shoulder. "I truly can't wait to see you in that throne instead of her. She says she pays us well, but we're all struggling. We all appreciate your kindness. Her, on the other hand..." She trails off, straightening up and offering me a weak smile.

"There's no need to thank me, Jane. It's the least I can do until I can get on the throne and get you all fair wages." I pause as a thought hits me. "Jane, would you care to join me tomorrow evening? I was going to go to the library and could use some company to pick out my next book. I've noticed a few novels in your apron from time to time. We can meet here after dinner. After we clean up together, can we go?" Jane hesitates at my offer.

"Is that allowed?"

"I don't see why not. So, tomorrow, yes?" I glance at her over my shoulder. *Please say yes.*

"Yes, Princess. I'd like that." Her excitement shines through her smile as she nods eagerly.

"Ember. Just call me Ember."

"Everyone is dismissed. Ember, you stay." Professor Soren sits at her desk while everyone leaves. She's been oddly quiet today. No comments on my posture. No comments on my work. Just quiet teaching.

I wait to rise until everyone's gone, but Jasper's taking an excruciatingly long time gathering his things.

"Sometime today, Mr.Wellington," she snaps. Jasper shuffles out of the room immediately. I try not to chuckle as I walk up the aisle of desks and stop once I reach her desk.

She's holding the same speech from yesterday.

Well, I'll be damned.

Jasper was right.

"For once, I'm actually quite impressed with you, Ember." Her voice is surprisingly gentle. "This is excellent. I will let the queen know I approve of this one. You may take it back now; I made a few markings for grammar. Rewrite it so you have a clean copy for the Winter Solstice ball. However, I suggest memorizing it." She lifts her hand with the papers, and I reach to take it, but then she pulls it back for a moment.

"I hope you know that I've only ever put pressure on you to shape you into the smartest person here. Amongst your peers, even you must be the best of them all. Otherwise, any of them would be suitable to be king or queen. You *must* be perfect. I'm starting to see it in you, finally." With that, she hands me the papers. My hands shake as I take them, and I'm too stunned to hide their tremor.

"Thank you, Professor Soren. For everything, I suppose." I offer a half smile politely, and she nods. I take that as my cue to leave and rush out of the room.

Holy gods—

I let out a bit of a yelp as two hands grab my shoulders,

pushing me into the alcove of the stone wall. The cold seeps into my back, and I look up, stunned, into a pair of seemingly frustrated green eyes.

"What the hell, Jasper?" He's got me caged in with both hands on either side of my head, so I can't really go anywhere.

"Can we just—" he starts.

"We can't—"

"Just listen—"

"But Jasper we're—"

And so goes our typical spats where we anticipate what one another is going to say and talk over each other. Truly, it's a gift and a curse. Something I love and hate about us.

But Jasper has forgotten one minor, yet major, detail in his ambush.

River *was* standing ten feet away by the entrance of the classroom, but somehow he crossed that distance in seconds. Without warning, Jasper's ripped off of me and thrown across the hall like he weighs *nothing.*

He lands in a heap, nearly knocking his head against the wall on the other side. That sight nearly has me seeing red. The well inside me bursts open, and it takes every bit of my will to close it before I send River flying on his ass, too.

"River." His name snaps off my tongue like a band. He whips around to look at me, rage flashing in his eyes, but it fades just as quickly as it came. "We're just talking. I'm fine. Back. Off."

His fists clench tightly, so tight his knuckles turn bone white. He turns to Jasper who's getting up and dusting himself off.

"Lay your hands on her like that again, and I won't be so forgiving," River says with such authority and such ferocity, that I have to blink a couple of times to make sure I didn't just imagine that. Jasper turns pale, nodding quickly.

River looks at me. He truly looks at me for a moment, and I realize he's assessing me for any injuries from the yelp I let out. The intensity of his gaze is so overwhelming that *I* have to look away. Once he's satisfied, he walks away, giving us a wide berth of privacy, but not enough that I'm out of his line of sight. Jasper sighs in relief, turning back to me.

"Gods, that man is intense." He shivers.

"Are you okay?" I look him over with worried eyes. Gods, River flung him like a rag doll.

"Oh, I'm fine. That was nothing." He chuckles, but I know he's lying. I won't press him on it, though, because I know it's more his pride that's been wounded than anything else.

"I'm sorry about that, but Ember, what's going on? Are you avoiding me? You didn't come to dinner. You apparently snuck out on your own last night, which you said you wanted to do this weekend. Why the rush?" He doesn't let me answer; he just prattles on. "You didn't come to breakfast this morning. You were about to skip lunch. You won't even *look* at me." His voice cracks, but he's not done yet, so I stay quiet, letting him continue.

"I don't know what that was yesterday, but I know you felt it too. I'm just trying to figure out what it means for us." His forehead leans against mine for a moment, and it's not intimate. It's simply an act of exhaustion, as if this has plagued him as much as it has me. It's that little movement that clicks things into place.

"Jasper, we spend all our time together. I think something like this was bound to happen. But I don't want things to change. I don't want to lose you. You're my best friend."

He's all I have, and if I lose this, what do I have left to lose? What would I become?

I wrap my arms around his torso and he sighs in relief, pulling me closer. One hand grabs the back of my neck, holding me firmly against his chest as he murmurs against the top of my head.

"You won't lose me, Em. You've always had me, and you always will." His promise sinks into my soul, branding me with relief that nearly brings me to tears. *Gods, please not him. Anyone but him. Don't let me lose him.*

He pulls back just enough to look down at me with my favorite crooked grin. "You're my best friend. If in ten years we both haven't found love, let's just get married. Otherwise, you're right. I've thought about it, and on second thought, we're just a couple of horny bastards." I burst out laughing before offering him my pinky. He hooks it with his.

"Deal." I return his smile, scrunching my nose at him.

Sweet, silly boy.

CHAPTER 5

I'm staring at the thick wood grain of my father's door, meant to keep all his secrets from being heard. I have to go in. There's no getting around this.

But this never gets easier, and the fear wrapping around my throat is starting to choke me. River stands unmoving behind me for as long as I wait, never questioning why I've waited so long to knock. The ache in my back has subsided, which is a nice reprieve from everything else. I'm not sure if it's the power that thrums in my veins that I have to thank for, but physical pain doesn't stick around as long as it should.

Without thinking, I raise my hand and finally knock.

A gruff voice from the other side answers, incoherently beckoning me inside for whatever consequences await.

My father's office is large, with the back wall being entirely made of windows, so he can get a good view of the front of the castle, who enters, and who leaves. Bookshelves line both sides of the other walls; with books I'm not convinced he's read. And there's one other door that leads somewhere I don't know, beside the bookshelves.

King Nicholas Canmore—the man I resemble, with short, black, waved hair peppered with grays and cold green eyes I hate looking into. He doesn't bother looking up as *I* walk in, but when River steps in behind me, his head snaps up.

"River, you can stand outside." River nods obediently and closes the door behind me. I hate to admit it, but without River, my fear grows. In his presence, I feel the safest. In this man's presence, well, I'd rather spend the night in Atravelien alone.

"Ember, in two weeks' time, the Winter Solstice ball will happen. Approximately two days after that, you, your mother, and I will be visiting Klyeria." The breath I was holding lets go quickly.

All my training remains on high alert within the walls of his office. In here, I don't dare step out of line, no matter how much I ache to stand up to him. But the question burns my tongue like tea that's too hot, so I can't help but ask,

"Is that safe?" We've been at war for so long, lost so many men, it just doesn't seem right.

"Of course it is, are you questioning my decisions?" He stands up, walks around his desk to the front, and leans against the edge of it. He crosses his arms and looks at me pointedly. I swallow, keeping my voice soft and quiet.

"No, sir, of course not. I apologize." I bow my head, waiting for his response. He must be telling me for a reason; otherwise, why tell me so early?

"We'll be going without River or Eli. I need you to be on your best behavior. It is important that we show up with an air of superiority. We won't have many guards at all, in fact. I want to show that bastard that we're not afraid of him." *But you are. This castle is patrolled twenty-four/seven.* "We need to make you as presentable as possible. The next queen must look and be at her best. Your mother mentioned today that she thinks you need new dresses, and quite frankly, I agree. Stop slouching." Instinctively, my shoulders straighten back and my chin lifts slightly.

When I meet his eyes, I'm met with a blatant look of regret. And not because he constantly has to reprimand me.

My father wishes I was anyone else but who I am. He wishes I was a son. Hells, he probably wishes I was Jasper. But he ended up with me, and every day, I'm a living reminder of his failure to have birthed a better heir.

"What else do you need me to do? Is there anything I can help with for the trip?" Why are you telling me this? What aren't you telling me? He swallows, and everything about him hardens even more. He stands up straighter.

"We've put bars on your windows. You think the guards didn't tell me about your charades last night? When will you *learn*, Ember? There will be extra patrols at night from now on, just to be sure you're not out whoring around. Gods know what you were up to last night. I can't have you ruining this for me. I've worked much too hard for you to tear it all down." The anger rolling off of him is tangible in the air.

And I absorb every bit of it.

If he's going to hit me, I'll make it count.

"Have you ever thought maybe, just maybe, if you just let me live a little, I wouldn't have to do half the things I do?" My hand turns into a fist at my side.

"You're lucky I don't chain you up in your room until the ball. At this rate, that's exactly what I'll do if you keep this up. If the law weren't written as it is, I'd have you held down, spread your legs, and make you give me an heir because that's all you're good for. Unlike your mother." He's come to stand right in front of my face at this point, and I know the blows will come soon. I can already feel them, so the next words feel like the heavens as they roll off my tongue.

"Fuck. You."

I expect a punch to my ribs, maybe my stomach. It's always blows to my body, so no one will ever know. But when he slaps me across the face, hard enough to knock me to the ground, I almost laugh.

Blood blossoms on my lip, and I know it's been busted. This is exactly what he usually avoids. He doesn't like to hear the whispers through the halls whenever there are visible marks on their precious princess. But I pushed him too far.

I'm pushing myself up when his boot connects with the right side of my rib, and all the air whooshes from my lungs.

Now that. That is what I truly expected. It takes a moment for me to bring myself back to my body. There's always a moment like this when I'm a heap on the floor, gasping for air that won't return. A moment when I'm no longer inside my head. There's a ringing in my ears while I piece myself back together.

There she is.

I take a huge, gasping breath before sitting up, coughing for a couple moments before looking up at him. The magic within me thrashes like a wild animal, *begging* to be unleashed upon my father. It's so protective in nature, but I never let it protect me.

"Is that it, King Nicholas?" I spit out his name like it has a bad taste in my mouth. "Don't worry about the trip. Your perfect little daughter will be put on whatever display you'd like." I pull myself up, wincing softly and hating the sound for how weak it is. "But don't, for one second, think that I'm doing this for you. I'm doing this for my people—something you have no idea about."

He raises his hand again, so I wait. I wait there for him to hit me again, staring him down. "Go ahead. Show your people just what kind of king you are. What kind of father you are. We can just get someone in here to cover it up again, right?"

And then he lowers his hand. He hates it, but he knows I'm right. *Gods, I hate you.*

"Get the fuck out of my office."

I don't waste a moment leaving that blasted place. My feet take me down the stairs that lead straight down from his door. The bravado I was feeling starts to slip, and in its place is the anguish I'm familiar with—the kind I feel every time I leave an encounter with my father. All I want is to make it to Jasper before he leaves dinner.

For once, I am thankful River doesn't look at me. Having flown out of my father's office, I don't think he could've seen my face. And with him behind me, there's no way he can now. The longer he can't put two and two together, the better.

The ache in my ribs is sharp and tender, and the more I move, the worse it gets, but I can't stop my haste until I get to the only person I know I can call safe. He's the only one who knows the truth. A servant opens the dining hall doors for me, and it takes all my will not to sprint to him. But the moment he sees my face as I approach the table, he's up and meeting me.

Those usually bright green eyes become stark with worry as they take in the gash on my lip and the agony I can't hide from him. His gaze shifts between me and someone behind me, and I don't have to look to know he's looking at River for some reason.

"What happened, Em?" He looks back down at me, using his thumb and index finger to grab my chin and lift it up, inspecting only the damage he can see. Then he lets me go, turning toward River again.

"Jasper." Still, he doesn't look at me. He's locked in a hard stare with River, neither of them backing down. "Jasper," I say a little louder. "Jasper, he wasn't there. Father ordered him out." Jasper reluctantly looks back at me, but when he sees my lip, which has begun to bleed again, he storms off toward River.

"Jasper!" I turn after him, wincing involuntarily, but they don't notice, thankfully. I ignore the stares we're getting from our peers as Jasper walks right up to him. River stands there unflinching, looking slightly down at Jasper like he's nothing but a pest. With just a couple of inches of height, he manages to make Jasper look small, even though Jasper's anything but.

"You have one fucking job, and you do it pretty poorly. Surely you heard something! Anything!" Jasper at least has the decency to whisper yell so nobody else hears my business. I grab Jasper's arm, but he doesn't budge. *Oh, for fuck's sake.*

"Jasper, what is he supposed to do? Fight the king? He wasn't even in the room. He didn't know. He didn't see my face or anything else," I whisper yell right back.

And then I realize my mistake, and want to shove my foot in my mouth.

I start backing up, but then they're both looking at me, and I'm shaking my head.

"What does that mean, Em?" Jasper asks slowly.

I can't do this here. There are too many eyes. Too many ears. And the way River's looking at me right now—I can't breathe. So, I step into the hall, placing a hand over the side that's throbbing, and take a shallow breath until they join me.

"It means you don't get to get mad at River for something he has no control over. I pushed the king too far tonight. River, I'm sorry for my friend here. He's a bit overprotective." Jasper scoffs. But I look at my guard, who doesn't look like he's breathing as he listens to me. "And you don't get to blame yourself for something you didn't know about, so wipe that look off your face before it kills me." River stares at me for a moment, and I have to look away.

I've been begging to be looked at by him.

And now under the weight of that ocean gaze I might drown.

"Don't apologize for me, Ember. I don't care who your dad is; it's not right." Jasper has never been this outwardly angry before.

"Jasper. I'm *fine*. We know this changes nothing. Twenty years and nothing has changed. Skin heals. Now, please, go grab your things. I want dinner, wine, and to uphold my end of the bargain, so will you *please* just shut up and help me get my mind off of tonight?"

"But—"

"Do not argue with me."

"Ember." It's not Jasper who says my name. And I never thought my name could sound like that. Like a plea. "Can we at least take you to the doctor first?"

My stupid, traitor heart warms a little at the concern laced there in his words. But I shake my head, offering him a sad smile.

"No, he doesn't allow it. You get used to it." I don't wait for a response. I don't want to hear one. I just want to move on. That's what I came here for. So, I walk to the kitchen and let them decide whether they're coming or going. Jane's sweet smile is a pleasant sight to behold when I enter.

"I packed up your dinner for you, Prin—I mean, Ember."

"Thank you, Jane. I appreciate it. I'm looking forward to tomorrow." I take the carefully wrapped meal.

"Me too! I have some novels in mind for you already." I'm about to respond when a sneeze startles us both. I turn, grimacing before glaring at Jasper. He leans in the doorway with his hands stuffed in his pockets, looking at Jane for a moment.

Then he gives us his signature goofy smile, his dimples wonderfully on display. He's such a cheeseball.

"Jasper, this is Jane. Jane, this is Jasper."

"Pleasure to officially meet you, Jane." He tips his head forward like he's tipping his hat at her.

"Y-you too, Jasper." She stammers adorably, and I refrain from chuckling.

"Hey, Jane?" I call over my shoulder.

"Yes?"

I grab a couple bottles of wine and hand them to Jasper. "You didn't see that."

"See what?" she asks innocently. *That's my girl.*

Jasper smiles at her again over my head before we head out.

River is quiet as we walk, but from what I've learned about him, I can tell he's in his head. Even without quite looking at me, I can see how stormy his eyes are, how far away they look as we near my room. It's rare when he's like this. In fact, I've only seen him like this a handful of times.

River's only ever stoic. But the shift happening within me is affecting his ability to stay so cold with me. And I'm not quite sure whether that's a good or bad thing.

"Don't worry, I've got her," Jasper tells River. And I know it's meant to be lighthearted. But I feel it when River hardens. I cast a questioning look back at River and find that he's already watching me.

"Come here," River says quietly.

"Jasper, I'll just be one sec." I don't wait for an answer before shutting Jasper inside my room.

"Why didn't you tell me?" He's still reserved, so there's not much I can read in his face or his voice.

"You can't protect me from him. No one can. It's my burden to carry." I keep my voice soft and without blame. "I didn't think you'd care," I admit.

I don't know why I admit that to him, but it's too late now.

"I'm not letting you go in there alone anymore. And later, when Lord Jasper is gone, I have a salve that can ease the ache from bruising. We can find someone to apply it—"

"No one else can know. Can you do it? Or I can try to do it myself, I suppose." I don't think I can feel my heart anymore; it's beating too fast. An almost pained look flashes across his face before he smothers it.

"I'll help you." There's something about his demeanor that still looks as if he's carrying guilt. And I can't have that.

"You're a good guard, River. Quiet, but good." I don't wait for his response.

I know him well enough to know one won't come. But that's okay. I let the door close quietly behind me and am pleased to find my dinner spread out on my desk along with both bottles popped open.

"Thank the gods and goddesses for blessing us with wine," I say as I slide into the seat he's pulled out for me in front of him.

"You can say that again," Jasper mumbles before taking a long swig from his bottle.

This isn't the first time we've done this. It's easier for him to come to me than for me to go to him. But we don't make a habit of it because, well, it goes without saying. I'm locked away for a reason.

I'm already branded a whore, and no one but my own fingers has touched this cherry.

"Alright, where's your homework?" I ask over a mouthful of bread.

"Come again? Couldn't hear you over your terrible table manners."

"Oh, I said fuck you." I cast him the middle finger as I take a long pull from my own bottle, relishing the sweet and bitter taste that coats my tongue.

"We didn't have any, remember? She was in an oddly nice mood today. So, even though you sorely lost our bet, you've been left off the hook. Lucky you." Jasper leans back in his own chair, stretching out his long, gangly legs. He intertwines our feet and rests his hands over his chest, content to stay just like that.

"Lucky me indeed." I don't mean to say it as sadly as I do, but he catches it and nudges me with his foot. A silent push to go on. To tell him what happened.

In order to do that, I take another long pull from my bottle of liquid courage, even though the effects of alcohol never seem to have the same impact on me as they do on everyone else. Those unjudging, sweet, silly pair of green eyes ground me as I tell him what happened last night and how that led into today. He doesn't interrupt me.

He listens. He's patient. Even when I have to pause because it feels like I can't breathe, he talks me through it. Murmuring softly as he counts in and out until I'm not shaking anymore.

I know I asked for today. Deserved it, even. And I'll stand by what I said to my father and receive those blows tenfold just to say it again. But my strength only carries me so far.

"Don't do that," he whispers.

"Do what?"

"Justify his actions. I can see it in your eyes. You don't deserve this life. And I'm finding a way to save you from it." There's a certain indignation in his voice that drives his determination. "Just a little more time, Em. A little more time."

I find myself nodding, because enduring is what I do. And enduring a little longer, I can promise him.

"Now, can you entertain me like I brought you here to do?"

A flash of dimples is answer enough.

EMPTY BOTTLES OF WINE. An aching belly from laughing so hard. An even more painful rib. But a happier heart. That is how Jasper leaves me, and it is how I hoped he would. His duties as my best friend have been fulfilled, as have mine, as I listened to him vent about Robert's latest antics, his weird dreams at night, and the stomachache he had after trying a berry from one of the bushes in the gardens.

Oh, how I love that boy.

An almost hesitant knock comes a moment later, and the tug I feel at the center of my core somehow tells me it's River. So, I open the door for him, and the sight of him never ceases to amaze me.

"Right, let me, um..." I don't even finish that thought as I leave him in the doorway and make my way into the closet.

The dress comes off, and then...pants. I need pants. I find a pair of wool leggings and shimmy them on. There. That's at least somewhat better.

Standing in front of my guard in nothing but leggings is not how I thought this night would end. *I'd be lying if I said I wasn't the tiniest bit thrilled.*

"You should probably sit while I stand, huh?" I ask as I walk out. "Yeah, that should probably work. It's mainly on the side, not my back this time." I'm rambling, giving away way too much, but the nerves are getting the best of me, and I can't help it. *Calm down. This will be over before you know it.*

The bruise, which I caught sight of in the mirror of the closet, is already a nasty shade of black and purple. I'm not looking at him because I'm too focused on walking toward the bed so I can stand in front of him and maybe use my blanket to cover up.

The hitch in his breath stops me dead in my tracks.

"What did he *do* to you?" His voice is ragged, torn as he stares at my ribs.

"I'm okay, really, this is nothing," I assure him, resuming my trek to my bed. I know he wants to argue.

But I can't stand it. That look on his face.

Like *he's* in agony.

I know I'm only seeing what I want to see, and I can't do that to myself. It's torture more horrid than anything my father could put me through—imagining someone cares about you.

So I grab a blanket to cover my chest as he sits at the edge of my bed. He opens the salve as I step forward, raising my arm to bare myself to him. Mint and earth wafts over me, and I know the salve is supposed to heal me, but that scent, *his* scent, does more than anything else could.

I breathe it in deeply, unapologetically, as he leans forward. My eyes close shut, unable to watch him, especially as his cool breath fans over my skin.

"This is not nothing." His voice is barely more than a whisper —raw and gravelly.

How did we go so quickly from silent and brooding to this?

When he presses his fingers into the wound, almost as an emphasis, I can't help the whimper of pain that comes as he rubs the salve as softly as he can over it.

"If he lays a hand on you again, somehow, in some way, and I don't know about it—I beg of you, Ember, that you do not hide it from me. Let me help you, at least like this. Let me make up for the ways that I cannot protect you from his wrath." The pleading in his voice sends tears prickling in my eyes.

"River, it's not your—"

"Ember, *please.*" And I can't deny him. I won't.

"Okay," I whisper.

He finishes in silence, but it's the first time it's not in tension, nor is it uncomfortable. But when he leaves, he doesn't look back.

CHAPTER 6

"You're wearing your hair down again." It's not a question, but a marveling statement, dipped in awe, made by Viola as I walk toward the table at the center of the dining hall.

"Does it look crazy?" I smile at her sheepishly, which makes her roll her eyes.

"Jasper move," Viola more so commands than asks.

"Why?" he groans.

"So I can talk to Ember without your big-ass head in the way." I can't help the laugh that barks out of me, but I quickly quiet down at the first ache that comes with it.

Jasper does as he's told, moving to the seat I normally sit in. I take his spot, centralizing myself more and placing me beside Easton, who smiles down at me warmly.

"There's something... untethered about you," Easton says quietly. And I don't know why it shakes me, but it does. *Untethered.*

"She lets her hair down, and suddenly you all are enamored. It's just hair," Robert says over a mouthful of bread that's already been set out on the table. Viola takes a piece and throws it at him.

It hits him in the shoulder, and he squeaks. *Squeaks.* Crumbs scatter over his velvet jacket, and he viciously wipes them off.

"Enamored is a big word for you," Easton retorts.

"It's not when all the ladies are into you." The sly grin that spreads across Robert's face has us all groaning and looking away.

"I'm simply trying something different." I bite into my own piece of bread, not minding the crumbs because I need something to focus on besides the attention I'm suddenly getting.

"I like it," Daisy says softly, sweetly, as if anything she ever says could ever be anything but those two things.

"Thank you," I murmur before leaning back, desperate to change the subject. "It's the last day—what are we doing to celebrate?"

Jasper's arm rests lazily on the back of my chair as he messes with a lock of my hair mindlessly. I fight the urge to look over his shoulder toward River, unable to shake the feeling of his fingers on my skin, even though they were causing pain. Cameron pipes up, a sly smile playing on his freckled features.

"We are going to Marb's for a proper celebratory celebration." Easton snorts softly beside me.

"Celebratory celebration. I like it," I tell him, nodding in approval. "What's the attire?" I look to Sierra and Viola.

"As least royal as you can manage. Short gowns. Unbuttoned tunics. Sexy as fuck," Sierra practically purrs. Her lips are painted in a bright red rouge, a stark contrast against her smooth porcelain skin. *Enticing. Even I'm drawn in.*

"Short gowns?" I've seen the town's women wear them, but never any of us girls. I don't own any, and I didn't know any of them did either.

"Don't worry, Ember, I think I have a few that could fit you. Just come get ready in my room," Viola offers with a warm smile, one that says she can see right through my worried thoughts.

"One problem," Jasper says, tugging on the strand he'd been messing with.

"What?" I glance at him, flashing a look of annoyance.

"How the hell are we going to get you out of here? And without that guy? No one look." And yet, Robert and Cameron look despite his warning. I facepalm, groaning softly before throwing visual daggers at them both. They both throw their hands up in defense.

"Jasper was too slow in instruction!" Cameron says quickly.

"I don't answer to Jasper," Robert says defiantly.

"You're both idiots," Jasper groans. "He'd wipe the floor with us all for even trying to sneak her out," he whispers.

"We're already looking way too suspicious." Daisy glances toward River, keeping her voice hushed like a baby mouse.

"He looked ready to beat you to a bloody pulp yesterday; what was that about?" Sierra asks curiously, glancing at me and then Jasper. Suddenly, my mouth goes dry. *Easy does it. Keep it loose. They like this, Ember—don't go somber now.*

"My dumbass—" I start.

"Finally, someone says it," Robert interrupts. Three more pieces of bread go flying toward him from Jasper, Easton, and Sierra. A long string of curses tumble out of Robert as Daisy and Cameron snicker at the crumbs all over him.

"As I was saying, I was reaching for a book on a high shelf when it fell and hit me in the face." I gesture to my busted lip, which is nothing but a scab now, healing quickly, as my injuries normally do. "And Jasper here—"

"Not my finest hour, I might say," Jasper says, taking over smoothly. "I immediately assumed he let something happen to her and let—"

"Your stupid masculinity get in the way," Viola finishes, nodding as she glances at my lip again.

"It sounds worse when you put it like that. Either way, we have to figure out a way around the scary man." Jasper looks down at me, a thousand words passing between us in one look.

He hates that I keep the truth from them. He wants nothing more than to tell them what really happened. He believes that if they knew, we could get my parents off the throne quicker, and therefore me to safety. I just don't think it's that simple, and then they'd know for no reason. Or worse, they wouldn't believe me. I mean, why would they? We've kept it hidden my entire life.

"I'll just tell him my parents already approved. Easy-peasy. Plus, it'll probably be Eli who goes, and he's way more easy-going, so we'll be fine. River will be glad to not have to deal with me outside of the castle." This is a terrible idea. Lying to my parents and to River? I'm asking for heaps of trouble, but a night out with my court is worth the hassle.

"You think it'd be that easy?" Jasper asks, at the same time that Viola says,

"You're actually blind if you think River wants you out of his sight."

I'm silent for a second, and so is the rest of the table, and suddenly they're all looking at me and then River. *Gods, if you wanted to strike me down, now would be the time.*

"I'm hoping it'll be that easy. I just want to get out of here." I address Jasper first by looking at him because he's all I can look at before I let my eyes glide to Viola. "Now, you and I must know two different Rivers. The one I know has said less than a hundred words to me in almost a year of being my guard. He won't look at me and he's probably the coldest person I've ever met, until maybe last night, when he showed a sliver of humanity."

"What do you *mean* he doesn't look at you?" I'm so grateful Viola's keeping her voice hushed and that the rest of our court is too busy listening to us and eating to chime in. I can't even touch the food that's been placed down in front of me.

"Every time I look at him, he's looking somewhere else. It's like I repulse him." I try and fail to keep the hurt out of my voice, but it's there. It's so *clearly* there.

"Do you bathe?" Robert asks. Every girl at the table turns and glares at him. Easton leans down and sniffs my hair.

"Like floral and honey. It is not a matter of smell, you buffoon." Easton looks down at me apologetically for our misguided lord. I can only chuckle because only Robert would be so ridiculous.

"Ember, that man cannot take his eyes off of you. In fact, I think he hates that he struggles so much to keep his eyes where they should be," Viola says fondly. Daisy and Sierra murmur their agreements. Cameron and Robert have launched into their own conversation, bored of this one, which is fine by me. Easton looks down at me, and so does Jasper from the other side. Easton speaks first.

"He walked out of the room when you and Jasper were dancing. It was as if it physically pained him to see him with you." *No, that can't be.*

"I'm pretty sure that's why he doesn't like me." Jasper shrugs. "I know what you see, Ember, but I also see what they see."

"All to say, I think he takes his job more seriously and cares about it more than you know." Viola looks at me with such confidence in what she's saying, but I don't quite hear it still. It doesn't sink in. No belief finds its way into me.

I look over at him, and as I suspect, his eyes are trained toward the doors that lead into the dining hall, nowhere near me. And that's okay. I'd prefer not to give in to their silly conjecture of what I believe is quite impossible of River. My heart cannot take such disappointment.

"What time should I be at your room tonight?" I ask, grateful when they take the change of subject without hesitation.

Lunch goes by quickly after that. After the library with Jane, I'm going to drag her with me to Viola's, and then we'll all head to Marb's together as a group. The guards are already aware of the outing, so they won't question us all leaving, which will make it easier for me to slip out with Eli.

When the table is cleared, everyone rises. But for some reason, I stay put. Jasper offers me his hand, and yet, I shake my head.

"I'll see you later. I just need a moment." I gave him a reassuring smile. He squeezes my shoulder softly before filing out with the rest of them.

The room becomes silent, and all I can hear is the rushing of my blood in my ears as my heart pounds steadily. Mindlessly, I tug my bottom lip between my teeth, so lost in thought I hardly notice when the blood from the scab blossoms on my tongue. It doesn't mean anything to me. Not as I wrap my arms around myself and press my hand into the bruise, letting the slight twinge in pain wash over me to remind myself what this is all for. *Endure until I rule. Endure to save.*

The salve he put on me did wonders, almost as if his touch healed me in and of itself. It'll be fully healed by tomorrow at this rate. I'm so busy swallowed up in my head that I don't notice his steps or his scent that blankets me.

"Stop biting your lip," he commands softly. "It'll never heal if it keeps busting open."

Immediately I release it, a quick breath following it as my eyes snap up to meet his, but they're not looking at me; they're staring at my lips that I'm sure are red from my nibbling. He looks away quickly, looking forward to where the servants are cleaning up around me. I hadn't even noticed them there either. I murmur a quiet apology, rising to leave so I can change for my next class, but he raises a hand to halt me.

It doesn't touch me, but I wish it did. I look up at him again, and without looking down at me, he says,

"The guards have informed me that your court has planned an outing to celebrate your final day of academic courses. If you'd like to attend, we only need to seek approval. Then I can escort you." His voice is so serious. So void of emotion I wonder if the rawness I heard in it last night is something I might've imagined. If the pleading he let me hear was a fluke. If maybe the humanity I thought I saw in him was nothing at all.

"They've already given their approval. But there's no need for you to attend something so late in the evening. Eli can take me." *Please, for the love of the gods, do not make this harder on me.*

"I insist." He turns and leads us forward; the hard planes of his back are tense, and I know there's no use arguing. I nearly growl at the back of his head as I follow him to my room, wishing I had a piece of bread to throw at him. *I insist you stop being such a royal pain in the ass.*

"No." Jane shakes her head adamantly. The kitchen is spotless, and we're enjoying our dinner sitting on the counters across from each other.

"I think it's against the law to tell the princess no."

"I'm telling Ember no." She raises her eyebrow at me.

"Jane, please. It'll be fun. We'll still go to the library; we have plenty of time to kill before we can get dolled up. I'm sure you'd love to wear something other than that maid gown for once. And I saw the way you looked at Jasper." I raise my eyebrow right back at her, to which she starts blushing.

"Aren't you...into him?" She gathers our bowls, washing them with her back to me.

"We had a momentary lapse in judgment. But no, he's my silly best friend, and that's all."

She peeks over her shoulder and then rolls her eyes in resignation. "Fine, I'll go tonight."

I smile in victory and drag her to the library. The smell of parchment and ink fills me like a welcome home. That, coupled with the sweetness of a new friend, makes me feel awake. Alive even.

Unburdened.

Classes are over, and now what looms over our heads is our kingdom's future. But for a blissful moment, a sweet break, we are free—if only for tonight.

There are rows and rows of books, filled with our kingdom's history from the very beginning to the present day. Every book, whether rooted in fact or made-up stories, is in here. There are thousands, and some are so old I'm hardly sure we could open them without them crumbling to dust. My personal favorites are the made-up ones. The ones that speak of romance are enough to make me swoon and yearn for something that I may never know in this life.

Jane walks straight to the section I've come to love, the section I've vowed to read in its entirety if I'm being honest, and picks out a book that holds no title.

"This one. This one is...incredible. The romance. The passion. The fighting. The risk. The sex." Jane hands it to me, marveling at it with a gleam in her eye.

"The sex?" I whisper harshly, and I'm so thankful for the wide berth River has granted us by standing near the only entrance to the library. We're well within his line of sight as he scans the room meticulously.

I flip through the pages, and words like "fuck" and "wet" stick out. I slam the book shut as a blush crawls up my neck. *Gods, I've clearly been missing out.*

"Yes, the sex. I've never read something like it before, but now I'm on the hunt for more. Their love is forbidden. It's tragic. But the yearning is deep, and, well, just read it. You'll see." She continues to scan along the bindings of the books, and I can't help but marvel at her for a moment.

Her short hair is a dark midnight black, falling in soft waves just above her shoulders. She has lightly tanned skin that makes her green eyes stand out. Her thick brows furrow as she looks on in deep thought. Her facial features make her look poised and graceful, and I think that's what drew me to her in the first place. Jane always seemed so sure of herself. Quiet and reserved, but steadfast.

I go and pick up my favorite book. It's about a girl who lives a double life, and how things begin to unravel when she falls in love with a girl from one of her separate lives. I hand it to her.

"This is my favorite. The writing is absolutely stunning, and the characters are beautiful. I wish I could've met the woman responsible for writing it; I'd thank her personally." She takes the book from my hands and runs her hand over the cover.

"Until You Came." She gets a faraway look in her eyes for a moment, and I'm struck with a question that comes tumbling out of my mouth before I can stop it.

"Jane, have you ever had sex?" Her eyes widen a bit, but she doesn't chastise me for asking. Instead, she sits on the couch we're near, and I follow suit.

"I have actually. Have you? I've heard you royal children are menaces outside the castle." I snort, shaking my head.

"No. No, I haven't. Though I can't speak for everyone else, my virginity is properly intact." I wonder who she's been with.

"Properly?" She tilts her head in question.

"Purity is important to the crown. At least until they choose a husband for me." I shrug. My body has never really been my own. "What was your first time like?"

"It hurt, and then it didn't. He was awfully gentle and kind. We did it a couple of times on the hay in his barn late at night, and when we got better, it got addicting. We'd find any time we could to get our hands on each other. Young and lustful, I suppose..." She trails off quietly.

"Did you love each other?" I lean my head against the back of the couch, staring at the ceiling.

"I think so. He's the only person I've ever felt something for. But like I said, we were young—only sixteen years old. Thinking back to it now, I'd say I was infatuated with him. It wasn't love, but it was sweet, and for that I'm grateful." She leans back too.

"What happened then?" I ask gently. She takes a deep breath, and suddenly I fear I'm pushing too far. "I'm sorry if I'm being too nosy; you don't have to answer. I've never talked about this stuff with anyone. I have no idea how to do anything in the realm of love, sex, and relationships. I've been shielded off from it, with the exception of books. I don't have a clear idea of what it should really look like aside from happy endings and one true love." She chuckles softly.

"No, you're not being too nosy. I quite enjoy your company. I'm glad to be sharing this with you. I sense you'll start experiencing more of those things soon. Henry went off to be a soldier, and at seventeen, after I finished my schooling, I was ordered here. Since then, I haven't seen or heard from Henry. I haven't been back home."

"Do you want to go back home?"

"I don't think so; there's nothing left there for me." And the way she says it finalizes the conversation. I find myself nodding.

"I'm sorry, Jane." I take her hand and squeeze it.

We stay like that for a while. Hand in hand, the moment seizes us into a comfortable silence of two women stuck here with nowhere to go, but at least having each other.

Eventually, we find ourselves at Viola's door, and when she opens it, my jaw finds its way to the floor.

"Holy goddess, Viola." Because that's what she looks like. A godsdamn goddess.

The dress is white chiffon, cinching at her waist before flowing out to the top of her knees. It fades into gold at the bottom, making her honey-colored eyes stand out even more. Her sleeves, which are the best part, flow past her hands in long wisps, billowing with every movement. Paired with gold heels that lift her to her tallest, I'm not sure how anything could top what she's got on tonight.

"Lady Viola, that dress... I mean you! You're stunning!" Jane gushes.

"Ah Jane, you can just call me Viola. But thank you, darling. Let's get you into something fun of your own, shall we? Step into my closet." A wild smile blossoms on Viola's face as she ushers Jane inside.

I take a seat on Viola's bed and glance around her room. Her walls are covered with her artwork. She has portraits of everyone, and I spot myself in one of them. It's drawn with charcoal, but the details are incredible. It's from when Jasper and I were dancing. It's the final moments of the dance where he's dipping me.

But we're looking at each other with something that nearly knocks me breathless. Drawn through Viola's eyes, I see something much different than what Jasper and I had gone through that day.

Here are two souls who understand each other. Intertwined not romantically, but in a way that's meant to save each other. They love each other despite each other's deepest and darkest flaws. A mirror of light and dark. Twin flames.

"You can have that one. That day was..." Viola trails off, her voice soft. "You two have something special. You always have. Take it." I pull it off the wall, touching the picture.

"Thank you," I murmur softly.

When I turn and look at Jane, my jaw hits the floor again. She's wearing a long-sleeve, wine-red dress that falls to her lower thighs. It's form-fitting and shows off more of her than we've ever seen from her maid gown.

"Wow, Jane, you look divine." She blushes, twirling for me to show off the silver heels that wrap up her calves.

"Jane, you can keep those heels; they don't fit me anymore. I just never wanted to part with them until I was sure they'd have a good home." Jane sits down at Viola's vanity, thanking her.

Viola takes her time applying cosmetics I've never seen before onto Jane. They only enhance the features that Jane already has, making them stand out more in an even more enticing way.

"You should get out of here while you can. Don't let this castle soak up your beauty." Viola touches the bottom of Jane's chin. Jane looks up and swallows, nodding silently. But her words find me too.

"Alright, Ember, your turn."

Viola's closet is color-coordinated and far fuller than mine is. From short to long, shiny to matte, she has it all. She goes straight to the black dresses and pulls out a short, black satin dress.

A truly tiny dress. *Sierra hadn't been kidding.*

I mean, there are no sleeves, just straps leading to a cowl neckline.

"Viola, no, I couldn't." I start looking at the other dresses.

"Nonsense, Ember, this dress is perfect for your body. Sierra already preselected it, so you have to wear it." She hands it to me. "Change, now." Still, I hesitate.

But then I find myself stripping, freeing myself of the long gown and putting the short one on. *Dear heavens, what am I getting myself into?*

And yet, when I look into the mirror, I love it. Because Sierra was right. I *don't* look like a princess. I look far from it. The hem stops mid-thigh, swishing loosely at my hips but cinching tight at my waist. The neckline dips, and my eyes flash to her mischievous ones. She tosses me a pair of black heels with a thick heel, and I oblige silently.

"I have a feeling a certain guard is going to be getting into a lot of fights tonight, and he'll be standing *extra* close by." I roll my eyes at her as we walk to her vanity. *One can only hope.*

By the end, I hardly recognize myself.

She'd lined my eyes in kohl, swiped my lashes in dark liquid, elongating and curling them; she tinged my cheeks in a soft blush color and painted my lips in a dark red rouge.

But that isn't the reason I didn't recognize the girl in the mirror. The girl looking back at me had a wild look in her eye. Something primal had awoken, as if tonight was the first night of her life stepping out of the confines of her invisible chains.

"Easton was right; there is something untethered about you lately. And I really like it," Viola says softly, running a hand adoringly down the back of my head. "I'll wait for you at the front entrance. Hide this under your other dress and grab a warm cloak from your room while you dump your things." Nerves start to settle in my belly as the reality of the risk starts to kick in.

It's worth it. I just have to keep telling myself that whatever the consequences of tonight might be, it'll be worth it.

With my old dress on, I bid the girls goodbye before grabbing the drawing and my bag to rush to my room. River, who had stood guard outside of Viola's door, follows silently on my heel.

When we reach our rooms, I quickly close myself in and hear his door shut as well.

Which means he's changing, but I suppose that makes sense if he wants to blend in. I crack the door open instead, so he can come in when he's done. The long dress comes off carefully, so I don't mess with the hard work Viola put into my appearance tonight. Cloak. Where's my bloody cloak?

Shuffling through my closet, I find it where I discarded it after my escapade and exit—only to drop it at my feet when I see River leaning in my doorway with his arms crossed.

He's wearing a black tunic, black pants, and the all-black suits him *so* well. His hair is a delectable mess of curls. Facial hair covers his cheeks and chin lightly, but it's trimmed neatly, which means he keeps up with it. He looks rugged, intense, and so godsdamn devastating that it hurts.

I'm staring. Staring unapologetically, until I realize I'm not the only one.

And suddenly, I'm set ablaze. For every place his eyes touch, my skin burns. Wherever he looks, it feels as if he's physically touching me, and I can't *breathe*. He clears his throat softly, and that's all it takes. I grab the cloak and wrap myself in it, unable to look at him as I rush out.

When we arrive at the front gates, my peers all turn to us at once. I immediately fall between Jasper and Viola, seeking normalcy to calm my raging heartbeat.

"Ah, the princess has arrived," Robert says, a smirk playing on his lips. "Prepare to be demoralized." *Little do you know, Robert, little do you know.*

The town square is already full of inebriated folk leaning against the walls of the buildings and each other. The lamps along the cobblestone road light our path. There's a warm glow from the butts of the cigars hanging from the lips of men and women who glance at the royalty. Then they're double glancing, shock lighting up their faces. Jasper's arm slides off my shoulder as we near Marb's. The wooden sign is worn down with weather and age but refuses to fall off.

Once we're inside, my court begins hanging their cloaks on the pegs that line the wall beside the entrance, a seemingly natural action for them, as if they've done this plenty of times before. I suppose they have. *That shouldn't hurt as much as it does.*

I'm about to mimic them when a hand wraps around my arm, the skin of his palm searing into mine, branding itself into my memory. A shiver racks my body when those fingers brush downward. My eyes find River's brooding ones, and for a moment all he does is stare at me like he's going to change his mind and march me back to the castle. Instead, he leans down to talk to me, tugging me forward so I can hear him above the loud music and clanging voices of the tavern.

"If one thing goes wrong, I'm taking you back. If you can't see me, you've gone too far off. You stay within my eyesight. You check in with me. I'm allowing you a night of freedom, Ember. One night. Don't make me regret it." His voice tickles the cusp of my ear. His scent is overwhelming, and I can't help myself as I turn my head inwards toward his neck and inhale deeply. Oh my gods. Did I just *smell* him? Did he notice that? *Fuck, why does he have to smell so good?*

"Ember," he snaps. "Are you listening?" Nonchalantly, or as best as I can manage, I turn my head back forward.

"Yes, but—"

"No buts. We leave at the first sight of any danger." Rolling my eyes, I glance away from him. I liked it better when he didn't pay attention to me. *That's a bloody lie, and you know it.*

"Okay, but we take everyone else with us too." He straightens up, the stubble on his cheek brushing against my own. He finally releases my arm too, realizing he'd been holding it the whole time, and when he does, my magic thrashes in me wildly. Fire licks the inside of my skin, burning me from the inside out. My breath hitches in my throat, and he immediately takes a step away from me as if he noticed too. But that's impossible because he doesn't notice things like that. Not like I do.

He nods curtly, and I take that as my cue to hang my cloak and leave. *Aye aye, captain, you need not say another word, Mister Grumpy Pants.* He plants himself beside the entrance, monitoring the place as if his life depends on it. No, not his life—my life. Ripping my eyes away, I find my way back to the girls, shaking away the encounter from my skin. I stomp down my suddenly raging power back into its box, and all that warmth leaves with it.

I lean my back against the bar, propping my elbows on the counter as I take a look around. Wooden tables and stools are filled with all sorts of people here. Soldiers, villagers, farmers, merchants—everyone. Women with even shorter dresses sit on some of the men's laps. Women in normal maiden dresses hold mugs of ale, froth spilling over the edges as they raise them to the band playing in the corner. Some patrons have taken to dancing in the small opening of space, creating a sort of dance floor.

They don't waltz or spin. They move against each other in unorganized movements. Hips swirl, finding the lap of another while arms entwine around the necks of others. It's mesmerizing, electric, and nothing like the precious balls I've been to. This is raw and unhinged. It's human and civilian. Improper, and *I love it.*

"First drink of the night, Ember, take this." Viola turns and hands me a tiny cup that has clear liquid in it.

"What is this? And why is it so tiny?" I ask, confused. Viola bursts into a belly laugh.

"You're supposed to take it in one shot. Like this." She demonstrates by taking the tiny glass cup, and drinking it in one swallow. She makes a funny face, slamming the glass back onto the counter. "Your turn." Jane comes around next to me, holding her own tiny cup. She clinks it softly against mine, making sure not to spill any. Tipping them to our lips, we knock them to the back of our throats, and it burns all the way down. Shivers rack my body as I slam the cup onto the counter.

"Ew, gods, Viola, that was terrible! Give me ten more." Make me forget I just *sniffed* my guard. *Help me forget who I am tonight.* Viola turns to the bartender.

"One more round of those!" Jane and I instantly grin at each other. I can't feel anything other than some warmth as it trickles down within me. A couple more of these and I won't feel so cold anymore. We take the tiny cups again and repeat the process. The second one goes down a little easier.

"Can we drink something less bitter?" Jane says beside me to Viola, her sweet face twisted in disgust. Viola chuckles at us and orders us something else. I can't decipher the name over the noise of everyone talking and the music, but it doesn't matter. Soon we're being handed tall glasses of a pink liquid. This one is sweet, and at the very end there's a hint of the alcohol we were just drinking, but it's much more manageable. With our drinks in hand, we find the rest of our court, who are nursing their own drinks. They quiet when I approach.

"I'm really so glad we got you out this time. You look incredible," Sierra says, smiling in satisfaction as her eyes roam over the dress she chose for me. She's dressed in a sparkly pink dress that stops at the middle of her thighs, hugging her figure in a way I could never mimic. Her hair is put up in a fancy bun. Next to her, Daisy wears a purple dress with a similar hairdo as Sierra.

"I am beyond happy to be here. You all look, and I quote, sexy as fuck." They all laugh, shaking their heads at me. I glance over at River, who meets my eyes for a moment, nodding before he continues his scan. I look back at my court, smiling before I say, "Freedom feels good even if it's just for the night."

Robert walks over with a mug of ale in his hands. "Let's all raise a glass to finally being done with our studies. Let us never see a math equation ever again in our lifetimes!" We all raise our glasses, laugh, and take a drink together. Jasper comes and slings his arm around my shoulder, and I'm grateful just for his body warmth. Short dresses are not convenient for the cold.

"You have to keep up with taxes, dumbass, so math is still a little important," Cameron chides, looking at Robert over the lip of his mug.

Robert's face falls. "Could we just get rid of taxes so I don't have to deal with that?"

Easton chimes in. "How do you propose to pay for things then? Like guards and servants? Trade and goods?"

"There's one thing for certain, and that is that they needn't be so high." I lower my cup onto a table. "They're suffering for no reason, and they desperately need a break."

"That, I can agree with," Jasper says, and Cameron nods.

"So, I still have to do math," Robert grumbles.

"I'm sure one of your advisors will be able to calculate for you," Daisy suggests. Robert's eyes brighten again, seemingly content with this.

"Great, because I learned nothing this year. Or any of the other years." He shrugs.

Simultaneously, we all groan, "We know." He feigns being hurt, clutching his heart only to down the rest of his ale and wander off after a pretty girl that ogles him. Gods, what am I going to do with him and his province?

Jasper squeezes my shoulder silently as if reading my thoughts, and honestly, I bet he can. He looks down at me, shaking his head like, *What can we do? It's Robert.* And all I can do is shake my head back in our silent communication. *You're right; it's just Robert.*

Then everyone launches into reminiscent horror stories of Professor Soren. And for the first time since I was a little girl, before I was separated from them, I feel like a small family again.

I make sure to keep an eye on River every now and then. Each time he'll give me a little nod telling me everything's fine.

It's not fine when I see a redhead saddled up beside him when I glance over a final time.

His head is bowed close to her, similar to how he was with me earlier, and something in me hardens. I watch, not being able to tear my eyes away as she places a hand on his chest. River can do whatever and whomever he wants. So can I. But why do I want to claw her face off for touching him?

I decide I want to dance. I'm on my second drink, which is doing absolutely nothing. Which is absolutely ridiculous because Viola and Jane are definitely on their way to inebriation. The world and my vision are still crystal clear, and my mind is still sound. Any decision-making will be rational, which is no fun.

I set the drink down on a nearby table and tug Jane and Viola onto the dance floor with me. The bar is steadily filling up to its capacity, and now we're all squished against each other. Scents of sweat, perfume, and cologne permeate the air, making a heady mix.

Jane is in front of me, and Viola is behind me, the three of us letting the music seep into our bones, driving our movements with the rhythm. Our bodies naturally flow together as I lay my arms on Jane's shoulders. Jane's hands grip my hips, and Viola touches my side above Jane's hands, keeping her body flush to mine. The three of us move as one, gliding and swirling like an asp. No organization. No performance. Just the raw need to release.

I close my eyes, losing myself in them, leaning my head back next to Viola's. Her hands trail down my arms, dragging a sigh from my lips. *This is exactly what I needed.* She spins me so that I'm facing her, and now Jane is behind me. My eyes pop open when the music speeds up and she lets out a whoop. The people around us mimic her, making Jane laugh behind me. I can feel her chest rumble against my back as my bum nestles against her, and we begin moving to the beat of the music again. Viola leans down, her lips right against my ear,

"The men are really getting a kick out of this." I slowly turn to look toward the bar, and sure enough, they're all looking. Except for Easton, who's on the other side, talking to another girl. Robert, Cameron, and Jasper—who has his eyes trained on precious Jane. I wiggle my eyebrows at him when he looks at me, and he wiggles them back suggestively. I mouth the words,

"Horny bastards." I watch as he tips his head back and laughs before stalking forward toward us, and then suddenly the warmth at my back disappears.

"Mind if this bastard gets a turn?" Jasper asks. Jane's eyes are bugging out of her head while a bright blush works its way up her neck.

"Only if you can keep up with her." I wink at Jane before waving them off. Jasper flashes me a goofy grin before sweeping Jane a few feet away, diving right into the fast music that just livens the night. I turn back to Viola and lose myself again.

We keep dancing together, our expertise from school coming in handy as we expertly move with each other. Her hands move across my body, and my own do the same. It's sensual. It's fun, new, and I can't get enough of the adrenaline coursing through me right now.

All too soon a beautiful girl comes and says something in her ear. Viola smiles at her, then turns to me. She gives me a questioning look. *Will you be okay?* I nod eagerly, shooing her away. She disappears into the arms of that beautiful stranger, losing herself in her own treasure for the night. Grateful for the break, I go back to my drink and take big gulps to finish it.

My court is scattered amongst the room. Daisy and Sierra are hopping up and down to the music, laughing giddily as Cameron comes to join them with another round of drinks balanced in his hands. Robert's face is being practically sucked off by an eager woman when another joins them, and then he has a handful of both their backsides. My attention gets torn away again by a figure appearing at my side, but I'm thankful for the distraction.

A tall man with bright blonde, almost white hair leans down in front of me. His breath smells like ale, and it fans over my face in a way that makes me crinkle my nose. I lean away from him, trying to put distance between us, but then I bump into someone else who mutters something incoherent at me. I'm stuck where I am, holding my breath, trying not to smell his putrid breath.

"Hey there, Princess. Mind if I get a dance with you? I've never seen a girl as pretty as you." He doesn't wait for my answer before gripping my hand, forcing me toward the dance floor. I try to tell him no. I try to tell him to stop. I try to rip my hand away from him, but his grip is like iron. Frantically, I look around for a way out of this predicament, but it's so packed in here now that I've lost sight of Jane and Viola. I try searching over people's heads for River, but I don't see him either. Damn it. I've gone too far.

"River!" I scream out, but it gets lost in the music.

The man pulls my back into his chest, running his calloused hands all over me from behind. I try to pull away again, but he doesn't budge. The protective nature of my magic starts to well up within me, but I remind myself that I can't use it. Not with all these people here. People crowd in on us from either side, swallowing us up like we're not here. One of his hands slides up my waist and grips my breast. His other hand snakes its way up my inner thigh, and I *lose* it. I slam my heel down onto his foot and throw my head back, hitting him in the nose, ignoring the throb in my head that follows. *Ouch, that hurt.* He finally lets go of me, and I run for the nearest exit, shoving people to the side. People yell at me as I push past them, but I don't care. I need to get out, and I need to do it fast.

The front is too far, but like a beacon of safety, a back exit calls to me, and I beeline for it. That is until my legs turn to mush and my vision clouds with fog. The edges of my mind become hazy, and everything that was clear before is suddenly blurry. *Come on, Ember. Push.*

Grip the wall. One leg in front of the other. Shove the door open. My mind barely holds itself together as I try to find my way to safety. The cool breeze blows away some of the fog as cold sweat slides down my neck.

I take a moment, leaning against the brick wall, willing air into my lungs. The ground starts to swirl as stars dance at the edge of my vision. *Something's wrong. Very wrong.* I need to get out of here. I need to find River. The door beside me bursts open, and the blonde guy comes running out, holding his nose, which is dripping blood.

"You bitch! You're going to pay for this! He'll get over it." In a flash he's in front of me, moving so quickly I must've missed it when I blinked. With hardly any fight left in me, it doesn't take much for him to press his forearm against my neck while his other grabs the hem of my dress, shoving it up. My skin stings as he rips my underwear clean off my body, throwing it to the ground. It's then that something cracks in me. Like the world comes to a standstill.

I don't scream. I don't whimper. I don't even cry.

Death looms upon me; I can feel it. Between the burning in my lungs and the dark edges clouding my head, dripping down into my heart. It won't be long. So I look at him with dead eyes.

"Take it. Take it like the slut you are. Putting on that little all-girls show for everyone to see? You're a godsdamn whore. I'll make sure everyone knows that the pretty little princess puts out for anyone. What will they think of their queen then?" He laughs darkly, shoving his pants down just enough to release himself. He uses his leg to spread mine, leaning forward to press himself into me.

Then there's a flicker within me. A wild, angry force that *refuses*. And when he's about to ruin me beyond repair, I lose control of my magic. My power makes the decision I didn't have the will to make.

I reach my hand out to the side and muster whatever strength I have left to focus on any loose object near me. A large rock flies into my hand, and I use it to slam it against his head before he's able to enter me—before he's able to take from me something I'd never get back. He crumples to the ground, and the rock drops from my hand.

With shaky hands, I cover my mouth, afraid I've taken his life. *Oh gods.* I lean over and empty my stomach contents onto the ground before stumbling toward the door. He groans, gripping his head, and relief fills me. I start to slide down the wall, the magic having taken all the energy I had to keep myself standing. It seeps back into its box, content with itself as the lid shuts. Shoving my dress down, I find my voice, or at least a shred of it, calling out to anyone,

"Help..." Barely audible, the wind carries out my cry. I try again when a dark figure comes outside, their cloak billowing in the wind. I can barely keep my eyes open as the figure reaches down and scoops me up into their arms. His body jerks underneath me as he gives my attacker another kick. Darkness tinges my vision as my eyelids droop before shutting completely.

"Stay with me, Ember." Heat encompasses my entire body as the figure cradles me against him, enveloping me in his cloak as best as he can. The last thing I smell is the scent of mint and earth before I pass out in my unknown hero's arms.

WHEN I WAKE UP, it's still dark out. My head throbs as I lift it from the pillow. *What happened?* My body aches as I try to sit up, so I settle for leaning on my elbows. When my eyes adjust to the room, I see that River has fallen asleep in a chair at the end of my bed. Seeing him makes something in me tug, and it tugs hard.

He's in my room. His wavy hair is unruly, and his chin rests on his chest with his arms crossed. I listen to his soft breaths as I lay back down, memorizing the way he sounds in this moment.

I'm met with a blanket of darkness when I try to remember what happened last night. I'm not in the black dress anymore, so someone's changed me. Who did that? Why is everything sore? I try to turn to my side and wince when a sudden pain ricochets down the back of my head. From that barely audible sound, River is suddenly at my side, kneeling beside the bed.

"Ember." He breathes my name like a prayer. Like an answer to all his questions. *Say it again.*

"What happened last night?" I slowly turn to face him.

"Last night? You've been asleep three days now," he says softly. More softly than he's ever spoken. My eyes widen, and I try to sit up again, but he puts his hand on my shoulder, stopping me. His touch instantly calms me, washing through me like a pain-relief tonic. I lay my head back on the pillow. "Don't try to move too much. You were poisoned, and your body took a heavy hit. You're still healing." *Poisoned?* My head swirls with memories from that night. The last thing I remember is coming back to my drink and finishing it.

"What happened, River?" I press for more information. "How did I end up here?" *Why can't I remember?* He gives me a pained look as if reading my thoughts.

He takes his time explaining what he knows about what happened, and I listen in stunned silence. He's horrified. Completely and utterly horrified by his performance. He's never failed before, and in his eyes, he's failed me. He let me down, and that is so far from the truth. Whether he had come with me or not, I would have been in that tavern. I would have disobeyed every single order to be there.

"You saved me, River. You didn't let me die. You didn't fail."

"But *you* stopped him. Not me. I let you get hurt, and my only job is to not let that happen." He clears his throat, looking away from me. His hands are shaking, and I wish I could reach over, grab them, and kiss them to calm them. The thought has me reeling. "I should go get the doctor; they didn't think you'd wake up this soon. Let alone at all." Panic rises up in me as he walks to the door.

"River?" I start to sit up again. "River, please don't leave me alone." He turns around instantly, rushing back over. The deep sense of care and worry set in his features is something I've never seen in him before. I try to commit it to memory.

"Eli is right outside the door; I'll ask him to come in while I go. I promise you'll be okay. No one can get to you here." I nod, reassured while lying back down.

Eli saunters in, his big muscular body filling the room. "Hey, party girl." I crack a weak smile at him. He lights a candle on my bedside table, allowing for a soft glow to light the room. He brings the chair by my bedside and sits, leaning forward on his knees. "Quite a time you had, huh?" The solemn smile he gives me makes the ache in my heart pierce just a bit more.

"You could say that." I take a deep breath. *What would've happened if River hadn't found me in time?* But he did find me. He did save me. "Eli, who changed my clothes?" My cheeks warm, hoping it wasn't either of them. He laughs softly.

"That's really what you're worried about?" I roll my eyes at him. "Jane and Viola came by that night and cleaned you up since there was some of the guy's blood on you. They've come every night to rebraid your hair and to sponge bathe you. You should've seen your hair; it was a rat's nest." Normally, I'd swat at him, but I can't lift my hand off the bed. I'd laugh, but I hardly have the energy for that either, so I just smile. Pain fills Eli's eyes, something I don't normally see from someone so easygoing.

"You had me really scared there for a sec, kid. Maybe if we'd both gone—" I cut him off.

"It's not your fault. It's not River's fault. It's just my own for going in the first place. I'm sorry I scared you guys. I didn't think anything like that could, or would, happen." I'm starting to understand why my life has been so guarded over the years.

"It's not your fault either, Ember. You're trying to *live* in a life that basically forbids it. Anyone would understand."

"Do my parents know what happened?" Eli grimaces, and my heart sinks.

"River had to tell them. We couldn't hide the fact that you were out cold or the fact that you needed a doctor. Your father was very angry with River. In fact, River was ready to resign, but I convinced him not to. So, maybe you ought to tell him yourself that this wasn't his fault. He wouldn't listen to me on that. He's been really hard on himself about it, which I get; I would be too." More panic than I care to admit to myself floods me. That damn tug comes back, and it's almost frantic. *He can't leave me.*

"Resign? No, he can't. I know this job may be boring for him, and at times I know I piss him off. But he can't." Eli gives me an incredulous look.

"Boring? He loves this job. Sure, you don't always make it the easiest with that hard head of yours, but he does care about it." *It. The job. Not you, Ember, quiet that silly heart of yours.*

"He hasn't left this room since he brought you back. I had to force him to go bathe and eat so you wouldn't wake up to a stinky, hungry man." We both chuckle softly. *He stayed.* I remind myself that he's just my guard. It's his job. That's it.

"Thank you for looking out for him and me. I'm sorry to put you through all this." Despite having slept so long, a yawn escapes me.

"You don't get to apologize either. This isn't your fault," he chastises.

I'm quiet for a moment until I notice my favorite flowers, white chrysanthemums, on the desk. Instantly, I know they're from Jasper. Only he'd know something like that.

"Jasper was here?" Gods, he must be horrified. I wish he was here right now.

"Well, River wouldn't let him inside. Something about not wanting to disturb you and unnecessary stress. I don't know, but I heard Jasper was really angry about it. River compromised by putting the flowers inside for you at least." I furrow my eyebrows. Why would River do that?

"What time is it right now?" It must be late if Eli is here.

"It's late. Maybe three in the morning. You should try and sleep. I can tell you're tired; your eyes are barely staying open." Just as he says that, another yawn escapes me. I nod sleepily, not having much energy to ask the millions of questions circling my head. Instead, he blows out the candle and touches my shoulder softly as he rises.

"I'll let you rest. I'll be right outside the door if you need anything. And I truly mean anything; just yell for me, okay? Or maybe not. We'll get you a bell. I'll check in on you later, though. Get some sleep, pretty girl. Just not for another three days, okay?" I nod slowly, already succumbing to the sleep that pulls me.

Faintly, I hear Eli open the door and close it behind him. Part of me panics at being alone, but I'm too tired to allow the panic to spread. As I fall asleep, images of that night resurface. Pieces start to fall into place, dancing around in my dreams, taunting me with uncertainty.

CHAPTER 8

The next morning I wake up to find breakfast and pitchers of water waiting for me along with a doctor I've never seen before. River's standing beside my door, watching the man closely as he approaches the bed. He's middle-aged, already graying, but there's a certain kindness to him. The kind you're born with. The kind that decides your profession before you've learned your first words or taken your first steps. This man was destined to help people in one manner or another from the start.

"My name is Doctor Jemar. Can I take a listen to your clock, Princess?" I nod, setting the food beside me, swallowing the bite I just took. It goes down roughly, scraping against my still very dry throat.

He takes a seat in the chair beside the bed before leaning over with a contraption, placing the two ends into his ear, and holding the other against my chest, listening for several beats. It's fascinating to watch, intriguing as his eyebrows furrow. You can see him process the information in real time as he diagnoses me from just a sound.

"When they brought you in, there was hardly a pulse. Somehow over the past three days, your heart has grown stronger, and now your pulse is practically normal." He sits back in the chair, crossing his arms, still wearing a stumped expression. "It just doesn't make sense. The poison we found in your blood kills soldiers in *minutes*. It enters your system and shuts your organs down before an antidote can even be thought of. If the accounts are true, you should've been dead on the dance floor before you ever made it outside, yet here you are hungry and almost normal."

"Are you sure it's the same poison?" I pick up a piece of cheese, nibbling on it.

"We took a sample of your blood and then took a normal sample of blood from River. When we placed your blood onto his, it attacked his in the same manner the poison does. You see, when the poison enters your body, it takes over everything. Your body becomes the poison; only one type of poison does that. The one that comes from the Hakalie Berry bushes." He uncrosses his arms, folding his hands in his lap. "I'm going to ask you a question, Princess, and I need you to answer very carefully. Do not lie." I swallow, nodding nervously.

"Have you ever been able to do something inexplicable? Something that may seem...magical in nature?" He looks at me with such a look of safety. So sincere and genuine that I nearly answer him honestly.

That rattles me to my core almost as much as his question does. But I keep my expression smooth, flat, and emotionless. Chef Jean is the only one who knows and the only one who will ever know.

"No, never. I don't even really understand what you're asking. Isn't magic impossible?" My voice comes out surprisingly calm and believable. He studies my face before shaking his head with a soft smile.

"Nothing is impossible, Princess. Continue to eat and drink plenty of water the next couple days, and then you'll be all set to resume normal life." He stands, brushing his hands on his pants.

"Wait, when am I exactly allowed to leave?" I don't want to be stuck here.

"I'd say another two days."

"But I already feel better; how about tomorrow?" I look at him with a sense of urgency, pleading with him. He gives me a look, but then nods.

"Very well, tomorrow. But if I hear anything that tells me that you're not feeling better, you'll be coming right back here." I nod eagerly, smiling because there's nothing I want more than to get out of this room. The doctor leaves, and I resume eating in silence.

And it's the silence that starts to berate me. Broken pieces of my memory play over and over on repeat. Never in order. But I've pieced enough together with what River told me to picture it.

This is why I can't be in here. I can't be left alone like this.

But I'm not alone; River's just as quiet as ever. It's like he's hardly there. It isn't until I start to move to stand that he lurches forward to stop me.

"What? What do you need?" It's hard not to look at him with furrowed eyebrows. *Where's River, and what have you done with him?*

"Nothing; I was just going to put this on the desk and take a bath before anyone comes to visit." My feet find the cold stone ground slowly, each movement a slight ache from being so stiff.

"I can help you." He moves to grab the tray of food from beside me as I slowly rise. And my stupid mouth can't stop the words that come tumbling out.

"You're going to help me bathe?"

His eyes slam into mine as his grip on the tray tightens until his knuckles turn white. I scrunch my nose at him.

"I'm kidding, Mister Grumpy Pants. I can manage. I won't drown. You know what you can do to help me?" I grab my robe that's laying on the back of the chair beside my bed and wrap it around me. "Pick a dress out for me. Will that make you feel better? Turn thy frown upside down?"

I realize right then and there that I've never seen him smile, and gods what I'd do to see it. When I turn to look at him, there's a glint in his eyes, one that, if maybe it grew, could turn into a small smile. A half-smile. A turning of the lip. Something, but it's gone before I can hardly register it.

He doesn't say anything as I make my way slowly to the bathroom, and he places the tray on my desk on the other side of the room. But right as I'm closing the door, I swear I hear him faintly say,

"I don't frown, Miss Sunshine."

And that's how I know the poison must still be in my body. Hallucinations are powerful, cruel things.

When I emerge, a lovely red-colored dress with lace trim has been laid out. Complete with a matching set of red undergarments, and I can't help the nervous chuckle that comes out of me. Imagining him—and his face—having to pick those out is just priceless. But there's also a heat filling me at the thought that he *wanted* to see me in those. They're a much nicer pair than the others I own. *Don't go down that road. He doesn't want to see anything. You asked him to do this.*

With my muscles finally relaxed from the warm bath, I make quick work of getting dressed. I'm impressed with my body. The aches and pains I woke with last night are already fading to a dullness I can withstand like I normally do. I think I've lived my life so thoroughly in pain it'd be a miracle if I weren't in it.

Clamoring voices outside break me from my thoughts. My door flies open, nearly cracking the wall with the ferocity with which it's pushed through. In its entrance stands a heated Jasper and an angry River.

"I told you she wasn't ready for visitors," River growls, his voice low, downright predatorial.

"She looks pretty ready to me," Jasper retorts, his words dripping with such venom I'm not sure how River doesn't drop dead right then and there.

But hearing Jasper's voice.

Seeing him there in his rumpled tunic, messy hair that looks like he hasn't slept in days, and hands that shake at his side so violently—well, it breaks something in me. A dam within me lets loose, and I can't help the sobs that follow. I let go of the brush I was holding and cover my face with my hands, horrified at what he must've felt.

Anger forgotten, Jasper rushes to me. I don't have to look to know it's his footsteps, large and lanky. And then I'm being wrapped in his arms—in the most comforting place I could be. I bury my face into his chest as my lungs heave and shake with the intensity of my cries.

Female voices sound behind him, and I realize that Jane and Viola had come with him. River's at the door, and before he can do anything, Jasper turns over his shoulder and commands with an authority I have never heard from him.

"Out. Everyone get the hell out." And then he turns back to me, lowering us to the ground as the door quickly closes.

He's real. He's here. I'm okay. I'm alive.

I repeat that in my head over and over again as he grips the back of my head, his fingers lacing through my wet hair. He murmurs soothingly, never once shushing me. Never once telling me to stop.

We stay like that for a long time; at least it feels like an eternity. He never complains. When I've calmed down enough, he gently turns me around so I'm sitting with my back to him. He grabs the brush I'd dropped and begins to comb my hair gently, and the gesture alone almost makes me cry again.

"I'd follow you," he whispers softly.

"What do you mean?" My voice is raw. Raspy and thick from the constant onslaught of sobs that tore out of me.

"Whenever my time comes in this life. My soul would find yours again. We're tied together, you and I. I'm not sure if platonic soulmates are a thing, but if they are, I think that's what we are. Two souls intertwined in eternal ways, destined to find each other in every life. Whether you went to the heavens or the hells, or even became a turtle, I'd be a turtle right there with you. And when I flipped onto my shell and couldn't roll over, I know you'd be there to nudge me with your head to make me right again." He pauses, the brush stilling in his hand, before leaning forward to kiss the top of my head. "I'd follow you."

"Jasper..." His name comes out with so much emotion. And I know in my heart and in my soul, like he said, that he's right. We've saved each other and have become permanent to one another in ways we can't explain.

When we were children, we loved to play in the rain. In one particular storm, we went a little too far into Atravelien. It was just him and I running through the branches when he slipped in the mud and hit his head on a rock.

I thought he was dead. I was only seven, and I was petrified I'd just gotten my best friend killed. It was one of the only times I used my powers so blatantly. I needed to save him. I needed to get him help. So, I lifted his body off the ground and let him float until we got to the edge, where I laid him down carefully and began to drag him, screaming at the top of my lungs until a guard heard me.

And then I prayed to Nythiem, the God of Death, and begged him for the life of my best friend. I didn't know the precarious balance of life and death. I didn't care what the price was. I was seven, and I needed him alive. I still don't know if Nythiem answered my prayers or if maybe Jasper was never dying to begin with.

He still hasn't let me live it down. He thinks I dragged him all the way through the forest, that I mustered all that strength to save his life.

That night was the first night I started to get hit. But it was worth it because I had saved him. My sweet, silly best friend was alive. So the pain didn't matter. And that's how I learned that sacrificing my pain for others wasn't such a bad thing so long as the outcome was for the greater good.

"What if we're both on our backs?" The brush resumes its gentle, soothing strokes in my hair until there are no more tangles.

"Then we'll stare at the sky until someone else comes along and saves our dumbasses," he says as a matter of fact.

"I'm sorry. I know I scared you. I know what it feels like to feel like...you'd lost the person who makes home feel like home," I whisper softly into the space in front of me. His hands find my sides gently, guiding me until we're standing again so he can turn me to face him. Then I'm looking into a pair of green eyes that make me feel like I can breathe again.

"I don't want to hear the words I'm sorry out of your mouth again," he commands again. And there goes that voice again. A borderline kingly voice I could get used to hearing from Jasper. "I hope to never feel that kind of ache again. That soul-piercing pain of feeling you being ripped away from me. But all that matters is that you're here. You're living. Breathing. With tangled hair, a rat would love to make its home in." He smiles down at me, and those dimples ease away some of the throbbing that hadn't stopped beating in my chest.

"I thought you got them all out!" I turn to grab the brush again, but he stops me, grabbing my arm.

"I did, Em, I did." He laughs, shaking his head. I roll my eyes at him before hugging him again, breathing him in for a moment until my lungs feel like they're filled with peace.

"Can you go tell Jane, Viola, and River they're not in trouble? Maybe we can go sit out in the garden? I need to get out of this room." I move out of his arms to find my cloak.

"Why would they be in trouble?" Jasper grabs his own that had been discarded on the ground as soon as he ran to me.

"You yelled at them." I tilt my head at him as I wrap myself up, watching him do the same.

"I...directed them," he says defensively.

"You were kind of mean."

"Was not."

"Jasper."

"Ember."

"Don't make me use my queen voice on you." I cross my arms, trying not to smile.

"Oh no, look how I quiver in fear." He holds his hands up in mockery before opening the door, revealing two concerned friends and a guard ready to murder. Jasper's fear becomes real within moments.

Holding on to the peace I found within him, I hook my arm with his, appearing at his side. The girls look at me, and something like pity flashes across their faces. I try not to let that bother me as I muster the strength to smile at them, to shake off any remnants of what I'd let slip moments before and plaster on the princess they know.

"Join me for a walk?" They both nod quickly, turning to lead us forward. And I'm thankful for the lack of conversation. We don't make it far before I'm being tugged backward out of Jasper's hold, which pauses everyone's stride.

"Didn't the doctor say tomorrow?" River asks, and not kindly.

"I feel fine," I answer just as harshly.

"You need rest." He takes a step forward, towering over me. But I don't back down. I stare up at him with indignation.

"It's just a walk," I say between gritted teeth. He breathes out heavily through his nose, frustration flashing through his gaze.

"Why are you so godsdamn stubborn? Why can't you listen to what the doctor told you?"

"Because I'll go mad if I do. Please, if this is you pretending to care, then do me the favor and listen to what *I'm* telling you I need, and that's out of that room. I need to be with them. I need out of my godsdamn head. I can't be alone in silence with a man who doesn't fucking talk." I turn around, anger flooding me faster than the sorrow had before. And it ignites that same fire that begins to beat against the firmly shut lid. The same fire that always wants out whenever River's around.

A thought hits me as I walk back to Jasper, who's trying not to smile proudly at me as we walk toward the stairs that lead outside. Jasper almost groans when I halt us again, but I shoot him a look that shuts him up. When I look at River, his face is void of all emotion.

"Is he talking?" I ask hurriedly, and suddenly I'm not so angry anymore. Not until he doesn't answer. "River, is the man who did this to me talking?" He doesn't look at me, but the slight dip of his head is all I need.

When we make it to the garden, Viola asks a servant to start a fire in one of the pits. Once that's going, we gather around it. Although it's only the early afternoon, it's exactly what I needed. The cold breeze blows over my face as the warmth from the fire warms my hands.

"What are you thinking?" Viola asks.

"I want to question him," I answer quietly. Jasper stills beside me; instinctually, he scoots closer, wrapping a protective arm around me.

"Is that a good idea?" Jane asks before thanking another servant who brings hot mugs of cocoa. I'm sure Viola was able to steal her away from her duties, pulling rank and, well, being Viola to get her way.

"I want answers." I shrug. "I want to see his face. It's all so blurry still. Pieces keep coming back, but it's not enough."

"Can I come with you?" Jasper looks down at me, and I can tell the idea of me being anywhere near that man is killing him.

"I don't think he'd talk to me if I were with anyone." Jane opens her mouth to say something, but before she can, River steps forward.

"He won't," he says as a matter of fact. When my eyes meet his, it's like the ocean has been set on fire the way the flames reflect in his irises.

"You said he was talking," Viola interjects for me. He doesn't look at her, though. He keeps his eyes trained on me as he answers.

"He is."

"So what's the problem? Why wouldn't he talk to her? He obviously wanted something from her," Jasper retorts. Then I start to see it—the shift in River's eyes—before he says it out loud, and I almost laugh.

"There's no problem. The princess will simply not be going anywhere near that man."

Would it be wrong to tackle him to the ground, hit him in the head, and demand to know why he is the way he is? Also, who told him he has such authority over me, *and why do I so readily want to listen?*

"Like the hells, I won't," I snap. Jasper's grip on me tightens as I nearly come to a stand, but he keeps me sitting.

"Can he do that?" Jane asks Viola. Viola's eyes are wide as they volley between River and me.

"I don't know," she whispers.

"He can't," I answer. Jasper leans down, pressing his mouth against my ear so only I can hear him as he asks softly,

"Will you be okay?"

It feels like everything pauses. The crackling of the fire, the chirps of the birds migrating, the swishing of the leaves—it all comes to a standstill. No one knows me better than him. No one knows that I push the limits more than he does. So when I pull my eyes away from River's hard gaze to look at Jasper, I know in my heart that I can face the man who did this to me, because I know Jasper will be waiting at the end. I nod, and Jasper doesn't question me. He believes me.

When I look back at River, there's something in his face that wasn't there before. Something that leaves as quickly as it came. But this time, I was quick enough to see it. Quick enough to see what looked like actual pain etched in his eyes before they became void again.

I don't question it. I don't let myself dwell on it.

Instead, I let myself fall into the company of my friends. And one by one, the rest of my court finds us. And step by step, River retreats until he's standing behind me, out of my eyesight. Close enough that he'd be able to save me. But far enough that it feels like I'll never quite reach him.

CHAPTER 9

My dress drags softly on the dirt ground as I follow River. Two guards flank me from behind as we walk down the hall lined with cells—cells filled with moaning bodies begging to be freed. The smell is enough to twist my stomach, and I'm grateful I hadn't been up to eating this morning. But it's not the stench of bodily fluids that makes my gut lurch with nausea.

No, I'm horrified by their living conditions. Completely and utterly appalled by the inhumane way they are being forced to live. *Do the others know about this? How did I not know of this?*

This is no way to live. And knowing my parents, there's no telling what these people are in for, or if they're even guilty. I'd never been down here until today. I wasn't allowed to. But then River knocked on my door and told me that we were going to see the prisoner.

At the end of the hall is a door, with two torches on either side lighting our way as we approach. It only has a small, glass window to look through. For a moment, River stands still at the door, his hand on the large metal beam that holds whoever is inside locked in.

Please don't change your mind.

As if reading my thoughts, he slides that beam up and opens the heavy door. A cold shiver runs through me as soon as we step forward into the completely dark room. There's no windows, and the smell of blood is so pungent that if I hadn't heard a groan as soon as we walked in, I would've thought he was dead.

More torches are lit by the guards behind me, and the sight of the man is worse than I'd imagined. Inside the room is a cell. The man is tied to a chair behind the bars with ropes so tight that blisters and rope burn have turned his wrists raw. There's not a single part of him not covered in gore. And I can't see his face because it's slumped forward, his once blonde hair now caked with dirt and dried blood.

"Wake up, Norman," River commands. He groans again but doesn't move. The door closes behind me, and then it's just River and I in the room. "Get up." River bangs on the bars, and the man jolts awake, sitting up.

A slow, menacing smile spreads over his swollen face.

And then he spits at me, but it lands in the dirt between us. River immediately moves forward with keys to open the cell, surely to dole out more punishment. But that's what this man wants. A reaction.

"River, no. That's enough." River doesn't look at me as he stands back at my side.

"You should be dead," the man rasps out, but he doesn't seem surprised. He tilts his head, running his eyes up and down my body. I restrain myself from shivering under his gaze, holding my chin up. I purposefully wore an older, baggy brown gown so he couldn't see anything. He coughs and sags against the chair.

He doesn't look like he's been fed or given any water. And somehow, despite it all, that still doesn't sit well with me. *This man wanted you dead, and you're worrying if he's fed. Get a grip.*

"Well, sorry to burst your bubble, but I'm alive and well. You on the other hand, well, you don't look so good. I caution you now; if you do well and answer my questions, I'll see to it that you get fed." My voice comes out authoritative and calm. Not reflective of the turmoil wreaking havoc in my chest.

He narrows his eyes at me, but something in him softens. He's desperate now. I nod and step forward from River. Something isn't sitting right with me. *Norman? Really?*

"What's your real name?"

"Smart girl," he says, tilting his head. "My name is Dracyl." He doesn't offer a last name, but that's okay. "I only want to talk to the princess." River visibly straightens beside me.

"Absolutely not." River looks at the man like he's gone mad. But Dracyl only looks at me.

"He can't hurt me in here. Not like this. Give me ten minutes with him." I turn to River, hoping he'll reason with me.

"Ember, I'm not leaving you alone with him. I'm not making that mistake again." There's something in his voice that has me softening when I was so ready to argue.

"Just a few minutes; I'll stay right by the door; if anything happens, I'll leave the room immediately. Trust me, River." I place a hand gingerly on his forearm without thinking and snatch it right back. He stares at the spot where my hand touched before looking at me with those blank eyes again.

"Ten minutes." And then the door closes behind him.

"Is he your lover?" Dracyl leans forward in his chair, smiling a bit when I turn back to him.

"Why did you lie about your name?" I ask, ignoring his question. Dracyl's smile falters a little.

"How about we play a game, Princess?" he asks venomously. "You answer my questions honestly, and I'll answer yours the same." Worth the risk. Plus, how could he know if I was telling the truth or not?

"Deal." I gesture for him to answer my question first.

"I only tell important people my real name, and I was waiting for you to arrive. Now, is he your lover?" I roll my eyes.

"No, he's my guard." I keep my voice low. I don't want him to hear this out there. "Why did you try to kill me?" He leans back in the chair, taking a long look from the bottom of my dress all the way up to my eyes again.

And suddenly the look in his eyes is one I've seen before.

Predatorial. Lusting.

I'm right back there on the dance floor, and then it's gone, and I'm blinking rapidly.

"Aw, Princess, don't tell me you've forgotten our fun night. I wanted to do a lot more to you before you passed out." He raises an eyebrow at me.

He didn't get the chance to. I'm alive. He didn't take from me. I didn't let him. Don't let him get under your skin. *Get your answers.*

"Answer the fucking question, Dracyl." I take a step toward his cell.

"I wasn't trying to kill you," he says flatly.

"But you—"

"Next question, how did you get the rock to hit me?" Now he sounds serious. He stares me down as I figure out how to answer that without telling the actual truth.

"It was right next to us." He shakes his head at my response.

"Try again; how did you get the rock to hit me?" *How does he know I'm lying?* "No point in lying to me, Princess."

"It was right next to us," I repeat harshly. He shakes his head again. *For fucks sake.*

"Princess, if you lie to me one more time, I'll have the guards come back in here to remove you myself." I panic at that, so I give him half the truth.

"I don't know how I got it. All I remember is that suddenly I had it, and I needed to stop you." I let vulnerability enter my voice, and this seems to appease him. "My turn, what were you testing?"

"Whether you are actually the king and queen's daughter or if you're from—" He's cut off when River comes back inside. I didn't realize it, but now I'm standing directly in front of the bars. Dracyl smiles at me as if he knew River was about to come in. As if he was never going to give that information, but there's no way he could've known that. Immediately, I back off and turn to River.

"I was actually getting somewhere with him." *Damn it, River.*

"You're too close to him. Time's up anyway." River gives a dirty look to Dracyl, who swallows audibly. *Not so big and tough now, huh.*

"There are bars between us. That wasn't even ten minutes. Let me finish this." I'm borderline begging at this point, which makes me want to throttle him, but what the *fuck* did Dracyl just say?

"A lovers quarrel is so much fun to watch," Dracyl says from behind me. "I don't feel like talking anymore. Get me that food, Princess. Maybe we'll talk more in the future." I turn to him, and he winks as River takes my arm and drags me out of the room. The door slams behind us, and the two guards who followed me earlier return to their positions on either side of the door.

I rip my arm away before turning on him. That fire starts to thrum, but I shove that box so far down within me before unleashing my anger on my ridiculously stubborn guard.

"What the hell was that River? You have to *trust* me!" I can feel other prisoners watching, but I pay them no mind.

"The last time I trusted you, I almost lost you!" River growls.

"How is that my fault? You're the one who got distracted by a red-headed bimbo." It's a terribly low blow, and I regret it the moment it comes out of my mouth. But gods, he gets under my skin, and I can't get him out. River takes a step closer to me, seething.

"That's not true. Once again, you have no idea what you're talking about." He glares down at me.

"I saw her, River. You were talking to her all night. I actually wanted you to have fun. I thought maybe you'd be less of an asshole if you got laid." One of the prisoners stifles a laugh. We both stop and give him a pointed look.

"Your memory is still wrong. She was only with me for a few

minutes—I only said two words to her." I shake my head again. I remember clearly seeing his head bent next to hers as they talked, or was it as he listened? Fuck. Maybe he's right.

"This is besides the point. You interrupted me. This could've been our only chance to get information out of him. You guys didn't even know his real name." I start walking again, not wanting to be near him. "I know more now than you did, but I don't understand any of it because you're too—"

"What did he tell you? It's imperative, we know." River's voice is back to being business-like. No emotion. *Don't scream. It's not princess-like.* Another guard at the end of the hall moves to open the door for us to climb the stairs. I recognize him right away as one of the guards that sometimes fills in for Eli at night, named Vangard.

"Oh, it's imperative, you know now?" I want to hit him. "I'm not saying anything until I have the chance to talk to him. Vangard, will you see to it that someone brings all of the prisoners some warm meals and water? Including the one at the end of the hall." Vangard looks down at me, giving me an unreadable look.

"Why would you give him that? He tried to kill you, Princess. He doesn't deserve your kindness," Vangard says gently.

"He wasn't trying to kill me. Apparently, he was trying to test a theory." A theory I need to know more about. "But he'll talk more if I stick to my word. I need to know the rest of what he was going to say." Vangard gives me another questioning look.

"What was his theory?" he asks tentatively. I hesitate. Just a little kindness, and I'm blabbing everything now.

"He didn't say. That's when River walked in." I glance back at River, who I know is listening, but he says nothing; he just keeps looking ahead of us.

"Bloody hell, River. I told you to give the girl a few more minutes. She's right, you know, he's probably been lying to us the entire time." Vangard huffs quietly.

"I don't trust anything he says. He could be lying to her for all we know." River shrugs, not caring that he'd cost me valuable information.

"He said he was trying to find out if I'm actually my parents' daughter or if I'm from..." I trail off, staring at the stairs. Vangard speaks first.

"From where?" He shuts the door, lest our voices travel up to the top.

"That's the thing. He didn't say. But why would he say that to begin with?" I lean my back against the wall, looking at Vangard, then River. "That's why I need to go back. I want to know why he might think such a thing."

"Ember, I don't think that's a good idea. He's delusional. How would attempting murder prove whether you're their daughter or not? If you died like he planned, what would that confirm? It makes no sense. He must be lying. He laughs while they try to beat him into submission. He still looks at you like you're *his* meal. I don't trust him. I think he's just trying to get into your head," River says. Vangard nods to my left. *That's the thing though; I didn't die, and part of him knew I wouldn't, but how?*

"He's right, Princess. The man is insane. He's from Klyeria after all," Vangard admonishes.

Every muscle in my body tightens. And when my eyes find River's, I find that he knew.

"It didn't seem important," he says before I can berate him. "At least, not important for you to know."

Does he truly think he's guarding some child? Some girl playing dress-up princess? That I'm not set to take the throne and make decisions for an entire kingdom, let alone question my own attacker in the safety of these very walls? And now he thinks withholding information from me is okay?

I don't dignify him with an answer.

"Still feed him; he may be a monster, but I am not." With that, I ascend the stairs quietly.

And as I make my way toward my father's office, I mull over

everything that's just been told to me. I ignore the fact that seeing his face did exactly what I wanted. Now more and more memories are flooding me faster than I can keep up, but it doesn't matter compared to what he said.

I can't let it matter right now.

If I didn't belong to my parents, then who really gave birth to me? How did Dracyl know of me before he found me? Especially all the way from Klyeria? Suddenly something he said hits me.

He'll get over it.

Who's he?

I'm so caught up in my thoughts that I stop paying attention to where I'm going and run into a hard figure.

"Em, I was looking for you," Jasper steadies me before pulling me close, and I let him. I soak up his sturdiness. My foundation. "How did it go? Are you okay?"

"I'm okay. It just was...not at all what I expected. And I'm this close to ending up in one of those cells down there for murder." I press my forehead into his chest, mumbling and grumbling.

"I mean, I don't think they'd lock you up for killing the guy." Jasper sounds like he's considering doing it himself.

"Not him. River." Jasper barks out a laugh that makes my head bobble up and down. The sound is enough to heal a thousand wounds.

"I wouldn't blame you for that either," Jasper whispers as he slides his arm around my shoulder. "Talk and walk; where are we off to, and why was it odd?"

"My father's office," I groan. I fill him in on what Dracyl said, as well as the conditions of the prison below us, and by the time we get to my father's door, he's just as stumped as I am. He looks at River over my shoulder with something like confusion on his face before looking down at me.

"He takes overprotectiveness to a completely different level. And me and overprotective go way back. We're very fond of you." He shakes my shoulders lightly.

"I just think he has a stick up his ass." I don't say it as quietly as I should and Jasper snorts a little too loudly. I hear the lock click open, and Jasper's eyes widen.

"Okay, I will think about this mystery, and fill in the others on what's going on below. Then you will meet me for dinner, or I'll hunt you down and make you hand wash my dirty socks for abandoning your best friend in his dire need."

"Yes, Your Majesty." I mock a bow for him, but it's poorly timed as the door opens, revealing my mother standing in all her glory. I immediately straighten up and try not to laugh as Jasper practically sprints away to avoid the wrath of the queen.

As I enter, I feel so much more at ease. I knew I'd get through this with a light like him at the end of the tunnel.

River enters the room behind me, and we wait quietly together as the door shuts behind us.

"Ember, take a seat. River, wait in the hall," my father says without facing me. River doesn't move.

"Sir, with all due respect, I think it would be best if I waited in here. The office has a secondary entrance in which someone might be able to get through. Danger is more likely in this office than it is in the hallway." River stares my father down, and I whip my head to look at him. His voice sounds so intimidating that everyone in the room might as well be bowing down to *him*.

My stomach tightens at the sight of him like that. I swallow looking at my father, who is staring right back at River. He doesn't seem to understand what River is truly saying because he starts to nod. *It worked. It actually worked.*

"Good, that is the thinking that we hired you for. You have a lot of making up to do." My father turns back to my mother, still not looking at me. "Ember, sit." I swallow again as I take a seat, crossing my hands in my lap. My heart begins to pound in my chest.

"Good afternoon, Mother. Father." My voice is decorous, my face is void of emotion, and my posture is pristine. They both nod once.

"How did the meeting with the prisoner go?" my mother asks.

"He said his real name is Dracyl. But not much more came out of the exchange. I'm hoping to meet again, seeing as he's given me something tangible compared to the fake name shared with the previous guards." I only plan to give them bits and pieces of the truth. My mother nods approvingly.

"Being a queen means being authoritative—making people listen to you and commanding the truth. Not quaking under fear. You may continue to meet with the prisoner as much as you want. See if you can get any information on King Bleren during your interrogations before we leave. You will help me make the arrangements over the next twelve days regarding the Winter Solstice ball as well as our trip. We also have the seamstress coming tomorrow to take your measurements. My hope is that you've gone down a few sizes. It's time you start looking like a queen. No more of those horrid baggy dresses. Have you been following the diet plan like we talked about?" You mean skipping meals and not finishing my food every day? That "diet" plan?

"Yes, of course. I think you may be pleased to see it's been working. But, Mother, if Dracyl is from Klyeria, then why are we still going?" Her eyes drop to my chest, which never goes down, but she says nothing, where she would usually make a remark about the size of them.

"For far more important matters." More important than a man almost murdering your daughter?

"Should we consider bringing River with us because of what happened?" As much as I want to throttle the man, I'd feel better with him there. If the people of Klyeria know who I am, there's no way I'd be safe.

"We'll consider it. Now onto why I called you here. Your father and I are very disappointed in the way those events transpired. I understand that the end of classes is a great feat to be celebrated; however, to wear such horrid clothes, or the lack thereof, is to ask for what happened to you. We hope that you have learned your lesson. We will not punish you, as we see that what happened is punishment enough. Let this teach you that being a queen comes with elegance and grace. It is not appeasing to be a skank or a whore." My mouth goes dry as I sit there expressionless, nodding to agree with her.

"You're right, Mother, it will not be happening again. I am extremely embarrassed and sorry for my behavior. It does not reflect well on the both of you, and for that I am extremely regretful. You have taught me better." The insincere apology rolls right off my tongue, but it seems they buy it. I glance at my father, who has been extremely quiet.

His silence petrifies me to my core. I know that if it weren't for River, I'd be on that floor bloodier than Dracyl. No punishment is a lie. River just spoiled the delight my father would've taken in my pain.

"There will be no more going out without prior agreement from us. It is important for the queen to not be seen as a commoner. Your presence amongst common folk is meant to be sparse, and this is especially why. You're lucky that your mother is releasing you from punishment. I feel differently, but alas, we have more to worry about." I nod to agree with him as well, knowing that's what he wants. He goes on,

"Today you'll be focusing on the guest list. You can get the list from your mother's office. No one is to enter without an invitation, so it is dire that we send them out tomorrow. There are approximately three hundred handwritten invitations that need to be prepared." I nod again, letting my reflexes take over.

My parents go over a few more technicalities, and I sit there silently, trying to stay in the present moment as I feel myself slip further away. The further I sink, the harder it will be to come back up. My mouth says the things I need it to say. My head shakes and nods on command. My spine stays straight as an arrow.

But my head is only full of loud roaring the longer I sit there beneath their scrutiny. The more hollow I become, the louder the voices inside me echo. Screaming at me the things I so desperately try to keep quiet.

Skank. Whore. You asked for it. You deserved it. That's your punishment—almost dying, almost losing yourself completely.

Then they dismiss me.

And it's the first time I've ever walked away from that office without a new cut or bruise. There's a triumph waiting to be felt, but I'm too far beneath to reach it.

The cold air is a reprieve against my blistering skin that'd become so hot, smoldering under the weight of my father's hatred. He didn't need to say anything. He didn't need to say anything at all to beat me down.

I did that all by myself.

We're almost to my room when a callused hand wraps around my arm and pulls me back. I nearly trip over my own feet as I spin into an impossibly hard chest, and I almost beat on it.

"River, please, I'm in no mood to argue with—"

Everything in my head shuts off.

All the voices.

The roaring and echoing.

Everything goes quiet as his strong arms snake around my waist tentatively, like he's never embraced someone before, and he pulls me against him.

My body acts on its own, accepting what my mind seemingly can't as I take in the comfort he's offering and burrow myself into him. Mint and earth fills me, and it feels like a salve against my aching soul. One of his hands clutches my back while the other wraps all the way around my waist; that's how much he encompasses me.

I don't cry. Here I don't feel like I need to. Here is a different kind of peace. A different kind of quiet I don't think I've ever experienced.

"I wish I would've known what I really needed to protect you from," he says softly into the top of my head. When I look up at him, my face is so close to his. I don't think I'm breathing, and neither is he.

"You can't blame yourself. And what I said earlier that wasn't—" His hand tightens on my back and he shakes his head.

"Don't worry about that." I nod. I listen this time.

I open my mouth to ask him why he's doing this, but a servant's footsteps down the hall break the spell. We rip out of each other's arms, remembering who we are. Princess and guard. Nothing more.

"Thank you, River. I don't think I'll ever understand you. But I'll learn to appreciate how hot and cold you are one day." I offer him a small smile before disappearing into my room.

Gods, whatever you're up to, I beg you leave my heart out of this.

CHAPTER 10

Winter Solstice has arrived, and it's colder than ever. The last twelve days have been nothing but grueling, long days spent in isolation as I've worked tirelessly on the preparations for today.

And finally, the day has finally come.

Everything has been taken care of: all of the invitations, the security details, the menu, who will be working the kitchen, who will be serving, and the musicians. *Everything.*

The sun is just beginning to rise. Its brilliant rays of burnt oranges set ablaze the dull stone wall, and I watch as the light slowly climbs over my sheets. The brisk cold has begun to seep in, but my fireplace is burning steadily to keep me warm as I relish the last moments of tranquility.

Until a knock comes at my door.

You gods have such a funny sense of humor.

The well within me hums and tugs gently as I near the door, more awake than it's felt ever before. More alive than I've ever had to manage. When I open the door, I know I'm going to find River. But what I do not expect is the way he looks.

He's already dressed in his royal guard uniform specifically meant for nights like tonight where appearances matter. He's wearing a black tunic tucked into black pants that are held up with a belt that his sword hangs off of. Thick black leather straps crisscross his chest, surely holding other knives or daggers somewhere I can't see beneath his velvet, forest-green jacket.

There are gold epaulets on his broad shoulders, and the lapel is complete with our kingdom's royal crest. Our kingdom's colors are red, and his uniform usually matches as such. So the green is new. But I'm not complaining because he looks incredible. He looks deadly.

He's devastatingly beautiful.

And then I realize I've only stared at him since the moment I opened the door. I clear my throat, trying to urge my heart to quit beating so hard. The thrumming beneath my skin becomes a constant hum as I look up at him to see him quirk an eyebrow.

"Forgive me. It has just been a while since I've seen the royal guard uniform. It is different from last time, right? It was red from what I remember, the colors of the palace?" There's still a slight morning rasp tinging my words.

"It was. But you're wearing green, and I am meant to match you, seeing as I'm *your* guard, not the kingdom's." He clears his throat, and his demeanor takes on a more serious tone. "I was hoping to go over the day's events with you; I wish to know the details so I know what to expect. I hope I did not wake you." He doesn't meet my eyes anymore. All business now.

"Oh, of course, just give me a couple of minutes, and we can talk over breakfast." I don't wait for an answer before shutting the door in his face.

Hugging. Talking. Either I'm dreaming, or River's been swapped with an identical-looking man who acts a lot nicer than the one I knew before. Over the last few days, as I worked in silence, there were times when he'd sometimes ask what I was doing.

He'd *talk* to me. It was like he was trying to make a genuine effort not to leave me stuck in silence for so long. Like he could tell when the quiet was a little too loud and I was sinking a little too much. He'd always say something small in the moments I needed it the most, somehow knowing.

And I really needed it. Especially since I wasn't seeing Jasper or the others nearly as much as I wanted. There had been many nights I worked past dinner and ended up eating alone because it had gotten too late.

Once I'm dressed in a plain blue gown and wrangled my curls into a loose bun on top of my head, I make my way to the door. Wisps of curls frame my face as I place my hand on the handle.

The door is only open a crack when the well within me floods me with fire so hot I almost yelp. The magic had become a constant hum, something I thought I could manage. But this was something else entirely. I had to release it, or it'd burn me from the inside out.

"Ember?" River calls, but I shut the door and lock it before he can see anything. "Ember!"

I let a breath go, and the fire in my hearth becomes wild with flames before going out completely when I will it so. Smoke fills the space, and I make quick work of opening all the windows with the flick of a hand and begin guiding the smoke out as quickly as possible.

When it's gone, I take a moment to relish the cold air against my hot skin, willing it to cool me down. The fire licking against my skin fades away into dwindling embers. Another flick of my hand has the windows shutting quietly.

Eventually, the magic running wild inside me seeps back into the box, almost painfully so, and shuts without any more of a fight.

I've never lost that kind of control before. Ever. But that almost felt like it *needed* to get out. Like something or *someone* pulled it out of me.

My magic tends to act up around him a lot more now. As if it wakes up when he's near. I grab my cloak from my chair and throw it on quickly as I open the door again.

"Forgot my cloak; it's quite nippy out this morning." I move to walk past him, but he holds out his arm, blocking my way.

"Are you okay?" The question has me doing a double take before I nod eagerly.

"I'm fine. It's just a big day. Lots of nerves running wild." He seems to accept this and gestures for me to begin walking. The thrumming in me doesn't quiet. Doesn't halt. It remains.

And it worries me.

"I'll be going around and checking on food preparations, decor, and also taking attendance of all the extra servants we've hired for tonight to ensure everything runs as smoothly as possible. Once that's taken care of, I'll meet with the king and queen. If they deem everything is as it should be, then Melana will meet me in my room to help me get ready tonight. I'm sure you can take a break or do whatever it is guards do in their free time. I don't know, punch a tree or a wall."

There goes my stupid rambling mouth again.

"Busy day."

I wait for him to say anything else, but I'm only met by silence.

I don't let it bother me. Instead, I enter the kitchen and inhale deeply.

"Happy Winter Solstice, everyone!" They all smile and bow toward me, murmuring it back. I weave my way through the kitchen into the large pantry to grab several fruits and two small bowls, balancing them against my chest. An apple slips off, and my hand shoots out to catch it. I place it back on the pile and make my way to the sink to rinse the fruit off.

The servants eye me as I cut up the two apples, some strawberries, and a peach into smaller pieces and place them evenly in the bowls. They've gotten used to me coming in here at odd times of the day to prepare myself something when I've missed normal meal times. They've stopped trying to offer to do it for me and instead work seamlessly beside me. And I always make sure to clean up after I'm done.

I don't usually prepare anything for River because the servants beat me to it. But today I've actually gotten here early enough that I'm able to.

The dining hall is empty and glowing in the morning sun as we enter. I place River's bowl on the table he always sits at near the entrance before taking mine to my seat at the center of the room. I try not to look at Jasper's seat. I try not to let the ache of missing him hurt too much.

I just focus on the sweet fruit in front of me.

Until nearly silent footsteps approach the seat in front of me.

The hells have frozen over.

He takes a deep breath as he sits down, setting the bowl in front of him. But then he doesn't touch it; he just stares at it.

"Is something wrong?" I furrow my eyebrows looking at the fruit. Maybe he doesn't like those? I should've asked.

"I'm allergic to apples," he says plainly, looking up to meet my eyes finally. My heart drops.

"Oh my gods, I'm so sorry I should've asked, and now I've just tried to kill you." I frantically get up to grab the bowl, but he grabs my wrist, stopping me.

"I'm only joking, Ember; thank you for preparing this." A slight smile settles on his lips before disappearing just as quickly as it came.

It's as beautiful as I thought it'd be. If not more. Everything that was cold and hard became soft and warm. But in less than a blink, he's cut from stone again.

"That was not funny; I thought I almost killed you," I mumble as I shake my head. "And what a pity that'd be. I was just starting to like you." A low rumble of a chuckle fills the space between us, and my whole body freezes listening to it. I look at him slowly, and he's looking at me with a whisper of a smile again.

"It'll take far more than an apple to kill me, don't worry." He's teasing me. Like we're friends who tease each other. *Gods, this is not me complaining. Don't spoil my fun now.* My shoulders relax a bit, and he tracks the motion, seemingly content with that for some reason.

"Are you actually allergic to anything?" I ask before licking one of my fingers of peach juice dripping from the fruit. He looks at my fingers and then back at me before answering.

"Nothing that I know of." He takes a bite of an apple slice; a hearty crunch echoes off the stone. *He's invincible.* "Are you? I probably should know that as your guard and all." River's voice, though deep and silky, is light and almost airy. As if he's let go of the stoic part of him for now and is content to be at least a little bit human with me.

"Um, no, not that I know of. Thankfully, I mean, imagine not being able to eat something you really love." River's eyes darken before they move away from mine.

"It sounds horrible." He pops the last strawberry in his mouth and licks his lip. I drop my eyes immediately before I'm caught. Thankfully, a servant appears with two glasses of water, setting them on the table for us. My mouth is suddenly dry, and I desperately need something to quench this thirst.

"Thank you," both of us say at the same time. The servant, a young girl, smiles, stifling a giggle before bowing and rushing back to the kitchen.

I finish the last bite of my peach and lean back with the glass of water, looking at him over the brim of the cup. He stands up, and it seems like he does so for an eternity because he's so tall.

"Ready to start your day?" he asks as I stand. I groan in response.

I HOPED SO FERVENTLY that nothing would go wrong today. Yet here I stand, in the middle of my father's office, listening to him drone on about one thing after another that "could have gone better." I nod where I'm meant to nod. I apologize where I'm meant to apologize. I thought everything was moving wonderfully. Leave it to my father to nitpick at it all and find the smallest flaws. I stare straight ahead, not really listening as he drones on, until suddenly there's silence.

"Am I free to go now?" I ask softly, daring to take a peek at him. His face is like stone. The hard lines of being a king are etched into every part of his face and stature. The once dark as midnight hair is now rippled with gray that he tries to cover in vain. Where smooth skin once lay is now rugged and wrinkled. Being a king has not sat well on him. But that is his own doing—karma at its finest—stripping away his beauty and leaving behind the ugliness he so desperately tries to hide.

"Fix what is wrong, and then you're free to put yourself together," he spits out at me. Beside him, my mother holds her chin high, a smirk playing on her lips as she watches me. She finally speaks up.

"Melana will be in your room; don't keep her waiting. She'll need plenty of time to make you presentable." She looks me up and down, the disgust in her eyes so blatant it makes me wonder why they don't just choose another heir.

I don't waste time leaving the office to rush down to the ballroom. My father mentioned something about the linens at each table being placed incorrectly and the candles not lit the way he wanted. I take my time in lighting each candle in its respective votive and adjusting the linens.

The ballroom is decorated in a magnificent display of the finest floral. Each chandelier hangs beautifully with white wisteria. The band is set up near a large dance floor that my court and I will use later to perform for the guests. The tables are all centered with grand bouquets of red and white flowers, blooming with radiance that has me stopping to admire each centerpiece. Red curtains with our royal crest line the long windows, letting in the sun that will be setting come dinner time.

The dance floor is placed directly in the middle, giving everyone seated at the tables a vantage point of the performances laid out for tonight. The rest of my court will perform in song, I'll play a song on my cello, and to finish we'll perform our final dance together.

Talent is the sign of power here. And tonight is the night we prove to our kingdom that we are no ordinary class. We will demand their attention visually and orally. We are meant to show them that they will listen to and obey us in every way we command. And I, most of all, am meant to show them why I am meant for the throne. Their future queen must show off the most.

The archaic tradition almost seems silly at this point. But our kingdom delights in the arts, and showing off the royal children and their talents on the Winter Solstice is just part of the fun. Part of the magic we create throughout the night to make our people feel as though everything is okay.

But I plan to be honest with them tonight. I want to show them the kind of queen that awaits them. I hope that my voice carries further than those that were lucky enough to be invited by my parents. And I will show them that I am much more than the suffocated embers they think I am. Embers can breathe a fire back to life. And that's exactly what I plan to do with this kingdom.

Satisfied I've done everything I could, River escorts me back to my room, where Melana squeals when she sees me. He politely excuses himself into his room as I shut the door to mine.

"My darling, it's been so long. Look at you!" She marvels at me, walking around to get a good look, which makes me chuckle.

"Thank you, Melana." I bow my head at her in thanks. She has a bunch of things laid out on my desk and some other gadgets I've never seen before laid out on my bed. I look at her quizzically, and she laughs.

"One by one I'll show you what these are. For now, I have a hot bath for you running; go bathe, but do not wash your hair, or I'll have to commit treason and murder you." She wags a finger at me as I shake my head at her.

Once undressed, I sink into the steaming water. It smells of roses and soothes my aching muscles. I close my eyes for a moment, leaning my head against the porcelain side. The peace lasts for all of two seconds as Melana barges in.

"No time for naps; bathe and come out quickly." She disappears just as quickly as she came, and I groan softly. "No whining through this process either!" I stifle a laugh and grab the soap laid out on the side. *Gods, grant me the patience.*

Fearing that we'll lose our best seamstress to treason, I make quick work of my bath and then lather myself in cream that smells identical to the floral soap I just used. When I exit in just my robe, she ushers me to the seat she's pulled out.

She starts with my hair by demonstrating how she heats up a hot tool to create soft, elegant waves in my hair. It's fascinating watching her in the mirror she's set up for me to see what she's doing.

As she works, she tells me the town gossip. Who's with who, who's having an affair with who, whose business is thriving while others are not. I half listen as I stare out the window worrying about tonight when a bit of information piques my interest.

"I also heard a little rumor that Prince Aris will be making an appearance tonight." I turn to look at her, but she taps my head, making me look straight again. "I see that got you to pay attention. Don't move or I'll burn your head." She lets down the final section of my hair.

"Where did you hear that?" I ask cautiously. There's no way the prince from Klyeria will be here. We're going to visit his kingdom in two days. Why would he come now?

"Heard some of the servants talking about it who overheard your parents talking about it. Something about him escorting you guys back home, blah, blah, blah. The important thing is he's going to be here. And if the rumors are true about his looks, then we're in for a real treat tonight!" She stops to fan herself for a moment, which makes me stare at her like she's crazy. Though, I've overheard Sierra and Daisy talk about how beautiful the prince from the other side is. "Although, once I'm done with you, Ember, no one will be able to take their eyes off of you. And hopefully, that prince won't be able to keep his hands to himself. You are as rigid as they come; you deserve a night of letting loose." She rubs my shoulders, and I loosen up immediately.

"I'm not going anywhere near that man. As far as I've also heard, he's a selfish womanizer and as disrespectful as they come." She runs her hands through the curls, loosening them up. I can feel them tumble down my back softly.

"We'll see about that." I narrow my eyes at her, but she just shrugs as she begins to sift through the cosmetics she's brought.

"I don't have much to do here. You have a beautiful array of freckles I don't want to cover. So, we'll liven you up a bit, elongate those dark lashes, and stain those lips so you can kiss whoever you want without it smudging..." She trails off, looking at the time, and her eyes widen.

"Gods, we have barely any time left—time to hustle." She falls silent, focusing on her task. I keep my eyes closed and lean whichever way she tells me to. I look up when she directs me, and she glides the black ink through my lashes as we finish. She runs to grab the dress that's been waiting to be worn and pulls it off the hanger.

"Robe off, no undergarments; this dress requires nothing underneath." She looks at me with enough seriousness that I freeze, realizing she's not kidding.

"What?!" *You crazy woman.*

"You heard me. Naked. If you wear anything beneath, it'll be seen, and it'll ruin all the hard work I put into this dress. Now, *strip,*" she commands.

I do as I'm told. She helps me into the dress, buttoning the very bottom of my back that cinches my waist tightly together. The lace and vinery that travels down my arms and over my chest reveals skin beneath it but covers the riskier areas of my chest by becoming denser. My hair tickles my back as it swishes across the bare skin, and the cool air brushes over my legs as they peek between the slits that stop mid-thigh.

I'm marveling at my reflection when she makes a tsk sound behind me.

"Don't fawn over yourself just yet. I have a few accessories for you." She sits me on the edge of the bed while strapping on a pair of gold heels that crisscross up my calf.

But when she reveals a golden crown adorned in emerald jewels, my heart stops. I look at her, and all she does is nod encouragingly. And when she places it on my head, it's not nearly as heavy as I thought it'd be. Still, she pins it in place to ensure it won't be going anywhere. Not even when I dance.

"Melana, why green? The royal colors are red and silver. You've donned me in green and gold. Everyone else will be in red tonight." I stand as she backs up to look at her handiwork.

Tears well in her eyes, and she begins fanning them frantically, afraid of ruining the cosmetics she's already applied.

"Red is the color of ruin, sweet Ember. Green is the color of growth. And since the day you were born, the villages, the towns, and the kingdom have known that you would bring us back from the destruction that your father has caused through the years of this awful war he has waged. It's like there was a ripple in the world when they finally showed us their beloved daughter. A tiny toddler with black curls and those sunny eyes of yours. We all knew. You were our savior. Your parents believe you to be dressed in red tonight, but I decided to dress you in a symbol of hope. And you make it look so sexy." She chuckles softly, dabbing at the corner of her eyes with a cloth.

"Thank you, Melana. I will not let you down." It is so often that I feign the strength people think they see in me. It is so easy to fall into my patterns, into my thoughtless actions that get me through the day.

But today real strength blossoms in my chest, spreading throughout me as I take a step toward the mirror. The woman staring back is not just the Crown Princess but a queen ready to take what's rightfully hers.

A queen ready to save.

The magic within me seems to enjoy that feeling, and the air around me electrifies. It presses against my skin, pushing and filling me as if eager to show off just how powerful I am. I focus on keeping it at bay while Melana gets ready.

She quickly dresses in a stunning cream gown that compliments her deep tan. She's probably only a decade older than I am, but she is nothing short of radiant as she finishes her own touches and gathers her things back into her bags.

"Oh, I forgot about River. I guess Prince Aris won't be the only man after you today." She winks at me while I roll my eyes and open the door. River immediately looks past me to Melana. *You're wrong, Melana. This man doesn't have any eyes for me.* I take a deep breath.

"Melana, this is River. River, this is Melana." Melana walks over and offers River a hand. He takes it softly, and it takes everything in me to keep the buzzing beneath my skin under control.

"Pleasure to finally meet the woman behind my guard uniform," he says smoothly, and that makes her giggle.

"You sure make it look good, River," Melana purrs, earning a small smile and a thank you from him. My jaw clenches, wishing that smile were mine. *Relax, nothing of his could be yours.*

Soon enough, I'm in line with my court. Jasper's dressed in a red and silver suit, of course, looking as dapper as ever. He's bouncing on the heels of his feet, his own nerves getting the best of him. I take his hand and squeeze it. *I'm here. You'll be amazing tonight.* One squeeze back and I know he's sending me that same encouragement.

I'm still covered by my cloak, waiting until I'm ready to reveal myself. Jasper leaves, and the audience goes wild. He's always been a kingdom favorite.

Finally, it's my turn, and a servant stands beside the closed doors holding their hand out for my cloak. I take it off and hand it to her. She gasps softly, her jaw dropping until she quickly recovers, shaking herself out of her awestricken moment.

"Your Highness, you look..." She trails off when I hear my name called inside.

"Breathtaking," River finishes behind me.

CHAPTER 11

My head snaps to River, so completely shaken that he steps forward, offering his elbow in encouragement to keep me moving. So, I take it. Tentatively, I weave my arm through his, settling my hand on his forearm as he guides me into the room. If I thought the applause was loud outside, inside it's *deafening.*

It shakes me to the bone, watching the crowd, my people, light up to see me. For a moment all I do is take it in. All I do is replay Melana's words as I look over them. I let the sound of their excitement and awe fill me to the brink, forming me into the queen I know they want me to be.

Until I meet a pair of onyx eyes, and suddenly there's only *him.* River leads me down the stairs, and I should be afraid of falling, but I can't pull my gaze away. I can only stare, locked into him in a way I can't explain.

He's *beautiful.* And I've only thought that of one man—River. Because "handsome" just didn't seem to do him justice. But the prince... That word could be reserved for him, too. With high cheekbones and a jawline sculpted by the gods themselves, it's no wonder he's known to be a womanizer. *Who could say no?*

His hair, so black and with just a slight wave from the way it's so effortlessly tousled, is longer than the standard. The bottom of his hair touches the collar of his black tunic that I can tell is made from expensive material as I walk toward him. The tips of the front pieces just barely brush his cheekbones.

I've never seen anything like him. Wouldn't have been able to dream him up on my own even if I'd tried. And when I notice a slight smirk on his plump lips, I immediately look back to his eyes.

He raises an eyebrow at me. And I can see it—him teasing me already, almost as if he's saying, "Whatcha looking at?"

That's all I need to remind myself of who he is and where I am. Suddenly, the crowd is back, and my father is already speaking before I've taken a seat. River pulls it out for me, and I take it quickly, unable to stop myself from glancing back at the prince seated beside my parents. I'd purposefully put myself at a separate table from them. They sit atop the dais to my right, and I sit below them facing the windows while they face the crowd.

He's leaning back in his chair, nursing a chalice of wine lazily in one hand, looking as if he's bored of listening to my father. And I can't say I blame him. My father talks of false promises. He justifies the taxation and the means by which they are all living. Basically, he's asking them to bear down, take it, and one day they'll thank him. He says it in a nicer, more roundabout way, but it's as plain as day. He doesn't care about them or their poverty so long as his coffers are filled.

Nothing is going to change. He's just saying nice words to make them feel good even though there's nothing to feel good about when they're starving. It's so completely different from what Professor Soren approved of me to say, and now I can only wonder if that was purposeful or if she's set me up for failure with my parents.

When he's finished, I know it is my turn to stand atop the dais to deliver my speech. But for a moment I'm frozen in fear. River takes quick notice of my hesitancy and offers me his hand to rise. So I take it. I stand, and he guides me to the first step of the dais before returning to his seat. Ever the gentleman. Just a princess and her guard.

I let some of my power fill me, letting it press up against my skin, letting it remind me of what I'm capable of.

Only then do I find my voice to begin.

"Welcome to everyone who was able to make the journey here and celebrate this beautiful day with us. And to those who couldn't make it, don't worry—we do this four times a year; we'll see you at the next one." My voice carries through the room, strong and firm. A few people chuckle before I continue, "The celebration of winter coming is probably my favorite one. When workers return from their voyages, we hibernate with our families, open gifts, and the warmth from our hearths is the perfect kind of cozy to lay with your loved ones while the snow falls heavily outside. It is the little moments this season brings us that I like to hold onto. The hot cocoa, the snowmen I see in the town square, and the never-ending smell of freshly baked cookies.

"However, I know that year after year, those moments have become far and few between as this war wages on. As I prepare to take the throne in the near future, I plan to bring back the warmth we have all so desperately missed by bringing families back together. The war will end, the soldiers will come home, and all the money wasted on this fight will return to you. We will rebuild. I hope not only to restore our towns to their original glory, but also your faith and trust in the crown." I pause, looking at the faces of my people, pride swelling in me as they gaze on with hope swirling in their eyes.

"It's a lot to promise, but I do promise to each and every one of you that I will make it happen, or I'll die trying. Because each and every one of you deserves a ruler willing to make sacrifices for their people. You deserve a ruler who will do anything in their power to better your lives. And I won't be the only one to make these changes. My peers and I will walk amongst you, work beside you, and do anything we can to make Agatharea feel like home once more. So, join me in celebrating this beautiful winter night.

Happy Winter Solstice, everyone!" The crowd erupts in thunderous applause as I finish.

There's only a sliver of our population here, but I'm hoping my words will travel to every nook and cranny of the kingdom. I turn and walk back to my seat and look at my parents, who are both stark white but remain composed beneath their anger.

When I get to my seat, I grab my glass and raise it to them. I watch with satisfaction as my father bristles, and I know I'll pay for this moment. But I'll pay it for my kingdom. I'll pay it to be a little more me tonight. A little bit stronger.

The prince eyes me in amusement and what looks like a bit of pleasant surprise, tipping his glass to me before taking a sip. *Gods, I'm sitting here eyeing the prince, the enemy of my kingdom, and I can't seem to look away. What is wrong with me?*

I let my gaze travel up to River, who looks down at me with a mix of emotions I can't decipher. But all too quickly, they're masked by the blank expression he wears so easily. I can't help but deflate a little. Still, I hold onto his compliment from earlier, reminding myself not to want too much.

I don't know why I seek any validation from him in the first place. Every time I think I'm making any progress with him, his stoic silence takes me right back to the beginning. But there's something about River that wakes up something inside of me. No matter how aggravating he is, I can't seem to stay mad at him. There's always a part of me that wants to reach for him. But he makes it clear he doesn't feel that same pull. So I shut down those thoughts and look away from him.

The servants have begun to serve everyone, bringing around platters and platters of food to each table where guests begin to serve themselves and dig in. I find my court and make eye contact with Jasper, who looks at me adoringly, with a look of praise and pride that makes me smile. Beside him is Jane, who looks bashful just to be seated next to him. I managed to get her the night off by placing all her duties in the morning.

Then I notice Cameron giving me a thumbs up, and one by

one, my court all raise their thumbs at me. I can't help but laugh heartily at the sight of them, shaking my head at their silly gesture. But I know deep in my heart and soul that it's with them that I can accomplish this.

With them, I can save Agatharea from my father's rule.

I begin to eat quietly, and the power I've let fill me begins to buzz with impatience. River shifts slightly beside me, and it takes all my will not to lean toward him. The heat radiating off of him is enticing enough to want to steal.

Dinner goes by quickly, and once dessert has been served, the musicians start to take their place in their seats. They prepare quietly for the performances that are about to start.

One by one, my court begins to take the floor, singing what they've prepared for tonight. This showcases a voice that people will bow down to, a voice that will command the room and the kingdom.

I take a moment to admire how the candles are lit at each table in their floating votives, illuminating the faces of our guests, warming their features as they enjoy the show we're putting on. But it's not lost on me how *tired* some of them are. They've put on their finest clothes, bathed, and groomed just for tonight. But the hollow in their eyes cuts through me like a knife to my stomach. They're run ragged and in desperate need of peace. I clench my jaw as I return my attention to the dance floor. *One thing at a time, Ember.*

Jasper is the final one to go, and I can't help but lean forward in anticipation. The anxiety building up in me finds release by bobbing my knee up and down rapidly. I'm after Jasper, and there's a certain vulnerability in playing for everyone that always makes me nervous.

Jasper commands everyone's attention right away. His baritone voice fills the room, and no one can look away. There are many times I've looked at Jasper and thought that he should be in my spot. As silly as he is, he is the most qualified to be on the throne out of us all. And the way none of us can stop listening to him and that silky voice is proof enough he was born to be a king.

I look over at Jane and can see her practically swooning from here. I don't blame her. When Jasper sings, there's something alluring about him. It excites me to know there's something blossoming between the two of them. As Jasper nears the end of his song, my knee begins to shake more rapidly.

I feel like I can hardly breathe until a rough, warm hand takes hold of my knee. It makes me pause, and the fire dancing in my veins comes right up to the surface as soon as he comes into contact with my skin. The candle lit in front of us starts to burn wildly, and it takes every bit of my will to stomp down the power back into its box.

When he squeezes my knee, a completely different type of fire fills my belly. He leans down to whisper into my ear, his soft breath fanning across my neck as he says,

"Your father is watching you. Take a deep breath." I shiver at the proximity of his lips to my skin. He leaves his hand on my knee for a moment before slipping it off, his fingers dragging across the top of my thigh.

It's the perfect distraction. My body stops shaking, and I'm able to pull some oxygen into my lungs finally to calm myself further. Shoulders back and chin up. Suddenly I feel like I can take on the world again.

I feel a pair of eyes on me and expect to see my father looking at me, but he's not; he's applauding Jasper with a sense of pride I've never seen him have before. My mother beside him is doing the same, then dabbing her eyes as if overcome by emotion. I join the applause while a painful pang hits my heart knowing I'd never make them that happy, that proud, but I shove it down. That's to ponder on later.

I find that a dark pair of eyes is watching me. The prince stares at me so intently, it almost makes me flinch under the weight of his gaze. I tilt my head slightly at him, wondering why he's here. Why would they invite him and not tell me?

Soon, I'm rising up out of my seat, not breaking eye contact with him as I walk toward the center of the dance floor where my cello is being placed. He's so enigmatic that it's hard not to stare.

There's just something about him. Something that reminds me of River and the way he fills the space every time he walks in. They're different, but they both have looks that not only command attention but also respect. Looks that command authority, and it makes me want to kneel before them. Heat floods to my cheeks as he gives me a look that says he knows exactly what I'm thinking. He looks me up and down, and it shakes me a bit. It feels like he can see *through* me.

I look away first, needing to clear my head of all the swirling thoughts so I can focus on performing. As I sit, I spread my legs slightly; the fabric between each slit in the dress falls between my legs, leaving my legs bare on either side of the cello.

I close my eyes, trying to find that sense of tranquility I find when I'm in the office playing. But it eludes me. It isn't until I frustratingly open my eyes and find a pair of blue ones that I feel grounded enough to start. It's with his look alone that I place the bow to the strings.

I nod at my pianist, who's accompanying me, and we begin together in a flood of harmony.

When the music begins to fill the room and in turn, fills me, my magic responds again. It feels like my chest has been cracked wide open and everything I'm pouring out begins to swirl around me. A small breeze shifts through the room, but no one bats an eye. A draft isn't out of the ordinary, but it is if I'm the one causing it.

I try my best to ignore my power, but it runs wild, like a child who's eaten too much candy—too hopped up on its freedom to rein in. It stays that way, toying with the flames of candles until I finish the song and can beckon it back into me. Applause fills my ears as I rise, taking a bow while two servants come and collect my cello. I avoid looking at the prince or River, afraid that whatever it is I'm feeling because of them will make me lose control again.

Suddenly, my court is joining me on the dance floor. Jasper grabs my hand and spins me into his chest before leaning down to murmur, "Ember, that was incredible. I swear I could *feel* the music. Everyone is going to be talking about it for ages."

"Says the man who single-handedly sang the panties off every woman and possibly man in this room." His chuckle is contagious. He gathers me into our spot to begin our final performance. A dance of unity.

The music begins playing, and muscle memory takes over as we dance the choreography we've practiced so much I could dance it with my eyes closed. But for the first time, I think my court actually feels like one. Like tonight, they realize what's to come and what this means for us moving forward.

It's unlike anything we've done before. When the last note rings, and I'm staring up into Jasper's eyes, I have to choke back tears. He looks down at me with understanding, and his grip on me tightens as we rise to bow before everyone at the same time.

For the final time tonight, the audience explodes in applause. Everyone comes rushing to the dance floor as the band begins to play something upbeat while Jasper picks me up and spins me, causing me to whoop with laughter.

"You hooligan!" I yelp. He laughs, setting me down before hugging me tight.

"I'm so proud of you," he whispers softly in my ear. I pull back to look at him, a bright and real smile filling my features.

"And I'm proud of you. Of us. In the end, no matter what, it's you and me." He nods before he releases me and grabs my shoulders, shaking them like he always does, pushing me forward toward the bar set up in the back serving wine and ale.

"Let's go get some more wine and really have fun tonight. Before everything changes." He grabs my hand, pulling me along. I grab Jane's hand when we pass her and tug her with us. *Before everything changes.* It echoes through my mind as we make our way through the rush of bodies and release each other's hands.

Soon we'll all be separated, and I'll be here still, waiting to be crowned queen. But who knows what the future holds? Especially given that our sworn enemy's son is in our midst at this very moment. Seriously, what were my parents thinking? Looks aside, I've heard he's ruthless—unforgiving just like his father.

As we approach the bar, I realize my parents are already standing there with the prince. My stomach flips, and immediately I straighten out my shoulders and tilt my chin up, observing them. They turn to me, and my father says,

"Ah, Ember, there you are. We would like to formally introduce you to Prince Aris of the Klyerian kingdom. Prince Aris, this is our daughter, Princess Ember." There's no sense of pride in his words as he speaks of me. Jasper and Jane immediately throw me an apologetic grimace before grabbing drinks and escaping back to the dance floor to give us some privacy. I narrow my eyes at Jasper for leaving me, but I don't blame him. I swallow and extend my hand to Aris wearily.

There's something about him I can't put my finger on. He's like a beacon of danger, and instead of wanting to run the opposite way, I want to run right where the warning signs are being pointed. He's the son of the man responsible for the demise of my kingdom. And yet those dark eyes have me pinned in place.

Aris bows deeply before me and then takes my hand, bringing it to his lips. My eyes widen at the sight of him bowing for me. One look at my father and pure anger is all that shines while watching Aris.

As soon as his hand meets mine, electricity zaps through me and straight into him. Something snaps into place within me, like a cord tightening and connecting us. It nearly takes my breath away, and I know he feels it at the same moment I do.

I refrain from looking at River. The last time I felt something like this was the first time he touched me. Aris' eyes flare briefly, and it takes everything in me not to snatch my hand away, full body chills running through me.

"It is a pleasure to finally meet the one and only Princess Ember," he drawls. His voice is smooth, rich butter, and it reaches me all the way to my bones. He releases my hand slowly. His presence is even more enigmatic up close. I clear my throat softly, finally finding my voice to respond.

"The pleasure is all mine, Prince Aris. Welcome to Agatharea. I hope your travels here weren't too harsh." I look him straight in the eye, wondering if I can get any information out of him. Dracyl has frustratingly refused all of my attempts to speak with him in the past two weeks, and I'm running out of time to find out more before we leave for Klyeria.

"Nothing I couldn't handle. We'll see how you deal with it in two days." Mischief plays in his eyes, making me swallow to try and wet my suddenly dry mouth.

"I look forward to it." I look at my parents, who are watching Aris and me. My father looks like he suddenly remembers he's present and puts on a fake smile. *What the hell is he up to?*

"Prince Aris will be escorting us back to his kingdom. We agreed it would be a good chance for you two to catch up on the way there." My father puts his arm around my mother, an odd sight to see, seeing as they don't normally show any affection toward each other. *For us to catch up?* I quickly swallow my confusion and put on my own fake smile.

"That sounds lovely to me; I'm sure he knows all of the shortcuts." I turn my eyes back to Aris, who's giving me a look I still can't quite decipher. The look quickly vanishes and is replaced by that same cocky glimmer in his eye that he's had all night. The music slows down a little, and Aris takes a step toward me.

"Princess, may I have this dance?" My eyes widen a bit. I hear someone shuffle slightly behind me and peek over my shoulder at River. His ocean eyes look like waves crashing relentlessly on the shore. And I don't miss the way his hand opens and closes into a fist. I'm sure having our rival kingdom's prince asking me to dance when someone from his kingdom just tried to kill me doesn't sit well with him. It doesn't sit well with me either, yet I still find myself nodding. There's something about him that I can't say no to. I look to my parents, who seem happy with the exchange, so I take his hand and let him whisk me off to the dance floor.

I try to ignore all the curious looks we are getting and focus on not stumbling over my feet. His hand is warm in mine; the heat seeps up my arm and through the rest of me as he spins me into his arms, bringing my back to his front. The cloth of his clothing brushes against my bare skin, and I stifle a gasp. Everything about this day has felt so sensitive. It's like my body is hyperaware of every single touch, and it has the magic in me soaring. He leans down and whispers in my ear,

"Show me some of those dance skills I saw earlier." I shiver even though it's not cold inside. He spins me back so I'm facing him again, and just like that we let the music take over our movements. Now that I'm closer to him, I study his features more. His skin is flawless—there are no hidden scars or imperfections. There's just smooth skin that I find myself wanting to caress. His eyes, which looked black from afar, are flecked with gold that I couldn't see earlier. He too studies me silently as we move skillfully around the dance floor.

Silent curiosity floats between us both. I've only just met him, but it's like looking in the mirror. The more we move, the more I realize we're cut from the same cloth, drink from the same cup, and bear the same weight of the same crown. It's as if a thousand words are passing between us, yet neither of us has said a thing. There's an unspoken understanding that the roles placed on both of us are one and the same. And for the first time in my life, I feel seen; I feel heard, and I haven't said a single word.

It makes me pause, and I know he can feel it too because he hesitates. We stand there for a moment, just staring at each other, our breaths ragged. Everyone continues to move around us as he holds both of my hands and finally speaks,

"Would you maybe want to take a walk with me?" There's a softness to the way he asks, almost like he's telling me it's genuinely my choice. I can say no. But again I find myself nodding. I drop one of his hands and hold tight onto the other as

I lead him off the dancefloor. We make it all the way to the exit when River steps in front of me, causing me to walk right into his chest. Which must be made of steel because I bounce off of it—hard.

"Ow, River. What's going on?" I look up at him, searching his face for an answer. His eyes flicker down to me for a moment and then back up to Aris behind me. I drop his hand immediately and take a step back from the both of them.

"Where are you going, Ember?" I open my mouth to answer, but before I can, Aris answers for me.

"She's with me, and shouldn't you be addressing her by her title? Where I come from, you'd be dead for speaking down to royalty like that. Who is this guy, Princess?" Aris takes a step toward River, and I swear I can see the steam rolling off of River in waves. *Oh boy.*

"Prince Aris, this is River, my personal royal guard. And don't speak to him like that; he knows I don't like being referred to by my title." Though I've never had to say that to him before. "River, we were just going to get some fresh air; I'm fine." River looks down at me finally and doesn't say anything at first. I watch as his jaw ticks with frustration.

"Ember, may I speak with you? Alone." He glances at Aris when he says the last word. I quickly glance at Aris, who looks at River as if he's grown two heads for addressing me that way. But I follow River into the hall, where it's quiet. The door shuts behind us, and he lets out an exasperated sigh.

"What are you doing? Are you trying to get yourself killed? It's my job to protect you, but you make it so damn difficult sometimes."

"What are you trying to say, River?" I cross my arms and look at him pointedly.

"That I wish you gave your life just a little bit more regard. If you did, then you wouldn't make rash decisions like going off with a man you don't know." I flinch at his words like he just slapped me.

Immediate images of *that* night flash through my head, and everything in my body turns to iron. That night wasn't my fault, I remind myself. But when he says that, I can almost believe it was. I take a deep breath, trying to remain calm. Immediately regret fills his features. "Ember, that's not what I meant." He pauses, and I look away, clenching my jaw.

"Look at me," he says softly, taking a step forward, and now there's barely any space

between us. I swallow and look up, hardening my features. The irony isn't lost on me. He's asking me to look at him when I've wanted to scream those words at him from the moment I met him.

"I hear you loud and clear, River. My parents trusted him as a guest at this ball; they trust him to lead us all the way to the Klyerian kingdom, so I imagine I can take a walk with him through this *heavily* guarded castle. I appreciate all the work you do for me. I know I make it difficult for you. I'm sorry I haven't made it any easier with my 'rash decisions.' But I do hope that one day you'll come to trust me."

For the first time since I got hurt, I can see a crack in River's demeanor, and there's a dam of emotion just waiting to be let out. I hold my breath, waiting for him to say something, but it never comes. He only releases what he's willing to, and that's very little.

A head pops through the door, causing River and I to take a step away from each other. Aris looks at me questioningly, as if asking if he can come out now, and I nod at him. He comes to my side and takes my hand. I look at our fingers entwined, wondering if he can feel the magic vibrating within me, mere seconds away from being released if I'm not careful.

"Is everything okay out here?" he asks, almost like he feels the need to protect me, which is ironic considering I'm supposed to be his mortal enemy, but here we are, somehow hand in hand. Did I not just meet him minutes ago?

"Everything's perfect. Enjoy your time with her," River says to him, but he never looks at Aris; he only looks at me. There's something about the way he says it that sends a ping straight to my heart. That pull I feel for River is now tugging me in two directions. He just wants to keep me safe, though that pull toward him isn't reciprocated. Aris turns to me as he says,

"Oh, I will." A sly grin plays on his lips. I swallow as River moves to the side, no longer blocking us. He stands beside the door we came out of and takes up post there, waiting for my return. My heart aches as we walk away from him.

I let go of Aris's hand and run a hand through my curls, letting out an exasperated sigh. *That man.* I shake my head clear of River and all the frustration he makes me feel while I walk toward the exit. Aris removes his suit jacket and places it around my shoulders before we get outside.

The cold is a welcome reprieve from the fire building in me constantly because of River. The breeze combs through my hair as we near one of my favorite parts of the garden. The willow tree is bare now, so moonlight cascades through the tangle of hanging branches that have lost their leaves. Snow clings to them, reflecting the light to make it just a bit brighter. I sit on the bench, leaving room for him to sit.

He doesn't, at least not immediately. He comes to stand in front of me, casting me in a shadow that makes it hard to see him clearly. But I can still feel the heat of his gaze nonetheless.

"You aren't anything like I thought you'd be." He sweeps a piece of hair behind my ear, never breaking eye contact with me. His finger trails down the bottom of my jaw before dropping his hand to his side.

I'm not entirely sure how I can tell, but he isn't bad deep down. There's something genuine and *real* about him. The mask he wears is simply that: a mask, hiding what's beneath. *Oh, how I know that feeling well.*

"And you're nothing like I thought you'd be," I divulge.

"I'm more handsome in person, right?" That makes me laugh, and finally he takes a seat beside me so I can see his face more clearly in the light. It's hard not to stare at him, not when the moonlight makes him somehow more breathtaking.

"I'd be lying if I said no." My honesty surprises even me. Being so forthcoming with the prince? Maybe River's right; I have little to no regard, but how could I when this feels so good? So risky and thrilling.

"I..." He stares at me, trailing off. I raise an eyebrow, silently urging him to continue. "I'm at a loss for words, honestly. I don't think there are any that would truly suffice to describe the ethereal beauty you hold. No poem, no book—past, present, or future— could ever write the words, the sentences, or the chapters to convey what it feels like just to look at you."

CHAPTER 12

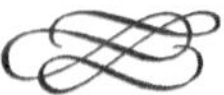

This is all just a weirdly terrifying but somehow sweet dream that I'll wake up from any moment. The Prince of Klyeria did *not* just say that. I am not swooning over my sworn enemy. I close my eyes and count to five, trying to get myself to wake up. Several moments pass, and then I open my eyes again just to meet his gaze again. *Oh my.* He studies me with a puzzled look.

"So this isn't a dream," I mutter and look back out toward the garden, unable to look at him without spontaneously combusting. A deep chuckle fills my ears, and *gods,* that sound makes its way all the way through me.

"No, this isn't a dream. But if you've been dreaming about me, sweetheart, I'm sure I can help make a few come true." His teasing voice only makes the electricity that's begun to course through me more intense. I shut my thighs close together. We're not touching, but it feels like we are. I can feel his eyes on me, beckoning me to look at him, but I don't. I can't. Or I'm sure the cap I have on my magic will be blown right off.

"How many ladies has that worked on?" I keep my tone light and playful. Play it cool; act unaffected. Instead, deep down I'm wondering how many people he's seduced into bed. Everything about this man screams power, and something tells me no one has ever turned him down. Not with those looks, and certainly not with that charm.

"I've never actually used that one before," he admits, and that makes me turn and look at him finally. There's a smirk playing on his lips that makes me roll my eyes. But then he continues, "People talk about you, even all the way in my kingdom. You're rarely in the public's eye, and every account of you always ends with them describing how absolutely stunning you are. And yet, that's not even the most attractive part. Sure, you're stunning in a way I've never laid eyes on before, but you're smart. You're talented. You're poised and graceful. You're nothing like the rest of your royal court. No, there's something about you that makes you radiate absolute power. And that? That's sexy." My lips part with a soft release of breath.

No one has ever talked about me like that, especially not to my face. I swallow, searching his eyes for honesty. It's all right there, right on the surface, like he's letting me in to see parts of him that he doesn't show anyone else. It's incredible really, not having to guess at what he's feeling or thinking. That voice telling me not to trust him is diminishing faster and faster, and it's *terrifying*. I've known him for all but an hour, and somehow the walls I've built all my life are being melted in mere minutes.

"Ember?" He searches my eyes, wondering if maybe he took it too far too soon, but he hasn't.

"Thank you, Prince Aris. I just..." I trail off trying to find the right words.

"Aris, just Aris for you," he says softly. I offer him a small smile.

"I don't think anyone's really, truly looked at me. Not like that. Not the way you are right now. I've always wanted to be more involved with the citizens of Agatharea. I don't want to be some mystery of a woman that leaves my kingdom reeling to know who their future queen is. I want them to know exactly who I am. I want them to trust their leaders. I want to be different."

"Well, you've certainly succeeded there tonight, Princess." He moves slightly closer, so his legs are just barely touching mine; the air beginning to electrify between us doesn't go unnoticed, but he doesn't say anything about it.

"Ember, just Ember." I try to control my breathing and control the swell of power rising in me. It's tugging right out of me and toward him. It's the same feeling I got when I opened the door this morning to see River. I grip the bench, willing it to stay put.

"Ember, I see you." He looks at me long and hard, and everything around us goes quiet. Not even a single hoot of an owl interrupts the thick silence between us. I expect him to say more, but he doesn't. And somehow he doesn't have to because the look he's giving me tells me he knows exactly what I'm feeling. He understands my position like no one else does. He has an understanding of the immense pressure bestowed upon us.

"Why was my father so angry when you bowed for me?" I ask, the question gnawing at me.

"Because I didn't bow for them," he says plainly.

"You didn't bow for them?" But he did for me? No wonder he was angry; Aris basically disrespected him in the biggest way he could—by respecting me instead.

"I don't bow for anyone." He gives me a look as if waiting for me to understand, but I don't. Why would he do that?

"But you—"

"I know what I did, Princess. And I'd do much more than just bow for you. I'd kneel before you if you asked." His words knock me breathless, and I can't find any words to respond.

His hair cascades around his face, and I can't help myself when I reach up to run my hand to touch the waves that fall around his ear. So soft. He tenses as if I've touched his skin, but I haven't. Not yet. But boy do I want to. *What is* wrong *with me?* The electricity intensifies, and I know he can feel it. I can see it in his body language as he responds to the way the air is shifting between us.

It's seeping out of me, making my skin prickle, and I can't seem to stop it as the wind picks up too. The damned solstice must be doing something to my power; it's the only logical explanation I can come up with. No solstice has done this before. Over the years my magic has grown to be stronger, but never harder to control. Not like this.

I lay my hand against his cheek, and even though it's freezing out here, his skin feels warm under mine. He lets go of a breath I didn't realize he was holding, and his eyes flare upon the contact. Finally, he laces his fingers through my hair, tilting my head up. And gods, it feels divine. Another rush of air sweeps around us as he moves closer, and it takes all my willpower to keep my body from trembling with the intensity of my power.

He searches my eyes, almost as if making sure this is okay. I answer by placing my hand on the back of his neck, twirling some of his hair around my finger, and that's all it takes for him to finally lean the rest of the way in; my eyes flutter closed, his lips a mere breath from mine when footsteps interrupt us. Immediately my power sucks right back into me and into the little box I keep it in. He pulls back, a thumb running over my bottom lip as he stares at me bewildered.

"Temptress." He shakes his head, leaning away from me, and I stare at him with wide eyes.

"Me? As if seduction isn't what *you* do, Prince Aris?" I roll my eyes. *Too close. Pretty words, and I'm a goner.*

A breath of air rushes from my lungs as I stand, walking forward to see who's out there. I watch as Jasper and Jane run hand in hand through the garden. They're giggling as they make their way around the corner of the castle where Jasper leans her against the wall.

I hide a smile as I walk back over. Aris slips that cool mask back in place. Charm oozes from him as he leans back and lazily gazes over me. We're on opposing sides of an ongoing war and somehow lost all self-control in the matter of minutes with each other. I imagine he's not sure how he feels about it either, but he's not willing to let that show.

"Let's get inside; it's freezing out here." I put some distance between us, suddenly angry with myself for being so stupid and naive. *I fell right into his trap.*

Jasper and Jane are too wrapped up in each other to notice us as we walk back through the door. At least some of us are getting laid.

I hand Aris his suit jacket back, and he takes it, slipping it back on. We don't say anything to each other as we make our way back to the celebration. My pounding heart settles back into a steady rhythm as I walk toward where River stands. Aris excuses himself quietly, slipping into the ballroom without another word. There's a strange relief in watching him leave, and an unexpected itch to follow my supposed enemy.

River hesitates for a moment, just looking at me before immediately coming to where I stand like he can't stand it. His eyes run over me, searching for wounds I imagine. I try not to blush under the intensity of his gaze.

"I'm fine, River," I say, just barely a whisper. He doesn't say anything as he examines me, so I stand still, letting him do as he pleases if it makes him feel better. The music is muffled through the door, but I can hear laughter and happiness seep through. It makes me smile.

River walks around me, lifting my hair to examine the skin on my back, still not believing that I'm unharmed. I've kept wounds a secret from him before; of course he has to see for himself. And again, I can't blame him for worrying about our sworn enemy. I shudder when he lets my hair back down, his hand brushing the skin on my back. That single caress is enough to make my back arch. He walks back to the front of me, looking at me like he didn't notice that reaction.

"Why is he here? We know how to get to the Klyerian kingdom, so why is he here?" he asks. There's such an edge to his voice that it takes me a moment to convince myself that the edge isn't directed at me. He's so rigid, bound so tightly, like it took all of his self-control to let me go alone with the man he was sworn to protect me against. I desperately want to reach out to him, but I don't. I have no right to. Not after almost letting myself go with that same man in the garden just now.

"I don't know. All they said was that he would escort us back to Klyeria and something about him and I catching up, but I didn't really understand that. They're perfectly content with having him sit beside them tonight. So something tells me they might be working on some kind of treaty. Why else would they trust him to be here? To be next to them—be with me." My parents may make questionable decisions, but they're not dumb. They always know what they're doing; they're always working several steps ahead, and most times they don't include me in the why. River's jaw ticks, and he huffs an angry puff of air.

"Why do you trust him?" His voice almost sounds hurt, but that can't be right.

"All I know about him is what's been fed to me by word of mouth. I owe him the benefit of letting him explain himself before jumping to conclusions. I'm sure he's heard worse about me, and he's given me the same respect. River, I know this is hard. I know your job here isn't easy, and again I'm sorry I make things difficult from time to time. I still understand if perhaps you want to take a different assignment." I offer him the same chance I did before. I don't want to lose River, but if he'd be happier doing something different, then I'd rather see him follow that path than continue being so miserable every day.

This morning, getting to see him laugh and enjoy an actual conversation with me meant the world to me. There's something just as riveting about River as there is Aris. There's so much depth just waiting to be explored, and if he gave me an opening, I'd dive into him. But I don't think he'd ever give me that chance. So as much as it would pain me to let River go, I would if that meant he could let someone else in.

"No," he answers immediately. His voice is firm, but then softens as he continues, "I don't want any other job than the one I have. And you have nothing to apologize for, Ember. I'm sorry for making you feel like the things that happen are your fault. That isn't fair of me, especially as your guard. I shouldn't have personal feelings about these types of ordeals." And that's when it all clicks for me. My lips part softly as I stare up into his stunning blue eyes. He looks down at me, almost pained to admit those words.

"Thank you, River, but I don't expect you to be a statue void of any feeling. You are human, and I am not ignorant of that fact." It's all I can manage to say in fear that I may say too much and ruin the moment.

He nods once before moving to open the door. He reaches from behind me, holding it open. His chest brushes against my back, and a whoosh of air releases from me in the process. No one bats an eye; they're too caught up in the atmosphere of drinking and dancing. I move forward quickly, not looking back at River to see if he felt that. I need to start saying my goodbyes and head to my room *now,* or else someone's going to notice if they haven't already.

I look around and see that the number of people present has already dwindled. Eventually, I spot my parents, standing with Aris and the lords and ladies of their court. I walk toward them as my parents beckon me over. River trails behind me as we move between tables to get to the small crowd.

"Ember, we were just talking about your speech and how wonderful it was," my mother says so sweetly it's almost sickening. I plaster on the smile I've practiced and smile at the group.

"Thank you, Mother. I made sure to speak from the heart, like you've taught me." My father's smile falters. "I'm very happy with tonight's turnout, but I do find myself exhausted from the day's events. I'm going to retire to my chambers now, but I hope you all enjoy the rest of your visit here." I curtsy for them and turn to leave.

"Perfect timing, Ember!" my father exclaims a little too

joyfully. "Prince Aris was just saying that he wishes to return to his room as well; would you mind escorting him there? We've placed him in the East Quarter in the room beside yours. Tomorrow you can give him a proper tour of the estate and perhaps take him into the village before our voyage the next day." My father wraps his arm around my mother again and smiles at us both. It's a shocking sight to see, and it takes all my strength in me to rein in my surprise.

"Of course, Father. I bid you all a good night." They all nod at me, and I turn and begin walking, glancing over my shoulder to make sure that Aris is following. He follows a safe distance behind me.

I turn and lead us toward the main entrance where a servant holds my cloak. I can feel the heat of Aris' stare on my bare back as I grab the cloak and fasten it around me. River walks beside me as we begin down the hall to the exit toward the East Quarter. Aris quickens his pace once we get outside to say,

"Does he sleep in the same room as you as well?" His voice is back to being playful. The arrogance is back on full display. I snort.

"No, he has his own room," I say over my shoulder. River opens the door to the East Quarter, allowing me to enter first, and then enters behind me, not holding the door for Aris. Aris huffs but comes right back up beside me on my right side.

"So shouldn't he be going to his room now?" I chuckle and go to answer, but River beats me.

"I am," River answers flatly.

"They allow the guards to sleep in the same hall as royalty?" Aris asks, but it doesn't sound like he's being demeaning. He sounds genuinely curious, as if the way we do things here is the most peculiar.

"River sleeps across the hall from me. I have a guard who stands by my door overnight, and then River takes over during the day. You don't have any personal guards?" I ask.

"Does it look like I do?" he replies sarcastically. "I don't need any."

"Must be nice not having to worry about people from your rival kingdom trying to rape and kill you," I mutter, the words slipping out so fast before I'm able to stop them. I slap my hand over my mouth. My heart begins to thunder in my ears as images of that night flash across my mind. River's eyes flash to me, surprised I said it too. Aris stops walking in the hall.

"Excuse me?" he asks, almost offended I'd say something like that.

"Don't act like you have no idea what I'm talking about." I whip around and face him, now standing in between our rooms. River stands beside me protectively but says nothing as he watches Aris carefully. I cross my arms, staring at Aris, trying to read his unreadable expression right now. How could I have gotten so carelessly close to him earlier?

"I have no clue what you're talking about, Ember. I've heard no such thing. He wouldn't..." He trails off, taking a step closer to me, but River steps forward, and Aris stops. "I wouldn't let that happen; that's not what we're trying to accomplish. What happened to you?" He furrows his eyebrows, genuinely bothered now, and now I can't tell if I want to explain or not, but I don't have to because River starts to speak.

"Someone from your kingdom," River spits out, "poisoned her, attempted to rape and kill her on the one night she was out of the castle, and you want us to believe you had no clue?" River takes another step toward Aris, anger rolling off of him in waves as he struggles yet again to keep his composure. It's such a sight to see.

Aris straightens up and stares River down. They're both the same height, but where River is thick with muscles, Aris is lean. They're two massive men, and the tension in the hallway expands to full capacity. It makes it hard to breathe watching them both. They continue to size each other up, forgetting I'm here. It's an impressive show of authority between the two, and I find myself somewhat entranced by them.

"If I wanted to hurt her, I already would have, but I didn't. Doesn't that speak to something?" Aris crosses his arms over his chest, his arm muscles straining against the fabric of his coat. I suppose he has a point. I could be dead right now if he wanted, but instead he's treated me with nothing but gentleness and kindness.

"I don't trust a single thing you do or say here. Your people hurt her; that's enough for me to never trust you." River's voice is low and lethal and makes me shiver at the thought of being on the receiving end.

"You act like I have complete control over every citizen and their actions. You must be some guard to have let it happen though, huh?" Aris snides. River's hand curls into a fist, ready to punch Aris straight in the face when I step forward.

"That's enough." I step between them. River backs up instantly, and so does Aris, but they don't take an eye off of each other. I turn to River first. "Give me a few minutes to talk to him. You can wait for me in the hall and see to it that I'm safe and sound." River opens his mouth to disagree, but I hold my hand up.

"I mean it, River, I'm fine. I'll just be a couple minutes." He huffs but nods in agreement. He stands off to the side, his back to the hallway wall. I walk into Aris' room with a silent command that he follow. He follows me in, and the door closes behind us. His room is set up the same way mine is, but there are no bars on his windows. I look through them, out to the night sky, with my back to Aris as I try to gather my thoughts. He takes a few tentative steps toward me, stopping just behind me.

I slowly turn around and look up at him, searching his face for honesty, desperately hoping I'll find he's telling the truth. Again he stares down at me, letting me see straight through him, and it's too much. I know he's telling the truth, but it doesn't stop me from fearing this is all one giant facade.

"Ember, I'm so sorry. I didn't know. I swear." He closes the distance between us and stops short of touching me. "We want to work toward peace. I want to end this bloody war just as much as you do. How would killing you do us any good?" He searches my eyes, looking for understanding.

"I don't know, Aris. I want to believe you, and deep down there's this voice telling me that you're telling the truth. I have the first inclination to trust you, and that goes against the very nature of my being. I don't *know* you, Aris. You're supposed to be everything I hate, yet somehow, you're nothing like that. Now, I'm at war with the image of you I've built and the one standing before me. I don't blame River for not trusting you. He's trained to put my life before his, so he's not easily swayed like I am, and you don't get to blame him for what happened to me. That is the doing of a Klyerian citizen." I take a deep breath and lean away. How fucking crazy am I to be here like this right now?

"I know, and I'm sorry. Your guard is already infuriatingly good at pissing me off. I'm sorry for what that man did to you, and I promise I can make it up to you. Get to know me, Ember. Tomorrow we get to spend the entire day together. Let me show you that you can trust me. Let me erase the images of the Evil Prince that you have and show you who I really am. I know this is all crazy, and trust me, I never would have thought I'd be here in a million years, but I am. So please, give me a chance." He stuffs his hand in his pockets as if he needs to put them somewhere else instead of touching me. I find myself nodding. My gut says I can trust him, but my head's saying I still need to be careful.

"You get one chance. If you fuck this up, there's no coming back from that." He nods eagerly, and I begin to walk toward his door. "Goodnight, Aris. I will meet you in the garden tomorrow before breakfast." I open the door and walk through, closing it behind me before he can say anything else. River walks toward me, worry etched in every feature he has.

"He didn't know, River. You have to trust me. Something tells me his father isn't being honest with him, just like my parents aren't." River looks away and simply nods. I can't stand that. Not right now.

So I do the boldest thing I have with him and grab his chin, making him meet my gaze. The turmoil in his eyes is enough to make my knees weak. "River, what happened isn't your fault. You are the best of the best. There's nowhere I feel safer than when I am with you. No matter what anyone may say about that night or anything else, you are the guard I want with me. I will always choose you." I let go of him with a shaky breath. He stares at me for a moment, his usually emotionless eyes now swirling with so much that I almost look away from the intensity they hold.

"There is no one else I'd rather be protecting, Ember. Go get some rest; we will figure this all out tomorrow. I'm not saying I will ever trust the man, but I am willing to give him a chance to redeem himself given the circumstances." I smile at him. He returns it with a small smile of his own, and it melts me all the way to my core. For the millionth time tonight, I try to shove down the rising magic in me as that smile becomes my undoing. He opens the door to my room and lets me inside, bidding me a goodnight.

My mind is completely overwhelmed by these two men. I've never felt so torn, so pulled in two different directions before, and either path is insane to walk. One leads to a man whose only job is to protect me and who won't let personal feelings get in the way of that, and the other leads to my supposed lifelong sworn enemy, whom I barely know. What have I gotten myself into? And will I make it out unscathed?

CHAPTER 13

S lumber doesn't find me until the early hours of the morning, and just when I finally feel my head shutting off, a knock sounds at my door signaling it's time to get up. Feet shuffle outside my door as Eli and River switch with each other. I groan softly as I sit up, rubbing the sleep out of my eyes.

I take my time getting ready, nervous butterflies filling my stomach as I think about the day I'm about to have. Walking around with both River and Aris. With my so-called enemy and protector. I sigh softly as I run my hand through the soft waves that tumble down my back, calming them from the mess they were from tossing and turning the whole night.

The well of power in me seems to vibrate like a pot of water about to boil over, heating up my skin like lightning about to strike. I was hoping it would have calmed down since the solstice is over, but that vibration of magic didn't dwindle one bit over the night. I have no idea how I'll control it knowing I'll be near the two men who made it most difficult to contain it yesterday.

I make my way to my closet and sift through the gowns I own and land on a black one I haven't worn yet. I slip off my night-gown and slip into the silk onyx dress. The long sleeves stop right at my palms, and the neckline dips into a V. The edges of the silk fabric turn into lace, lying snug against the curves of my breasts. The entire dress fits me like a glove.

I let my hair stay loose today, cascading over my shoulders and down my back. It feels good to wear something that fits me the way it's supposed to. It's like I'm finally in control when I don't have to hide myself.

When I get to the door, wrapped in my cloak, my core tugs rapidly as if my magic is eager to see who's on the other side. I grit my teeth as I turn the knob and find River and Aris standing there.

My eyes flare at the sight of both men. *How could they both be this gorgeous?* Aris is dressed in all black, his clothes cut from the finest cloth money can buy. They hug every muscle in the delectable kind of way that doesn't leave much to the imagination.

River is back in his everyday guard uniform; the golden sword at his side swings slightly with his movement. The dark brown pants hang perfectly on his hips with a black tunic tucked into the waistband. He wears a warm black coat over it with the kingdom's crest sewn into the breast pocket. I swallow as I meet both of their eyes. Aris looks unbothered, leaning against the wall to the left, a lazy smile playing on his lips. River stands rigid, but much more contained than he was last night.

"Good morning to you both." River bows his head slightly in return. I turn my attention specifically to Aris. "How long have you waited here?" I stick my hands in the pockets of my cloak and begin the journey toward the exit.

"Not very long; I didn't want to piss off the brute too much." Aris lands in stride with me, leaving River at our back. I snort softly.

"You know he can hear you right?" I raise an eyebrow at him as Aris reaches the door, holding it open for me as I step through. He lets go of the door before River can walk through, the same maneuver River pulled on him last night. River huffs behind us, and I stifle a laugh at the two.

Aris just shoots me a sly grin as we continue our walk through the garden. It's even colder than last night, instantly chilling me down to the bone. I take a deep breath of the frigid air, cooling the warming magic beneath my skin that keeps tugging toward both men.

But the fight to keep it contained is futile as invisible tendrils of power seep out of my skin, yearning to caress them as they flank me at either side. Panic begins to build in my chest as I try to tug on those tendrils as if they're a leash, but it's no use.

It sweeps over both men, who don't seem to notice the extension of me trailing over their skin. But I can feel them as if I was touching them with my own hands. It's terrifyingly delectable as I take in both of them at once. I want to stop, but I can't. So, I speed up my pace, reaching for the door to the Main Quarter. As if getting away from them would stop whatever's happening with me, but distance doesn't change a thing. This strange new magic takes its time reveling in the strength and power of each man—marveling over the muscles sculpted by gods themselves.

Aris shoots me a strange look as I whip the door open and continue my fast walk that's turned almost into a jog at this point.

"Princess, I promise the food will still be there if you slow down a bit." He reaches for my hand, but River lets out a grunt from my other side, causing Aris to retreat. Aris narrows his gaze at River, who simply ignores him. I'm barely able to pay attention to both of them while I try to rein in those invisible hands.

But I can hardly breathe, so I stop abruptly and lean my forehead against the cold, stone wall, closing my eyes. I practically beg for my magic to listen to me. *Focus. Please come back to me.*

River moves to my side, placing a hand on the small of my back as I focus on calming myself down. I suck huge gulps of breath down. At this point I'm practically vibrating as their scent washes all over me. That hand feels like it's burning my skin even with multiple layers separating it from me. I don't have to open my eyes to know that Aris leans a shoulder against the wall, facing me with concern.

My magic tracks every bit of their movement, moving right along with them as if it can't get enough of them. They're both quiet for a moment while I struggle for control. River finally speaks first, but not to me.

"Aris, go down the hall and take the first left; three doors down on the right, the doctor should be in his office. Bring him here." Aris pushes off the wall, surprisingly quick to do as he's told. I glance up, my eyes wide as I look at him.

"No, no, don't do that. I'm fine; please, I just need a moment," I beg him and then turn to River. "I just need a moment." River looks down at me, those ocean eyes swirling with a mixture of worry and confusion. His jaw ticks as he struggles between listening to me or doing what he thinks is right. I don't wait to see what he decides. I turn away from him, putting my forehead back against the wall.

Aris leans back in place, and River keeps his hand on my back, steadying me. I feel another hand, Aris', press against my upper back, and suddenly it's like I'm on fire. Electricity zaps through me while I burn from the inside out, but it's exactly what I need to suck it all back in.

With both of their hands somehow grounding me, I'm able to rein all that magic back into my body with a powerful whoosh that almost sends me to my knees. Finally, I'm able to take some deep breaths and stop shaking.

It's silent for a while, and neither of them rush me until I'm ready. I push off the wall and away from their touch as the lid comes to a tight close. The panic subsides, and I'm able to look at them both with clearer eyes, seeing parts of them I'd never noticed until those tendrils had explored them.

"I'm so sorry. I don't know what came over me; I just felt ill for a moment, but I promise I'm fine now." I don't have any more of an explanation for them. They don't look convinced, but they don't seem inclined to push me further on it. Aris pushes off the wall, gesturing for me to take the lead again. Both of them resume at my side as I walk at a much more normal pace toward the dining hall.

"Have you ever had spells like that before?" Aris asks curiously.

"Not like that, no, but I've noticed slight oddities since the poison." I offer a bit of truth in hopes that they won't inquire too deeply about what just happened.

"You never mentioned anything," River says from my left. "I still think we should talk to the doctor; maybe there's some medication or treatment to help the leftover side effects." River opens the door for the hall, allowing both Aris and I to pass through before coming to my side again. The heat from the proximity of both of them warms the chill in my bones, calming my still tingling nerves. I shake my head.

"Really it's nothing to worry about." I brush it off.

"Doesn't seem like just nothing." Aris says, and River grunts in agreement. I ignore them as I walk toward the table where Viola sits rubbing her temples.

Her hair is a wild array of curls sticking out in different directions. That stunning stranger she met at Marbs sits beside her, leaning onto Viola's shoulder. I turn and look at Easton, who is leaning back in his chair, arms crossed with his eyes closed. Sierra and Daisy, who would never be caught looking anything other than pristine, both look worse for wear. Their long blonde hair is pinned up in half-assed buns. Daisy leans her head on the palm of her hand while Sierra glares at the light spilling through the windows.

Cameron, who sits across from them, cradles his ginger-haired head in both hands, elbows propped on the wooden table. Robert is nowhere to be seen, probably still in bed if I had to guess. Jane and Jasper sit beside each other, murmuring quietly to themselves with their heads bowed close together. I can't help but chuckle at the sight of all of them, hungover and cranky as they wait for food to hopefully cure the remnants from last night's actions.

No one looks up as the three of us walk forward toward an

empty table where the three of us can sit together, seeing as there are no spots left with my peers. Aris pulls out a chair for me, the scrape of the legs ringing through the quiet hall. Someone groans behind me, and I stifle another giggle. Aris shoots me a sly grin, a telltale sign that he did it on purpose.

I untie my cloak and set it on the back of the chair. I don't have to turn to see Aris take in my appearance. I can feel it. I pretend not to notice and will away the blush that threatens to tinge my cheeks. A second pair of eyes does the same, and I turn to look at River while I sit. He matches my gaze with a sort of intensity I've never seen before.

I swallow, not used to the attention from River, who is usually so good at being indifferent with me. Yet now, it seems like he can't help himself after something shifted between us last night. He breaks eye contact and takes the spot next to me, so Aris reluctantly takes the seat in front of me, his back to all my peers.

Viola's eyes widen as she takes in both River and Aris. She arches an eyebrow at me, and I just shrug. A mischievous glint appears in her eye, but her attention quickly shifts to the girl beside her, who whispers something in her ear. Viola nods in response to whatever her date just said.

Breakfast comes soon after, and I make a point to eat silently. Both men don't say a word, thankfully sensing that I don't want to talk about what transpired anymore. It doesn't stop them from glancing at me worriedly the entire meal as if I'm about to sponta-neously combust. Though it's not completely put away, my magic is still a hum compared to the roar it was before. The over-whelming feeling of it coursing through me and around me is now a dull stream. Once the dishes are cleared from the table, I find the strength to finally speak.

"I figured I could show you around the castle and then we can ride into town. There are a few spots I want to take you to before sundown. I still have to pack before we leave tomorrow. Do you know how long we'll be in your kingdom?" Aris leans back in his chair, looking arrogant and full of grace all at the same time.

"The king and queen didn't tell you?"

"Does it sound like they told me?" I respond sarcastically. He rolls his eyes at me and hesitates before saying,

"You're scheduled to be there for at least a month." He stands, lifting his jacket from the back of the chair.

"A month," I echo as I stand, making a move to grab my cloak to find it gone. River stands with it in his hand, stepping closer to place it over me. I tie the strands in the front, welcoming the warmth it brings. I glance at him quickly, murmuring a thanks to which he simply nods in response. The River, who never used to even look at me, is now helping me put my cloak on. Did I wake up in the same realm as yesterday? This must be a dream. *Silly Ember, wake up.*

Someone clears their throat from the other table; I look over to see Viola raising an eyebrow at me and then making a pointed look to Aris. Right, I should introduce him.

"Aris, come meet the rest of my royal court." He nods and follows me over to their table. Now awake and a little less hazy, all of my peers, save for Robert, look up at us. Most with a look of disdain, some with curiosity. Aris stands to my right, River on my left.

"Good morning everyone, I'd like you to formally meet the Crown Prince Aris of Klyeria. He'll be touring the estate and Balle with me today, and tomorrow we leave for his kingdom." I peer up at Aris, who looks at everyone with that same arrogant, bored look he wears normally.

Jasper scoffs quietly, his hands balled up in fists in a not-so-subtle manner. Jane lays her hand on his forearm to calm him, but Jasper looks like he's about to combust. He looks at me, questions filling his eyes. *Trust me,* I urge him with pleading eyes. "This is my court. They will take over for their parents when I ascend to the throne. This is Lord Jasper Wellington and our lovely Jane. Then there's Lord Easton Cadrel and Lady Viola Cadrel—they are twins, so don't be confused; they will each rule their own respective lands separately. That is Viola's lovely date. Lady Sierra

Whitlock. Lord Cameron Stallard. Lady Daisy Lucertia. Lord Robert Walton is probably still in bed, nursing a hangover. " Cameron nods in confirmation, a sly grin playing on his lips.

"It's a pleasure to meet you all," Aris drawls from beside me. Sierra eyes him with both curiosity and something like seduction. I try to rein in the instant jealousy that bubbles up. Aris doesn't return the stare. He simply looks over all of them before nodding to himself. Jasper glares.

"Can't say the same," Jasper mumbles. I shoot him a look, and he looks away.

"Right there with you, Jasper," Viola murmurs, then looks Aris in the eye, and if looks could kill, Aris would be dead at my feet. "You have a lot of nerve coming here. I'd watch my back if I were you." Aris bristles beside me, but his stance remains lazy, unbothered.

"Is that a threat?" Aris says calmly. "Because for your sake, I hope it's not." I shoot him a look too. He picks an invisible speck of dust off his coat, not sparing Viola a glance.

Viola's eyes flare. She goes to stand, but her date puts a hand on her arm that stops her in her tracks. Viola swallows and looks at me, something like betrayal flashing in her eyes, but before she can speak, Easton is getting up, ready to pounce.

"Don't talk to her like that," Easton sneers. I've never seen him so quick to anger before, and I know if I don't step in, they're all going to go for his throat. Easton stalks forward and I take a step in front of Aris.

"That's enough." I use an authoritative voice over them that I've never used before. They all visibly flinch, and something hardens in the pit of my stomach. I don't want any animosity with them. The last thing I want to do is pull rank, but I will if need be. "He is a guest in our kingdom, and despite any assumptions, he is here amicably. Give him the same chance that he is also giving us." I turn to Aris. "The same goes for you: do not be so quick to anger. Forgive my peers; none of us were prepared for your arrival. They mean no harm." Aris simply shrugs. I glance at my peers once more. They nod, jaws clenched but, thankfully, no longer displaying hostility.

Not able to take any more of this awkward encounter, I bid everyone goodbye. As I turn to go, Viola says,

"Be careful, Ember. Find us later if you can. To talk." I look over my shoulder at her and give her a reassuring nod before the three of us exit. We're quiet for a moment until Aris says,

"Such charming friends you have." The sharpness in his voice causes me to pause in the hall, on our way to the stables.

"You don't get to joke about them." I cross my arms over my chest; River stands behind me while I face Aris. "We've spent our whole lives hating your father and everything he stands for. They've lost people because of this war. Cut them some slack for not understanding your presence here amongst us."

Aris looks down at me, anger and hurt swirling in his onyx eyes. His jaw tightens, but he doesn't speak for a moment. I hold his gaze, unwilling to back down.

"I am not him," is all he says. A wave of understanding floods through me, and I find myself nodding.

"I know. Just give them a chance to learn that on their own." He nods, and we continue toward the stables. I glance up at River, who meets my gaze for a moment, giving me a look of pride that makes me smile.

THE REST of the afternoon goes by as best as it could with two men who won't stop bickering and belittling each other. We ride the horses around the estate, and I show Aris my favorite parts of the village.

All of my favorite little shops and merchants that sell some of the best items we have to offer in Agatharea. As the day goes on, we all seem to relax a bit, the tension melting from our shoulders as we explore together. The peace doesn't last long for River as he becomes rigid and tense with worry as people come rushing up to my horse, eager to meet the Crown Princess. I scold him a couple of times as he glares at everyone who tries to come near me.

Some of the children bring me drawings and little toy figures, giggling when I thank them and tell them I'll be pinning up their artwork in the castle. The parents in turn bring me lists of issues that need addressing. I take it all, keeping a smile on my face as I interact with my people, trying to keep a friendly face for them to remember as their future queen. Most don't know who Aris is, and it seems he prefers it that way from the way he remains behind whenever someone rushes up to us. Those who do recognize him spit in the dirt at his feet. He takes it all in stride, never wavering from the cocky facade he wears so effortlessly.

I place all the drawings and lists into a satchel on the back of my horse, Snowball. She's as white as fresh snow, spotted with mud that's building on her hooves from all the travel. I take a deep breath, enjoying the way the cool air stills the buzzing within me. I don't know when I begin to shiver, but at some point I can't stop. River notices my chattering teeth immediately and decides it's time to head back to the castle. Aris miraculously agrees with River.

I was hoping to stay long enough to see Olga. I haven't seen her since the bars were put on my window, and with the Winter Solstice ball and everything else, I didn't have the time. There's no sight of her on her usual bench, and my heart sinks. With the weather being this cold, I just don't know how she survives the winters.

I huff and turn my horse down the main path back to the palace, whipping the reins so we can take off ahead of the guys. My cloak does well to keep my legs covered as my dress is hitched up from how I'm sitting in the saddle. I laugh giddily as the wind whips through my hair, the hood of my cloak falling back with the speed. I hear River curse behind me and a chuckle from Aris as they get their horses to do the same.

My heart beats wildly in my chest as I pick up even more

speed. The thrill rips through me, setting me ablaze as we enter an open field that is now covered in snow, dead flowers poking out from beneath. Snowball's hooves pound against the earth as she picks up more speed.

"Slow down, Ember!" River bellows not far behind me.

"Make me!" I yell over my shoulder, laughing. I look back at him for a moment, and the sight of him nearly makes me slow down so he *could* catch me. But Snowball flies across the field, almost as if she's just as giddy to be running so wildly, so freely.

I lean forward, squeezing her reins to keep steady on her back as the castle comes into view. My heart thunders in my ears as we slow at the entrance of the stables. I laugh as I slide off of her, leading her into her stall as Aris and River arrive, busying myself getting her some dinner and much-needed water before latching the lock on her door. When I turn around, I find River with his arms crossed and Aris, who looks bemused next to him. I smile at them both, a real smile.

"Well, that was fun, wasn't it?" River just continues to look at me with those brooding, unimpressed eyes. "Oh, come on, River, lighten up. I'm alive." River huffs but doesn't say anything as I join them to walk back to the Main Quarter.

"River, when's your birthday?" I ask suddenly, the thought striking me that I may have missed it. He looks down at me with cautious eyes.

"Why?" River asks.

"Mine is in February. The twenty-fourth," Aris says from beside me. I chuckle.

"Thank you, Aris. But seriously, River, when is it?" We enter the dining hall, now empty.

"In four weeks. The twenty-fourth of January," River mumbles, barely audible.

"And how old will you be turning?" I ask.

"I will be twenty-five," Aris answers again. I shove his arm and he chuckles.

"River," I say in warning. River sighs, pulling out my seat for me this time.

"I'll also be twenty-five," he grits out, uncomfortable with being the center of attention. *Interesting.*

"When is yours, Princess?" Aris asks as he sits across from me. I shiver, keeping my cloak on even inside.

"March twenty-fourth, I will be twenty-one." Servants emerge from the kitchen with bowls of something steaming that smells amazing. When the bowl is set in front of me, I hover my fingers above it, letting it thaw my ice-cold digits.

"How peculiar," Aris muses out loud. I hum in agreement. I'm about to bring the spoon to my mouth when the door opens; I peer over and nearly drop my spoon into my bowl when my parents walk in. I straighten up immediately and cool my features into the stone-cold look I've mastered over the years.

My heart pounds painfully in my chest as they near our table. We all rise to greet them.

"Ember, a word," my father says, his face a mask of cool authority. I move away from the table, and River moves to follow. "Alone," my father says to River, and River halts, looking at me with a torn expression that nearly breaks something inside me. I turn away from him, unable to bear that look, and then River does something I *never* thought he'd do.

"No," he says lowly and with so much conviction it almost makes me shudder.

"You're dismissed for the night, River," my father says with no room to argue. Aris looks between us all, confused at River's show of disobedience.

"She's not going anywhere with you alone. I won't stand for it." River takes a step toward me, but as he does, so do the two guards that trail my father. Nicholas takes a couple of steps forward and has to look up slightly as he speaks lethally.

"One more word out of you, and I'll find her another guard. You are dismissed to your chambers. Now. You can wait for her there." My father smiles at him. *Smiles.* It's then that I realize my father knows that River is fully aware of what's going to happen, and he wants to make this even harder for him. He'll make River wait, powerless, for me to arrive beaten and bloodied, and there's nothing he can do about it. I don't know when I began to shake, but Aris watches quietly, calculating as if beginning to understand.

My father turns and walks with my mother. He looks at me with a silent command to follow, and I do so until I'm yanked back by River. *Oh gods, River, please don't do this to yourself.*

It takes not one, not two, but three guards to hold River back as I follow my father with my head down. I blink back the tears as I listen to him bellow and fight against their hold. I faintly hear Aris murmur something to River but can't make out what it is.

As we walk down the hall toward his office, I empty my head of all thoughts. I know this one is going to be bad. I'll pay for whatever it is I've done *and* for River. I'd take his punishment any day.

My mother and I file in as my father closes the door with the two guards standing outside of his office. And then I see it. Everything in me turns to ice as I behold a whip laid out on my father's desk. He's never used anything but his own hands on me. This is an entirely new level of punishment. I should've known something was coming when they seemed all too kind after my speech and beheld my scandalous dress. My father's voice is a scary kind of calm as he begins to speak.

"I have never felt such shame, such embarrassment, as I did last night. Unzip the back of your dress," he orders me.

"Father, please, I—" I back up against the door, looking to my mother in desperation, but she doesn't bother to look at me. She studies her nails, as if this is boring her. In one swift movement my father is in front of me, wrapping his hand around my neck, slamming my head against the door. Pain ricochets throughout my skull. I find myself struggling to breathe as I try to pry his fingers away. Magic in me swells with the desire to defend myself, but I stomp it down.

"I should've killed you a long time ago. If you weren't so important, if you weren't the only thing that could secure me what I need, you wouldn't walk out of this office. This will teach you to cover up. This will teach you to keep your godsdamn mouth shut. This will teach you that what I say goes and you do as I ask. You think just because you'll be queen one day that you'll have a say in anything? That I'll step aside just like that? You're sorely mistaken. I won't let some whore like you do a single thing for this kingdom. You'll just be a pretty face on the cover. Now unzip the fucking dress and lean over my desk," he rasps out, pure hatred filling every word he spits at me. He finally lets go of my throat, and I gasp for breath, nearly tumbling to my knees as the room spins.

With shaky hands I reach to the back of my dress, grabbing ahold of the zipper, pulling down, and baring my back to him as I walk over to his desk and lean over the cool wood. I press my cheek to the surface, forcing my tears back as I stare at myself in the reflection of the window. He walks over, pulling the fabric away to fully expose my skin.

Some small part of me begs for me to fight back, to not give in to this madness, but the bigger, more prominent part of me allows me to just take it. To take the lashings I deserve. To accept that I am who they say I am. To accept that I have no power. My magic recoils even further, almost feeling disappointed that I could think such a thing.

I barely hear anything as he grabs the whip. I don't even hear the crack of it when it hits the skin of my back, breaking the surface. My body arches at the burning, but I force myself to still again, making no noise.

"You want to act tough?" He laughs wickedly, and the whip comes down again, harder. I can't help the wince that falls from my lips then, the pain flashing through me like lightning. "That's what I thought. You weak, stupid, fat bitch. I fucking *hate* you." The whip keeps coming, and coming, with more and more insults. His voice is a deep, dark thing scarring me from the inside out.

The words sear themselves into my skin, striking somewhere deep in my soul as all the terrible things he's wanted to say come tumbling from him. My mother snickers from somewhere in the room, and a sob escapes me at the sound. I should fight back, but something keeps me planted there.

Eventually I can't hear my cries, whimpers, or groans. Everything becomes silent as roaring fills my head.

I focus every piece of my will on keeping the magic welling within me to stay put. The aching pain from keeping it inside as well as the burning from the lashes causes black to tinge my vision. Sweat begins to build on my brows as the whip keeps on coming. He slows as he tires, and he raises the whip for a final time. I almost whimper in relief. My knees buckle, and I nearly fall to the floor when the final blow comes. Blood pours down my back, the skin raw and on fire as I begin to rise up.

"You're making a fucking mess; clean it up." My father grabs a handkerchief from his coat and dabs his forehead, sweat building up from exerting himself on me. He throws the cloth at me, and I use it to wipe up the blood that has dripped onto the floor and what has splattered on his desk. I zip up my dress carefully, wincing loudly at the sting as it lays against my back again, allowing the fabric to soak up the trickle of blood. Whatever adrenaline coursing through me is the only explanation for my ability to move at all. My mother speaks next.

"You are to act normal. Every time you move, every time you so much as breathe, you'll feel the pain. Every time you wince, remember this moment. The doctor is under strict orders not to heal you. Let this be your reminder as we travel to Klyeria that we own you. That you do as we say. Your job is to shut up and be a pretty little thing, and that's it. If you mess up, this will continue to be your punishment. Do you understand?" She looks at me pointedly. I merely nod, averting my eyes in the submissive manner I know they're looking for.

"Very well, be ready to leave tomorrow morning. It's a two-day journey, and you'll be there for a month, so pack accordingly. Now get out of my sight." My mother turns to my father, placing a hand on his shoulder, but he shrugs her off. I don't stick around to ask any of the questions that fill my head. I'm going to be there for a month; does that mean they're leaving me? Would River stay? Why am I staying and they aren't? What are they planning?

The door closes behind me, and I struggle to find my way down the stairs. The halls are eerily quiet, and for a moment I think of going to Jasper. But I think better of it and hold onto the wall as I make my way to my room one slow step at a time. Tears stream down my face as I realize I won't be saying goodbye to him, or any of them, and that hurts more than the lashes on my back.

Black edges my vision as I push through the pain, the cold biting into my skin as soon as I make it outside into the frigid night air. My throat becomes ragged as I sob through the torment of crawling up the stairs. There's a guard in front of River's room and in front of Aris' as I approach my door slowly.

When they see me, they take their leave, not sparing me another glance. I'm still crawling on my hands and knees when I get to my room, silently crying as I rise to turn the knob.

Between the exhaustion from the day, having not eaten since morning time, and the pain ricocheting throughout my entire body, I barely make it to my bed before collapsing.

Roaring begins to fill my head again as the images of what happened play through my head, my father's voice sounding like he's still in the room with me. Flashbacks of the night at Marbs start to spill over, and the rest of my horrifying memories start to meld together. I can't breathe. I can't move. I can't do anything but lay there, curled into a ball as I fight to calm down. The scent of blood fills my nose, and I know that the blood's soaking into the bed, but I can't find the energy to move. I can't do anything as the tears keep falling.

All I can do is wish Nythiem had mercy on me.

CHAPTER 14

I stay in the same position, afraid to move, afraid to do anything as I stare out my window. The night glares right back at me. Flurries have begun to fall, and I silently watch them in the moonlight, attempting to empty out everything screaming at me in my head. All that power has retreated into its box, and cold seeps into my bones. It's as if it's disappointed that I didn't fight back, that I didn't use it to protect myself. But how could I?

Without the well of power swirling in me, I feel hollow. And I suppose that's what I deserve for being so powerless against my parents. What I deserve for not being the strong woman I so desperately try to be.

It's not long before River figures out the guards have left and his door flies open. My own is already ajar because I had no energy left to shut it.

There are no words to explain the painful sound that comes from his throat when he lights a candle and sees me lying there, unmoving. I swear I can feel his own agony pulsing toward me, as if his emotion is flooding into me through what I recognize now as a tether that connects him to my very being.

I still can't fucking move. He says something, but his voice sounds muffled. Like he's speaking underwater. The roaring in my head is so loud I can't hear anything else. He says something again, louder this time, but still nothing registers.

I can't look at him. Can't move. I'm trapped in this hollowed-out version of myself. Can't do anything as he rushes over, and then there's another presence. They drop to their knees at the foot of the bed, taking in the sight of my blood, I imagine. I can't see out the window anymore. I can only see the flickers of the fires creating a mirror with the inky black night beyond the glass. Mint, earth, something like spice, and cedarwood swirl in the air, and I take a deep breath of it. The only thing it seems I can do. Breathe. Breathe. Breathe.

They're talking. No, yelling? I can't tell. I can't tell who they're talking to. My head—it's too loud. Someone leaves and enters my bathroom. The other says something to me, kneeling down to unzip the dress. I breathe. The zipper moves slowly, and the sting is almost as unbearable as receiving the lashes all over again. I breathe. The zipper halts at the bottom. I breathe. Warm hands peel the fabric from my skin. I breathe.

New blood gushes, and someone swears behind me. I breathe. Someone helps me sit up. The pain washes over me, and a flicker of me comes to the surface.

"Get out; let me undress her." River. River's talking. Who's he talking to? I try to focus on the reflections in the window. A flash of black hair and onyx eyes. He doesn't move. He can't move. He's staring at the lashes. I stare at him, watching the blood trickle down my spine. Something like horror flashes in those eyes. No, not horror—disgust. He looks like he's going to get sick. I think I am too. Nausea rolls through me as the pain comes to a full roar.

"Aris. Get. Out," River repeats, borderline growling in command. Aris swallows and nods.

"What else do you need? Bandages? Salve? Where's the doctor?" Aris moves away, still staring at the raw skin.

"He won't come," I say, my voice barely a whisper. My voice sounds foreign and not my own. River whips his head to me.

"Ember, oh Ember." He breathes a sigh of relief at the sound of my voice. Aris moves back toward me. I track the movement in the reflection, unable to look at either of them directly.

"Strict orders. No healing," is all I can manage to say before that voice disappears again. Aris' eyes widen with realization, followed by pure rage. I can't stay up. I lean to lie down again, but River stops me; he quickly turns to Aris.

"In my room, on the desk, is a first aid kit I keep; grab that and bring it to me in the washroom." Aris nods; his face has gone pale. He turns and briskly walks out of my room. I return to the hollow—the space where nothing resides. I breathe.

River comes to the front of me, gripping my elbows as he helps me to my feet. Carefully avoiding my back, he turns me, guiding me one foot after another into my bathroom toward a tub that's filling with warm water. The air smells like lavender. I breathe. River lets me stand while slowly pulling the dress completely off me. My knees threaten to buckle as I stare straight ahead; the muscles in my back scream with the tension of holding me up. He pulls the rest of my undergarments off before grabbing my hands to guide me into the bath.

I scream as the water touches the open wounds, but the sound of my voice is muffled in my own ears. It stings so much it feels like tiny knives are digging into each individual lash. The water turns red from the blood. The rushing of the water fills my head, and I let that be the only thing I can hear as I draw my knees to my chest and lay my cheek on top of them. The skin of my back stretches and aches, but I ignore it, seeking solace in the warm water now that it doesn't sting as much.

With my back to the door, I can feel Aris walk in and hear him say something to River, but it's all quiet again. River responds, and then Aris leaves after one long look at my back once more. I don't say anything, don't make a noise as River takes careful measures to clean my back and my hair from the caked-up blood at the ends. He rinses me off, trying to be as gentle as he can. I can't think of anything as he pulls the drain, the red and pink water washing away. I can't think about him seeing me naked. Can't dwell on being weak and injured again. Something sours in me, but still I say nothing.

He applies a cream to my wounds, and I can't help the whimpers that come with the direct application. I think he apologizes. I can't bring myself to tell him he shouldn't. The bandages come next, and he takes extra care with each wound, making sure it's covered to his liking. After the lashes are attended to, he focuses on the bruises forming on my throat, rubbing another cream into the tender skin there. Finally, he takes a brush from the counter and carefully brushes my hair as best as he can.

He lifts me up by my elbows again, drying the rest of me off as carefully and respectfully as he can. I should feel embarrassed. I should feel angry, or sad, or anything. But I feel nothing as he wraps me in the towel and leads me back to my room. He grabs a warm nightgown that has been laid out on my bed. I lift my arms wordlessly, painfully, and he slips it on over my head. I look down at the bed, now stained in my blood, then back at him. He follows my gaze before he nods, understanding. We can't ask a servant to change these. They'll know. They'll gossip.

"I can get extras. Just stay here; stay where it's warm." He turns to pull a chair near the fire, and I raise a hand to stop him. He looks at me. I look back at the blood and shake my head. *I can't sleep there. I can't sleep alone.* He seems to understand the look in my eyes and nods again, taking the sheets off the bed and piling them to the side. After blowing out the candles and putting out the fire, he comes to where I stand and puts his arm around me, holding me up by my elbows once more. He's very careful to not touch my back as he leads me across the hall to his bedroom.

River takes his time getting me into bed. Every touch, every caress is more gentle than the last. He doesn't say anything to me and I realize that he's at just as much of a loss for words as I am. I don't have to ask for him to join me in bed. He does it all on his own, carefully getting comfortable beside me.

The fire flickers, sending shadows over his beautiful face. A storm rages in his eyes, a whirlwind of thoughts and questions clashing in the battle within his mind. Still, he lets the silence settle between us.

He leans forward eventually, brushing his lips softly against the furrow in my brow, loosening the tension there with a single touch. His forehead finds mine and everything quiets eventually.

He may not have been able to protect me this time, but his presence alone calms the ache inside me for a brief moment. It allows me the ability to breathe deeply. His scent and warmth lull me into a deep sleep I didn't think I'd find tonight.

It is with him that I realize I may be able to endure after all.

MY HEAD POUNDS the next morning as I lift it from the pillow. The sun shines through the window, revealing an empty bed beside me. My heart begins to race in panic, but I force myself to get up, pushing on my hands beneath me. I groan loudly as my back stretches against the already forming scabs. More whimpers escape as I sit on the edge of the bed. His room is a mirror of my own, but somehow more rugged, more suited toward River.

Some of his guard uniform lies on the chair near his desk; books lie everywhere in piles scattered throughout the room.

Standing causes the scabs to crack, and my back becomes wet with fresh blood. I'm cursing silently as River walks in, fully clad in his uniform already. His eyes widen when he takes in that I'm awake and standing.

"Sit down," he orders me, and I give in instantly, knees buckling as I sit back on the edge of the bed in relief. He sets down several bags near the door, and realization dawns on me that I haven't packed. He seems to recognize the look in my eye immediately.

"I packed for you. As best as I could, at least. We'll be gone for a month, so I pretty much packed as much as I could fit in the bags and then some. If not, maybe you can go shopping while we're there." His voice sounds sheepish. It's cute as he seems to fumble his words.

"Thank you, River. I'm sure you did a wonderful job. I'm also positive you didn't think your morning would start with rifling through my panties," I joke softly, hoping to ease some of the tension vibrating in his body. He raises an eyebrow at me, knowing I'm covering the pain with humor. He steps forward, kneeling in front of me as he searches my face. In this position, we're eye level with each other. The rage simmering in those ocean eyes causes tears to burn in my own.

It's not you he's mad at.

"I'm okay," I whisper, trying to assure him.

"Don't," he says.

"Don't what?" I dare ask.

"Don't lie to me." River reaches up, wiping away a stray tear from my cheek. I lean into his hand, closing my eyes as I try to still my shaking. "I could kill him," River murmurs low and deep. The sound of his voice is almost primal, so soaked in rage. He rises, taking a step away from me, and I already miss the heat from his hands. He begins to pace back and forth, contemplating the murder of the king. "I could fucking kill him." And somehow, I found myself wondering the same thing: how I could be rid of the man for the rest of my life. *But there is no escaping.*

"You can't. We can't. We have to pretend like nothing happened. They don't want anyone to know." I glance at the window, knowing we're biding our time. I stand, taking a couple of painful steps toward his door. "No one can know. That's part of the punishment."

"Well, he should've thought about that before whipping you raw. There's no way no one's going to notice you're hobbling around, Ember. I can't..." His jaw ticks. "I can't just act like he didn't do anything. I can't pretend you're okay. I can't pretend that yet again I haven't let you down." His hands shake, and the guilt in his eyes almost brings me to my knees. *But he's letting you in; he's letting you see.*

"No one denies the king, River. Not me, not you, and not even Aris. And the fact that you tried is something I'll be eternally grateful for. As much as I hate this, I'd do it again just to give my people a fighting chance. We just have to get through the next few days, and then we'll be rid of him." He shakes his head even as I try to use a soothing voice with him. My heart swells at how protective he's being.

"How are you okay? How can you... How do you have the strength to do any of this right now?" He walks over to me finally, his gaze intense, making me swallow. *Gods, I don't know if I can take him looking at me like that.*

"Because I have to be. Last night was... That was a fluke. I don't know where I went, but I'm fine now. I promise I can do this." I take a few steps without grimacing or wincing just to prove it. My body screams on the inside, but I calm my features, making it convincing. He narrows his eyes at me, wanting to argue, but he knows there's no other way. Not right now. He only nods, not convinced but defeated.

I walk into my room silently, and I head for the closet to grab the warmest clothes left in there. I quickly slide on a pair of underwear since River didn't put any on me last night. Not that I blame him; he had to get intimate enough with me as it is. My cheeks burn at the memories of him seeing me completely naked. Part of me wishes circumstances would have been different. *I wish he never had to see me like this at all.*

I grab my warmest dress and a tunic to put under it and set them on the bed. I'm preparing to change when River knocks on the door. His soothing presence fills my room after I call to him to come in. He holds up some wraps and the salve he used on me.

"We should change the dressings before you put all of that

on." He gestures to the bathroom, and I follow him, slowly getting used to the burn that accompanies each step that I take.

He turns around to give me some privacy while I take the nightgown off. In one hand, I hold it to cover my chest. I use the other to brace the sink, leaning forward slightly. The image in the mirror has my heart pounding with the way I'm displayed for him in nothing but my underwear. I clutch the fabric flush against my breasts, but there's no mistaking the slope of them from the side. He turns and pauses for a moment, and it's as if he can't help himself as his eyes roam over my body. My skin sears in every place he looks, and it takes everything in me not to pant under that gaze.

All this time, begging for him to look at me, and now suddenly it's too much.

He clears his throat softly before moving to undo the bandages. His fingers work gently, one by one, removing the bloody gauze. I hiss as the air stings against the raw skin. He murmurs an apology before wetting a soft hand towel and begins cleaning the newly spilled blood. He works slowly, but the pain is blinding. My knees wobble, and he instinctively grabs hold of my hips with his free hand, steadying me. His fingers grip against my skin and the lace of my panties.

I focus on those fingers and the way they feel to try and distract myself from the burning pain. He drops the bloody rag into the sink and grabs the salve he used yesterday and begins working that onto the wounds. His thumb moves against the skin on my hip, and I can't help the little pants for air that fall from my lips. They turn into whimpers I can't suppress as the pain becomes unbearable. He moves closer, working his way up my back, the heat of him pressing right behind me. *Focus on him. Focus on him.*

I dip my head, biting my lip to control the way I'm reacting to him. But I can't stay still; my body is too confused by the pain and pleasure signals being sent to my brain. I lean back a little more, my bum dangerously close to his groin. Fuck, if I just lean a little more, he'd be perfectly nestled into me. I look at him through my lashes in the reflection, and the circular motion of his finger on my back stops as he meets my eyes.

Fire burns in my gaze as I drink in the sight of us. I'm almost completely bent over at the waist for him; his grip on my hip is the perfect anchor for him to drive himself into me. I don't even bother trying to hide the dirty thoughts, too caught up in how much I just want to feel good in the middle of all this bad. I need his touch to replace all of the terrible things scarred on my skin. Both visible and invisible.

He swallows, and I watch the bob of his throat go up and down. I wonder what his skin tastes like. Is it as delicious as the way he smells? His eyes trail down to where I clutch my nightgown and where I've now started to let it go, letting my breasts free of the fabric. My nipples ache for his touch, and the throbbing in my core becomes almost unbearable as he drinks in the sight of me.

The burning in his eyes matches my own, and the lust-filled air becomes intoxicating. His hand starts to trail up my hip, across the sides of my ribs, and I nearly arch at the touch if it weren't for the pain that would follow. When I push back, my bottom brushes against something hard. Our breaths are ragged, mingling together as he continues to trail up, almost reaching my breast until his eyes catch on the lashes of my back once more, and suddenly he stops. We both do as if remembering who we are and what we're doing. I swallow, bringing the nightgown back to my chest as he picks up the gauze and begins wrapping the open wounds.

Neither of us says a word as he finishes. I can't look him in the eye as I turn and let him apply the second cream to my now blue and purple neck. Can't breathe as those rough hands rub the tender skin. I swear he doesn't breathe either, not with me facing him like this, so close that another step would bring us flush against each other. So, we don't move. We don't breathe. He takes a step back, both of us pretending nothing just happened as he gathers the rest of the supplies. He clears his throat before asking,

"Do you need help getting dressed?" His voice is husky, and the sound drags itself over my body. I try not to act affected.

"No, I think I've got it. Thank you, River." My own voice rasps, thick with arousal. He nods and walks out of my room without another glance at me.

Where the hell did all of that come from? I've never been so bold with him, and now I'm terrified I've just scared him off. I don't want him to go back to that silent, stoic River. But gods, I can't help the effect he has on me either. I can't help that silent tether that tugs on me wherever he goes. I shake my head of the aroused fog and quickly make my way back to my bed. Painful groans fill the air as I struggle to get dressed. All the pleasure I felt moments ago fades quickly as the pain rushes back, replacing it once again.

The turtleneck of my dress covers the bruises on my throat, which I'm grateful for. The fewer stares, the better. River meets me in the hall with his own bags, and I move to grab mine, but he gives me a look.

"Not a chance," he growls. I snort but listen nonetheless. Aris enters the hall with his own bags and sets them beside the door as he closes it. He immediately turns to me, those stunning dark eyes stark with worry. I offer him a smile. *I'm fine. I'm okay.* Still, he swallows the distance between us in a few short strides.

"Princess..." he breathes. So many questions simmer on the surface, but he doesn't ask any as several servants come up the stairs at the opposite end of the hall. They pause, taking in me and the boys before hurriedly grabbing our things to take down to the carriages. I place my hand gingerly on Aris' arm, hoping to soothe the worry.

I let go as I follow after the servants, walking as normally as I can without grimacing. It's not the most graceful of movements, but it'll do if no one's paying attention. I try to calm my racing heart by taking deep breaths, but the stretch of my lungs pulls at the skin on my back. *Every breath soaked in pain, to remind you they own you.* I swallow the acid rising in my throat and push forward.

River falls into step behind me alongside Aris. I can feel both of their stares on me like they can see straight through my clothes to the wounds that lie below. The brisk air is cutting as it whips across my face. The journey to Klyerla will be brutal in these conditions, and I know that's part of this punishment.

Aris splits apart from River, and it feels like two leashes tethered to my core move apart in different directions as Aris approaches our carriage, where some of our bags are being placed. River comes up beside me as I stand still in place, awaiting the arrival of my parents. He places a comforting hand on the back of my arm, rubbing softly. I sigh into that touch, my breath clouding in front of me as I breathe out.

Aris returns to us, stopping in front of me with a knit hat in his hand. He lifts it and puts it on my head with a goofy smile as he adjusts it and my hair, moving some pieces to my shoulders and tucking others away from my face.

"Is this necessary?" I ask.

"If it'll help keep your clattering teeth to a minimum, then yes, I believe it is." I smooth my wild curls beneath the hat. He's right, though; I savor the warmth it brings to my ears, and my shivering eases. But the smile fades from my face as the king and queen begin to descend the stairs, hand in hand, toward their royal carriage.

River immediately drops his hand from my arm, and I try not to care. The horses at the front huff and dig their hooves into the ground impatiently. We all wait as the king and queen are escorted into their carriage; the queen enters first, followed by my father. He leans down and says something to the servant before they close the door. The servant walks to Aris and says,

"You three will ride in the front carriage, followed by the king and queen, and then the final carriage will carry the rest of their belongings and a few of us servants. His Majesty would like to stop for a meal…" I drone out the rest of my father's requests and orders, my eyes glazing over as I retreat inwards. I focus on those two shimmering tethers, wondering what they mean and why they're connected to both River and Aris.

I remember the first time I felt it; it was a little over a week after I had met River, the first time he'd ever touched me. I was walking, and my ankle rolled over on a loose rock I hadn't seen. He had caught me, steadying me with his hands beneath my elbows. He hadn't said anything to me then, but in that moment it felt like something had snapped into place, as if a lasso had been thrown around the both of us, connecting us with an invisible rope.

If he had felt it then, he didn't show it. But in the beginning, he was even more closed off than he is now. I never paid it much attention until it happened again with Aris.

I drag an invisible hand up each chord, and I'm vaguely aware that both men straighten at my sides. Then I tug, paying attention to the way they react. They both take a step closer to me, their warmth flooding me from either side. *How peculiar.*

I stop messing with those tethers, even though a million questions bombard me at once about what they are and how they work. Perhaps I did something involuntarily with my magic.

Finally, Aris and the servant stop talking, and we make our way to our carriage at the front. Aris says something to the coachman and then gets in first, sitting against the window. I climb in, taking River's hand as I raise myself inside. I can't help the wince that falls from my lips as I bend to sit. Aris flashes me a worried look, but I ignore it, trying to ignore the pain. I settle beside him, my shoulder pressed into his as River takes the spot on my right. River's thigh is flush with mine, and I press my lips into a thin line as Aris' does the same. It's a tight squeeze for all of us here, but not uncomfortable.

As I look out toward the castle, a different type of ache fills my chest. One that brings me back to tears as the carriage begins moving. I'm leaving Jasper and not saying goodbye. There's a part of me that's grateful. He doesn't have to know what happened to me.

The much larger part of me yearns to have had a moment with him before I left. To tell him it's going to be a month, not a couple of days. To tell him I'll be back before he knows it because as much as I need him, he also needs me. We make that castle feel like home to each other.

I quickly wipe away my tears, sniffling softly when River looks down at me.

"We'll be back. He'll understand when we get back," he reminds me soothingly. All I can do is nod.

All I can do is lay my head back and shut my eyes. The exhaustion just from moving has already settled into my bones, and quickly slumber finds me. It takes me and drowns me in my sorrows. The only thing that doesn't let me get pulled too far down is the heat radiating on both sides of me. With them, I have a way back to the surface.

CHAPTER 15

Murmuring voices bring me back to consciousness. I don't open my eyes right away, too comfortable with where my head lies on Aris' shoulder.

"There has to be a way to take her away from this. River, he whipped her so hard and so long there wasn't a single inch of untouched skin," Aris whispers.

"I know. Aris, I fucking know. What do you suggest we do? If we take her away, they'll hunt her down, and then us. If we say anything, they'll deny it, and then our heads are on the line for speaking ill of them. Every single route could end with all of us dead. I spent the entire night trying to think of a way out of this. The only way it stops is when she becomes queen. So, we need to make that happen. Do you know anything else about why they're finally meeting after all this time?" River's voice is so soft, but the rage and hurt underneath are loud and clear.

Aris stops breathing for a moment. Almost like he wants time to stop right along with him so he can figure this out.

"My father does what he wants, when he wants. I'm just at his disposal to carry out whatever ridiculous plans he comes up with. Including pushing me onto her." Aris' voice is hoarse as he speaks; I can tell there are hidden scars beneath what he's saying.

"I'm sure they'll do whatever it takes to remain in control, even if that means trading off their daughter to our enemy," River grits out. "Fucking bastards," he adds. I stir quietly, feigning that I'm just waking up with a soft groan as I lift myself from Aris' shoulder.

"Hey there, sleepyhead, did you know you snore?" Aris says first, in a much more pleasant voice, like they weren't just talking about how to save me. *I don't need to be saved. This life is what I'm supposed to live.*

"I do not." I look over to River for confirmation, but he can't help the small smile as he nods in confirmation. "Oh gods." *Nythiem, strike me down now.*

"Don't worry; it's cute; it sounds like a little mouse snoring," Aris says while chuckling. I look to River again, who again nods to confirm. *Oh, come on.* Before I can respond, my stomach growls. I cover my face with my hands, my cheeks reddening with further embarrassment.

"Throw me out of this carriage now," I mumble into my hands.

The warmth radiating off of both of them has made me much too hot. So I begin to peel off layers where I can. The hat comes off, but when I try to take my cloak off, the stiffness in my back brings me to a halt.

Without hesitation, they both jump in to help me, pulling it off of me gently before discarding it at our feet neatly. I welcome the cool air against my clammy skin, breathing a sigh of relief.

Aris slides the window open and leans out to call to the coachman to stop for a moment. I watch curiously as he disappears outside of the carriage to retrieve who knows what. He's quick. When he enters with a sack of what smells like fruits and cheese, I just about groan with delight. But that wouldn't be very princess-like, and I'm trying to preserve at least a little bit of my dignity.

"I had the servants pack some snacks for the road; I figured you'd get hungry." I offer him an appreciative look before we dive into the much-needed nutrition.

I can practically hear my body singing with relief as I finally get something into it. Once we find ourselves satiated, we place the sack at our feet. It's quiet for a moment, and I find myself itching to fill the silence.

"Aris, what are the camping conditions going to be like tonight?"

"We'll set up the tents in an area I scouted while coming here. I marked it off. I didn't have any issues with the creatures in Atravelien. So we should be fine for the night. If not, we'll just offer up the brute and then run for our lives." River cuts Aris a look but doesn't say anything. He hasn't said a word to me since he took care of my bandages. I try not to care. I fail—miserably.

"As in, we're staying in the open wilderness, like bait to all of the animals out there, while it's also simultaneously below freezing outside? My parents somehow agreed to this?" I ask in astonishment.

"They did, and I hope they suffer as much as I think they will," Aris says, his tone lethal. "But yes, we are bait for the wild in the blistering cold. It's going to be so much fun." He flashes me a grin.

The cold begins to seep back into the carriage as the day carries on and the sun begins to set. I don't remember dozing off, but I wake up on River's shoulder when the carriages come to a halt.

My cloak has been placed over my shoulders like a blanket. Aris orders me to stay in the carriage while everything is being set up, and I don't argue with him. There's a part of me that hates feeling helpless. I would be out there helping if I could but aggravatingly, I can't.

I watch as River scouts the area for any security faults, even though the only thing that's actually a danger to me is my father, who'll be in the next tent over.

It's not long before I'm getting out of the carriage, letting my legs stretch despite the ache in my back.

The clearing in the forest is perfect. It looks like it's been used as a campsite many times before. The moon shines down through a patch in the trees, illuminating areas of the forest that otherwise couldn't be seen. The wind rustles throughout the leaves of the bushes, carrying with it that sweet but sickening scent Atravelien is known for.

So alive but so wicked and dead. I walk slowly toward one of the fires already roaring and hold my hands over it. The servants quickly finish putting up the tents. I start counting them and then freeze. There are only four tents, the largest being for the king and queen. Which leaves one for the three servants, one for the three coachmen, and then one for... *Oh gods.*

I look back toward the carriage. Maybe I can just sleep inside there. It wouldn't be ideal, but the thought of sleeping in between Aris and River? I shiver—not from the cold. Everyone is rustling around, setting up the camp, so I grab a blanket from the pile placed near our tent and slowly make my way back to the carriages.

Someone rounds the back end and almost crashes into me. Somehow warm and steady hands grab my arms to keep me from toppling over. I inhale the now-familiar scent of spice and cedarwood and look up to find Aris raising his eyebrow at me, then at the blanket in my hand.

"Where are you going, Princess?" He looks at me and then the carriage and furrows his eyebrows. "Absolutely not. You need to eat and rest properly, and you cannot do that in there."

"Where else am I supposed to sleep? I don't want the bears to mistake me for dinner." I try not to pay attention to his hands still on my arms, but the tingling rushing along my nerves makes it hard.

"You're more likely a snack for a bear than dinner, and I don't know if you noticed, but there are tents designed to keep you warm and safe." He looks to the tents as he says that and realizes the dilemma we're in. "Your mother and father have poor planning skills." And of course, as if right on cue, the king and queen step out of their carriage. The king looks straight at Aris, who immediately steps away from me. I turn to look at them and curtsy, biting my lip to silence the cry that I almost let loose. When I rise up, I catch a satisfied look pass over my mother's face.

"What have we so poorly planned, Prince Aris?" my father drawls, putting on what looks like an amused look instead of the fury I know lurks beneath. Aris straightens beside me.

"We are one tent short, Your Majesty. It seems there was no tent packed for the princess and her privacy." Aris' voice is clear despite the intimidation rolling off of the king.

"We hadn't planned for River to come along, but the princess insisted he should be here. So, it is her poor planning at fault, and as we discussed, Prince Aris, Ember was to stay with you at all times during the trip. You all can figure out where to put River or her. We don't care about such trivial matters." And with that he moves on, not waiting for us to respond. I watch them enter the largest of the tents where servants are waiting with warm food and blankets for them already. I snap my head to look at Aris.

"They had always planned for me to sleep with you?" I narrow my eyes at him.

"I was going to figure something else out." He drags his angry gaze to look back down at me. River finally starts walking toward us, but I pay him no mind.

"When were you planning on telling me that? What else has been discussed with them?" I clench my hands at my side.

"I was going to trade with a servant so you wouldn't have to be uncomfortable." Aris crosses his arms over his chest, avoiding my question.

"I'm going to sleep in the carriage; you and River can share." They're adult men; they'll be fine. River snorts.

"Not a chance, Ember," he grumbles from behind me. "I can sleep near the fire, and Aris can squeeze in somewhere else." River gives Aris a pointed look, to which Aris rolls his eyes.

"Absolutely not." I turn slowly so my back is to the carriage with both of them facing each other on either side of me. "You'll freeze to death out there. The tent fits at least three people, does it not?" I aim the question at Aris.

"Three people max," he answers, though not very happy about it.

"Then we'll fit." I look at River, who looks less than pleased, and then at Aris, who just seems uncomfortable with the idea of being in the same place with River for another extended period of time. Civility be damned; these two can't help but jab at each other.

"I don't know, Princess, he's kind of a behemoth of a man. I'm sure if you slept on top of me, then maybe we could fit," he purrs. I scoff, and River's jaw ticks.

"You'll keep your filthy hands off of her," River practically growls at Aris.

"Or what?" Aris challenges. I look between the two beautiful men and shake my head, laughing softly. They break their stare to look down at me.

"Shut up, the both of you; let's go eat. I can't feel my hands or feet, and I think there's frozen blood on my back." I walk toward our tent where servants wait for us with bowls of steaming stew. The inside of the tent is big enough to fit a plethora of blankets and cushions to lay on. It's slightly warmer inside without the blistering wind but still uncomfortably cold. I eye the blankets we'll huddle under tonight and fight the blush crawling up my neck. It takes me a moment to lower myself onto a cushion before the servant hands me my bowl. Thankfully they don't ask any questions.

After I'm done eating, I find that no matter how much I slept today, fatigue still plagues my body. I just want to lie down and find some semblance of warmth. The servants take the last of our bowls and close the flaps to the tent tightly.

Immediately, I quickly take off my shoes and climb into the

center of the makeshift bed. I'm on my knees when River clears his throat beside me.

"Ember, we should clean them again. I don't want them to get infected." I nod in agreement. "Aris, get out," he orders while moving behind me so he can help me up to undress.

"It's fucking freezing out there." Aris shakes his head. "I'll just turn around." River looks like he's about to argue, but I shake my head at him.

"It's fine. He can stay." River huffs angrily but concedes. Aris grumbles something I can't hear in response but turns around as River helps me back to my feet. He unzips the dress, pulling it off my arms slowly so it drops to the floor at my feet. I can't help the whimper as it pulls away from the bandages. Next he takes the tunic off, and another groan escapes as the cold air clashes with the exposed skin. Aris balls his hands into fists at his sides but doesn't turn even when he begins to tremble. *How could someone you hardly know care so much already?*

I hold the tunic to my chest and glance down, noticing the blood has soaked through to the shirt. Now, I'm left in only thick wool leggings.

"This might be easier if you lie down, Ember," River says from behind me, the tickle of his breath ruffling my hair a bit. I nod silently and lower myself onto the cushions, grateful to cover my chest. He kneels down beside me and wraps his fingers on the inside of my waistband. "Lift your hips," he whispers softly, and I do as he says so he can pull the band down slightly to get to the lower lashes.

"Aris, you don't have to face the wall anymore," I mumble softly, lying with my head facing away from River as he begins to peel the bandages away. I can't help the tears that prick my eyes and begin to fall as the pain wrecks through my body.

"Yes, he does," River mutters from behind me, but Aris doesn't listen to him; he immediately comes to my side, moving the hair behind my ear in a gentle caress. He grabs my hand, which I squeeze tightly as River continues to peel away the gauze.

Breathe.

Breathe through it.

Yet, every touch, every sting of pain is coated in my father's malice.

"Actually, Aris, can you have one of the servants fetch some water and have them warm it? I need to clean these before I redress them." Aris nods fervently, immediately leaving to fetch someone.

I hate making the servants do more work; it's freezing out there, and it's enough that they're on this blasted trip with us. River removes the last of the bandages and curses softly. He moves my hair completely to the side, brushing the top of my shoulder where the skin is untouched. I shiver beneath his touch, goose-bumps following in the wake of his fingers.

Aris comes back not much later and kneels down with River; they both take washcloths and begin to gently clean away the dried-up blood. I bury my face in the pillows to muffle my cries. *When is this going to end?*

"Almost there, Princess," Aris says soothingly. Once they finish cleaning the wounds, they both begin massaging the salve on. I can make out whose hands belong to whom based on the roughness of the fingers. River's fingers are tougher, whereas Aris' are smoother, less worked with.

Once they finish with the salve, Aris cuts pieces of the gauze for River to place, the fabric sticking to the wounds because of the salve. Aris grabs the bloodied tunic and gives me his black one.

"Wear this one instead," he says softly before turning around. I place my hands beneath my chest and push up, bringing my knees up so I can sit back on my feet. I pull the waistband of my leggings up slowly, but when I go to put the tunic on, I grimace. River moves to help me, but I shake my head.

"I have to do this." I have to push through; I can't be coddled.

"Ember," River says quietly, and I can't help the sob that leaves my lips from the way he says my name. I hate this. I hate how vulnerable I have to be, how weak I am right now.

"I *have* to do this," I whisper. *They didn't break me completely.* I force my hands through the sleeves, the whimpers making it less graceful than I intended. I pull the hem of the shirt down and sigh in relief once it's on.

River looks at me with a compassion that nearly cracks my chest wide open. As if I'm the warrior and he isn't. As if I'm one of the soldiers who just walked off the battlefield bloodied but victorious.

I'm not worthy of this. Of them.

"I want to go to bed," I tell them as I pull back the blankets and bury myself within the pile of them. The makeshift bed beneath us isn't comfortable, but the relief of lying down is enough to release the tension in my body in a whoosh of a breath.

I lay on my back carefully, able to bare it tonight as I try to get comfortable. Aris lays on my left, far enough away that there's no chance of him touching me. River does the same on my right after blowing out the lamps. I stare through the inky black of the night and focus on slowing my breathing, trying to lull myself to sleep, but even under several layers of blankets, the cold seeps in.

I can't help the shivering that comes next, or the clattering of my teeth. Aris rolls over first, closing the distance between us by lying on his side flush against me. He wraps his arm around the bottom of my torso, and the warmth from his breath tickles the skin of my neck, but I welcome his body heat gratefully. I gingerly reach a hand for River and touch his shoulder softly. *I need both of you.*

He rolls over, wrapping his arm around me above Aris'. With them both at my side, the trembles subside. We lay like this, absorbing each other's warmth for a long time before I can feel them both start to relax near one another. Their breath slows, coming to an even rhythm that forces my own eyes to close. Somehow, in the middle of the beautiful and terrible Atravelien, with my parents a mere ten feet away, I've never felt safer, never felt more at home than I do right here in their arms. As I drift off into the dreamworld, I caress those tethers one more time, and I swear they both move closer.

CHAPTER 16

Peace and tranquility.

I don't think I've ever felt anything like that until I fell asleep in their arms. There were no nightmares, no tossing and turning. No pain, internal or external. I was simply there with them, and they were with me.

I'd somehow made it onto my side with my back against Aris, facing River. Waking up like this is something I could get used to.

Light floods in from the top of the tent, illuminating the stunning features of River's face. I fight the urge to run my fingers down the ridge of his cheekbones, over the sharp slope of his nose, and against his plump lips, which lie slightly ajar. He looks so peaceful like this. No tension lining his brow or worry pursed in his lips. His hand lays between us, and I settle for tracing the lines of his rough palms, unable to keep myself from touching him.

From behind me, an arm tightens around my torso, and I brace for the impact of pain, but it never comes. I stifle a gasp of surprise as Aris pulls me closer to his chest and nuzzles his nose against my hair. The strong planes of his body lay flush to my own. I take it all in, the way my knee lays lightly on top of River's bent legs. The way Aris' breath tickles my neck. The warmth radiating off of them both mixed with the frigid air around us makes for the perfect combination. I don't want to leave this cocoon of safety, this bubble of perfection.

The rustling of the servants bustling around the camp wakes River eventually. A soft smile comes and goes so quickly I almost miss it. He hones in on the arm wrapped around me that isn't him, but then he notices where I'm still tracing his palm, and he softens again.

And then he leans forward, laying his head on my pillow. His forehead touches mine, and his nose brushes against my own. We stay like that for a while, simply basking in each other's presence.

Until we know we can't anymore. River pulls away, lifting himself out of the makeshift bed. I detach myself from Aris, who groans and mumbles something incoherent about needing more sleep. I stretch carefully, but still, hardly any pain comes. The wounds don't feel like the scabs are on the verge of continuously breaking. The constant burn of the torn skin has subsided. I can move, and the constant reminder of their existence could be forgotten if not for a moment. A moment of relief. I turn around and take Aris' tunic off, clutching it to cover my chest.

"River look," I say softly while Aris rises from bed with another groan. I chuckle softly, facing Aris with my back to River, who's moved toward the entrance of the tent. River takes a step toward me and peels back one of the bandages. "How does it look? I can hardly feel any pain! Whatever salve you put on must've worked wonders last night." Aris wanders toward me, and I don't miss the way he looks me up and down, taking in the sight of me topless. I raise an eyebrow at him, to which he merely winks at me before joining River behind me and gasps.

"Ember, it looks so much better. The wounds are closing, and the redness and swelling have subsided substantially. I've never seen anyone heal like that," River tells me as he places the bandage back down.

"You just needed my healing touch," Aris drawls next. I laugh softly, shaking my head.

"Something like that." I tug the tunic back on and quickly

wrap myself in my cloak before stepping out into the frigid morning. A servant quietly hands me a bag of my toiletries and some water for me to wash my mouth and relieve myself in a private area away from possible peering eyes.

Out here in the open I take a moment to bask in the morning beauty of Atravelien. I gaze between the canopy of trees where sun rays fall into the thick forest and listen for something, anything. Magic begins to crawl up my arms slowly, almost tugging me forward like there's something waiting there for me. Something to be found. I take a tentative step forward before shaking my head, signaling it to go back to where it's kept. It's too dangerous to be wandering around here. It almost hurts to put the lid back on top and turn away.

The camp comes apart as quickly as it was put up. Before I know it, we've eaten, and we're being packed into the carriage again to finish the rest of the journey. Aris tells us we should be there just in time for dinner.

I busy myself by answering the list of complaints given to me by the people in my village, handwriting a personal letter to each of them. I'm hoping to send it back with our servants so they can be distributed properly.

My attention is so wrapped up in the letters I don't notice when we've entered Klyeria. Our arrival is announced loudly as we begin descending down a road that looks like it leads straight to the castle.

"Don't fall for my father's charm. He may seem kind, easy on the eyes, and might even be a flirt, but don't fall for it. He's never what he seems," Aris says carefully.

"Sounds a lot like you," River mumbles without looking away from the window. Aris narrows his eyes at him with a look that could kill. But I can't say he's wrong. Even if I did just share a bed with him.

"You'll just have to see for yourself," Aris mutters as he turns and looks out the window himself as we approach the tallest castle I've ever seen.

It puts our estate to shame in comparison. The stone is the darkest black imaginable, the kind of black that darkens anything around it just for its mere proximity. I try to see the top, but end up having to lean over River to get a better look. His thigh goes taut under my touch as I use it to steady myself over him. But instead of telling me to move, he simply snakes his arm around my back, allowing me a better vantage point.

Even then I can't see the top of the castle; it's that large.

River's hand is nothing but a whisper against my clothes, but it feels as if he's branded my skin with his touch alone.

Large iron gates open slowly, and the carriages begin moving again. An almost sheer layer of snow lays over the garden that still looks pristine despite the weather. Naked bushes are still shaped into various animals; the lawn is cut with the utmost precision. I can only imagine how much my father might be seething right now.

"Ember look," Aris calls to me.

River's hand leaves me as I lean over Aris instead. He clutches the fabric of my cloak at my hip as I peer out of the window. On the left side of the cobblestone road that leads up to the entrance lies an entire field of the largest horses I've ever seen in my life.

"My father has a thing for them. They're purebred and trained by our finest trainers. Mine is the all-black one all the way in the back over there, near the spotted brown one. His name is Coal. I would've taken him with me on my journey, but we had just gotten back from a different trip, and I didn't want to tire him." I marvel at the animals, at the sheer size of them. The horse he brought is helping pull our carriage as we speak.

"I can understand his love for them; they're absolutely breath-taking." I can't look away; there are so many of them. Most are huddled in groups, some frolicking around. I can feel the heat of Aris' gaze but can't pull myself to lean back. A lone horse, completely blonde and glistening in the evening sun, stands far away from the rest of the group. "Why's that one all alone?"

"That one hasn't been broken yet; she has one hell of a will and won't let anyone get close enough to train her. My father may put her down if she doesn't give up soon." Aris' tone is solemn.

"He can't do that." I lean back in my seat as the carriages come to a halt. "He can't do that, Aris, would he?" I look up at him, my chest cracking. I couldn't fathom the thought of killing such a beautiful mare just because she wouldn't back down.

"He can, and he has," Aris admits gravely.

But how could I expect anything else from a tyrant such as his father? Destroying beauty is a talent of his. He's desecrated some of the most beautiful towns in our kingdom, for what? In the name of this war over land we have no claim to?

And my father's no better.

Once the other carriages pull up, the servants hurry themselves to open the door for my parents and then for us. Aris is the first to step out, stretching out his hand for me to take as I descend. River follows after, taking his spot slightly behind me to my right. Always protecting my back, always staying vigilant.

I try not to grimace when I realize my appearance is far from what it should be given whom I'm about to meet. I run a hand through my long waves, hoping to smooth it down some. Aris leans down and murmurs,

"You look perfect; don't worry." I can feel him smile against the shell of my ear, and I fight off another shiver. I offer him a bashful smile before turning my attention to the servants pouring out of the main entrance. They come to gather our belongings and lead us into the huge steel doors. I stifle a gasp once we get inside.

The floors are white marble, so clean it doesn't seem like anyone has ever stepped foot on them. In their reflection are giant chandeliers sparkling against the glossy finish. Black and what looks like real gold curtains line the floor-to-ceiling windows that overlook the rest of the estate, which seems to stretch for miles and miles. Old metal knight uniforms line the wall in varying positions with different weapons.

I steal a glance at my father, whose face I can't read, but I can sense the simmering anger beneath. Our castle is beautiful but bland. It's nowhere near this level of artistry.

A servant comes to Aris and bows before us before murmuring something soft to him that I can't hear. He goes back and forth with the girl for a moment before nodding and turning toward us all.

"My father has had them prepare a welcome feast for you. It's been a long day of travel, so he'll allow you to freshen up, of course." A hint of humor peaks through his voice.

"Allow?" my father mutters, but Aris pays that no mind.

"The servants will show you to your rooms, and I will see you at dinner." And with a small bow to me, Aris disappears down one of the many halls. My father huffs angrily, watching the daring prince walk away. Two beautiful, young girls step forward to lead River and I down a different hall than the one Aris just went through and away from where my parents are being led. One of the girls keeps stealing looks at me and then at River; a small blush creeps up her neck, and I can't help the small smile that forms on my lips as we walk. *Trust me, I get it.*

One of them, with fair blonde hair pulled into a bun, opens the door to one room on the right side of the hall.

"For you, Your Highness. We will be in to help you get ready." Her voice is so soft and sweet, but still I find myself weary. I nod in thanks while the second girl, with mousy brown hair and thin wire-framed glasses, opens the door across the hall for River. Her voice shakes a bit when she speaks to him.

"And for you, sir, just ring the bell if you need anything." She almost squeaks at the end and it takes all of my will not to chuckle. River gives her one of his good smiles, and I swear she almost faints, before he turns that smile to me.

"Yell if you need me. I'll be right here." His gaze lingers on me for a moment before entering his room. The two girls follow me into my own door, and I take a moment to take it all in.

My bags have already been brought in, emptied, and placed into the armoire, I assume. The bed is huge; four long wooden posts almost reach the ceiling where sheer fabric lays across the beams and then ties to the posts. The comforter is soft beneath my touch and thick to keep me warm. A fire is already going in the hearth. There's a beautiful vanity across from the bed and a gigantic armoire beside it. I can hear water rushing through one of the doors, so I move toward the bathroom. Both of the girls follow me, and I look back at them.

"You don't have to help me," I tell them softly. "What are your names?" I ask. I really don't want them to see my back. The blonde girl cocks her head to the side, confused as she says,

"My name is Layla, and hers is Melody. But of course we'll help you. Don't you have servants who help you get ready back home?" She doesn't ask with malice. Her confusion seems genuine.

"I don't actually. And I... I can't..." I can't voice it. I don't know how to voice it. Melody's face softens with sympathy. Her voice is much calmer now that she's out of the presence of River.

"Prince Aris told us, Your Highness. You needn't worry about a thing; we will take care of you. We have some of the best healing ointments on the way, and the oils we'll put in the bath will help too. Come, come, we mustn't waste any time." She rolls up her sleeves as we walk toward the bathroom.

I'm really doing this. I'm baring myself to them. *You can do this.*

They do everything. They take my dress off and all the layers beneath. Carefully they strip the bandages off of me, and the rush of cool air is somewhat pleasant against my skin. I sink down into the bubble-filled bath, inhaling deeply at the floral scent that fills my nose. They scrub me until my skin is brand new and a soft pink from their rigorous effort. They massage my scalp in a heavenly rhythm that almost lulls me to sleep. They even go as far as shaving my legs. Suddenly, Melody looks up at me.

"Your Highness, would you be comfortable with a waxing of your lady areas?" she asks politely. My eyes go wide as I look down my stomach to where the lower half of my body lays beneath a layer of suds. Images of River seeing me naked but ungroomed flash through my head, and I grimace. There is nothing wrong with hair; it's perfectly natural, but then other images flood my brain from my books. Words like slick, glistening, and soft bombard me, and I find myself nodding.

"If there's time, then yes, I'd like that." I can't help the blush that crawls up my cheeks. The girls exchange a look, hiding their own sheepish smiles. They lather me in lotion that smells like the heavens and put a thin layer of ointment onto my back that feels divine.

The rest of it all goes by in a blur as I fall deeply into thought. They recognize my need for quiet and focus simply on their tasks at hand, thoroughly enjoying what they're doing as they fall into their own chatter.

It doesn't feel like much time has passed at all when they're finally turning me around to show me the finished product.

The girl in my reflection is one I hardly recognize.

"Wow, I really need to learn how to do this back at home. Thank you, both of you." I smile at them, and they return it back.

"Of course, Your Highness, we can teach you. You are truly one of the most beautiful women we've ever laid eyes on. Now, come on, dressing you is our favorite part. We know that you've brought some of your own gowns, but we've also picked out a few from our own seamstress here. We think we have the perfect one to impress the king," Layla says as she excitedly throws open the doors to the armoire.

She pulls out a stunning sleeveless black dress. The bodice is a sheer corset with gold lace woven into it. The gold flows down the skirt on a sheer layer in swirls of flowers and vinery. The sheer layer lays over onyx silk that drapes to the floor with a slit in the right leg that comes dangerously high. It's beautiful. Elegant. And they're absolutely right, perfect to impress the king. Though I'm not sure how worthy *he* is to see me in this.

"It's perfect." I say as I run a hand over the fabric. They waste no time getting me out of my robe. Melody rustles through the armoire before holding a pair of black lace panties out to me. I shimmy them on, catching a glimpse of my body in the mirror, and even I shock myself with how much I like the way it looks. I step into the dress and they pull it up.

Melody laces the corset, pulling it tight, but not tight enough that it hurts. It's then, when I feel the ghost of pain in my back, that I start to freak out.

"Wait. Wait, I can't wear this. They'll see, and they can't see." I try to calm down, but suddenly it's all on the surface. The panic, my power, my embarrassment. The girls have been so good about my wounds; they haven't said a thing or made any faces, but I can't face the king, my father, or my mother.

"Breathe." Melody comes and takes my hand. "Deep breath in." She breathes in with me. "Deep breath out." She breathes out. I do it several times, calming the ache in my chest and pulling that well of power back into the box I've kept it so tightly in. "Good. Your hair covers it all, and if it moves slightly, then so be it. They should have thought of that before they did that to you. But I doubt anyone will notice; your hair is thick, and as long as you keep it swept over your shoulder, then all is well. You have to wear this dress; I refuse to take you out of it. It looks too good." She offers a kind smile, and my heart calms a little more.

"You're going to knock everyone off their feet, Your Highness," Layla says sweetly. Melody squeezes my hands and lets them go.

"Thank you, both of you. I look forward to my time here with you." I turn and take in my appearance in the long mirror that has been hung onto the wall. They're right; there's no way I can take this off. I might have to sleep in it; it's *that* pretty. It gives my Winter Solstice dress a run for its money.

A knock sounds at my door and I find myself involuntarily moving toward it. The tugging in my core pulls frantically, pleading and begging to reveal the man on the other side. Melody opens the door, stealing my breath when she reveals the prince waiting there.

Aris leans against the frame, adjusting his sleeve while he looks at me. His tunic matches my dress, with gold-laced throughout the stitching; it's subtle but reflects in the light enough to be shown. They're the kingdom's colors I realize. Those onyx eyes roam over me, drinking me in so thoroughly my own throat becomes parched.

Eventually, he meets my eyes, his own ablaze with heat and need. He opens his mouth to say something, but the door behind him opens. River steps through; his hair is slightly damp and curling at the ends. He wears a dark red tunic, our color, with the sleeves rolled up to reveal his veiny forearms. I swallow, soaking them both in, and it's almost too much how beautiful they both are.

River takes in my dress, the slit, the sheer bodice, and does it unapologetically. Somewhere, at some point, something has shifted, and gods am I glad that it has. Melody clears her throat from behind us, and we all snap out of it.

"You boys clean up nicely." I walk forward, and they both scramble to walk beside me. Aris takes the lead to guide us to dinner. The dress whispers against the floor, dragging ever so softly. My heels click against the marble, and it sends a wave of power through me at the sound. Faintly down the opposite side of the hall, I can hear Melody and Layla giggling amongst themselves. I can only imagine what they might be saying. We approach another large set of doors, eventually arriving at what I presume is their dining hall. Aris pauses before we enter.

"Princess, you look absolutely incredible. I don't know how, but you're more beautiful every time I see you." There's a slight hoarseness to his voice that I feel all the way to my toes. I smile up at him, a real, genuine smile. He returns it, but it wavers slightly when he continues, "Don't let your guard down." Then he nods at the servants to open the doors. He steps in first, and River puts a hand on my arm, stopping me from going in just yet. He drops his head low to my ear.

"At the first sight of danger, we leave. If you so much as give me a look, we leave. I don't care who's in there or what say they have over us. You are my only priority. Just..." River searches my eyes before saying, "Just be careful, Ember." I nod, words stuck in my throat. There's something about the way he says my name that sends a wave of heat to my core.

It's almost unbearable how much I want him. *Them*. Damn them for looking so good. River extends his arm, and I take it, entering the dining room. A table almost as long as the room sits in the center, full of a feast that could feed a hundred people. At the head is an empty chair that's so big it might as well be a throne. Beside it are my parents; on the other side is Aris. Two place settings sit beside Aris, so we make our way there. River pulls my chair out for me, and I stand, waiting for the king.

My father looks me over quickly, a look of disgust washing over his face before he cools it into authoritative indifference and looks away. They're both clad in their finest red, fit with a crown and everything. He's trying to be impressive, but he looks so out of place here. So small compared to the grandness of the palace. I almost wish River wasn't wearing red, just so he wouldn't be matching them.

We stand there for a while, waiting for the king to make his entrance. My father continuously huffs, hating to be the one waiting, hating to be the less superior one. I stifle the smile threatening to take over my face. A servant enters and announces the king's entrance, and we all stand a little straighter. A tall man dressed in all black walks in with such grace I struggle to keep my mouth from dropping open. The entire air shifts as he stalks forward, like a predator having just found its prey.

His hair is midnight black dusted with silver streaks; his face, though aging, is just an older version of Aris. He's a handsome man, and he knows it. He wears a magnificent golden crown atop his head, making the one my father wears seem like child's play with all the jewels that adorn it. He flashes me a smile, and if I didn't know any better, had I not been warned or knew what he was capable of, I might've swooned for it. But thankfully I can see right through him, and under all that ego, underneath the charming smile, I can see an ugly, ugly man. So I smile back, but not so sweetly—no, I let him see a hint of my own malice. If he notices, he doesn't show it. He finally gets to his throne of a seat and clasps his hands together.

"Welcome, welcome!" His voice booms too loudly throughout the grand room for such a small group of people. "I hope you have found your accommodations to your liking and that the journey didn't tire you too much. We have much planned before you two leave." He gestures to my parents. "And a welcome ball tomorrow to truly welcome you to Klyeria," he says to me specifically. "Now sit, sit. Let us eat!" Gods Aris was right. This man is all charm. I look at my mother, who's falling for it, her own eyes lingering on him a little too long as she moves her gown to sit.

The servants come around with the dishes on the table, serving us what we pick and choose. My mother eats lightly like a bird and gives me an expecting look to which I oblige. But every time I tell a servant no thank you, Aris is right there to tell them to put it anyway because I just "have to try it." At some point I have to stop him because I can't eat anymore, or I'll bust through the corset. But he's right. The food here is just as good as Chef Jean's, if not somehow better, or maybe I was just hungry. My mother looks disappointed, but so be it. Once everything is cleared, the king clears his throat to speak.

"So, Princess Ember. Can I just call you Ember? You are just *such* a sight to see. Has my son been good to you? It seems you two are...well acquainted." He gives me a serpentine smile that slides down my back uncomfortably. Aris goes rather still beside me.

"Yes, he has been incredibly welcoming, Your Majesty," I offer politely.

"Bleren. You may refer to me by just Bleren." It's not an offer but more of a command. "But I'd hope he'd be a bit more than welcoming to his betrothed."

It was my turn to go utterly still. I swallow, hoping to wash away being caught off guard, but the king catches it regardless. He sits back lazily, looking between me and Aris, who still hasn't said anything. *Betrothed. Marry him. No choice.*

"Oh well, you know it's only been a couple of days, I can't make it too easy of a chase now, can I?" I purr. Whatever game he's playing, I can play too. I glance at Aris, who doesn't seem surprised in the least, and the food in my stomach turns to ash. *He knew.* The king smiles knowingly. My parents don't look the least bit bothered either. I should have known. Suddenly it all makes sense. Them nudging Aris toward me. Us coming here in the first place. *How blind could I be?*

"You're right. No one likes an easy lay. Though no one wants too much of a fight when it comes to the bed either. The easier to spread, the better." The king chuckles. "Perhaps it is a good thing to keep you in separate rooms for the next three months. We don't want you spoiling the wait now, do we?" I can't help the shiver that runs through me this time.

"Makes the reward all the sweeter," I drawl, but it's not as convincing. Even my own hackles rise at what the king implies. River moves his hand slowly, hovering near the pommel of his sword.

"Tell your guard dog to stand down or I'll put him down myself," the king sneers, throwing a look in River's direction that would have killed him on the spot if looks could kill. I reach over and squeeze River's hand softly, but it does nothing to calm the rage I can feel boiling over in him. So I try stroking that tether softly, sending a wave of calm down it, and his shoulders visibly sigh in relief. I remove my hand and look toward the king when he speaks again. "I ought to have him sent away when you two are married. There's no need for him."

"She needs me the same way you walk around with four personal guards at any given time in your own castle," River spits out, to which the king's eyes flare wide with anger at the blatant disrespect. But the king quickly recovers.

"You're pushing your luck, boy; you'll be on your way out of here with Nicholas and Eloise." My father looks like he's been slapped for not being referred to by his title, but he doesn't say anything, surprisingly. In fact, my parents haven't said anything at all. They're letting Bleren walk all over them. For the first time ever, I'm watching them be *weak.*

"River stays." I turn my attention back to the king and lean forward, staring him down. "I stay; he stays. You haven't given me much reason to trust you, Bleren." Something like pride emanates down the tether from Aris. My father perks up at this.

"You shut your mouth; you're in no position to negotiate," he snaps, and I can't help but flinch. *Nothing but a placeholder with a pretty face. You are nothing.* River's fist tightens but he keeps his composure. I recover swiftly, tilting my chin up while leaning back in my chair.

"Let her keep the brute. If only to keep her compliant. It doesn't bother me, and he knows if he steps out of line, then he's out of here." Aris leans back in his own chair, a perfect mirror of his father, even down to that arrogant tone that's made its way back. "Anything to keep her from complaining." The king nods at this.

"Very well, he stays. As for your trust, dear Ember. I don't care if I've earned it or not. You're mine now. You are at my disposal; you do what I say, when I say it, and how I want it. I say jump, you jump. I say marry my son; you become his bride. I say fuck him and give me an heir? You give birth to a boy. This is your life now. My son knows what he's supposed to do, and if he's anything like me, then you should already have started to fall for him. We're quite the charmers." The king looks at his son, studying him for a moment before nodding to himself as if confirming that Aris is just like him. A sense of disgust washes over Aris, but his face reveals nothing.

"She makes it easy when she's desperate for even an ounce of affection. You should see the way she glows when you compliment her." Aris looks at me up and down, and suddenly I feel sick to my stomach, even though I know he's playing his part. I can feel just how terrible he feels having to say it out loud. Even though he's right. "Yes, I will have an heir in no time." Aris looks at his nails, as if bored by this conversation. The king turns to my father.

"You've provided your side of the deal, so it's only fair I hold up my end. We'll pull our soldiers back for now. I'll keep you updated, Nicholas." My father nods as they shake hands, like they're old friends or something. Like we haven't been at war killing each other for decades. "I understand it's been a long day, so for now you both are dismissed if you'd like to return to your chambers. Ember, I'd like a word before you may leave."

My father and mother rise together in sync, bowing their heads to the king before a servant comes to lead them away. I watch them as they leave hand in hand, gripping each other like they're a lifeline. It's so odd seeing my father as the inferior one in the room, answering to someone else's demands and doing so without any hesitation. It's like he's given up, like he knows he's somehow powerless against Bleren. I just want to know what it is Bleren has over them to allow them to act like this, to make this bargain in the first place.

A bargain. Stop killing our people, and we'll give you our daughter as a truce. My mother once told me when I was a young girl that they would choose who I'd marry, just as they had chosen her for my father. I just didn't believe it. *He's never what he seems.* I turn my attention to Aris, who won't look at me.

Was that a warning against himself? I'm angry he didn't tell me. I'm disappointed I let myself trust him so easily when he didn't trust me to tell me.

And then actual tears prick my eyes when I realize I truly never got to say goodbye to Jasper and to my court. This isn't a month-long trip where I'll return to him.

There is no return.

I don't know if I'll ever see him again—if I'll ever be *allowed* to see him again.

Rapidly, I blink the tears away before they can be noticed, but they sink into me, settling in my chest where pain curls up and makes itself at home.

Three more months and I'm no longer the heir to the throne of Agatharea but the wife of the Crown Prince of Klyeria.

That should scare me, considering his dishonesty.

But the tether between us is already pulsing with immense guilt, and because of that, the anger in my belly doesn't put up as much of a fight.

CHAPTER 17

Bleren watches my parents leave, his eyes lingering on my mother, who makes a good show of swaying her hips as she walks away. He stares off for a moment, lost in thought, before Aris clears his throat. That slimy, serpentine smile comes back as he clasps his hands together.

"Just a couple of rules, my dear, now that you are living under my roof. Now that you know you are to marry my son, that means no suitors. I don't want you caught with another man, let alone look or think about one. You will go to planned outings with him, act as a couple, and do everything a royal couple would do. I heard about the little tavern fiasco. You're still a virgin, right?" He looks at me expectantly. like it's a normal question to ask a lady. I pretend my heart doesn't squeeze at the memories. At what could've been and at what was.

"And if I'm not?" I ask, unable to cool my own temper.

"You better pray to the gods you are. I was promised untainted goods." Fire brims in his eyes.

"I am a virgin, Bleren." I try to keep the growl crawling up my throat at bay. But I can't help the heat rushing to my face.

"Untouched?" Bleren pushes. River's leg vibrates beside me; he opens and closes his fists but keeps his face blank.

"Ask your son." I pick up a piece of my hair, studying the ends that split, trying to keep my hands busy so they don't shake. Aris chokes softly on the glass of wine he was drinking from. Bleren gives him a look, asking him to explain without having to say anything.

"Nothing worth noting, Father. Just enough to keep her coming back for more," Aris purrs, looking me up and down, and I hate to admit it, but I *will* keep coming back, even if I don't want to. That godsdamn tether will always tug me back.

"Good, she must remain as such until your wedding day. Otherwise, I don't care what you do. Feel free to roam around; you have access to all parts of our estate, save for my office. Don't go getting into any trouble; you are now a reflection of my name, Ember. Tread lightly." With that last warning, Bleren stands nodding to his personal guards as they flank his sides once more. I watch as he leaves, barely breathing until the door shuts and uncomfortable silence is left in his wake. *He lied, he lied, he lied.*

"Ember..." Aris voice is back to that low, velvet tone he uses with me. Soft and sweet.

"I need space. I need to process what the fuck just happened. You said I'd be here for a *month*. You led me here knowing I'd never see my home again. Just let me think that through for a moment." It tastes bitter as I swallow and rise from my seat. River stands with me, offering me his hand as I leave the table, turning my back on Aris.

"Don't touch her," Aris snaps at River, but River ignores him, replacing his hand on my lower back, leading me toward the way we came in. I lean into that hand for support, still trying to make sense of what's happening right now. Aris comes rushing from behind us, standing between us and our exit.

"You think he was joking? River, you *cannot* touch her. Ember just became the most coveted woman of our kingdoms. She has to stay pure, wanted, and desirable, and I'm the *only* one who can claim her. From here on out, you can't even spare her a second glance. If you so much as share a look, he will have your head on a stake, and then she'll be next for good measure. Ember, please just let me explain," Aris begs as he steps forward toward me. I step back further into River's side, but River seems hesitant. I look up at him, and I can see the turmoil in his eyes. I recognize that battle, the battle he's always having with himself. *His feelings or my safety. They can't coexist in his mind.*

"What is there to explain? I'm to be your wife. That's it. Spread my legs like the whore my parents think I am, and listen like a good girl. Right? We can fake it until we make it, *right*?"

"That is not who you are and not who you'll become. Ember, you'd do anything for your kingdom. You said so yourself, right? That's all this is. I play my part. I do his biddings. I take over, and I do *better*. Marrying you is the easiest thing I could do for them. I thought you'd be some brat. Some entitled woman who wouldn't have a care in the world about her people, but I was sorely mistaken. Please. *Please,* give this a chance. A real chance. Listen to his stupid rules for the next couple of months, and we'll figure it out. Together." He takes a shaky breath, running a hand through his tousled hair.

"How can I help *my* people from *your* throne? What good does this do me? I play housewife? Pop out a baby or three whenever *he* says?" My magic begins to crackle on my skin, heating me up, but I can't tamp it down. *I'm more than this.*

"We make our own rules. We could join the kingdoms and rule both. Bring peace for once. We just have to listen to him." His voice is so soft, so broken, and my stupid heart falls for it, raging a war with my mind that doesn't want to give in to him.

"That's exactly what your father wants! He wants *my* land! He wants *my* people to be *his* slaves!" I laugh; it's so comical. This can't be happening. My yentire life has been spent learning how to be a queen, learning how to be perfect or as close to it as I could be, and for nothing. To be pawned off like *nothing*.

"That wouldn't happen," Aris says, seeming so sure of himself. I look at River, who's so quiet, so still as he tracks me pacing back and forth. "We just have to play our cards right."

"It's not that easy," I mumble, trying to think this through. "Is there anything else you're hiding from me?" I turn and face Aris, coming to stand directly in front of him. His jaw clenches, and just like that, *there's more.*

"I can't tell you," he says, looking away.

"Oh come on, Aris! We can't do this if you're not honest with me. If you want any semblance of trust from me, you need to start by coming *completely* clean." I cross my arms, lifting my chin.

"I can't. At least not when you're mad at me. I trust you'll do the right thing, but I need the calm and collected princess. This one scares me." He meets my stare, cracking a smile. I grind my teeth, beyond livid and seconds away from losing the withering control on my magic. As if River can sense it, he takes a step forward from behind me and rubs my shoulders. Relief fills me instantly and my shoulders sag beneath his touch. Aris glares at him over my shoulder.

"I think we're done here," River finally says. "She will seek you out when she's ready. She's smart. The smartest person I know, maybe a little naive, but that's because her heart is too big. I'm here to protect her whether you or your father like it or not. We will be careful. We will tread lightly, but she will not dim her light for anyone." He rubs his thumbs over my skin, causing goosebumps to spread in their wake. I look up at River, admiration for him shining through my eyes. Aris struggles with his words, having a war with himself before he finally nods.

"Okay. Okay." He runs a hand over his face. "Get some rest; the girls will take care of you. I'll be busy until the evening, so take the day to look around." He pauses again, looking me up and down with a yearning that washes over me. "They should've saved that dress for the ball tomorrow; you look so fucking good." He says the last part more to himself than to me before heading toward the doors. Then he stops, and without looking at us, he says,

"River, don't underestimate my father. Keep your hands to yourself. If not for your sake, then for hers." Aris leaves with that final warning, leaving us alone. The crackling of wood from the huge fireplace fills the silence as I stare after Aris.

And despite my anger, that tether shines brighter than it had before, stretching as he leaves, following him somewhere in this fortress of a building. I stare at the door, taking in everything that just changed. *Breathe. Breathe. Breathe.* The ache in my heart doesn't dull, not as I remove myself from River, not wanting any of the servants to see us.

I turn and look at him and he meets my gaze with such heat it nearly melts me where I stand. He's just been told he could never have me, and whatever that means for him has finally pushed him past his breaking point. We both know what will happen now. We know that all this progress we've made will end tonight. The choice I thought I had has been made. Tomorrow starts a brand new me, and we have to go back to the way it was before.

I swallow the lump in my throat as I move for the exit. River walks beside me, careful not to touch me as he opens the door for us. We retrace our steps back to the hall that leads to our rooms, where Melody and Layla stand beside my door waiting for us. They straighten up when they see us and bow low at the waist.

"Your Highness," they both say. Everyone is so proper here. No wonder Aris was taken aback by the way we do things. No one does any of that unless my parents are involved.

"You don't have to do that; it's just me, but thank you, both of you, for waiting for me. I need to be alone tonight, but I promise to call on you in the morning." I offer them the best smile I can muster, but it falters despite my best efforts. They seem to understand as they both nod, bidding us a good night.

We wait until they disappear down the hall before River opens my door, letting himself in. I swallow my shock and follow him. He takes a look around inside the various doors to make sure the room is empty.

I lock the door behind me and lean against it, putting my face in my hands, trying to hold my sanity together. *Wife, mother, slave—not queen, savior, or hero.*

I listen as River takes some deep breaths. Then quietly, his footsteps find their way toward me, and my hands are being pried away. Immediately his touch burns my skin, branding it so I'll never forget what his hands feel like. We stay like that for a moment as he holds my wrists, searching my eyes, looking for answers to the questions swirling in his head.

We spent so long denying ourselves of each other.

Months and months of playing our part. Guard and princess. The little brushes of skin were all mistakes. I'd convinced myself that he didn't care for me. He wouldn't return my yearning gaze. There was no humanity in him. There were no feelings until he almost lost me, and I can't *breathe.*

I can't breathe while he's looking down at me like that. Like I'm the only thing that exists in his world.

"Ember..." My name comes out like a prayer. As if he were praying to Kienah, the Goddess of love and desire. "I've never needed someone the way I need you. And now you're slipping through my fingers. I spent so long..." He doesn't finish, the words getting stuck in his throat.

"I know, I get it now." I whisper softly, unable to stop the tear that spills down my cheek. He gingerly reaches up to wipe it away before taking that same thumb and running it over my bottom lip. I watch him quietly as he does it again, making them part. *We could die for this.*

Yet, that doesn't scare me as much as it should. I'd gladly have him now and die for my longing than go through this life not knowing what it would've been like to have him. Even if it's for one night. He seems to come to the same conclusion as he looks at me with a silent question in his eyes: *Is this okay?*

"River," I plead.

His name from my lips becomes his undoing. The world seems to still, as if everyone else on this earth is gone but us. We share a breath before he closes the distance between us.

His lips brush over mine softly, still making sure that I want this as much as he does. When I lean up to meet him the rest of the way, he lets go of my wrist and grabs the back of my neck. The kiss becomes carnal, and my legs nearly buckle as my body itself becomes fire, burning for him.

He tugs softly on my hair, causing a moan to slip out, but it gets swallowed by his skillful attack on my lips. That sound only seems to rile him up more as he takes from me everything I'm willing to give him. I almost can't take it, the flood of pleasure pulsing through me. I've *dreamt* about this moment, but I never thought it'd be the last.

He separates from me for a moment, his eyes dark with desire. It's as if he can't believe that this is real. That I'm real. As if he's also trying to convince himself this isn't a dream.

He crashes back into me, like waves crashing onto the shore, kissing down my jaw to the sweet spot on my neck beneath my ear. Breathless sounds release from my lips, and from his kiss alone, I feel as though I could come undone right there in his arms.

His hands find mine, and then he's leading me toward my bed. *I'd follow him wherever he wanted me to.*

He sits against the edge of the bed, tugging me between his legs. His hands grip the fabric at my hips as he drives me forward right into his lips. *I need more.*

Almost as if he can read my mind, he turns my waist around and begins expertly undoing the laces. Once it's loose enough, the dress falls to my feet.

I place it on the chair beside the bed, somehow weary of facing him. Weary of him seeing my body even though he's seen it in its entirety. He stands behind me and silently moves my hair away from my back before dragging a single finger down the hollow line of my spine.

"You've healed so quickly. They're almost scars already," he whispers, before kissing the scar on my shoulder blade. It nearly brings me to tears as he tugs me back, leaning against the edge of the bed again before planting more kisses on the ruined skin.

"There's not a single part of you that I don't find beautiful.

Not a single part of your skin I don't want to run my lips over. I only wish to ravish every inch of you until your skin is covered in my yearning. Until your body knows just how much I want you." The rawness in which he speaks, in which I can feel his eyes look upon me, cracks my chest wide open.

When I turn to look at him, I'm only met with desire. *Body, heart, and soul.*

I take my time pulling his tunic off of him. He stands for me when I find his belt and lets me slip that off of him too.

I take a step back to admire him in all his beauty. Perfect. There are no other words to describe him as I run my hands over the hard planes of muscle, so defined you'd think he was sculpted by gods themselves. He vibrates beneath my touch but doesn't rush me. His pants are taut where he's hard and ready for me— straining beneath the fabric, just asking to be freed.

"Then teach me. Teach my skin what it's like to be enraptured instead of ruined."

I look him in the eyes as I run a finger over his long shaft. He takes a shuddering breath, trying to stay in control. His hands come up, unable to keep them off me as he drags them up my hips and over my ribs. My nipples are hard buds, erect and eager for him to touch. He lightly runs a thumb over them, and I whimper. *More, I need more.* He palms my entire breast, and then the other, so enthralled with the curvature of my body.

"So fucking perfect." He leans forward and takes one in his mouth, his tongue circling the tip before sucking on it. I throw my head back, gasping as my power fills me up to the brink at the rush of pleasure that washes over me. My hands become tangled in his hair as I try to shove it way, way down, focusing on the way River's lips feel all over my skin instead.

Suddenly, River picks me up. I instinctively wrap my legs around him as he lays me down in the bed, lowering me like I weigh nothing.

There's nothing, no words, I could use to explain what it is to look at River when he's leaning over me.

He lowers his body onto mine, his hard cock brushing against the lace of my panties, which are now soaked beyond repair. I try to stay quiet, but the more he moves against me, the harder it is to silence my moans. He swallows it all, kissing me with such fervor I think I might see stars. When he lifts himself off of me, I moan in protest, but he just smiles up at me. I swear to the gods I could've climaxed right there and then. I commit the sight to memory, hoping that every time I close my eyes, I'll see that image instead of the ones that haunt me.

He hooks his fingers into my underwear before commanding me to lift my hips. He rolls them off of me so slowly I almost growl in frustration. But still, I let him take his time. I try not to think about the cruelty that the gods have bestowed upon us for the limited hours, minutes, and seconds they've allowed us.

When my panties have come completely off, he settles on his stomach with his head between my legs. He hooks his arms under my thighs, gripping my hips to keep them open when I move to shut them.

"Stay still," he commands. I obey. I think I'll always obey. He takes his time, kissing the insides of my thighs, the bottom of my belly, everywhere except where I need him. Everywhere except where I'm absolutely soaked and throbbing.

"River, please." *I am not beyond begging.*

"So pretty and wet, just for me," he says before he dines like a starved man.

He sweeps his tongue over my swollen clit, and I instantly arch at the explosion of pleasure in my core. I throw my hand over my mouth, silencing my moans as best as I can.

He continues to lick and suck and stroke, and I'm not sure I can take it. My orgasm instantly starts to build, threatening to come undone, but he takes his time, bringing me to the brink and then bringing me away. I think I might go mad, might go crazy with how good it feels. I whimper and plead. I moan his name, and only then does he concede.

He slips a single finger in and ups his speed, never wavering, never getting tired, and the pressure finally tips over, sending me soaring into the clouds.

I bite down on my arm to keep from screaming as waves and waves of pleasure wash over me. He keeps going, pulling me beyond the brink of sanity.

"River, I can't," I pant as my clit becomes overly sensitive. He pulls away, kissing up my stomach until he reaches my lips.

He kisses me slowly, and I revel in the way he tastes. Sweet like wine mixed with the remnants of my arousal. It wakes something primal in me. I reach between us, sliding my hands into his waistband, and begin stroking him from shaft to tip. He releases a growl mixed with a groan against my lips, and the pulsing in my core returns at the sound.

There's no other thought in my head but the need for him in me. *Now.* Using my momentum, I flip him onto his back. Just for now, I can take what I want. I sit back, grinding my hips softly against him; the fabric of his pants is rough against my skin, but I can't get enough. He looks up at me with so much emotion in his eyes it makes me pause.

I smile down at him, my hair cascading over my shoulders as I rest on him. He takes a strand and twirls it between his fingers.

Mine for tonight. Just a night.

I'd ruin myself for him, I realize. To the hells with the consequences. I slide down so I can take off his pants, tugging on the waistband of them and his briefs beneath. He helps by lifting his hips, letting his cock spring free, glistening at the tip, and gods, is it *glorious*. A vein pulses along the side, and I can't help but dip my head, dragging my tongue up his impressive length.

"Ember," he hisses, his own hips bucking, and I can't help but smile at the effect I have on him.

I do it again, but when I get to the tip, I wrap my mouth around it. *Gods, he barely fits.* Moans muffle on the soft skin of his cock as the thought of him stretching me open becomes the only thing I can think of. My throat relaxes as I suck him further down until it's almost too much. His hands find their way into my hair, moving it into one fist as my head bobs up and down. I come up for air, gulping in big breaths when I look up at him through my lashes.

"You taste even better than I imagined," I purr, and those ocean eyes of his go feral. "River, I need you in me now," I beg as I sit back on my heels, reaching between my legs to feel how wet I still am for him. He sits up so fast, pushing me onto my back. I land with a thud, chuckling softly as I look up at him.

He pauses, looking at me long and hard, the tip of his cock propped at my entrance. Tendrils of his hair curl around his face and right here, right now is the most beautiful he's ever looked. A chain hangs down from his neck, tickling the tops of my breasts. When I look up into those dark ocean eyes all I find is turmoil.

"What's wrong, River?" I reach up and stroke his cheek softly. His eyes flutter close as he leans into my palm. He sits back with an exasperated sigh, kneeling in front of me. I sit up on my elbows, watching as he wars with himself.

"If we do this, we can't go back. If he even thinks to have a doctor check for your virginity... Ember, I can't do it. I..." He looks at me, so torn between what he wants and can't do. I scramble forward, kneeling in front of him, knee to knee.

"We'll deal with the consequences when they come. Whatever they are, damn them to the hells. Because right now, right here is all we have left, and no one gets to control my body. They may have taken most of my choices away, but River, I get to choose you. We can't stop here." I rub my thumb over the top of his thighs where my hands rest. He grabs my other hand, kissing the inside of my palm, and a small breath lets loose from my lips.

I'll never recover from him. But at least I have tonight.

He contemplates for a long moment, and I let him take his time. His eyes rake over my body, taking in all its curves in the moonlight streaming through the window. Then his gaze flicks to my own, and it nearly takes my breath away. Not just need lies there. No, it's something else entirely, and I can't stop the burning in my eyes or the tears that follow.

He lays me down softly, taking his time to kiss my breasts, my neck; he even nips at my ear before grabbing hold of himself and settling right at my entrance. I arch my back softly, ignoring the ghost of pain that comes from back there. I need him in so many ways I can't take it.

"This could hurt, and the moment you want me to stop, you tell me." It's not an offer—it's more of a command, and I'm more than ready to listen. I nod, eyes on him as he pushes forward, sliding right into me. It's not like anything I could've imagined.

He slides in further, dropping his head to my shoulder, groaning into my ear as he keeps stretching me open. I wince softly as he breaks through me completely, and he freezes. "Baby, I can stop," he whispers against my skin. I shake my head.

"No, I need you, River. Please don't stop." I grip the skin of his back, raking my nails down as he pulls back and then slides forward again. *Oh gods. This is what the heavens must feel like.*

The tether between us shines so brightly from within me, and I wonder if he can see it or feel this bond between us. My magic purrs with him in me as he continues moving slowly to accommodate for the sheer size of him.

"Gods, you're so tight, Ember," he moans again as he brings himself to the hilt, and I can't form a coherent thought, let alone actual words. He leans down and kisses me, swallowing my own moans as pleasure soon takes completely over the pain. I wrap my legs around him, needing him deeper, and he concedes, driving forward at a steady pace. It feels like sparks explode all over my skin as my orgasm starts to build once more.

He chases after his own, looking down at me with his lips slightly parted, and I just can't take it. I arch beneath him, my breasts coming up to meet his chest as the most powerful orgasm I've ever had rips through me. He crashes his lips into mine to silence any sound I make as I ride out the incredible waves of ecstasy.

Seconds later he pulls out of me, spilling his climax all over my stomach, groaning my name. He drops his forehead to mine, panting softly, our breaths mingling as we both come down from our high.

He slides off of me, and I lay there with my head at the foot of the bed, skin glistening in the moonlight. He comes back a moment later with a soft rag to clean me up. He takes his time getting every last drop off before cleaning himself up, and I can't help the flare in my core watching him. *That really just happened.*

He picks me up, setting me on unsteady legs that still shake, and grabs the top sheet we ruined. I see the remnants of my virginity, gone and given to him. He crumples it up and puts it in the corner to be dealt with later. He pulls back the comforter and lets me climb in. For a moment he doesn't join me as he looks at the door, and I panic, thinking he's going to leave.

"No, please don't go," I beg.

"I'm not going anywhere, Ember. I promise." He moves the comforter back to lay with me, pulling me to his chest. I lay my head in the pocket of his shoulder and intertwine our legs, resting my hand on his stomach. My fingers begin to trace the lines of his abdominal muscles, marveling at the design of his body.

"You're so beautiful," I whisper. I feel him chuckle in response and look up at him.

"Beautiful?" he muses.

"There's no other way to describe it. Sure, you're handsome, but you're also more than that. Beautiful just seems like the right word." I smile at him and he returns it. And it's devastatingly... *beautiful.*

"See, you're breathtaking. Quite literally, I feel like I can't breathe sometimes when I look at you, but you're also more than *that.* You radiate in ways I've never seen before. The first time we met, I almost forgot how to speak. I was so tongue-tied I could barely say a word. I was completely caught off guard by your sheer beauty." He pauses, looking over me before continuing,

"I have never had an issue paying attention. I was a part of our army's undercover operations, where we searched for Klyerian spies in our villages. So being observant is one of my specialties.

Until you." He looks up at the ceiling, and I realize I don't know a whole lot about River before his time here.

I only know the River I've come to know over the year he's been assigned to me. I absorb every word, memorize every detail, desperate for more.

"For over a year now I've had to fight to focus on everything else but you, but my eyes have a mind of their own; it's like they're magnetized to you. I'd look away, and then suddenly somehow I'm right back to watching you. Which is dangerous for someone in my profession. I need to know everything that's going on at all times. You make that very difficult." He chuckles softly before he goes on, and it's music to my ears.

"I've memorized everything there is to know about you. What face you make when you don't like the food. The little shiver that runs through you every time you sneeze. The way the very atmosphere changes when you play your cello. Every. Single. Detail. And it's not enough. You've got me parched like a madman, always ready to drink more of you. I've never felt like that before." He absent-mindedly trails his hand up and down the curve of my hip.

All this time...I was wrong. Completely and utterly wrong.

"I had convinced myself you hated me," I confess as I stare out the window. "Every time *I* looked at you, you were looking somewhere else. You were so quiet. So stoic and...cold. But even then I couldn't stop myself from thinking about you. About the way you tick your jaw when you're angry or don't agree with me. I couldn't help but relish every touch or the way you started to say my name. I've felt this pull to you, River, for so long, and I never thought... I never thought that you'd felt anything toward me. But then that night at Marb's happened, and Eli told me you hadn't left my side, and I could see how upset you were. Like your worst nightmare was playing out in real life." I pause, taking a deep breath.

"It *was* my worst nightmare. I thought I had let you *die*, Ember. There is nothing sweeter than the relief I felt when you woke up. And not only were you alive, you were already healing. I vowed then that I'd show you at least a fraction of what I felt for you. I hated that I had waited until you almost died to actually act human for once. But you still didn't believe I cared about you.

"That tore me apart, realizing I had fought so hard to push you away, fought so hard to try and pretend you had no effect on me that you believed I hated you. You thought there was no passion for me here, nothing to wake up and look forward to. Yet, you are the sole reason I can get through my day and not think about the atrocities I've seen in my lifetime. So, I started to let it seep through a little more, and once I started, I couldn't stop." There's so much emotion in his voice; any doubts I could have had about the way he feels toward me are properly destroyed.

"Is that why it was so hard to see me with Aris?" I wonder aloud.

"Yes. Not only did I not trust him, but I didn't want him to touch you. I never wanted anyone else's hands on you but mine. I couldn't stand to watch you dancing with Jasper—I had always wanted it to be me even if I can't dance." I chuckle at that, moving as close to him as I can. "But I could see the way you looked at Aris. You had never looked at me like that, or so I thought. It was infuriating—I almost had half a mind to walk into that garden and rip you away. And gods, the way you looked in that dress? It took everything in me not to touch you. And even *then* I failed. You drive me crazy, Ember. The sheer willpower it took not to follow you into your room that night..." He shakes his head like it was the hardest battle he's ever been through.

"We wasted so much time," I whisper, the rush of reality threatening to crush me as the weight of it all settles on my chest. He pulls me closer, brushing his lips over the top of my hair. I wrap myself around him, bringing my leg up higher on his thighs.

"I know, I'm sorry. I'm so sorry. I thought I was doing the right thing, pretending not to care, pretending I didn't..." He trails off, swallowing. "I thought I was protecting you by pretending you didn't affect me. But you do, and now I... Now I don't get to have you, and part of me has always known I wouldn't. The brute never gets the princess. But I'd rather be a part of your life than not at all." His hand trails up the sides of my ribs, causing more goosebumps to spread.

"We'll find a way. We have to. We can play our part. We can have tonight, and then we can go back to playing princess and guard, and we'll figure it out. This can't be it; I won't stand for it."

But I know we won't figure it out. Even though my feelings run so deep for River, even though I've ruined myself for him, there's another name that owns the other part of my soul.

A little voice in my head whispers his name. A name I choose to forget for tonight, a tether I ignore. I've never hated my magic more than I do now, when that other tether tugs in my stomach, aware he's moving around somewhere in these walls. I shove all of those thoughts away as I trail a finger down the center of River's abdomen, reaching his waistband, and then I start the trail back up. His heartbeat quickens and his breath falters, so I do it again.

"We'll figure it out. And if we can't? We run away." But I can hear even in his voice that he knows we can't do that. He trails his fingers back down my ribs and runs lazy circles over my hip. He grabs a hold of my ass, squeezing it before rolling us over, smiling down at me. "We have tonight, and I'm going to make it worthwhile." I giggle as he dips his head, kissing all over my neck and chest, his erection growing hard against my inner thighs, which become increasingly wet.

I lost count eventually, how many times I lost myself in him. At some point, I didn't know where he started and I ended. We tried our best to stay quiet. We even tried to sleep. But we couldn't keep our hands to ourselves, let alone our mouths off each other.

For one night I was able to love him.

One night where we could pretend that every night would be like tonight.

By the end, my skin finally knew what it was like to be loved instead of hated. To be ravished instead of ruined.

When my eyes could no longer stay open, I fell asleep on his chest, listening to him murmur sweet nothings into my ear.

But when I wake the next morning, I find myself alone in bed. His clothes are gone and so is the bloody sheet. The crack in my chest finally caves in, and I can't stop the waves of tears that come after.

Once the tears have dried up, and the ache in my chest has become a constant pain, I pull myself out of bed. Just moving sends an array of pain and pleasure as the night's effects on my body become apparent. My hips are sore, and when I look in the mirror, I can see faint bruises where he gripped them tightly, taking from me so unabashedly that my cheeks burn bright red with the memory.

When Melody and Layla arrive, I've already bathed, washing away the remnants of our only night together. Still, his touch lingers on my skin as if unwilling to let go just yet.

"Good morning, Your Highness. How did you rest?" Melody asks as she walks over to where I sit wrapped in a robe at the vanity. Layla sifts through the armoire.

"So good; the bed is very comfortable." I look at it through the reflection of the mirror and do my best to keep my face neutral. *Yet that bed is where I ruined myself so willingly, so thoroughly. How could I ever act like nothing transpired?* Layla looks over at me.

"Wonderful! You let us know if there's anything you need changed; we'll see to it that your time here is as comfortable as we can make it." Layla gives me a reassuring smile, coming over with a simple cream gown. It's long sleeved to accommodate the cold and an expensive silk I never would have had in my own closet. She produces a lovely set of white lace undergarments to go underneath. "How about this?" she asks.

"I think that's perfect. What about later for the welcome ball?"

"Prince Aris requested that we dress you in, and I quote, 'Something dark green; it's her color whether she knows it or not.' So we have our seamstress working on something for you right now," Melody answers. That blush makes its way up my neck again. *Is he ever not charming?*

"He really loved the dress I wore for the Winter Solstice. How sweet." The tether that ties me to Aris warms.

It makes the ache in my chest feel even worse.

For how could I want two people at once?

How could I still be feeling anything toward him when he let my life get ripped out from beneath me?

"Can we do an updo on you today?" Melody breaks my thoughts while lifting some of the drying curls. I nod quietly.

I think they sense my need for quiet because they begin to work on my hair silently. Curls frame my face with the braided bun they've placed at the nape of my neck.

I slip into the dress quickly, hoping they won't notice the love marks that weren't there before. The dress is snug all the way to my thighs before it falls elegantly to the ground. The tight form accentuates my waist and the curve of my bottom. The neckline scoops, revealing the hollow between my breasts, and a golden brooch lies flat against the abdomen.

"I can't walk a whole day in heels as much as I wish I could," I say when Melody pulls a pair of low heels. She quickly changes to a pair of matching cream flats, and I nod obligingly.

"Thank you, ladies." I smile at them through the reflection of the mirror as they admire their handiwork.

"You must be starving; we can retrieve your guard and lead you to the dining room to enjoy some breakfast," Melody tells me as she retrieves a heavy cream winter cloak, some green gloves, and even a green scarf from a large bag they brought in with them. I chuckle.

"Are these also courtesy of the prince?" Layla nods with a swoon-type look on her face.

"He said you get cold really easily and had these delivered for you this morning. We'll carry them for you to the dining room." Melody smiles down at the scarf. "He really is so thoughtful," she murmurs, though it doesn't seem like she meant to say it out loud. *He really is.*

"I know Aris said he'd be busy today, but do you think you could send him a message for me?" I move toward the door as they open it for me.

"Of course, Your Highness," Layla replies.

"Just let him know that if he gets a moment in the day, I'd like to speak with him." I smooth my hands over the dress as I look toward River's door. I can do this. I'm the princess. He's just my guard. *That's not all he is to you.* I shove down the memories into a little box, using every bit of my willpower to act unaffected.

"We will let him know right away," Melody answers. Layla knocks softly on River's door, and it opens almost immediately, like he was waiting right on the other side. He's back in his guard uniform, a warm coat slung over his arm as he closes the door behind him. His hair curls around his ears, and his facial hair is trimmed down nice and neat. I want to run my tongue up his neck; he looks *that* good.

I realize this is going to be much harder than I thought it would be. River nods at me, much better at this sort of thing than I am. I nod back, swallowing to contain myself from making a fool of myself. *Princess and guard.*

My heart pounds in my ears as we make our way down the long hall. I focus on nothing but the sounds of our steps, counting them to keep myself from thinking anything other than the thought of his gods sent tongue. I nearly run into Layla, and a blush creeps up my neck in embarrassment. She chuckles before opening the door for us.

I take a seat, and an array of fruits, eggs, bacon, and sausage plated for our choosing lines one side of the table. Melody lays my coat and other winter wear on the seat beside me, while River takes the seat across from me.

"The prince has arranged for two of our finer horses for you both to take around the estate. Is there anything else we can get you, Your Highness?" Melody asks.

"No, this is lovely. Thank you, ladies. What time should I be back to prepare for the ball?" I begin grabbing some of the fruit and a couple of pieces of bacon.

"Four o'clock would give us a good amount of time; the seamstress would like to make sure she had the right measurements. Guests should begin arriving around six," Layla answers.

"Wonderful, I'll make sure to find my way back here then." I smile at them both, and they turn to leave when River speaks up.

"Where might we find the horses?" he asks, the morning rasp still very present. Just the sound of it makes my toes curl.

"Oh, of course!" Melody squeaks, turning on her heels to face River. "They have them ready outside of the main entrance. If you leave out..." She goes on to explain the different ways of getting around castle grounds and even a few places she suggests we visit. We both nod and thank them both again, bidding them goodbye. They both scurry off, giggling when they leave out the way we came in, and I can't help but smile at my plate, shaking my head at them. Taking my time, I enjoy the succulent fruit that's somehow sweeter than back home.

I peek at River through my lashes, watching him bite into a strawberry, and I nearly moan out loud as his tongue darts out to lick the juice off his lips. *You've got to be kidding me.* He looks over at me, the glint in his eye giving him away. *Bastard.* I shake my head, trying not to laugh.

He's not going to make this easy on me.

So I won't either.

I take my time getting up, reaching for my cloak but not putting it on just yet because I can feel him looking.

His eyes rake from the bottom up, pausing at the curve of my hips and the slopes of my breasts before settling on my lips. I hold his gaze before slipping the cloak over my shoulders. I wrap the thick wool scarf around my neck and slip the fur-lined gloves on. He shakes his head slightly, muttering something I can't hear.

River quickly puts his coat on, retrieving a black knit hat from the pocket. He tugs it on, and I can't help but smile at the curls of his hair peeking out of it. He returns the smile, and I know we're doomed. There's no way we're going to be able to keep this up.

Just the exchange of smiles could lead to our demise.

I welcome the cool air when we find our way outside. Two stunning, ginormous horses wait at the foot of the stairs, saddled and ready for us to mount. Servants hold the reins as we descend, bowing to me once I reach the ground. Even with the saddle, I'm not entirely sure how I'll get on top. I walk up to the slightly smaller of the two, placing my foot in the foothold, and grab ahold of the saddle, preparing to throw myself up on it when I hear footsteps come toward me. I turn to look at River.

"Allow me," he murmurs softly. He grabs hold of my hips and lifts me up. I use my arms to twist as he lifts, landing in the saddle perfectly. I bend my right leg slightly, letting my legs dangle over the side. It's the only way to ride in such a dress. With his back turned to the servants, they can't see when he drags his hand down my legs before releasing me fully. *Gods, you have no merciful bone in your celestial body, do you?*

I watch as he mounts his horse with ease. It's hard not to admire the way his body works so fluidly, but I turn and face forward, glancing at the servants who don't bat an eye. It's just a guard helping his princess mount her horse. *Nothing to see here.*

I lift the reins, tapping them lightly to send the horse into a trot. We ride in silence at the start, looking around the grounds and everything the king has crafted to perfection. I have to give it to the man; he's meticulous.

Every stone, every hedge is placed with a purpose. Even though most of the plants and trees are bare for the season, everything is still somehow beautiful. I run my hands down the soft hair of the mare beneath me, entranced by the way her strong muscles move under me.

Eventually we come upon a small stretch of forest; cobblestone lines a pathway that winds through the trees. The path is big enough that River comes up beside me on his horse. I look behind me and around me, making sure there's no one within hearing distance.

"Hi." My voice comes out sheepishly; a small blush creeps up my cheeks. He smiles down at his horse before glancing at me.

"Hi, Ember." Gods that voice. So low and seductive. He could talk me to climax; I'm sure of it.

"Tell me about your family. Your time in the army. Tell me your favorite colors, foods, and animals. Tell me everything you've never told me before." I run another hand down the hair of the mare, keeping my hand busy and my eyes forward, lest I jump off of her and run to him.

"Let's see. I'm the youngest of three brothers. I'm from the small village at the southern tip of the kingdom, Jeran. My father was a soldier and died early on when I was about ten. After that it was just us three boys and our mom. We did everything we could to take care of her, and she did everything she could to take care of us. You really would have loved her." I peek over at him, and he smiles sadly.

Parentless. But well loved from what it seems.

"She would have loved you. She died while I was away training to be a soldier at only eighteen. She got sick, and it took her pretty quickly, from what my brother, Hawthorne, says.

He's the oldest, about five years older than me. He works as a blacksmith for the town. My other brother, Fern, is three years older than me. He's the general of the army. He's the reason I have this job." River pauses, and so do our horses; he takes a deep breath that comes out in a cloud of steam.

River doesn't seem like the youngest brother. There's so much wisdom and maturity; I just can't imagine him bickering with his siblings. I find myself wanting to meet them.

"We can stop there. I have a lifetime to learn about you. I just want you to know I want to know everything there is to know." I offer him a smile, wishing I could squeeze his hand, touch his face, kiss the furrow out of his brow. He gives me an appreciative look, and our horses begin moving again.

We spend the afternoon relatively in silence, but it's comfortable. Like a blanket of safety has wrapped around us, and we're just happy to be in each other's presence. We sneak glances and gazes, and as we make our way back to the estate to return the horses, we both straighten up. Princess and guard once more. In the distance I can see that blonde horse, still alone, frolicking through the field at her own leisure.

We find two servants ready to take our horses back at the main entrance. River dismounts smoothly, walking over to me to help me off mine. He grabs my waist, and I place my hands on his shoulders as he lifts me with such grace and ease. He sets me down on the ground and gives me a heated look before promptly letting me go as if I'm on fire and stepping several feet away.

We make our way back inside, and I wander around until I find the library and strip from my cloak, laying it all on a chair. River does the same, following me around as I journey deep into the stacks. The library is even bigger than ours, rows and rows of shelves lined with thousands upon thousands of books that go on and on and on. Long, large windows let in the afternoon sun, setting the room ablaze in beautiful golden light. A fireplace crackles in the distance, far from where we are now, warming the room. As we travel further from it, the cooler the air becomes. But it's just us in here, and I find myself completely at ease despite being on enemy territory.

My finger drags softly along the spines of the books, waiting until a book calls to me. When one does, I pause, pulling it from its place on the shelf to begin reading the first page. I'm so entangled in the text already that I don't notice River stalking closer to me until he's right behind me. My body goes rigid at his proximity.

I wait until he does something. It's so dangerous doing this out in the open, yet we are so far into the rows that the likelihood of someone seeing us before we heard them is slim to zero.

My eyes flutter shut when he grabs my waist, stepping into my back where my bottom nestles perfectly into his hips. He runs his nose up my neck, groaning softly when he places a kiss on my burning skin.

"This dress, Ember. I just can't help myself." He nips softly at my ear, dragging his large hands up my ribs and over my breasts. I drop my head back against his shoulder, trying my very best to stay quiet. My nipples become hard buds, and he pinches them through the fabric.

"River..." I murmur softly, pleasure ricocheting through my body as he presses his hard body into my own.

"Hmm." He takes my hips, pushing them harder against his hardened length. "I could take you right here if this dress wasn't so damn hard to pull up." He turns me in his arms, gathering me close.

"How are we going to do this?" I ask, looking right at his lips.

"I mean, I'm sure no one's going to come in here," he answers absentmindedly, gazing at my mouth. I laugh softly.

"I meant, how are we supposed to keep our hands off each other? How am I supposed to pretend I don't want you?" I whisper, tilting my head toward him.

"We're doing well so far if we have an audience. But if it's just us, I'm not sure we can. Or at least, I'm not sure *I* can. A year later, all my self-control is gone. I've finally gotten a taste of you, and I'm a goner. A complete and utter addict." He rubs his nose against mine, his lips mere breaths away.

"So we become a secret. Touch behind closed doors, or I guess in this case, deep in the back of the library. It's risky." I intertwine my fingers into his hair, tugging softly.

"A necessary risk I'll take so I don't go mad." He finally presses his lips into mine, and a glorious burst of pleasure rushes through me, igniting a fire within me. My magic slips out of its box, pressing up against my skin as if eager to meet the man we're tethered to. It's aggravating.

It's so frustrating to split my attention between his lips and pull that power painfully back into its box where the lid shuts begrudgingly. When it's tucked away, I tilt my head back so I can look into my favorite pair of blue eyes.

Suddenly, guilt pierces my chest so fiercely that I almost whimper at the ache. He furrows his eyebrows, looking at me worried while I look at him in agony.

"I can't..." I swallow, gathering the words to explain the pain. "I can't do this to you, River. I can't put you through this. I'd be forcing you to watch me go between you and my future husband. You'd have to watch me as I split my heart in two."

River's watched me with two other men, and suddenly I feel like I'm going to vomit. I push myself out of his arms, taking a couple of steps away.

How could I be so cruel? I didn't know about River's feelings, but now that I do, it makes everything feel *vile*. I think back on the moments with Aris, sitting under the willow tree with him, almost kissing him, and all the heated looks we exchanged during the ball. I think about the subtle way he'd touch me when we were out in the village, how he held me in the tent, and how he let me sleep on his shoulder. And then my chest crumples in on itself thinking about how River had to watch all of that and not say a word. He said it himself; he never wanted anyone else but him touching me. And I basically flaunted it in front of him. *Oh gods, what have I gotten us into?*

"Ember." River grabs my hand, pulling me back to him. "Ember, look at me." I do, and he smiles down at me. A rare smile I don't deserve. He cups my face and plants a soft kiss on my nose that makes me sigh softly.

"Do not blame yourself for things you did not know. Do

not worry for me. You are allowed to be and act as you are. Even when I want to tie you up so you'll stop getting yourself into trouble. Even when I want to order you away from things that might hurt you. I do not control you. And I never will. I will bow before you. I will protect you until I can no longer hold my sword. I will ravish you in secret, even if you swear your oath of marriage to him. Because even a fraction of your love is more than enough for me." He caresses my cheek. *I don't deserve this.*

"River, please, I don't want to hurt you. You can't tell me this won't hurt you." Or *him,* I add silently. I lean into his hand, closing my eyes.

"You won't. You can't. I knew what I was getting myself into when I walked into your room last night. I kissed you anyway because I'd spend the rest of my life adoring you in secret if I at least had the chance to show you my affections. I'm willing to share if it means I can have you.

"As much as I hate him, I'm not naive. I see how you look at him too. But I trust you, Ember. Your happiness is my own, and I'll do my best to behave when you touch him. But you're a grown woman. You're *my* queen. The only one I'll ever be on my knees for. I can't blame him for wanting the same." His breath fans across my lips as he leans his forehead against mine.

I'm willing to share if it means I can have you.

"I don't know what I did in this life to deserve you." I lean up and kiss him with everything I have—with all the unsaid words and feelings I can't quite voice. And he pours right back into me.

Eventually, we part, out of breath with swollen lips, and I don't want to stop, but we have to. I take a moment to catch my breath, my forehead still against his. We untangle from each other, which feels way too difficult to do.

Gods, what have I gotten myself into?

When we finish straightening ourselves out to return to our former state, no longer looking like we momentarily lost ourselves in each other, we find our way back to our rooms.

He nods at me before disappearing into his door, not casting another look back.

The girls relish taking their time for tonight's look. It's not long before my skin is scrubbed raw and perfumed with floral and honey scents. My hair is organized into soft waves that tumble down my back, and cosmetics are applied only to enhance my features and nothing more.

The seamstress pulls a dark, shimmering emerald dress that takes my breath away. We quickly get me in it after I put some matching green lace undergarments on. Thin lace sleeves fall off my arms, exposing my collarbones and the tops of my shoulders. Tiny emerald jewels encrust the bodice, which dips into a heart-shaped neckline, pushing my breasts together. The skirt of the dress is layers upon layers of dark green tulle with a slit in the right leg.

My back is covered by the bodice, and my hair covers the tops of my shoulders, so I should be safe as long as my hair doesn't move too much. The lashes have turned into white lines that layer over each other. Still noticeable but not to the degree it was before.

The seamstress even provides a beautiful matching pair of jewel-encrusted heels, which Layla takes her time to buckle on. When I stand and face myself in the mirror, I can't help but smile. *Aris was right; this is my color.*

"You look absolutely radiant, Your Highness," Layla says in admiration. Melody seconds her, nodding in approval at their handiwork. I offer them thanks in appreciation.

"Prince Aris was only able to find some time before the ball is to start; he'll meet you on our way to the ballroom," Melody tells me. I nod slowly, following them into the hall where River's already waiting.

There's nothing like setting eyes on him. Every time feels like the first time.

His Winter Solstice uniform has been washed and pressed for tonight, so he's matching me once more. The girls lead us away, and for a moment, behind their backs, we drink each other in until we no longer can. Instead, I train my eyes on the ground in front of me.

Footsteps approach, and I look up to find Aris walking toward us in his finest all black. He looks drop-dead handsome. I can't help but swallow as my heart quickens. Images of River kissing my neck from behind while Aris lowers himself to his knees flash through my mind, making my knees quiver at the onslaught of fantasies now corrupting my focus.

His eyes darken as they roam over me unapologetically before his gaze flashes to me. A slow, seductive smile takes over his features, and I find myself returning it. Then I remind myself to act like the innocent, polite princess and not the one horny for both of the men in the hallway. The girls quickly bow and walk in the other direction, peeking over their shoulders at the three of us and then bowing their heads together as they walk.

"Ember, I'm so sorry I couldn't get to you earlier. I was stuck in meeting after meeting after meeting. I hope you enjoyed our estate this afternoon. I'm told you were able to explore a good amount of what we have to offer today." His tone has that arrogant charm that sends flutters through me, causing me to take an involuntary step closer to him.

He's so hard to resist. It's *infuriating.*

"Your grounds are stunning, Aris. It'll be a beautiful place to live. I only have a few suggestions."

"Of course, we can decorate however you want when we're sworn in. I want you to feel at home. I want you to be comfortable here." *Home. Could these walls ever really feel like home?*

A servant with a cart full of linen moves to walk past us; Aris puts his hand on my arm, moving us to the side so my back is to the wall and he's in front of me. It's a natural movement, almost like we move like this normally. He looks down at me, not dropping his arm. River stands off to the side, looking anywhere but at us. "What did you want to talk about?"

"Just tell me one thing," I answer softly, not wanting others to hear us.

"Anything."

"Well, make that two things." I take a deep breath, trying to do this calmly. "I want to know why you didn't tell me. And two, I want a promise that whatever it is you're keeping from me, that you *will* tell me. If you can promise me honesty, then I can promise you my devotion." I tilt my chin up, making sure he knows I mean it.

"Done. One, I didn't know how to tell you. Was I just supposed to say, 'Hi, I'm Prince Aris, your future husband'?" He gives me an incredulous look when I nod. "It just didn't feel right. I just wanted you to get to know me first. The real me before anything else got in the way. So that you might trust me a little more, which I realize now was stupid. They told me to tell you it was only a month so you wouldn't make traveling there difficult; they thought if you knew it was to marry me, you wouldn't go."

"It really was stupid," I admonish. "But they were right; I would've been way bitchier."

"Two." He swallows, shutting his eyes for a moment before opening them again. "There's a lot at stake here, and there are a lot of listening ears around us. I can't afford to have anyone eavesdropping. But when the time is right, I promise you'll know everything." He drops the veil he keeps up, the one that shadows everything he feels, and lets me in for a moment, honesty and genuineness shining bright and sure. I'm about to respond when more footsteps sound down the hall, and I peer over quickly to see none other than the king walking our direction.

"Quick, act like you're flirting—" My whisper is cut off swiftly as Aris boxes me in with his arms and swoops down to kiss me. I suck a quick breath in before his lips brush mine, a mere feather of a touch, but it's enough to rock me to my core. Where River is fire that burns me from within, Aris is lightning that zaps throughout me. *What a dangerous combo they'd both be.*

The king clears his throat from behind us, and Aris leans

back, dropping his hands from where they were on the stone wall behind me. He gives me a lopsided grin that I return as he turns and faces his father.

"Father," Aris says, as if irritated to have been interrupted.

"Looks like you two are getting along quite fine. I hope to see more of you two together at the ball; people will want to see the betrothed in their love bubble," Bleren says with an undertone I don't quite understand. He doesn't stick around for a response; he moves on quickly with his entourage of guards and continues toward the ballroom where we'll be headed next. Aris turns to me, moving to tuck a piece of hair behind my ear. I hold my breath, hoping my thrashing heart will calm.

"Shall we?" Aris extends his elbow, and I take it, walking forward with him as River falls in step behind us.

As we reach the door, River appears at my other side, and with both of them there, their tethers pulsing with power, passion, and need—I've never felt more at ease than with these two strong men by my side.

CHAPTER 19

Our names are called, and when we enter the room, my breath is stolen from me at the grandness of it all. The tables seem to go on for an eternity. Civilians dressed in their best sit patiently, watching us with scrutiny that I almost want to wither under, but I don't. Not with Aris at my side.

I find myself searching the crowd for my court by reflex. The reminder that they won't be found amongst the hundreds of faces pierces me with a yearning agony that nearly makes my steps falter.

I miss Jasper so fiercely, and it's only been a couple of days. How will I spend the rest of my life away from him?

Ice sculptures of the bodies of beautiful women stand tall behind all of the guests, facing the crowd like they're watching over them. A rectangle of white tile cuts out a massive dance floor. Off to the corner a quartet of strings is set up, and my heart lurches at the sight of the cello, my fingers instantly itching to play it.

Aris and I wave to the crowd as they erupt in applause. When the noise dies down, he gingerly places a hand on the small of my back, leading me toward the table where his father and his court sit.

I watch as a servant leads River to a separate table to the right of us, where he sits with his back to the windows. It's a good vantage point for him to be able to survey the crowd and also us. The muscles in his shoulder are taut as he turns and faces me, a mixture of anger and worry settling into his features. Weariness floods the tether between us.

I send back reassurance, but even then I can feel River watching me wearily. Even as he sits so much further from me, I can feel those eyes as if they were my own. But I can't look at him, can't match that gaze. All I can do is act my part as a bride.

So, I grab Aris' hand and squeeze it, both reassuring him and myself that we can do this. Food that tastes better than I care to admit is quickly served; chatter and the sounds of metal on porcelain fill the room, echoing off the tall ceilings.

The king chats with my father, who sits on his right as they eat and drink. Neither of them spared a glance at us, which is fine by me. People watch us. They watch the way we eat, watch the way we drink, and the way we're not talking. I watch as some of them bow their heads together, whispering as they continue to glance at us. *Can they see right through us?*

"Act more like my fiancé," Aris says as he picks up on the same thing.

"You first," I mumble, taking a long gulp of my second glass of wine. The edge on my nerves begins to calm.

"Careful there; we don't want them thinking the bride-to-be is a drunk," he warns.

"Don't worry, they'll think she's fun." I flash a smile at him, leaning toward him for good measure. Aris chuckles, shaking his head down at me.

A bride. I am a bride. He is to be my husband. River is my guard.

I repeat the mantra in my head until I almost believe it. My heart doesn't, but it's easier to ignore the bleeding thing in my chest when our lives are on the line.

"Care to dance? I'd love to see some of those moves again." He leans down so he's only mere breaths away. I look down at those soft lips, replaying the ghost of a kiss he gave me, as if he was holding back on purpose earlier.

"I've been meaning to ask if you have a studio here and perhaps a pianist I can steal to practice every once in a while?" I look up at him through my lashes. Something flashes through his eyes as they roam over my face, settling on my own lips.

"We do; I can take you there tomorrow. I won't be as busy, so maybe we can have lunch together and do whatever we'd like." He sounds unsure, as if I'd say no to spending time with him.

"Yes, please, that would be lovely." I plant a soft kiss on his lips, a whisper of a touch to repay him for earlier. "Let's go dance now, show them how good we are together." I finish the last of my wine before he takes my hand and leads me down the steps toward the dance floor.

A hush falls over the tables closest as curious eyes peer over at us. I turn and face the king, curtsying for him. He nods approvingly, a delighted smile appearing on his lips. Aris says something to the players, who nod eagerly at him. He joins me back at the center and smiles at me wickedly.

"Follow my lead." He grabs my hand and pulls me close as a breath whooshes out of me.

I open my mouth to say something snarky, but the music begins, and he whisks me away. A hearty laugh escapes as we begin to dance to the rhythm that slowly starts to pick up.

It's not hard to keep up when I can anticipate what we'll do next. From rigid to smooth, we let it all flow away, only allowing the sound of the music to move through us as we expertly dance across the floor. Oohs and ahs flutter from the audience as Aris lifts me with ease into complicated positions that send my heart racing. It's exhilarating, and as much as I hate to admit it—fun.

Time passes so quickly that if it weren't for his lead, I

would've kept dancing through the end of the song. He dips me with the final note, holding all of my weight as if it were nothing.

Our chests rise and fall rapidly as we catch our breath. His hair falls forward, framing his face as he smiles, his dimples and sharp canines making an appearance. He's so handsome he almost doesn't seem real.

He brings me up, settling me down as my hands come to his shoulder. With one arm wrapped tightly around my waist, he brings the other up to grab the back of my neck, pulling me as close as he can. I look up at him with wide eyes, as if to say, *right here, right now?*

He tilts my head up, leaning down to kiss me softly as an answer, and the entire audience sighs in awe. *Oh, I get it.* I grip his shirt, shutting my eyes and letting myself pretend it's just us. I let myself think of only his lips and the way they feel on mine. Sparks tingle throughout my body, like little zaps of lightning pulsing against my nerves. I almost forget where I am. All too soon, he pulls away, searching my eyes as if I'm the answer to his wildest dreams.

The audience eats it up. And somewhere in me, something whimpers softly. The pain of knowing we're just for show makes my chest ache. *What I feel for him isn't an act, and I hate that.*

I don't want to feel for him.

Or do I?

"Bravo! Bravo." The king's voice booms throughout the room. "Give it up one more time for my son and his beautiful fiancé!" He claps, smiling at us with that evil gleam that never quite leaves his eyes. Aris pulls me tightly against his side, as if he's protecting me from something. He moves to lead us toward our seats when the king puts his hand up to stop us. I look at my mother and father, who sit pleasantly to the side with smug looks on their faces.

My mother's hair shines gold beneath the shimmering chandeliers, tucked into a slick bun at the nape of her neck. Her red silk dress is cut modestly, barely showing a whisper of her collarbone. My father holds her hand, his tan skin stark against the porcelain of her own. He's shaved, and his hair has been cut neatly. Something flashes in my father's eyes as he beholds me with Aris. Something that sends my heart into an even more chaotic rhythm than it already was.

"It has come to my attention that the bride-to-be has an extraordinary talent," the king begins. I glance at the cello, taking a deep breath as I prepare mentally for what I might play. "A magnificent singing voice, and she has agreed to perform for us all tonight. Such a treat."

The king merely nods at me to begin, and I can't help but stare at my parents as the king sits, content in making me a fool. My mother smirks, raising her glass to her lips as my legs threaten to give out from beneath me. My father levels me with a glare, daring me to embarrass him. There's an excitement that vibrates beneath his skin as he revels in the way he might punish me before he departs tomorrow.

I swallow as Aris separates from me, and I immediately miss the heat and the strength he gave me. He gives me an excited smile, oblivious to what is about to occur. Ignorant to the fact that I didn't even sing for my *own* kingdom.

Because I can't. No one could hear for as long as I tried growing up. And I can't even look at River to get me through this. I walk over to the quartet, asking them quietly if they know how to play an older ballad I fell in love with as a girl. A haunting love song dedicated to a forbidden lover. They all eagerly nod, and I smile as I take a spot in the center of the dance floor.

"I would like to dedicate this song to my dearest beloved. To the man I never thought I'd have, but soon will be mine for as long as I may live." I look over to Aris, whose onyx eyes shine brightly back at me.

And despite those words being for show, there's truth in them I find myself wanting to deny.

It has been years since I've tried to sing. I'd given up on trying when we couldn't figure out why no one but me could hear it. I nod at the quartet to begin, clearing my throat softly in preparation. The melody begins, and I find my entrance.

"In shadows' embrace, our love took flight..." My voice rings out, echoing into every corner of the hall, carried with it as a string of magic that snakes its way up my throat, intertwining with each note. I use the pause before the next line to wrangle it down, separating my power from the lyrics as I carry on. An eerie hush falls over the room, almost as if everyone's holding their breath as they wait for the next line. So, I continue.

"Forbidden whispers in the silent night." I close my eyes, losing myself in the melody as the quartet continues, following my lead. My voice vibrates in my chest, carrying the deep notes that transition into high ones throughout the massive room. The tethers in me tighten painfully as I continue, yearning to pull me closer to the other ends, but I stay put despite the pain. Because in different ways this song is about them. One forbidden before, one forbidden now.

> *"Heartbeats sync in a clandestine dance,*
> *Bound by fate, our love's forbidden trance.*
> *In moonlit murmurs, secrets entwine,*
> *Two hearts collide in a love divine.*
> *Though the world forbids our fervent flame,*
> *In each other's arms, our souls lay claim.*
> *In the void where love once thrived, now bare,*
> *Echoes of solitude, heavy in the air.*
> *Emptiness lingers, a silent, haunting trace,*
> *Alone in a world devoid of love's embrace.*
> *Apart, our souls wither in desolate rue,*
> *Dying echoes of a love that couldn't be pursued.*
> *Separated hearts, aching in the parting quest,*
> *Alone we fade, yearning to coalesce."*

The quartet looks to me, and I nod as we finish the last notes in sync. I hold my breath in the silence that follows; the last of the violin fades into the corners of the room. *They heard me; they really, really heard me.*

It's so quiet I can hear the blood rushing in my ears. But it's not actually blood I'm hearing; it's roaring applause that fills the room to a borderline deafening volume. I take a shaky breath, vibrating with power that wants to flood out of me like water through a broken dam. I look to River finally, and those turmoil-filled ocean blue eyes shatter any sense of self-control I thought I had as I take an involuntary step toward him.

He shuts down that momentary lapse in judgment and sits straight up, squares his shoulders back, and looks away from me. That stone-cold, stoic look returns in full force, and I stop mid-step, realizing where I am and what I'm doing.

My head snaps up to look at the king, who looks at me with all-knowing eyes. *Stupid, stupid girl.* I straighten up and look to Aris, who waits at the edge of the dance floor. I walk quickly toward him, taking his outstretched hand, and follow him away, out of sight of all the patrons, but within sight of his father as he leads me to the wall behind our table. He leans me against the cold stone wall, blocking anyone's view of us as we sink into the shadows.

More instruments join the quartet, and people flood the dance floor as merry music begins to fill the hall, and only one pair of eyes watches us closely—watches me closely. I've just revealed who part of my heart lies with, and that makes this all the more dangerous for River.

"Ember, that was—" I don't let him finish.

I kiss Aris like I've never breathed before, and he's my oxygen. I kiss him like the sunset kisses the earth goodbye. Like he's all I need and all I can see. He matches with the same fervor, even though I know he knows the song wasn't entirely meant for him. He kisses me like he's laid claim to the soul I laid bare on that dance floor tonight. He takes everything I give him and returns it tenfold. And for a moment, for a whisper of a moment, I can pretend I didn't just put a target on River's back.

He pulls back too quickly, grunting softly as if trying to stay in control. I release an involuntary whimper of my own with the loss of his lips. The ends of his hair tickle my cheeks as he catches his breath, his chest rising and falling rapidly. Someone clears their throat from behind Aris. I rise up on my tippy toes to look over his shoulder and lock eyes with my furious father. Aris sighs and turns around, keeping me behind him.

"Can I help you?" he asks irritatedly. I move out from behind him, staring my father down. My father ignores Aris and glares at me with a fiery rage that makes me want to curl into a ball. But I won't let that show, so I lift my chin.

"How?" he grits. My mother stands beside him, ever the silent supporter.

"What do you mean?" I ask, tilting my head in fake innocence. My father borderline hisses, taking a step toward me, to which Aris takes a step back in front of me; his arm covers half my body alone. My father takes a deep breath to calm himself and then tries again.

"You never could sing before; what changed?" His tone is significantly calmer, and that alone is startling.

"You mean how come I didn't make a fool of myself? How did I not embarrass you like you wanted me to? I don't know. I sang the same way I did when I was little, just this time you could hear me." This isn't what he wants to hear, and I can feel the words laced with poison about to attack, but Aris chimes in before my dad can deliver the blow.

"Careful with your next words, Your Majesty. I will not tolerate ill will toward my fiancé." The authority in his voice surprises even me.

"Who do you think you're talking to, boy?" The rage in my father's eyes shifts swiftly from me to Aris, who looks bored to be having this conversation. But I can tell by the way his muscles go taut just how angry he is too.

"This is *my* kingdom. You are a guest in *my* home. Who do *you* think you're talking to? You'd be lucky I don't send you on your merry way right now. We have what we need. So, you're going to leave us alone for the rest of the night and return home tomorrow morning without so much as another word or look toward her. Am I clear?" It's hard not to admire the certainty in his voice. I step deeper into his side, and he wraps his arm around my waist, his fingers digging into my hips where remnants of River reside. I bite my lip softly in response. My father only stares at Aris until Bleren walks over, dripping with charisma and authority.

Right into this fight for power.

"Everything all right here, son?" he asks. That voice—so, so easy to obey.

"I don't know; is everything okay, Your Majesty?" Aris asks, staring my father right in the eyes. A smirk plays on his lips, daring my father to defy him. My father, who is a couple inches shorter than Bleren, turns to him and says,

"Of course, everything is fine."

"Then maybe you'd like to explain why you lied to me?" the king replies.

"I beg your pardon?" My father swallows deeply.

"You said your daughter could not sing, and then she did. Wonderfully done, by the way, my dear. You have an incredible voice," the king drawls. He turns to me and smiles, almost seeming kind for a moment. *He really risked setting me up for failure?*

"Thank you, Bleren." I return the smile, digging my nails into my palms behind Aris' back.

"Because she's a lying bi—" He catches himself, taking a deep breath before continuing. "We've never heard a note from her throat until tonight. Your future daughter-in-law is finicky and shady. I warn you to take caution with her." My father looks me up and down in disgust. The king hums in response, rubbing the skin of his chin as he contemplates something.

"I see. We'll talk later, my dear; for now, go dance with my son some more; the people are eating it up. Have fun." There's something in the king's voice that immediately has me nodding and tugging Aris with me. Bleren nods at his son and then turns to my parents, his demeanor turning volatile as he begins speaking to them in a much angrier tone than he had with us.

As we escape from the wrath of his father, I snag two chalices of wine from a servant and hand one to Aris wordlessly. He takes it gratefully, and we both take long, deep gulps until the bittersweet taste is coating us from the inside. After emptying its contents, the edge slicing against my nerves eases a bit as the alcohol swirls around in me. *Deep, calm breaths.*

I look around for River and find him conversing with some of the other guards. He holds a pint of what looks like ale, and the buttons at the top of his tunic are undone. As if sensing my gaze, his eyes find mine. He takes a sip of his drink as he looks me up and down for any signs of injury. Content with what he sees, he turns back to what the guard is saying and responds, but I can't hear from where I am. I grab another glass from a passing servant and take a big gulp before setting it down, half-drunk. Aris chuckles from beside me.

"Does drinking help your dance moves? Because you seemed a little rusty earlier," he teases. I gasp and throw my hand over my heart.

"Oh, how you wound me so." I fake pout, and his eyes drop straight to my lips as he smiles wickedly at me.

"C'mon, Princess, prove me wrong." He rolls up his sleeves and unbuttons the top of his tunic before he tugs me onto the dance floor where people dance with each other. I chuckle, following him, denying myself the urge to look back at River. A few people smile and give us a wide berth as we begin to dance with each other. And so the night goes, dancing and drinking to try and forget the treachery of the course my life has taken.

I try my best not to think of Jasper.

I try my hardest not to think of my court and how they'd be dancing themselves silly into the night, getting absolutely trashed.

I try and utterly fail.

Because no matter how much I drink, no matter how much I try to drown my sorrows of missing them, no haze comes to fog the longing for the comfort of my friends.

Aris doesn't kiss me again, and something tells me it's for good reason. But his hands roam everywhere they can as we dance skillfully to every song they play, never faltering. And even then, his touches are resigned, like he's holding back. At a pause in the music, I pull away from Aris, needing a break to ease the pain in my feet and my bladder.

He tells me he'll wait for me and takes a seat at a random table to down a glass of water. His face gleams in the light from the chandeliers, pieces of his hair waving even more with the moisture, and his smooth chest looks enticing enough to lick. I flash him one last smile before slipping out of the doors, looking to my left and right. It's only then that I realize I don't know where the nearest bathroom is. *To the right it is.*

My feet ache terribly, so I slip off my heels, carrying them in one hand instead. The cold stone floor feels much better as I stretch out my toes and roll my ankles. I continue walking down the hall, flickering oil lamps illuminating my path.

I feel a presence just moments before they pop out of a shadowed alcove.

"All alone, princess?" That voice. I could never forget the voice that haunts my dreams. I take a few steps back, gaping at Dracyl. "What? You surprised to see me?" He flashes a white smile.

Suddenly the wine rises up in my throat. I swallow quickly, pulling myself together. He's clean now; his hair shines bright again, and all those bruises and cuts are gone. He's the picture of perfect health, as if he wasn't beaten within an inch of his life.

"How did you get out?" I ask, tilting my head as I take in the quality of his clothes. They're expensive, cut from the finer material I've seen the king's men wear.

"I walked right out of there, took a horse, and now we're

here." He walks toward me, towering over me in a way that has me gulping again.

"They let you go?" Confusion and fear wrap a hand around my throat, restricting my airflow.

"Courtesy of your soon-to-be husband." His eyes rake over my chest, causing me to take another step back. "You're so lucky you're untouchable now. We have unfinished business. It's such a pity that I didn't get to take you how I wanted then. I just love when they put up a fight." His words slice through me, and it takes every bit of my will to keep my lid shut tight and my lip from quivering. He sidesteps around me, and I let go of the breath I was holding.

"Watch yourself, Princess. You never know who's lurking around here," he adds over his shoulder.

I don't move until he's out of sight. Mindlessly, my body goes into autopilot, finding its way back to my room instead. In a moment of clarity, I flag down a servant and ask that they notify Aris that I've fallen ill for the night and returned to my chambers. They nod eagerly before I lock myself inside my room.

My body keeps moving on its own as I begin to remove all of the jewelry, the dress, and scrub the makeup off. I need to get out of here. *Out, out, out.* That's all I can think as magic begins to crackle and simmer in its well, and this time if it comes out, there will be no shoving it back in. I need to leave the castle before it's too late.

In a haste, I dress in warm wool leggings and a thin white tunic. I don't bother with a bra; I'm too wrapped up in my eagerness to get out from these walls. Once my cloak is on, I leave again, putting the hood up to conceal my identity.

No one glances my way as I exit with some of the other patrons already leaving for the night themselves. No one bats an eye as I jump up onto a horse, not caring who it belongs to.

As if sensing my need to get far away from the castle, the horse takes off at high speed, the wind ripping the hood from my face. The simmering turns to a boil, and it's almost unbearable as I hold onto the last shreds of control. I ride and ride into the forest until I can't anymore.

With the mare tied to a tree, I take off running as fast as my legs will carry me. Wind whips around me, matching the rapid beating of my heart as my magic begins to pour out of me with no restraint left.

It's as if it's on a path to vengeance. Seeking retribution for all of the times I've forced it into the dark. For all of the times I refused to use it even with my life in peril. It has finally stopped listening to my begging for it to stay put and is taking control instead.

The force of it stops me in my tracks and brings me to the floor.

As my knees hit the ground, air whooshes from my body, blowing with such force that the trees groan against it. Electricity pulses from my hands, and shadowy tendrils flow from me, tangling into the long grass and bushes. It relishes in its freedom, flowing with relief. Flowers grow, branches stretch, and *gods* my power just soars and soars all around me.

There's no end in sight. No limits to my magic, and that *terrifies* me.

I grapple for control, gritting my teeth as I wrangle in the power rushing out of me so forcefully.

Inhaling slow breaths brings me a sliver of tranquility, and slowly, the wind calms, the electricity simmers out, and the greenery stops rustling. Those tendrils stay out, coming to me like they have a mind of their own as they wipe the streaming tears from my cheeks and move my hair away from my face. My face tilts up toward the moon, and I breathe in the sweet air. Using a bit of the breeze, I dry my face, relishing in the coolness it brings to my hot skin.

For so long I've struggled to keep this burning power away from the surface. This primal part of me I've kept in a box, locked away so deep inside no one would ever know. But it's growing, and with each day it becomes harder and harder to control the more I refuse to use it. Every time I shove it down, I can almost feel it groan in agony, yearning to be let out. Screaming at me to let it protect me.

Slowly, I stand. The forest is eerily quiet as if it's holding its breath as it waits for what I'll do next. The tendrils, which used to be invisible, have taken on a shadowy-like color, billowing black from my fingertips. Making a lasso with it, I whip it toward a tree branch and then snap it back. The branch cracks and flies into the woods where I direct it.

My power continues to amaze me. Continues to prove me wrong when I think I've found the extent of what I'm capable of. There's always something else waiting for me to discover.

I let it flow back into me, my body practically singing in delight with the newfound feeling of release. All of the tension eases out of my muscles, relaxing me into a calmness I don't think I've ever known. That calm doesn't last long as the horse I stole whinnies in the distance, a wild and panicked sound that sends me racing toward it.

The brown mare jumps up and down on its hind legs, terrified of something in the dark I can't quite see but can *feel*. The power in me sings to it, as if called to whatever lays out there. I grab the cloak off of the saddle and untie the reins, slapping the mare's behind to set her racing toward where we came from.

It's too dark to be able to make out the creature in front of me because those aren't animal eyes, and it isn't human either. But something deep in my soul is calling to it. Something so irrevocably *certain* fills my chest as it takes a step forward.

Wicked and beautiful green scales glint, almost sparkling, in the dark as it cocks its head to the side, watching me with a sense of curiosity. A slight warning goes off in my head that I should be scared, but I'm not.

No, I'm not scared at all as it fully comes into the moonlight, its giant body practically slithering as it comes to a standstill. I didn't think the legends were true. Dragons had always been a rumor. Big-scaled creatures with four legs and massive wings had only been drawings and stories told around campfires, but none had actually been seen in I don't know how long. But what was impossible is now truly standing before me.

It should be eating me alive. Burning me to a crisp before I can take my next breath. What little I do know is that they want nothing to do with humans. We're the very species responsible for wiping them out and forcing them off somewhere we could never find them.

Yet, there's nothing vicious about the way it's looking at me.

It takes another step toward me, huffing a puff of hot breath over me through its nose. I wrinkle my nose as the smell of its dead prey wafts over me. Those emerald eyes, both so young and so old, narrow as it cocks its head to the other side. It huffs again, pushing its massive snout into my chest.

The touch ignites a third tether. Glowing hot, red pain brings me to my knees before the dragon. It feels as if I'm being torn apart and put back together. A scream rips from my lips. Not a single part of my body is spared from the pain as the tether is stamped into my very essence.

The dragon leans its forehead against mine, a soft whine escaping its throat as if it's feeling the same pain I am. As if it understands what's happening to us at this very moment.

There's something so different about the tethers connected to Aris and River compared to this one.

No, this one is *more* somehow.

This is soul binding. It goes beyond the physical natures of our bodies and connects me to it on a level I didn't know was possible. It's as if our hearts begin to beat on the same rhythm.

Suddenly, the air becomes crystal clear, and the chatter of the forest almost becomes too loud. And *good gods,* its breath—

"*Watch your mouth,*" a sensual and bold voice says directly into my head.

In less than a second I'm back on my feet, staring into those glowing green eyes.

"You should try eating a mint bush every once in a while." I cross my arms, staring up at her. A female dragon. A female fucking dragon is talking to me right now.

I couldn't see her as well in the dark before, but now it seems as if my vision has also become stronger. A bold scar of claw marks slashes down the side of her neck to her shoulder. Her underbelly is a softer shade of sage, whereas the rest of her scales are varying shades of dark green that seem to shimmer and change as she moves. She watches me with the same fascination. Which I can *feel*, along with a growing irritation.

"I will do and eat as I want." But I can feel her contemplation about the mint and whether it's worth a try. It's too much feeling her feelings and my own. My head feels like it's going to combust. *"I do not know enough about this bond to help us. You have to come with me now so we can learn."* She nudges me with her snout toward her back.

"I can't just leave. And what does this bond mean? Why are my senses suddenly on overdrive? What is your name?" I have about a million other questions starting with, *am I really talking to a dragon? Did I hit my head? What the fuck was in my wine?* But I stop when she levels me with a glare, and her annoyance washes over me.

"Insufferable," she huffs. *"My name in your tongue is Asteria. Your magic called to mine, Ember. And now our abilities have intertwined with each other. We are now connected for the remainder of our lives; your heart will beat as long as mine does. If one of us dies, the other perishes with them. I have just become your fiercest protector. And for that, you* must *leave with me. One of the Elders will teach us how to utilize the bond and block each other out."* She turns to the side expectantly, but still I don't move.

"I can't leave. I didn't mean to call you here." I didn't mean to do this. Whatever this is.

"It would have happened one way or another." She lowers her head, nudging me softly. I run a hand over her large head, up the onyx horns that curl up. Her head is nearly half my size, her long neck snakes down to a toned, beautiful body, and if she stands

straight up, she'd be as tall as the evergreen trees. I take a moment to explain a short version of my current situation and why I can't just leave all whilst continuing to feel her slick and cool scales. She purrs beneath my touch as we both fall into the comfort of each other's presence.

"If I leave, Bleren very well may punish my people as a punishment for me. I cannot let that happen," I finish. She ponders for a moment, contemplation filling the both of us.

"*I will have to go back alone then.*" An ache pings in my chest at the thought of being separated from her. There's something about her being far and not within reach that feels so *wrong*.

She's now a part of me I can't live without. This is insane. I've just met a dragon, which I'm now bonded to for life, and now feel as though a part of my soul is being ripped from me. What the actual *fuck* is my life right now? Despite the lack of logic, panic spreads through me in a frenzy, and beside me she growls softly.

"*Breathe, Ember. I will be quick, and we will be okay. When I return, I will have learned what we need so we can be in each other's presence without overwhelming each other.*" She leans her head against mine once more as she sends a wave of calm through me before she continues. "*Please be wary and on guard. Even I have heard of the evil that lurks within those castle walls. Guard your magic. Come, I will see to it that you get back safely.*" I touch her face again, memorizing the details as best as I can.

"Will I be able to talk to you?" I lean back, wrapping my cloak tightly around me, pulling my hood up to darken my face once more.

"*Once I leave and become far enough away, then we will no longer be able to speak. But until then I can answer a few more of those pestering questions.*" I can hear the grin in her voice, causing my own to match.

She takes a few leaps and bounds into the sky, flying so high up she disappears into the clouds, but I'm sure she can still hear me. I can feel her, up there like a part of me is missing in the sky.

"Where have you all been? Are there a lot of you? Do dragons normally form bonds with humans?" Gods, there's so much I want to ask.

"In hiding, deep in the mountains on the other continent, Holarthia. That's where some of us are, and some of us are here. I am a scout. I was on patrol when your magic called out to me. And finally, no, dragons do not form bonds with humans. They can't." She sounds so wise and yet my age at the same time.

"I am considered young by dragon means, but to you I may be considered old. I am one hundred and twenty-seven years old." There's a warning in her voice that makes me bite back my retort. A terrible thought washes through me as I realize I've just tethered her life to mine, and I will die fast by her means.

"Is there a way to undo this? This doesn't seem fair to you. I'm going to kill you one day with my miserable human—" I'm cut off immediately by another thought. "You said you don't bond with humans. How am I an exception?" I jump off of another log; now being able to see clearer allows me to move much more gracefully.

"You're not an exception, and we will not be dying for centuries and centuries. We don't bond with humans," she repeats as if that somehow makes sense. But if I'm not an exception to the rule, then...

"That's impossible." My parents are human.

"Do humans normally heal fast and have unspeakably powerful magic?" Sarcasm drips from her tone, and irritation at my ignorance flows from her, but so does sympathy because there's so much she knows I don't know. I stay quiet as the castle comes into view.

Breathe; I just need to think this through. It'll make sense.

Except it doesn't. My parents have no magic to my knowledge, so either this bond really is a fluke or they gave birth somehow to something not human. But then what does that make me? I've never heard of any other species.

"We will answer that when I return, Ember. For now I want you to start training. Your magic is already some of the strongest I've

ever seen, but now mixed with mine, it'll be even stronger. You need to learn how to contain it, but you also need to use it. If you leave it locked up like you have been, you risk it taking over when you least expect it, and that is control that is very hard to get back. I will even have to train to learn the new powers you have shared with me. I am gifted with the earth, and I can make myself invisible." Up above, I can feel her circling in the clouds, trying to stay with my pace.

"You have many, many gifts. Learn them. Find the extent of your capabilities. Train with my new gifts to you and find a willing teacher who will teach you hand-to-hand combat and how to use weapons. I need you to stay alive; therefore, that means you can't always rely on your magic. Learn to fight. Your body is going to feel different now; it's stronger, faster, and every sense of yours is now heightened to my abilities. It will help you. But be careful. Be watchful for wandering eyes. Do not tell anyone about me, Ember. I will be back as soon as I can."

I draw in a deep breath, absorbing everything she's saying and feeling. She's worried about leaving me on my own, but at the same time, she's proud that I'm the one she's bonded with for life. I swallow, feeling more comfortable in my skin than I ever have before.

I will do my best, I promise. When should I expect your return? I speak to her directly in my head as my boots hit the cobblestone path that leads me toward the side entrance of the castle.

"No more than seven days. May the gods watch over you until I come back, Ember." The tether between us stretches long and far. I look up at the sky, wishing I could see her, wishing she could stay.

Be safe, Asteria. She snorts at this, but washes me with what feels like unconditional love. It roots me in place. There's nothing like it, no words to describe the way it feels to know that I am hers and she is mine. We are not alone.

I wait, feeling that tether stretch and stretch and stretch— feeling the speed at which she flies, covering a massive distance in mere seconds until the bond becomes a mere whisper and then she's gone.

I find my footing again, lowering my hood as I enter the castle with a sense of ease. The guards nod at me, giving me a surprised look that I know I'll hear about later. I slink along the hallways, attempting to stay in the shadows until I find the hall that leads to my room. Upon reaching my door, I'm immediately back on my guard. The familiar and now overwhelming scent of cedar wood wafts from beneath my door. He's in there. When I open the door, I come face to face with an angry Aris.

"Where in all of the hells have you been?"

CHAPTER 20

It makes me wonder how he and River don't get along when they act so similarly sometimes. I'm too frustrated to give him an answer, so I focus on removing my cloak and boots, then shoving them into the armoire.

Anger rolls off him in waves, filling the room and pulsing down our tether. But he waits, he breathes, and he watches. I turn to him finally, rolling up the sleeves of the tunic. He's lit a couple of candles that set the room in a warm light. He drinks in my attire, his eyes flaring a bit when they pass over my chest, a bit see-through as my breasts poke through. Instantly his gaze flicks up to my eyes, fire burning in his own. And there, right there in that look, I can tell he knows something is different about me, but I don't acknowledge it.

"Well, I needed to relieve myself. And you just wouldn't believe who I ran into." I lean back against the door of the armoire, crossing my arms over my breasts to cover them. He narrows his eyes at me as he mirrors my position, leaning against the post of the bed.

"Who?"

"Dracyl. Looking free and slimy as ever." I watch his expression, which instantly softens. He moves forward to take a step toward me, but I put my hand up, stopping him. "He went as far as to tell me who released him."

"Ember, my father ordered me to. There's no arguing with him." He sounds earnest; I can even feel the honesty flowing from him; scent it even.

"Why wouldn't you tell me? Aris, he..." The words get stuck in my throat. It's right there to tell him the grimy details of what Dracyl did to me. But I can't. "How could you not tell me that the man who almost... That he would be here?" My own anger rolls off of me, and with it waves of my magic. The flames on the candles burn brighter. I crush it down, shutting the door on the box and locking it deep until I can figure out how to deal with it.

"My father said upon his arrival that he would take care of him, that he'd be locked up in our own prison. I didn't think he'd let him be *free*. Ember, please; I didn't think you'd ever have to see him again. I wanted to tell you. When I saw what your father had done to you..." He runs a rough hand through his hair, pulling at the ends. "I couldn't. Ember, this whole thing has been a mess. I haven't handled this as well as I should have, and I'm truly sorry. I will find out what's going on." He pins me with a stare, waiting for me to believe him, and I do.

I study him. I can hear his breathing from here, and I'm sure if I took a moment, I'd even be able to hear his heartbeat. The crackle of the candle wick fills the rest of the silence. The candlelight glimmers off his toned chest that peeks out from his unbuttoned tunic. He takes another tentative step toward me and looks to me for permission. I nod once, and he swallows the distance in just a couple strides and stops just short of touching me.

"You're going to be my wife," he says confidently. "I don't plan on letting anything else happen to you. You're here with *me*. I want to protect you. And even though I know there's something between you and River, I'm going to fight for you too. I have never met another woman like you, Ember." He moves a piece of hair behind my ear, and there I go, softening beneath his touch.

The stupid bond makes it hard to keep a tough exterior with him. "I'm drawn to you like a moth to a flame. I'd gladly burn in your fire, if only to feel your warmth—if only for a moment, and I know you feel it. This thing between us." He grabs my hand and places it on his heart, his muscles taught beneath my palm. But there it is: a steady and strong heartbeat.

"This beats for you now. It has since the moment I laid eyes on you. Don't give up on me yet. We can save our kingdoms." Then he cups my face softly, and something cracks in my chest. "But more importantly, I think we can save each other." His voice is hardly a whisper, but I hear him so loudly, so clearly.

For a moment all I do is stare into those gold-flecked onyx eyes.

"Those things you said to your father at the first dinner about me being desperate for affection? How I glow when you compliment me?" He winces.

"Ember, I didn't mean those things. I'm just playing my part for my father." He strokes a thumb on my cheek, and I have half the mind to pull back, but the other half keeps me rooted where I am.

"I know, I know, but you weren't wrong. I was desperate, but I'm not anymore. I can't be as easily swayed by pretty words. So, if you're telling me you're going to fight and that you're going to make things right, then I need to see it. I can't just keep forgiving you. We'll be miserable together if we can't trust each other."

"I will do everything I can to prove it to you. Three months, Ember. When you say 'I do', they will be the easiest two words of your life. Our wedding bands will not be shackles. No, they will be signs of our freedom. My father doesn't know what I have planned for us. For our futures and our people's futures." He leans forward, planting a soft kiss on my lips, leaving me reeling for more before moving away from me and toward my door. *Godsdamn him.* He looks back at me, drinking me in unapologetically. "Get some rest, Ember. I'll see you tomorrow."

A glint of something passes over his face, and from here I can hear the way his pulse quickens as he leaves. I look at myself in the mirror, and my cheeks redden as I realize just how exposed I was to him with the candlelight casting the perfect glow to showcase my breasts.

I begin to undress and change into a nightgown when I hear Aris outside of my room again, talking to someone. Moving toward the door, I hear River. He's heated, and I can hear the way he huffs an angry breath.

"The guards told me she was outside. What was she doing alone? Why weren't you with her?" River demands in such a way that even makes me shiver. He's lucky Aris is so forgiving; talking to the Crown Prince like that could not end so well.

"You need to give her more credit, River. She's not a damsel in distress, and if you cannot see the power that woman holds in just her eyes alone, then you do not know her as well as I thought you did," Aris retorts.

"You were not the one who picked her off the ground half dead," River growls. "I know my princess. I trust her with my life, but I do not trust the world with her. Not when you have that man walking these halls."

"You need to trust she can handle the world. She'll be our queen one day, and she's equipped to do it on her own if she had to, and don't worry, he'll be taken care of. She's resting, so leave her be. Take the day off tomorrow while you're at it; she'll be with me, and I don't need you growling every step of the way." I hold back my snort. *He's not wrong.*

I can hear the growl work its way up River's throat, but he contains it. He doesn't say anything, but it's like I can feel his eyes cast toward the door. It takes every ounce of control not to go to him. To show him I'm okay the way I know he needs to see for himself. I blow out a soft breath of air, and instantly all the candles go out.

Once I'm in bed, rest doesn't come. I find myself wishing I could talk to Asteria about it. Or Jasper. He'd know how to get me through this.

THE SUN RISES SLOWLY, and I bask in the heat that shines on my face while the rest of my body shivers from the cold. The golden, shimmering horse is frolicking around the frost-covered grass, neighing in delight as she prances around like the wild spirit she is.

My parents are leaving. I can hear the carriage being prepared, but I don't want to say goodbye. I don't have to. I'll be here for the rest of my life, and I know they don't care, so why should I bother?

Layla found a nice pair of tight, black pants so I can ride comfortably. She paired it with a black tunic made of fine material that whispers on my skin as I move. My feet are warm in brown leather riding boots that come to my knees. And finally, a warm black jacket instead of a cloak and some brown leather gloves. My hair is pulled up into a ponytail with wisps of hair framing my face.

The way the air smells, feels, and even tastes is all so much different than it was before. The smell of the animals and their manure is overwhelming now. I can hear the lapping of water as they drink from a trough across the field, like I'm standing with them with my ear to the surface. Not much I do can calm the buzzing and vibrating of my magic.

I let an invisible tendril float from me toward the blonde horse, stroking her hair softly. Her head snaps up, looking at me directly, but there's no animosity in those light brown eyes. There's nothing but curiosity as she trots forward to where I stand by the fence. I lift myself up, standing on the wood to bring myself closer to her height.

She stops just in front of me, still too far to touch. Those all too knowing eyes size me up as if she's figuring out whether I'm worthy. So, I use that tether to stroke her silky hair again, causing her to huff.

"I'm not here to hurt you." Another stroke. She tilts her head, cautiously taking a step forward until I can stroke her snout softly with my hand. She leans into it, huffing softly again. I climb up the rest of the fence, swinging my legs over it until I can drop down in front of her. She lightly pushes her head into my chest, leaning down substantially to reach me. I rub the side of her jaw before beckoning her toward the stables. She takes one look toward where I want to take her and huffs louder, stomping her front legs. That's a strong *no*. Stubborn girl.

"Oh c'mon. Let's go for a ride; I can't ride you without a saddle. I promise, that's all I need." I talk to her like she can understand me. Maybe she can, because she seems to reluctantly agree and begins walking slowly beside me. One of the stable boys lifts his head as I approach the opening of a long hall of stables for the horses. The wood is painted a bright red, not a chip in sight despite the weather conditions. He pauses from lifting the hay and bows for me, looking quickly between me and the blonde horse.

"G-good morning, Your Highness. How can I be of assistance?" His voice breaks, and I can't help but smile at him. He can't be more than fifteen or sixteen years of age, but he's tall and looks strong from the work he's done in these stables. He should be in school, not here.

"I need to saddle her up; can you show me where I might find what I need, please?" I ask politely. The horse stops right behind me, her head leaning over my left shoulder as she stares down at the boy. He gulps, turning pale at the sight of her.

"Your Highness, if I may be frank with you, perhaps we can choose one of the other horses? She won't let me near her, and my older brother is still recovering from having his shoulder dislocated from just trying to remove the dirt from her hooves." He shivers just thinking about it. I can hear his heart beat faster as he looks at the horse, who huffs at him for good measure. I shoot her a look, and she just shakes her head in response as if to say, *I did what I did.*

"What's your name?" I ask softly.

"Hayden, Your Highness." He gulps in response.

"My name is Ember, and this girl here is?"

"We call her Bedelia for her strong-willed, stubborn nature." He smirks, and I can tell there's other strong-worded names they call her that he wouldn't dare say in the presence of a princess. I chuckle softly, looking up to Bedelia, who seems to huff in agreement.

"Well, Hayden, Bedelia has seemed to take a liking to me, and seeing as I don't want to see anything happen to her, I would like to make a point that she listens—at least to me. So, let's get a saddle on her so I can take her for a ride." An excited twinkle enters Hayden's eyes as he nods eagerly.

He gives Bedelia a wide berth as we walk into the stables. He quickly grabs what he needs and brings over a step-stool to raise even his tall frame to the proper height. He looks at her, and then me, checking for permission to start. Bedelia stands still for him while I give him a nod.

"I can't believe she's doing this," he mutters.

"She just needed some kindness. Perhaps when we get back from our ride, I'll try to convince her to let you guys groom her. Stubborn thing could use a good spa day." Bedelia neighs at this but keeps still regardless. I use one of those tendrils only visible to me to scratch beneath her jaw, and if she could, I swear she'd be purring. After a few adjustments, Hayden finally gets the saddle on her comfortably.

"There we go. Would you like a hand up, Your Highness?" He offers his hand as he stands beside the step stool. I nod as I take it and walk up, lifting myself up into the saddle. She trots slowly in place, becoming more impatient.

"Thank you, Hayden. I'll see you when we get back." I dig my heel into her side, and she takes off. I let out a startled laugh at her speed and lean into it, tightening my legs to keep me in place.

"Be careful!" I hear Hayden yell after me, but to the hells with caution.

The wind whips around me as she leads me through the field, heading right for the fence. Fear lurches in my stomach as she speeds up. *Oh no, no, no, no.* I go to pull on her reins to stop her from crashing us into the woods or throwing me off for my foolish attempt at saving her life, but she doesn't listen. Hard headed indeed. Instead of doing either of those things though, she takes a massive leap over the high fence taller than herself, and we land perfectly on the other side.

"You're fucking crazy," I mumble to her. She neighs in response, and I swear it sounds like she's laughing. She takes off, zooming through the trees with expert accuracy. Her strong muscles work beneath my legs at a tireless pace. My own heart beats wildly in my chest as the trees go passing by in a blur. The crisp sounds of the forest chatter fill my ears.

Rodents that skitter across the damp floor. Birds who haven't migrated yet. Squirrels who snack on collected acorns in the warm holes of the trees. Down to the very buzz of insects that somehow withstand the cold. It's incredible, and if anything somewhat overwhelming, but I find that when I focus on one thing in particular, the rest drowns out, almost as if my ear will cock the way Bedelia's does toward the sound I want to hear.

We spend hours exploring the edge of Atravelien, never straying too far as if Bedelia can sense the danger that lurks deep within the shadows. She never wavers, never falters as she presses on beneath me. When we pause for a break so I can stretch my legs, she drinks from a nearby stream while I stand in the center of a clearing.

Closing my eyes, I breathe in that sweet, sickly scent. I let myself calm down and prepare for what I'm about to do. Bedelia nudges my shoulder when she's ready. *So bossy.*

She navigates us back to the castle grounds, but I lead her toward the front, wanting to make the big entrance I've planned all morning. As we emerge from the thicket of trees, I see Aris waiting at the main entrance, his father standing right beside him. Exactly where I hoped they'd be.

They both look less than happy, but even from here, I can see an amused glint in Aris' weary eyes. Bedelia comes to a halt at the bottom of the stairs, and I swiftly dismount her, landing on my feet with much more grace thanks to Asteria. Otherwise, I would've face planted on the cobblestone. Bedelia stands behind me, facing both men over my head.

"How?" Aris asks, coming to walk toward the horse. She huffs angrily, her hot breath wafting into his face. He takes the warning and backs up, his hands raised as he does.

"A little kindness goes a long way." I shrug.

"We've tried everything for the better part of the last year. It couldn't have been that simple." He eyes the horse wearily before shifting his gaze back to me.

"You'd be surprised by how far a sweet caress could go. How willing a woman might be."

Then I do what is probably the most reckless thing I've ever done and let an invisible tendril caress his cheek. Nothing but a sensual wisp of air against his skin, but he visibly straightens at the sensation. His eyes narrow in on me, a smile playing on those thick lips. I bite my lip as my gaze drifts from him to his father, and my own smile falters at the pure anger directed right at me. That anger is quickly covered up with boredom, as if he hadn't meant for me to see such loathing.

"Have it tied up in the stables," Bleren says before turning swiftly on his heel and begins walking toward the door. A couple of servants move forward to grab the reins from me. *I wouldn't do that.* Then right on que, Bedelia jumps up on her hind legs, letting out a loud whiny in contempt.

"She answers to no one but me." I stare right at the back of the king's head. He spins around so fast I almost lose my stance. Bedelia huffs angrily at the servants now backing away. The king seems inclined to fight me on it, to put down his foot that there is not an animal or human on this planet that answers to me over him. But he thinks better of it, choosing this as a battle he's willing to lose. He nods. He *nods.* I wonder how I'll pay for this.

"Then she is yours. Consider her an early wedding gift." With that, the king enters the doors, leaving Aris, who watches me with fascination. I've just stood up to his father, went against his orders, and lived to do so. And there in his eyes is heat. Lightning. Burning like a caged animal, ready to sear every inch of my skin in the most delectable of ways. I swallow, clearing my throat.

"Let's go put our wedding gift back where she belongs." I turn and begin leading Bedelia back toward the large field with the rest of the horses for her to frolic.

When we arrive at the stables, she surprises even me when she doesn't make a fuss out of the saddle being removed. Then she really blows us away when she lets Hayden lead her toward a stable to be groomed. Hayden turns to me with wide, excited eyes and gives me a thumbs up. Bedelia huffs at me as if to tell me I owe her one. *Insufferable, beautiful beast.*

Aris takes my hand, and I let him lead me back toward the main entrance. His large hand swallows my own, warming it when I didn't realize I had gone so cold. He doesn't say much, but the silence isn't uncomfortable. We eventually reach the dining hall, where he holds the door open for me.

"You must be famished." It's not a question, but I answer anyway.

"Starved. Hungry as a horse." He chuckles, shaking his head at me. Then I sense *him* before I see him. River looks up, as if sensing me too, as if he can feel the instant tug on that tether that draws me to him. His eyes flash to where my hand is still in Aris', and I fight back the urge to rip my hand away. But nothing shows on his face, even when I can feel the yearning ripple down the bond. He simply bows his head to the both of us, ever the guard, showing his respect.

Aris nods back at him, and I can't do anything but the same as I follow Aris toward another table. I ignore the ache in my heart and remind myself to act like a betrothed. Yet I don't need much convincing when the other tether feels like it's caressing me from the inside out. My eyes shift up to Aris, who pulls my seat out for me, looking down at me with so many mixed emotions I can't sort them out.

"I was in the middle of discussing Dracyl with my father when a servant came to notify us that 'the girl has broken the stubborn horse and left the fields.' You should have seen the look on my father's face." The sound of Dracyl's name is enough to send my stomach roiling.

"He certainly didn't look pleased. What did he decide about Dracyl?" I set my fork down, suddenly not as hungry. Aris pales a bit, swallowing.

"Dracyl was new to the court before he left. He had been brought on as an advisor for his knowledge on certain topics that were of interest to the king. My father claims not to know about the motives behind Dracyl's attack and believes Dracyl has received enough punishment from the beatings he received from your guards. As a result, he doesn't deem it appropriate to put him back in prison and will return to his position with the king. But he is on strict orders not to touch or bother you. I'm sorry, Ember. I wish I could've done more, but my father wouldn't listen no matter how much I argued." He takes my hand, rubbing his thumb over the back of it, soothing the ache in my chest. I'm not surprised, and can I really blame Aris for his father's actions?

"I want to train, and I want you to promise you'll stop not telling me things because you think you're protecting me." My voice comes out more steady than I expect.

"I can't promise that, seeing as there's still information I'm withholding for the greater good. But I promise that the sole reason I didn't tell you about Dracyl or our arranged marriage is because I am a stupid male. I thought I was protecting you from more mental strife by withholding said information if I could deal with it on my own and reveal it at a later time with a better plan in place. Obviously, that backfired. I'm so sorry, Ember. When the time is right, I'll explain it all. But why would you ever need to train?" he asks, as if it's the most ridiculous notion for a princess to do such a thing. I rub my temples, trying not to groan in frustration. Can't be unprincess-like.

"I appreciate your honesty, but the lack thereof makes me want to punch you in the throat. I don't know what to do with you." I take a deep breath. "I want to learn how to fight and defend myself. I want a fighting chance. My mornings can be dedicated to training while our afternoons can be reserved to do whatever business your father has for us as far as our marriage goes." I give him a look, one that tells him either he agrees or I leave.

"You'll understand one day." He pauses in contemplation. "I don't have any women instructors—there are no women in guard positions here." He looks over to where River sits with some of the other guards, his head bent as he eats.

"That's a problem; why? Any male instructor can teach me, preferably River, since I'm already comfortable with him." I tilt my head as if this is obvious.

"Too comfortable," he mumbles.

"What's your point, Aris?" I raise my eyebrow at him. He stands, abandoning his mostly finished plate of food, and comes around the table. He leans against the edge right beside me as I tilt my head up to look at him. He grabs my chin softly between his thumb and index finger, searching my eyes. That thumb then reaches up, tugging on my bottom lip until they part slightly, releasing a soft breath.

"My point is that I don't want his hands on you. I know you might." Another stroke over my lip, and I fight the urge to shiver, holding his gaze fiercely. "I sure know he does. But I don't particularly want to share." One willing to share, the other not so much. Of course. "So I'll train you." He releases me, pushing off the table to come behind my chair, which he swiftly pulls back. "Come, I'm going to take you into town; we're going shopping."

"What do you know about training?" I put my coat back on.

"I've trained alongside the guards here my whole life. I'll be king one day, and I don't ever want to be weaker than my opponents because I rely on someone else to defend me." He places a territorial hand on the small of my back as he leads me out of the dining hall. I don't spare River a glance, even as I feel the heat of his anger drilling a hole through Aris' hand. Maybe he's not so willing to share either. But I knew that, didn't I?

"When can we start? You're a busy man." He leads me to a carriage already waiting for us outside, opening the door to let me in first. The door closes behind him as he sits beside me.

"I'll make the time for you. I'll empty my mornings for you like you said, and we'll begin tomorrow. Bright and early, we'll begin with a run to warm you up, and then we'll see what you've got, Princess." The carriage begins rolling, and I lean back in my seat, aware of every intentional inch of space he's put between us. Such soft caresses, ghosts of kisses—it's like he's scared to really and truly touch me.

"Can I get in on any of these meetings you're always in?" I glance at him, but one look tells me no.

"If I could, you would have already been a part of them." He frowns, looking out of his window.

"And all that secret information?" I push a little harder.

"In time, Ember." And the warning that's laced with my name shuts me right up. I look out of my own window, staying quiet. What is it that's so important he can't just tell me? That he worries even our coachman can hear?

We stay in silence for a while as I take in the scenery of the town. Everything near the castle is built meticulously. Stone houses tower over us, casting shadows onto the cobblestone road we roll over. Spices, bread, and even wine fill the air as we pass merchant after merchant. It's a city of mass trade. The people close to the royal family seem so happy and so well off. But I know that there are towns and villages plagued with poverty and slavery —the true face of this kingdom. The people Aris wants to free.

I listen to the trot of the horses, steadily pulling us along. To the steady inhale and exhale of our coachman sitting just outside the front window of our carriage. Aris' leg bobs up and down lightly as he flexes his hands.

Something's gnawing on him; I can feel it even down the tether. With the intention of calming him, I place my hand on his thigh softly, which startles him. He whips his head to me, exhaling through his nose sharply. I remove my hand instantly, heat flooding my cheeks.

"I'm sorry I..." I'm cut off by him swallowing the distance between us. He grabs my chin and forces me to look at him. He angles his body so his leg brushes against mine as he towers over me, making it hard to breathe with the sudden proximity.

"You don't apologize to me." The soft command in his voice has me nodding obediently. "You can touch me however and whenever you want, Ember. I am yours for the taking. But I must warn you that my control falters with every moment I am in your presence. Every look. Every single breath you take is another blow to the crumbling wall I have tried to build to maintain a respectable distance from you." He leans further down, his eyes molten, silencing every single thought in my head. I swallow, biting on my lip softly to keep me from closing the mere centimeters of distance left between us. He tracks *every* movement.

"Why must you exhibit such control?" I whisper, my breath mingling with his.

"Because I would've fucked you in front of an entire audience for the way you kissed me after you sang that ballad. Because I would fuck you right now, in the middle of this busy street, and not care who sees this carriage rock. Because when I make you scream, Ember, it will be for my ears and my ears only. And when I touch you, really and *truly* touch you, I won't be able to stop." His chest brushes my own as we both struggle to breathe normally. I stifle a soft moan at the promise he's making me.

I nod, understanding the precarious line we're both walking. He brushes his lips against mine in barely a kiss before leaning back in his spot just as the carriage comes to a halt in front of a beautiful boutique. I sit up, gaining whatever composure I can muster as the coachman comes to open my door.

"Now let's go buy you anything you want," Aris murmurs into my ear as we exit.

CHAPTER 21

"Are you always this demanding?" I mumble as I duck back into the dressing room, where I've been trying on at least a dozen dresses, all handpicked by Aris.

"I'm the prince," he says flatly.

"And I'm the princess, but you don't see me bossing you around." The navy blue dress I just showed off to him slips to the floor as I step out of it.

"Oh, you can be bossy when you want to be." I can hear the smirk in his voice.

"I am nothing but fair and just." Yet, I can't hide my own smile, even as I try. *Ugh.*

"Tell me your favorites," he says, yet another command. I open the curtain wearing the short red dress he'd ordered me to try on next and find him leaning back in the chair the owner brought over for him to sit in.

"You'll have to be more specific than that." My right eyebrow raises as I plant my hands on my hips, but he doesn't say anything.

His eyes drag up the long expansion of my legs, lingering on every bit of exposed skin as they trail over my chest and finally to my eyes, where I find molten black and gold staring back at me.

"That's my favorite," he says a little breathless, a dimple peaking out as that charming half smile comes back.

"What on earth would I wear this for?" Crossing my arms, I pop my hip out. *Stay strong, girl. You heard his warning earlier.*

"Me." He stands and starts walking toward me with a predatory look in his eyes.

"Atravelien green. The green that's rich and dark all at once," My feet stumble back away from him.

"Hmm?" He's hardly paying attention as his eyes drink in more of me.

"That's my favorite color." I continue to back up until I've backed myself into the dressing room. "Turtles are my favorite animal. I have a weakness for apple pie—" The snap of the curtain behind him cuts me off effectively as he comes to crowd my space. I open my mouth to continue, to ignore the pounding in my heart and between my legs at the ravenous sight of him.

But he puts a finger to my lips.

"Turn around," he demands.

And I do as I'm told.

I turn and face myself in the mirror. He trails a finger down the side of my arm as he presses his front into my back, aligning all of the hard planes of his body with the curves of mine. I can't help the shiver that follows as the vibration of thousands of tiny lightning bolts flickers across every inch of my skin.

"Look at you." His breath tickles my ear as he leans down to speak softly enough the owner of the shop wouldn't hear. That finger comes back up agonizingly slow. "I can't stop looking at you. You're making me a madman, Ember. The sight of you nearly drives me to my knees. Gods, *look at you.*" He grabs the bottom of the hem as if he dares to pull it up, but he doesn't.

I don't say a word. I don't want him to stop, and I know if I beg for him to continue, he'll snap out of this stupor.

"Call me crazy. Call me insane. Call me whatever you want. I know I've only just met you a mere handful of days ago, but every time I set eyes on you, my soul feels like it's come home. Every time I stop breathing—because you make it almost impossible for my lungs to work—it feels so *familiar*, as if I was born to suffocate in your beauty." He pauses, coming closer if that's even possible.

My eyes flutter shut when he plants a whisper of a kiss on my shoulder, and then another. The act is so soft, almost innocent. Yet, the effects are anything but.

"Let me tell you some of my favorites," he whispers across my skin. My eyes open wide as I listen intently. "I love this little birthmark here. It's almost shaped like a leaf." He kisses the brown mark on my other shoulder, and I can't help the sharp inhale of breath, not even if I tried.

"My favorite color is the color of your eyes. A thousand burning sunsets right there in your irises." He undoes the strings slowly, his gaze searing into mine. I swallow. Hard. The fabric falls away to my feet, but I don't dare look at it. I don't dare look anywhere else but him.

A soft groan works its way out of his throat when he beholds my body in front of him. Laid bare save for the undergarments I'm in.

"You're torturing yourself, Prince," I finally murmur quietly. It's as if Kienah herself has caught us in some type of trance. Neither of us are able to pull or look away.

"I'd torture myself for the rest of my waking days just to bear witness to you," he says almost thoughtlessly, as if this is simply a fact. Those onyx eyes darken further as they glide over my chest, down the soft flesh of my stomach, right down to my legs that had begun to quiver ever so faintly. "My favorite sound is the sound of your voice in the morning when there's a slight rasp to your words. My favorite smell is floral with a hint of honey. The scent you permeate and intoxicate me with every time you are near. Have I mentioned that you drive me *mad*?"

His eyes close as he inhales deeply. His hand tightens on my hip, right where the bruises from River are.

No. *Were.*

Every mark that was left on my skin has faded to nothing, having healed that fast.

He turns me, bringing my front to his. I have to press myself on to the tips of my toes just so he's not bending as much. But still, I force myself as close as I can, my lips mere breaths from his.

"My favorite feeling..." A soft brush of his lips over mine sends me reeling. "Are these on mine."

"And your favorite taste?" I watch nothing but the way his mouth moves as he speaks.

"I have yet to taste the glory between your legs, Princess. Ask me again when I have, though I'm sure you know what my answer will be." His eyes are dark with desire, brimming with lust, and so much more I can hardly sort it out.

My cheeks redden at his eroticism.

It seems fitting that the gods would tether me to one man of little words and one man of plenty. Where River shows his adoration in action, Aris pours it out in lyrical confessions.

River taught my skin what it *felt* like to be loved.

Aris is washing away layers and layers of insults and replacing them with loving words my skin has never heard before.

He places one last soft kiss on my lips. It's not enough. Not nearly enough to calm the raging storm crackling within me, right under the surface. But he steps back nonetheless, even when I so desperately want to demand more from him.

I don't. I don't push him, or the control I know is slipping because honoring the tradition for his father is important to him, and I don't want to make it harder than it already is for him.

"I'll tell you more of my favorite things at the next store. Get dressed. I'm going to go pay." Before I can get my questions out, he closes the curtain behind him.

"But which ones are we getting?" I call out after him.

"All of them," he says as a matter of fact. I can only chuckle softly as I slip back into the clothes I came here in, the ones I wore to ride Bedelia.

He keeps true to his word and shows me all of his favorite

spots. He buys us a bunch of sweet, little cakes to take back for dessert tonight and more than enough jewelry and clothes to last me quite a while. He insisted that I deserved nothing but the best, and according to him, he had the best to offer.

Besides Melana, I can't say he's wrong.

But the best part of our day out in the village isn't the sweets or the clothes.

It's when we stop, and he leads me toward a brown stone building with a red awning. It's what looks to be a tavern as we enter, but all of the tables are empty.

"We're not open for dinner yet!" A loud, booming voice shouts from the back, which I presume is where the kitchen is.

"Jeffrey, I've got someone for you to meet," Aris calls out, placing a hand on the small of my back. Something he's done all day long as if reminding himself I'm here and real. As if he needs to have one hand on me at all times lest I disappear from him.

A few curses and shuffling ensue before a large man in a chef's hat walks out. His white apron is splattered with what looks like red sauce, and he's wiping his hands on a towel that he drapes over his shoulder.

"Aris, it's good to see you." Jeffrey smiles warmly at Aris, coming forward to shake his hand before he turns to me. His eyes widen a bit as he swallows. "Your Highness, what a pleasure it is to meet you in the flesh."

He bows before me, and before I can return the sentiment, Aris speaks up.

"She's like me, Jeff; though I know she appreciates the gesture and title, she doesn't care for the formalities as much either. Even though I think the entire kingdom should always bow to her," he mumbles the last part more to himself than to either of us. Jeffrey rises quickly, a faint splash of red tinting his cheeks.

He reminds me of Eli.

And that thought alone is enough to send me reeling back to what I thought was home. Eli's soft smile. His endearing listening face. His boisterous laugh and crazy stories in his venture for love.

It all flashes across my eyes at once and fogs my vision for a moment.

Green eyes and deep dimples from a crooked grin make an appearance next. Jokes about flatulence and the smell of my feet sound in my ears. Brown curly hair and a short black bob. Ginger waves and kind smiles. Scrutinizing brown eyes and pretty blondes.

Imagery of my court. Of my best friend. Of the *people* I called home, strike me so fiercely that I forget where I am momentarily.

Aris says my name so softly, like a caress that snakes its way down my spin. Then a smile snaps on my face, and I extend my hand to Jeffrey, hoping not too much time has passed.

"The pleasure is all mine. This is a lovely place you have here." I gesture to it once my hand leaves his callused one. Hands of a hardworking man.

"Thank you!" He grins wide, looking around, proud of his restaurant. "I couldn't have done it without the prince here. It's his coin I work off of seeing as I don't charge my patrons."

My brows furrow as I look to Aris, who bows his head sheepishly. He rubs a hand on the back of his neck before glancing at Jeffrey.

"We feed the displaced families from the war here. Breakfast, lunch, and dinner. Jeffrey and his staff are paid by me, and I entrust him with a sum to buy the food needed to cook." He finally looks at me again, and there's a glimmer of hope amongst the gold flecks in his eyes.

"Aris that's..." Words elude me as I take in what this place really means.

"There are a couple other spots I've commissioned across the kingdom. I want to open more, but it's hard to come up with reasons for the missing money. My father doesn't know I do this. He thinks I spend it on ridiculous things." Aris glances at Jeffrey, who only smirks a little.

"Like brothels, taverns, and cards? Do you not actually do those things? Even Agatharea has heard of your antics." I raise a brow at him. "I didn't think you were a womanizer for no reason, Prince."

"I needed to keep up the illusion of where the money was going. So did I partake in some wild nights? Perhaps. But for a good cause." He gestures to the restaurant, and I can't help but chuckle.

"I see, I see. It was for the good of the kingdom," I muse.

"Exactly. You get it."

Jeffrey and I exchange a look that only makes me laugh more.

"This is wonderful, Aris." I walk around, touching the scratched polish of the tables.

"I wanted to show you that I've always been serious about saving them," he says quietly. "I want you to see that your being here is going to make a difference. Without you, I can't do this."

I turn back to him, looking over the prince in front of me.

The prince who has lied and is still keeping secrets from me.

The prince who pays handsomely with no reward other than the pride he has for taking care of his people as best as he can.

The prince who slandered his name straight into the mud so his father wouldn't know that he was picking up the pieces of his kingdom so there might be something left when he gets to the throne.

Suddenly, the secrets don't matter as much. Not when he's showing his hand like this. Not when he's baring other parts of himself to me, even if it's not in its entirety.

"I'm here, Aris. I am with you." I'd come to stand in front of him at some point, not even realizing I had moved. It's as if I'm drawn to him—pulled to him.

Jeffrey clears his throat softly, which pulls us out of the haze we keep falling into with each other.

"I can serve you both dinner. Would you like to stay?" He looks at us hopeful, but I hesitate.

"I don't want to take away meals from people who actually need it." I frown at the thought.

"Nonsense, there's plenty. I normally have too much and box

it up to take to anyone who couldn't make it. Two meals can be spared," he pushes politely.

We concede. Jeffrey serves us tomato soup with toasted cheese sandwiches to dip in, and yet again I find myself marveling at someone who could rival Chef Jean's cooking.

We eat quietly in the back of the room, away from any window or peering eyes. Aris tells me more about his efforts to take care of the people. How he arranges for donations of blankets, clothing, and any necessary goods others can spare in order to take to the towns that are now nothing more than camps.

He has servants who do a lot of the behind-closed-doors work that he can't see to himself, and as he talks about it, the more my walls melt. I'm willing to give him a chance to let him in over the next three months to see if this will work, because it has to for the sake of our kingdoms.

Even if it means I can't listen to the other half of my heart.

The carriage ride back is spent in peaceful silence, indulging in the little cakes he insisted we get. He holds my hand, running his thumb continuously over my knuckles, memorizing the way my skin feels beneath his fingers.

When we stop in front of my room, I notice the door is slightly ajar. I can hear Melody and Layla filling the tub with water.

"I asked them earlier to prepare a bath for you upon our arrival." He pauses, looking down at me with lots to say but no means to say it. "Thank you for giving me a chance today. I'll keep proving it to you. Get some rest, Princess. I'll see you in the morning." He plants a soft, sensual kiss on my lips before pulling away too soon.

He walks away with his hands in his pockets, charm and confidence oozing from him. My attention pulls toward River's door, where I can feel him inside. There's a part of me that contemplates knocking on his door when I remember Melody and Layla are waiting.

After thanking the girls, I send them on their way, needing to be alone with my thoughts.

Needing to sort out all the shit swirling in my head.

Needing to figure out exactly what it is I want from this arrangement.

Soon, I find myself lowering into the large tub full of hot water, oils, and petals, filling the air with a wonderful floral scent. The water is a milky lavender color, and I groan softly as I plant myself on the smooth porcelain floor. The concoction relaxes my taut muscles tense with need from things Aris can't give me yet. Tense with worry. Tense with yearning for River.

I take my time scrubbing my skin, massaging soap into my hair, and rinsing until I've relaxed enough to lean back against the tub. My head lays against the lip as the water comes up just above my chest, concealing me from the cool air and trapping me in soothing warmth.

And then the silence becomes too loud, and my thoughts begin to storm.

To rage.

When will I find the courage to set River free? Free from the torment I've put him through. Free from only having part of me when my soul is split in pieces, drifting around with him and Aris in this godsforsaken castle. But how could I? When he is a living, breathing part of me? An extension of myself I can't bear to separate from; the thought is as terrifying as cutting off my own limb. My heart hammers in my chest, the ache so strong it feels as if someone has reached in and squeezed with all their might.

I think back on the moment Asteria washed me in her love. On the moment where she touched my chest and connected us down to every fiber of my being. With each day she's gone, the hole where she resides becomes larger, aching and slicing through me as that tether begs for its other half to return.

When will *she return?*

The air around me charges as my power begs, *pleads,* to be released. It beats ferociously against the lid of my well that I struggle to keep locked tight. The pain from the will it takes to conceal it and isolate it deep within me makes me shutter, the water sloshing as I grip the sides of the tub.

My eyes snap open when my doorknob turns. Rushed footsteps barrel inside before the lock turns and clicks in place, almost as if he sped in here so as not to be seen. Earth and mint in its heady concoction waft toward me, instantly intoxicating me. His steps slow as he leans in the doorframe, and in just a mere breath, my head empties completely.

His bare chest glows in the light of the candles. The flickers cast perfect shadows over his muscles to where his guard pants sit low on his hips.

I take him in unapologetically, just as he does me.

My eyes trace every line sculpted on him, from his abdomen to the V pointing straight to where his pants have already begun to tent. Slowly, I bring my gaze up to meet the fire in his, almost moaning at the delicious scent his arousal brings into the air.

"You spent the whole day with him," he says roughly, the husky desire so rich in his voice. It's not a question, nor is it a jab, but it is slightly jealous.

My stoic, stone cold guard is *jealous.* If someone had told me this is what my life would be like a month ago, I would've laughed in their face.

River feeling anything for me at all, even after what we did—after his admission—it still takes me by surprise. As if it isn't quite true. Even as he stands before me with obvious desire.

"I did," I answer softly.

"He touched you." It's not a question. No, he knows somehow. He looks over me as if somehow able to see exactly where Aris remains on my skin. He takes a couple steps forward, coming in front of me. I bend my knees, the tops sticking out of the water as I spread my legs in the very wide tub.

"He did." I don't try to hide it.

"You liked it." His eyes track every bit of my movement, the fabric of his pants becoming more and more taut as he zones in on my body beneath the milky water, as if he can see through it. I nod in response. "Say it out loud," he chides.

"I did like it," I say breathlessly. He nods, watching me bite my lip as he slides his pants off of his hips, his long, aching cock springing free with the motion.

In the candlelight, he looks like a godsdamn sculpture. Naked and honed like a god. How is it humanly possible for someone to look like that? To actually exist? And want *me*?

He brings a hand to wrap around himself, pumping slowly. My mouth falls open, watering at the unholy but tantalizing sight. My hands drift toward my own throbbing center, needing so much release it almost hurts. I've spent all day in frustration.

"Not yet." He watches me with such patience, but I can feel it in him—the withering self-control. I pause my hand on command and grip the sides of the tub to keep from doing anything else as I wait for his next command. "Get out and on your knees." He walks to the side of the tub, holding a towel for me so I don't leak water everywhere.

The less evidence of what we're doing, the better. I dry off quicker than ever before dropping to my knees on top of the towel. It cushions my knees as I rise up on them, steadying myself in front of his rock hard, glistening cock that he still pumps slowly.

I don't wait for his next words before wrapping my mouth around the tip, sucking him slowly. So slowly. I savor the taste of him. The feel of him. The way he throbs against my tongue and I memorize it. He hisses between his teeth as his hand drops to let me work my way down his shaft; instead, he weaves his fingers through my wet hair.

Water drips down my back, sending shivers down my spine. Pure desire brings my nipples to hard buds, and the groan he releases makes my toes curl as I look up at him through wet lashes. He takes in the sight of my naked body, my mouth working him up and down at an aggravatingly slow pace, and his pupils dilate further. The black almost takes over the ocean blue.

I suck him further down my throat, breathing harshly through my nose to make up for the burning in my lungs. I don't care to breathe, as I find myself needing him more than air itself. He pushes his hips forward, not being able to help himself as I take as much of him as I can before tears prick the sides of my eyes. He watches me with such fire I could come undone just from that look alone. I slide back to his tip, running my tongue around it before slamming him back down my throat.

Gods, if this is wrong, then send me to the hells because I don't know if I can give this up.

"My gods, Ember, what did he do to you?" He stares down at me with wild adoration and savage desperation.

"It's what he didn't do. He's abiding by his father's rules. I've been wound up all day." I don't wait for another word, too eager to feel the soft skin of his cock against my tongue. He growls softly, gripping my hair harder as I lick from the tip down to the bottom of his balls and then right back up. "You taste so good," I purr.

He tastes like hot cocoa on a frigid day. He feels like the rain on your face after a day spent in the sweltering sun. He is a balm to my aching soul. My words are all it takes to snap the rest of his control before I'm being pulled up and his lips come crashing into mine.

Yes. Gods, yes.

His hard length rubs against my thighs, which become wetter and wetter as each moment passes. Hot pleasure washes through me as his tongue mingles with mine, and I press myself against him, yearning for some kind of friction as his skin presses to mine.

"Please, River," I beg. His hands roam over me lazily, up the sides of my breasts, and then back down to grip my bottom. He gives it a spank, and I can't help but delight in the pleasure that shoots through me at the slight tinge in pain. I tug on the hair at the nape of his neck as he kisses that spot right beneath my jaw. He takes my hips, spinning me around so my curves become flush against him.

"Be a good girl and bend over for me," he murmurs into my ear.

I swallow, moving forward toward the sink, and do as I'm told, matching his gaze in the reflection of the mirror. Flashes of this very moment from back home blur my vision between River then and River now.

The sight of me before him like this is one straight from my dreams. The hazy look in his eyes tells me I'm not the only one who's thought about this since we left. I lean forward, placing my elbows on the counter to brace myself as he positions himself behind me, pumping against my slick entrance, coating his tip in my arousal. I drop my head down, panting already.

"Look at me while I fuck you, Ember." He grabs hold of my hair and wraps it in his fist, tugging my head up to look at him, and if fire could burn in his irises, the ocean would be set ablaze. I moan at the sight of him as he finally presses into me with one swift push. He fills me up to the very brink, and stars explode behind my eyes as pleasure washes through me. He moves agonizingly slow, paying me back for the sweet torture I doled him earlier.

"River..." I moan softly, moving my hips against him, desperate for the friction. He shoves me forward, pinning my hips to the sink as he fully bends me over it, pushing my breasts into the counter. He releases his grip on my hair, letting it cascade to the side as he presses one hand into my back while the other grips the flesh of my bottom. He pulls out, just to slam right back into me, and I moan again, not being able to help it with the ecstasy coursing through me.

This is not the princess I was raised to be, but gods, it feels good to give into my depravity.

I feel him reach forward, wrapping his hand around my mouth to keep me quiet from listening ears as he begins to pick up pace. The orgasm builds in me, and as it does, the flames of the candles begin to burn brighter. There are windows at the very top of the ceiling, too small for anyone to be able to climb through. I nudge one up silently with a small tendril of power, letting in a cooler breeze to excuse the candles' wild behavior. River doesn't falter as he reaches down between my legs, one hand silencing me, one hand bringing me to the brink of glory.

"Do you want to come?" he asks in a low, seductive voice that nearly sends me over. I nod eagerly, holding his beautiful gaze in the reflection. He smiles at me, and I swear I could cry at the sight. "Then come for me, baby. Let go, but be quiet." His fingers speed up their pace against my clit, and my climax comes to a peak as it tips over the edge, sending me crashing into the sweet abyss of never-ending pleasure.

My entire body sags, my knees buckling as it rocks through me, pulling me apart and putting me back together again. He holds me up, slowing as he pulls out, and I whimper at the loss of him. When I open my eyes, all the candles have been blown out by the woosh of air that must've been released from me. I hope he blames it on the open window. Now we're in the dark, illuminated only by the moon shining through those small windows.

"Get back on your knees," he commands, and I oblige, twisting as I fall back to my knees, my legs trembling as the remnants of my orgasm sweep through me.

"I want every last drop," I tell him softly before taking him back into my mouth, savoring the way I taste on him, bringing him as far down my throat as I can muster. My head begins to bob up and down, and I use my hand to make up for the distance I can't take. My throat relaxes, taking him easily as he pulses in my mouth. I come back up, paying special attention to the way he groans as I suck on the tip, the hand in my hair tightening in response. I keep going, chasing his orgasm, wanting to taste his climax so bad.

"Just like that baby, you're doing so good," he rasps, and I can't help but moan against his skin, relishing in his praise. I look up at him, letting it all shine in my gaze. He takes one look at me, and suddenly my throat is coated with his release. The sweet but salty taste continues to pour down my tongue, and I swallow every bit of it, licking off the remnants on his tip as I pull away, satisfied. He pulls me up, kissing me sloppily with one hand in my hair, the other pulling me close by the waist.

"You're so beautiful. I wish for nothing but to be with you always. Not just to make love to you, but to really *be* with you." Something like pain flashes in his eyes as he lets me go. I watch as he grabs his pants, slipping them on, and I realize he came in no underwear. He knew exactly what he wanted. My mouth waters at the realization.

"You're leaving?" My voice comes out small, and I hate the sound of it. He swallows the distance between us in a few strides. He takes my face in his hands and kisses me again, the apology clear on his lips.

"I have to. We have to be careful. But do not forget, Ember, that I yearn for you every waking moment you are not near." His forehead leans against mine, his eyes shut in seemingly agony.

"You're right. We can't get caught. A part of me eternally belongs to you, River," I whisper against his lips, hating the truth in which I speak to him. He looks at me, really looks at me for a moment, honing in on that small word. *Part.*

I'm so sorry.

But he doesn't get angry, sad, or jealous like he did earlier. Something akin to understanding passes over him and it shakes me. He brushes a kiss over the top of my head before turning to leave. I hastily grab my robe and yank it on as I follow him to my door. His hands are on the doorknob when a sound shuffles in the hall.

My heart plummets to the floor with fear.

I stop his hand, shaking my head vigorously. He cocks his head at me in question because, to a normal ear, nothing can be heard. I only shake my head again. *Trust me.*

We wait as I listen to that person's breathing and silently sniff the air. Alcohol. Rank, drunken breath. There's only one person I know that smells like that. He must've seen River come in here and is waiting to catch us when River leaves.

"I'm going to start crying and become very agitated. You've come in here to check my rooms because I thought someone broke in since the window was open." I don't leave any room for him to argue before I reach deep down in me, yanking on the darkness I store down there and burst into tears. I open the door as I blubber, "I'm so sorry; I'm just being so silly. I swear someone's been through my things, and I j-just thought someone might be hiding while I bathed." River slides right into character. Shirtless and breathless, as if he came rushing to the rescue in nothing but his pants.

"No, no, Ember, it's okay. I'm glad you called for me. It's what I'm here for. We'll make sure they place locks on those windows, no matter how small they are. Get some rest." He walks out of my room, his posture making him the effortless warrior he is. He bows his head to me, and I nod at him, hiccuping as I rub away the tears.

"Thank you, River, for always saving me. Sleep well." I glance down the hall as I close my door and see a flash of Dracyl before my door shuts, and I lock it. For added measure, I shove a chair beneath the door handle.

When I'm finally in bed, a breath I hadn't realized I'd been holding whooshes out of me. My skin still prickles with remnants of both River's and Aris' touch. The ghost of their fingers and lips haunting my mind, body, and soul.

They're inescapable.

No matter how much I'm not supposed to feel for one.

No matter how much I hadn't wanted to feel for the other.

I am left a mess of tethers and emotions I can't free myself from.

I don't want to be free, not even from this torment of being caught between them both. Because Aris was right, I'd torture myself just to bear witness to them both for the rest of my waking days.

CHAPTER 22

"Oof," I grunt, landing on my back on the red training mats in the guard's training hall. Ungracefully, I jump back up to my feet, putting some distance between me and Aris, scowling at him while he smiles. "I thought you said we'd start with the basics."

"I just wanted to see how much work you'd need," he drawls. My scowl deepens; even with my new senses, strength, and agility, I don't know what to do with it all. I can anticipate his movements but don't know how to counter them in time. I take a deep breath, calming myself.

"Haven't you seen enough?" I cross my arms, and my hip pops out. This only makes him smile wider.

"Plenty. We're going to train your muscles, and then I'm going to show you some fighting and defensive stances." He beckons me over toward the exercise equipment. "We'll start with the simple stuff and work our way up. Don't worry, Princess, you'll be able to kick my ass one day—when I'm old and frail perhaps." He snorts, and I can't help but glare at the back of his head. Heat rises in my eyes, and I blink it out as if the anger had manifested with fire. He glances back at me with a smirk and pats the mat.

"On your back, Princess." A sly glint plays in his eyes as I plant myself in front of him. The girls showed up with comfortable clothing to spar in, courtesy of Aris, of course. A bead of sweat drips down my back beneath the short-sleeved tunic, and my pants stick to my legs.

He drops to his knees, and I ignore his stare, watching the dark-stoned ceiling instead. "Knees up," he commands, and I oblige. He leans forward, planting his hands on the tops of my feet. I intertwine my fingers behind my head and lean up; the sit-up feels easy enough. I breathe out and then lay back down, relishing in the newfound strength my body has.

"Question," I say as I come up again, face to face with him.

"Answer." He leans forward a bit so we're only a breath apart. Despite the seriousness with which he's taken upon himself to train me, it hasn't stopped him from teasing me for brief moments here and there. And I am no better than he is.

"What happens if I'm not a virgin?" I ask softly enough only he can hear. We're not the only ones training this early. He visibly straightens and tightens his grip on my boots.

"It's a long-standing tradition here that the queen be pure of touch, so that the king will be the first to take control of her body, his first act of duty to the kingdom—giving them a queen. They hang the bloodied sheet for what she's given to the kingdom and her king." I continue the sit-ups, even as my heart begins to race.

"And if there's no blood on the sheet?" I murmur, not really looking at him.

"Then we find some. The tradition is archaic." He grabs my chin as I come up. "Are you telling me what I think you are?" He's lethally calm. He's not angry, but there's something else in that tone. Something territorial. I nod, swallowing. He releases my chin and stands up, offering me a hand to stand, which I take.

"When?" I don't answer him as I turn away, aiming for the pitcher of water set out for us. I take long gulps, some water drips down my chest. He watches every movement. *Three nights ago, and again last night.*

When I don't answer, he swears softly beneath his breath, as if figuring it out on his own. "In my own castle," he mutters, and I whip my head to look at him. Anger now leaks from him, swirling with cedarwood and sweat. I set down the glass, pushing wisps of hair away from my face that have escaped from my braid.

"What does this change?" My own anger begins seeping through. My body is my own to do as I please with whom I please.

"Everything." He levels me with a stare, so much swirling in those eyes I don't know how to decipher what is what. "Nothing." He turns away from me. I told him because if I expect honesty from him, then he deserves the same. I wait, watching him as he looks out the window, the sun shining down brightly.

"I didn't think you'd care this much," I mumble, looking away from him, hating the feeling working up my spine. He turns, swallowing the distance between us in a few strides. He opens his mouth to say something, but then he recognizes the shame in my eyes, and his gaze softens.

"Ember, I..." He takes a deep breath. "I am not accustomed to...sharing. I never had to give up my toys when I was little. Never had to worry about someone stealing from my dinner plate. And women? The only one ever ravishing them was me. So forgive me as I learn. But you must be so careful, Ember. If he finds out..." He trails off, fear settling in his face. I nod in understanding.

"He won't." I touch his face softly, and he shutters at the contact. "Does this mean we still wait?" I murmur, taking a step forward. He chuckles.

"I meant what I said. I'm already on thin ice with my father, and I can't push him any further, and once I've started, I won't know how to stop. If I get caught with you..." He shutters at the thought. "I'd just rather be safe and wait. Plus, I look forward to seeing who can last the longest, but you have an unfair advantage of release at night if you've been sneaking around. All I have is my hand, images of you, and that pretty mouth of yours," he whispers, his breath mingling with my own. I swallow, licking my lips as I take a step back.

"I can level the playing field for the time being." Mischief dances in his eyes.

"It's only fair," he says, shrugging. But the smile he's fighting back gives him away. I shake my head, chuckling.

"Let's finish up; I'm starved." I walk back toward the training equipment laid out. He works my body until it's shaking with exhaustion. Eventually, we finish and head straight to the dining hall. Silence plagues us while we eat, simply too tired to say anything besides consume the energy we've just expended. He even brings me to my room before we part to bathe, kissing me swiftly before leaving me breathless.

River exits his room right as I open the door to my own, freshly bathed and dressed in his guard uniform. His eyes widen in surprise, taking in my sweaty appearance.

"What have you been up to?" He crosses his arms, leaning against the doorframe of my room while I look at the gowns I might wear today.

"Got a little training done today." I grab what I need and turn to him.

"Training for what?" he asks slowly.

"To protect myself." I shrug as if this is obvious.

"That's what I'm here for." His voice is protective, almost as if he feels like he's being doubted. Quickly, I rectify that.

"It's not because I doubt your abilities. It's just...if you're not there for whatever reason, I want a fighting chance." I lift my chin, meeting his gaze. He nods quietly. "It is not an insult to you, River. I promise."

"Can I help?" His voice softens again.

"Train me?" He nods. "I'd love that, but you'll have to take it up with Aris." He grunts at this, and I turn to enter my bathroom, pausing with my back to him. "I told him about us," I murmur softly. The air stills; I wait, unable to move until he responds.

"And?"

"And..." I turn and face him once more. "And he doesn't like the idea of sharing. Nor the idea of us getting caught, but he wasn't apprehensive about it. I did make an agreement though." He raises his eyebrow at me to keep going.

"I agreed to abstinence for now. Keeping my hands to myself." I bite my lip, looking him up and down, swallowing a groan of my own. "We have to be careful anyhow, with last night being a close one and all." I can't read him from here; I can't see what floats in his eyes, but I can feel the grumbling annoyance from him through the tether. It's safe to say he doesn't want to agree to keep his hands to himself, but he understands what's at stake.

"For now?" His husky voice rakes over me. He shifts off of the doorframe.

"For now," I repeat. "I'll find you later; Aris will meet me in a bit to show me a couple things, and then you and I are free until the evening. I have some research I'd like to do in the library if you'll accompany me."

"Always, Ember." He tips his head to me before closing my door for me. With half a thought, I lock it from where I'm standing with those shadowy tendrils. The small release is a blissful reprieve.

I take my time bathing, relishing in the way the water relaxes my already sore muscles. The simple burgundy chiffon dress I've chosen swishes around me as I move. The thin straps reveal my shoulders, but I welcome the coolness of the castle. I carefully pin up half of my hair, wisps framing my face. I even put one of the new necklaces Aris picked out for me—a simple gold chain with a diamond shaped like a teardrop lying in the hollow of my neck. It's stunning and probably the most expensive thing I've ever worn, but I love it.

I don't have to travel far out of my room before I can scent and hear Aris approach, the tether growing warm as he nears. His smile broadens as he takes in my appearance.

"Gods, you get more radiant every time I see you." He extends an arm for me to take, and we slide into step together.

"I was just with you not even an hour ago." I chuckle.

"I stand by what I said." He leads me down several halls and corridors that I make note of. It's easy to get lost in this never-ending castle, but I make mental notes of the paintings and busts of gods that line the walls. I might need them to find my way later.

"Where are we going?" I peer up at him.

"I didn't get to show you the dance studio yesterday like I had promised. So I'm showing you now, and I'm introducing you to my piano teacher." He lets my arm go to open a pair of wooden doors, revealing a grand room lined with mirrors on the right, center, and left side. The floor is dark cherry wood polished meticulously, and windows line the walls above the mirrors, letting in the sunlight to brighten the room in the afternoon rays. A black grand piano sits in a corner, where a small frail woman with a stern face but a warm aura stands beside it.

"I didn't know you played." I take in the room in awe. It's beautiful in comparison to the one back home.

"I dabble. She wouldn't call it playing." He chuckles. "Madame Celine, this is Princess Ember, my betrothed." Celine curtsies.

"It is a pleasure, Your Highness."

"Oh, please, Ember is fine. It is lovely to meet you." I offer her a smile, leaning into Aris' side a bit.

"Madame Celine is the finest piano player I know. She's agreed to be at your disposal whenever you want to come in and need to get away from everything and let loose. She lives here in the castle, so you can call on her whenever. I'm pretty sure she's memorized every piece of sheet music in existence." Aris flashes a sly smile.

"That's too kind; you don't have to—" She puts a hand up, cutting me off.

"Your Highness, if you will, playing is the one thing in my life that brings me purpose. Playing for you would be an honor."

Though her voice is stern, the warmth in her tone relaxes me, and I find myself nodding.

"Listen to her play; I think you'll find yourself understanding what she means," Aris whispers, his breath tickling the cusp of my ear. Celine sits at the piano, her posture picture perfect as she readies herself.

As she begins, my entire body goes still. It's not just a purpose; she was *born* to play. The magic in me stirs like a cat waking from a nap, stretching and lifting itself to go out and meet the sounds in the air. I pull it back, attempting to leash it, but it yanks, and it yanks *hard*.

I remember Asteria telling me that the longer I keep my powers in, the less control I may have. Celine continues to play in a manner that reminds me of when I lose myself in the cello, when I become the music itself and the sound travels through me. My magic responds to it, aching to dance through the air and sing with the notes and the melody around us. Aris glances at me as I fidget, trying to breathe like a normal person as I watch Celine.

Out, out, out, my magic seems to scream. It needs release as power begins to push against my skin, warming me from the inside out. Even Aris' proximity is too much, as the tether seems to glow as my power wakes. I take a step away from him, needing space to cool down. It feels like the magic is trying so eagerly to find a way out that it's burning even in my eyes. Aris glances at me again, eyes widening a bit when his gaze meets mine.

"What?" I whisper.

"Your..." He trails off, staring like he's not quite sure. "Never mind." I shrug as I glance back toward Celine, closing my eyes and tilting my head up like I'm just losing myself in her music. Whatever he just saw, I need him to think it was a trick of the light. I let a small tendril loose through the air, dancing invisible to everyone else, but it's enough to calm the aching burn building in my core. It's enough to not lose complete control for right now.

I'll need to slip out tonight to expend some of the power I've left locked up for so long. The little wisps to lock a door or close a window aren't going to cut it anymore. Even the tendril dancing through the studio is hardly enough to calm the throbbing pain from keeping so much kept inside. I've kept it locked up in a small box for so long; I've let it build and build and build, shoved it deeper into the well, and now there's nowhere else for it to go.

Asteria's right, it's going to take over me soon if I don't figure out how to start using it more often. Especially with her powers combined with mine and the way mine continue to grow, I'd explode surely. It would melt me from the inside out.

The piano rings with the final note, the chord pulsing through the air like a final exhale of breath. Aris places a tentative hand on the small of my back, meant to tell me he's here for me, but it only riles the power within me more. That touch once grounded me back home, when my powers had begun to take control then too, but now he just excites it more. The tendril I'd let loose shoots over, running through his hair.

It could be blamed on nothing more than a breeze, except there's no open windows and we're in an enclosed room. I swallow, wondering how much he's really paying attention. I lasso the tendril of power that's so eager to touch what we're bound to and pull it back into me. I look up at him innocently, leaning into his hand. He looks puzzled, as if he can't really explain what he just felt and what he just saw a moment ago. He doesn't say anything as Celine walks toward us, and we both turn to her.

"I have never heard someone play with their soul like that. It was like everything else in the room melted away, and it was only you and the music." That feeling is very familiar. Aris looks at me.

"That's how you play or even sing," he says fondly. "The entire room electrifies. You both have something rare." Celine smiles softly.

"It is for that reason, Your Highness, that I would love to play for you whenever you need reprieve from your other duties. Talent recognizes talent." She bows her head slightly.

"Thank you, Madame; let's meet tomorrow in the afternoon." She nods, offering another curtsy before taking her leave.

Aris walks me back to my room quietly, not saying anything about earlier, thankfully.

"I'll be busy until evening with meetings; will you be okay until then?" he asks softly, leaning over me. I tilt my head up to stare into his dark eyes, searching them for answers to what he saw earlier, but he reveals nothing. I'm tempted to ask him about the meetings but decide against it. Instead, I nod.

"I'll be fine; I'll be in the library. Go ahead." I offer him a tight-lipped smile as he leans back.

"We'll have dinner together; be at the dining hall at six." I nod as he slips away, shoving his hands into the pockets of his pants. I lean my shoulder against the dark stoned wall and watch as he walks down the hall, his steps graceful, that of a prince ready to be a king.

Even after he's long gone, I stay there, lost in thought. What does he know? What is his father's end game? And what are my parents going to do back home? What *am* I? The torches in the hall that are pinned to the wall burn brighter in response to my growing frustration. There's so much I'm realizing I don't know. So much I've let myself be ignorant to. I'm the only one, to my knowledge, with powers, and I really somehow thought that made me human? I scoff at my own stupidity.

Soft, almost silent footsteps sound behind me, and with it the swirling scent of mint and earth. I whirl around, his presence gratefully breaking me from the torment of questions I don't have answers to.

"River," I breathe. It pains me not to be able to embrace him. To kiss him.

"Ember." He bows his head, ever the guard with his princess. Servants pass us, their glances not as hidden as they think. Some disappear into both our rooms carrying fresh sheets and blankets; others carry our laundry.

"Let's go read about dragons, shall we?" I turn and walk toward the library, careful to avoid all the bustling servants going on about their duties. River walks slightly behind me, careful to protect my back but also keeps a respectable distance between us.

"Dragons, huh?" He raises an eyebrow when I look at him over my shoulder.

"I had a dream last night that one swooped down and ate Bedelia." I shivered thinking of what Asteria's going to have to eat when she gets here. River laughs, and I can't help but smile at the sound.

"So now you want to read about them?" he asks, still chuckling.

"Growing up, they told us they were nothing but myths. I just want to see if Klyeria has anything different in their library. I used to read about all of them, and then me and the others would choose a creature to be. Dragons, nymphs, sirens—monsters of all sorts." I pause at the door to the library, my hand settling on the long golden handles of the double doors. "I'd forgotten about those times. It didn't last long, for me at least; my father found out, and I was ordered to stop playing with the children. The pretend games were ill-suited for the princess. Those things didn't exist, and he would not have me prancing around as such."

I push open the doors; the sunlight immediately warms my skin, which had become cool from the cold hallways. The fireplace crackles softly in my ears, and today I notice what must be the librarian who takes care of the books. I'm sure he could point us in the right direction.

"He stole your childhood from you." River shakes his head. "Is that why you're not close with the others? It always struck me odd that Jasper was the only one you spoke to." We pause before walking toward the man hunched over a desk littered with several stacks of books.

"It's a very large part, yes. We were all close at first. One big group, like a family. But once they removed me, the hierarchy became apparent to them, and then slowly the struggle for power and creating themselves became more important. Jasper never cared about any of that. It was really lonely."

I look past River, toward the books, rubbing my arm softly. Though my magic has calmed down, it still thrums against my skin more consistently now.

"We could hire someone to deliver a letter to them. I'm sure there's someone Aris could appoint that would be discreet." We begin moving toward the librarian again.

"I could try. It never crossed my mind as a possibility with the war. You know, despite the divide that we grew up with, something has changed. At the Winter Solstice ball, they were all on board after my speech, even despite their parents being present. And they ride my parents' dicks the hardest." The librarian's head snaps up, and River coughs as if he's choking on something.

My cheeks warm; I hadn't intended to use such language; I don't normally speak like that because that's not how a princess speaks. I've trained myself to keep a tight leash on my language, but there's something about being in enemy territory that just makes me want to be bad.

"I am so sorry; please forgive my language. I have no idea what has gotten into me. Allow me to introduce myself—" The librarian puts his hand up, cutting me off. I snap my mouth shut. The man can't be more than his mid-thirties with dark blonde hair, big green eyes, and a large round nose that holds up thick-rimmed glasses. He studies me for a moment. He's shorter than average, dressed in plain brown pants, a white tunic, and a sweater. If I found a book in here to look up the word librarian, I think I'd find his picture as the definition. I offer him an apologetic smile.

"I know who you are, Your Highness. You were in here a couple days ago, yes?" he asks expectantly.

"Yes, we were." I cross my arms.

"You took a book." It's not a question—no, he somehow knows I took one. How the fuck does he know that?

"I did; was I not supposed to?" I ask, tilting my head. River shifts his weight behind me, looking down on the man.

"You didn't check it out properly, is all." The man glances up at River, losing some of that bravado.

"I'm sorry; we didn't see you here that day, and I wasn't aware of a system. We didn't have one back home. I have the book in my room; I can retrieve it and bring it back tomorrow. Now two questions: what's your name? I'll be in here a lot for the foreseeable future, so we're going to have to be at least acquaintances, and where might I find books on magic and/or magic creatures such as dragons?" I plaster another pleasant smile, hoping to win the guy over and get on his nice side. He narrows his eyes a bit at me and then nods slowly.

"Okay, bring the book tomorrow, and I'll look past the infraction. My name is Zephyr Molthaven. These books are my pride and joy, so you will follow my rules. I don't care who you are or what your role is; some of these books are thousands and thousands of years old and must be treated with the utmost respect." He cowers a bit when River takes another step closer, his chest brushing softly against my back, but the point is made. I may not be thousands and thousands of years old, but if Zephyr disrespects me, he'll equally regret it.

Zephyr swallows before continuing, "The section you'll be most successful in finding what you're looking for is in the, well, come, I'll just show you."

He pushes up his glasses before walking at a much faster speed than I expected. I take off, following him not far into the rows of shelves. We're still very close to the entrance and lounge area of the library. I had figured this stuff would've been buried further back.

"Here we are. These two rows should have plenty. If you need more or something more specific, let me know and we can go from there. If you want to take something out of the library, bring it to me so we can catalog it. If not, place the book back on the shelf before you leave." He bows his head before rushing back to the desk we found him at. I look up at River, and he starts shaking his head slowly. I roll my lips tightly to keep from laughing. A snort escapes from my nose, and I slap a hand over my mouth to contain my giggles, as even River can't stop his soft chuckles.

"What a guy," he mutters. "At least he's very helpful. Now, put me to work. What do you want me to read, and what do you want to know? Are you just curious about the overall history? Do you want crazy fictional stories about dragons?" His curious voice warms me up from the inside. I take a look at some of the titles on the spines, surprised at how many different books they have on just dragons alone.

"Perhaps start with the overall history of dragons and if there's anything interesting about whether there were ever human interactions with them? I just wonder..." I trail off reading more of the spines. River pulls off a couple of books and brings them toward a couple of comfy-looking lounge chairs and couches.

There's books here on sirens, griffins, nymphs, fairies, and nearly every other creature to exist. So much of this was taken out of the library after I was banned from playing with the children. It's why I could hardly remember anything about Asteria and what the myth had said about the dragons leaving.

I almost wonder if my parents had something to hide from me. As if there was information there they didn't want me to know. I grab a book titled "*The History of Magic and All Its Creatures*" and another about dragon biology and bring it over to River. I take the black velvet chaise lounge and sprawl out on it, kicking off my flats. My elbow leans against the armrest, and my dress rests over my legs in layers of chiffon.

River has one hand behind his head, his bicep so wonderfully on display even through his tunic as the other holds the book in his lap. He glances over at me and slowly drags his gaze over me before dragging his tongue beneath his bottom lip. He returns back to the book, widening his legs a little as he leans further into the couch. I don't dare glance down, because I know what I'd see —I can smell the way his scent changes in the air. Gods bless these new heightened senses.

CHAPTER 23

As I read, I toy with the fire in the distance mindlessly, making the fire bigger and smaller. It helps ease the burning within me; the ache remains, but my skin begins to cool. The room itself grows warmer, and I notice River roll up his sleeves and unbutton the top buttons of his tunic at some point, so I stop playing with it. Instead, I pry open a window in the back just enough to coax a breeze over him. My ears pick up on a sigh of relief from him as he relaxes. After a long while of sifting through the biology book, I sit up.

"Okay, what do you have?" I ask, folding my legs beneath me.

"There were hundreds of different dragon clans, or so the legend goes. They lived all over the world, but the heaviest concentration was here. There's a mountain range they lived in within Atravelien, on the edge of a heavily warded area that the humans couldn't get into. The problem was that there wasn't enough livestock to sustain the diet of that many dragons within the wards, so they ventured beyond them and started to eat wherever they wanted. The humans, of course, got mad. You can see where this is going and why they started hunting them. Now, it also says that within their wards were several different species, not just dragons. The way it's explained, though, is confusing, and I don't really think the author has it right."

His voice rolls over me like smooth silk. I could listen to him talk all day long. He leans forward, setting his elbows on his knees and holding the book open. Waves fall across his forehead as he looks up at me, and the sight knocks me breathless for a moment. He makes it hard to concentrate, but luckily what he's saying is equally as enthralling.

"Why? What's confusing about it?" I cock my head to the side, setting my book beside me.

"Well, he has a map here of our kingdoms and Atravelien, but he makes Atravelien seem so much bigger than it actually is in the center. It's as if he's claiming that where the dragons' warded lands preside is in the center between Klyeria and Agatharea. He calls it Ereltis." River pats the seat beside him so I can see the map inside the book.

"How could that be? We literally traveled through the center this past week; we would have seen it, right?" I get up, padding over barefoot, and sit beside him, folding my leg beneath me as he places the book between us. But sure enough, the way the map shows is as if Ereltis is an entirely new kingdom between ours. The mountains the dragons stayed in that were protected within the wards of this so-called kingdom are on the very edge of the border of Ereltis, but northwest, closer to Klyeria. Which means that they were probably raiding their farms or anything in the forest they could find.

If the humans started hunting in packs and picked the dragons off one by one, saving the scales as trophies, no wonder they had to relocate. If there wasn't enough to feed them in Ereltis because they were already overpopulated there, then they had to leave. But where in all of the hells was Ereltis? The author had to be mistaken about its actual location. As if reading my thoughts, River says,

"He must be wrong about where Ereltis actually is. It can't be exactly centered between the two kingdoms. Atravelien extends east and west for hundreds and hundreds of miles; maybe it's somewhere further down. If it's real at all. Do you actually believe dragons existed?" He bumps his knee into mine, an innocent touch to anyone else. I glance around and see Zephyr's the only one in here with us, and he's murmuring to himself while pouring over his own book. I bump my knee back into his.

"I don't know. Wishful thinking, I suppose. Something to get me through the day. I'm at a loss right now, so why not dive into the world of magic and dragons?" I shrug nonchalantly.

"My mom used to tell us stories about why Atravelien smells sweet but sickening. She told us that it was crawling with creatures. Creatures like hound hybrids that had canines so sharp and so long that they stuck out of their mouths past their chins and could rip straight through your ribcage in one bite. I think she called those 'rythars' and it scared us shitless. There was another, one that was eight feet tall and white as bone, skinny and gaunt; its eyes were completely white, no pupil because it was blind, but they could hear incredibly well, which made them good hunters. Their fingers aren't fingers; they're just claws. One slash and you're turned to ribbons. 'Wilps' I think." He pauses, a shiver running through him, and I can't help but chuckle.

"She really got you guys, huh?" I lean my elbow into the couch, watching him.

"Oh, we believed her. They were responsible for the death. They were responsible for why it's so sickening. But she said that the goddess, Atravel, tried to make up for it with all of the flowers in Atravelien, which accounts for all the sweetness. Hence, why it's so sweet and so sick at the same time. Either my mom had a very overactive imagination, or there's some seriously fucked creatures in the forest." He raises an eyebrow at me to suggest that he believes the latter.

"All the unexplained disappearances might suggest your mother is right," I argue.

"Atravelien messes with your head. There's strict orders that you can't be stationed within it for more than three nights, and you can't be in a group of less than three men. Anything less than that is a recipe for losing the entire group." He pauses again gravely. He looks away, toward the fire, the light in his eyes draining. The sudden onslaught of pain down the tether cracks my chest open. I grab his hand, my body covering us from Zephyr's eyes just for the moment.

"I'm so sorry; we don't have to talk about it if you don't want to. We can go back to the dragons or something else completely. I didn't mean to bring this up for you." I brush my thumb over his knuckles and focus on sending soothing waves down the tether. He looks back at me and smiles, sadness still tinting those deep ocean blue eyes.

"No, no, it's okay. I don't mind...sharing that part of me with you. It's just not easy." He takes a deep breath, and the sadness washes away. He returns back to the River who was talking about scary forest creatures, and glides past it instead. "So, the humans drove the dragons from Ereltis to go live and repopulate on another continent, and that's the last Klyeria or Agatharea has heard of or seen them for almost three hundred years. Which doesn't seem as long ago as I thought. It also mentions that the people who live in Ereltis, the Erelt, are their own kind of species. It says they were the protectors of the eggs and that their magic helped coax the hatchlings to hatch. They're essential to one another, so the Erelt must exist on the other continents. It did mention something interesting though." He flips through some pages, trying to find what he read.

There's a part of me that wishes he'd open up to me. There's another that understands not being able to speak the pain out loud.

"Does it say how the humans were killing the dragons? It seems crazy to me that such strong and magical creatures fell to us mere humans." I move away from River, sitting on the far end of the couch in case anyone were to walk in on us. Pulling my feet close to me, beneath my dress, I grab the book on dragon biology.

"They had catapults designed to capture the dragons when

they swooped in for the livestock, and then they would slaughter them by beheading them with large ax contraptions sharp enough to sever their heads in one swoop with them trapped by the catapult. They also poisoned some livestock purposely to spread disease, and then they'd find unconscious dragon bodies in the forest. They'd bring back the dragon heads in victory. The interesting part is that the Erelt and the dragons sometimes formed special bonds, but they were so rare it's only mentioned once in the section. He didn't know much about it. How cool would that be?" He glances up at me, closing the book, leaning his arm over the back of the couch to face me. My spine goes ramrod straight.

Rare. No wonder she went back. I wonder if she knew anything at all about the bond. When was the last time a bond happened? How rare is rare? Once every couple decades? She said her Elders would teach her—did any of her Elders have a bond?

"I wonder how he knows any of this," I murmur softly, chewing on my lip as I look toward the windows, wishing more than ever I'd see her green scales glinting in the clouds.

"What did you find?" he asks.

"Dragons live thousands of years. Their eggs take up to a year before they're ready to hatch. I did read something similar that magic is needed to coax them out, a very specific type to deliver them essentially, but this book didn't name the Erelt by name. They have special birthing ceremonies for them when the eggs are ready. Dragons have magic, but it's limited to a few different types. Some have two gifts, while most only have one. Most dragons are gifted with one of the elements; all can breathe fire, but it goes further than that; some can manipulate the earth, some the air, some the water, some can turn invisible, some have incredible speeds, and that's all they really name here." Asteria has two, which I'm excited to test later. I already was able to manipulate the earth somewhat, but I'm sure it's going to feel different now.

And now I can turn invisible? I wonder if I could get into one of the meetings Aris refuses to let me go to. It's a risk I'm willing to take if I can perfect it. And Asteria can do what I can? What does that mean for a dragon? Imagine the power that means for her. I suppose that she's learning exactly what that means with the Elders. If we're not close, do I lose access to those powers? I guess I'll find out.

"Ember?" River says softly, causing me to look at him. I think he was talking, and I completely zoned out.

"I'm sorry, I was just thinking. What did you say?" I smile apologetically.

"I asked if this is what you were looking for." He looks like he wants to reach for me, but we leave the space between us.

"Essentially. I haven't started this book yet; I think I'll take it with me. Maybe it'll talk more about the Erelt. I didn't realize how late it's gotten; we might've missed dinner." I stand, stretching like a cat. With the book on biology in hand, I slip back into my flats so I can put it back onto the shelf before heading over to Zephyr. River puts his books back before following me.

"I'd like to take this one with me, please." I place the book on magic and creatures on his desk with a soft thud. He looks up at me over his thick lenses.

"What do you want with it?" he asks, raising an eyebrow.

"I saw a small, pretty little fairy outside my window yesterday, so I'm curious," I tell him in all seriousness. River shifts behind me, and I don't have to look to see him smother a smile. Zephyr sputters.

"What did it look—" I cut him off.

"Zephyr, honey. Relax; I'm just kidding. I simply am curious, though. I will keep my eye out for any fairies, and you'll be the first to know if I see one. Do I need to sign anything?" I smile sweetly at him, but this only makes him scowl.

"No, I'll catalog it; you're free to go." With that, he turns, effectively dismissing us. I grab the book, flashing a smile at River as we hurry out of the library and down the hall toward the dining room.

I flag down a servant, handing them the book and asking

them to take it to my room for me. As we enter, several scents hit me at once. Cedarwood and spice, a dark, dirty musk, and something like leather and smoke bombard me. My eyes settle on Aris first, who's burning holes through me as I walk slowly toward the dining table. At the head sits the king, responsible for the leathery smoke, and beside him, smiling like a snake, is Dracyl, the dirty musk.

My heart beats so fast I can hardly feel it. I swallow the panic and school my features into the picture of calm and confidence. There's two place settings beside Aris, so I walk toward them, not daring to glance at River once to gauge how he's reacting. He's better at this than I am. I can picture his stoic, cold face that dares anyone to fuck with me or him.

The king's eyes watch me carefully, and down the tether I can feel Aris' anger. Swallowing, I take my seat beside Aris, and River takes his beside me. Aris never mentioned his father would join us. He hadn't joined us any other night beside the first and at the ball.

"How wonderful of you to join us," Dracyl drawls, a glass of amber liquid in hand. I stare at him, seeing him under good lighting for what seems like the first time.

The sides of his hair are shorter, but then longer on top, shining bright blonde, almost white beneath the chandeliers. Up close, his eyes are gray, almost silver; they're so light. His face is sculpted like it could cut ice, each edge sharp. He would be handsome if he wasn't a sadistic piece of shit. "Like what you see, Princess?" he purrs. I think I'm going to be sick. Aris' snaps his head up, a growl working its way up his throat, but the king beats him to it.

"That's enough, Dracyl," he commands, but there's not much bite to it, so it doesn't stop Dracyl from smirking. River sits so still beside me that I almost want to turn and check that he's breathing. We're sharing a meal with my attacker right now. I'm not sure how either of us are going to eat or how Aris expected for this to go. "Do you care to explain your tardiness?" Bleren asks.

"I was in the library reading and lost track of time. You have my deepest apologies; I didn't realize I would also be keeping you waiting." I glance at Aris. He narrows his eyes at me.

"If my son tells you to be somewhere at a specific time, then I expect for you to be there at that time. Not off with another man sharing a couch. I should have him punished for being so close to you." I snap my head up to stare the king in the eyes, my blood and magic starting to boil at a rate I can't control.

"Right, right, I just said I was sorry, and correct me if I'm wrong, but reading on a couch is just that—reading on a couch. Would you prefer I grab a measuring stick and ensure that we are six feet apart at all times? For fucks sake, Bleren, I wasn't fucking him." I stand up and the fireplace burns almost uncontrollably. Some servants come to douse it with water to calm it down. Bleren seethes, opening his mouth to reprimand me, his own fist clenching with the intention surely to hit me. I've seen the same look in my father's eyes.

"Ember, sit down," Aris says calmly, lethally, and it's the *last* thing I expect from him. The last thing I wanted to hear. I stare at him, and he stares right back before I glance at the king, who watches, waiting to see if his son can break the will of his betrothed. He looks content to see his son taking control. Can he saddle his bride and bend her will to his? I can't. I can't do that. Can I? What *am* I doing here? Playing a part to save my kingdom, right? Brokering peace so there's no more burned-down villages? No more innocent lives taken in a senseless war?

River hasn't moved, and I'm sure it's because if he does, he might end up killing someone at this table with the rage he's radiating down the tether right now. If I sit, then I lose a part of my dignity. I effectively tell them I can be walked all over. If I walk away, I have no idea what consequences await me. Would I be whipped again? Would Aris face consequences? Would River? That thought alone puts the fire out. The fireplace turns into nothing but ash as the fight within me goes out and I sit down. Instead, I stare straight ahead.

"Good girl." The king nods approvingly, and they resume their meal, talking in murmured voices I don't care to listen to. Dracyl watches me for a moment with knowing eyes before giving the king all his attention. I don't move a muscle, and neither does River. Aris pushes his food around his plate but doesn't eat. Eventually, the food is cleared, and Bleren and Dracyl rise from their seats. Bleren takes a good look at me while I still stare straight ahead.

"This only works if you listen, Ember. He only stays if you follow the rules. If I catch you too close to him again, I won't be so forgiving. That will be the last time you ever speak like that to me ever again, is that understood?" His voice scrapes against me. My magic pushes against my skin, almost as if it's begging me to say no. I shift my eyes to meet him.

"Yes, Your Majesty." I speak softly, obediently, and submissively. He nods approvingly and leaves with Dracyl in tow, who only sneers as he follows. Once the door closes, there's a beat of silence before Aris attempts to open his mouth. I stand, pushing the chair back, not looking at him. River follows suit.

"Ember, stop," he begs, catching my wrist. I snatch it and jab a finger into his chest.

"Give me one more command, and I swear to the gods, Aris, I'll find you another bride to make this work." Gathering my dress in one hand, I move around him.

"What did you want me to do? Let him hit you like your father?" he hisses at the back of my head. I spin around, all of my attitude gone in one moment just like that.

"Does he hit you, Aris? Has he ever hit you?" Familiar panic worms its way into my chest.

"No, he hasn't. Never me, but I've seen that look in his eye before. I've seen him clench that fist, and then my mother wouldn't come out of her room for days. So tell me, Ember. What else was I supposed to do?" He looks at me with so much pain in his eyes, taking a step toward me. I can feel the heat from River at my back as River steps toward me too. It's not me who answers his question.

"If you stopped to think about her for one second, you could answer that question. It's hard enough for me to sit there at that table without wanting to rip him to shreds, let alone *her*. On top of that, he's *taunting* her. Your father is reprimanding her for reading after giving her the freedom to do what she pleases so long as it doesn't ruin his reputation because she's now a reflection of you both. You could have easily made an excuse for her. You could have sent servants to her. You knew where she was. You could have found a way to warn her he was here so she could've prepared herself. Instead, you let them ambush her. For what? To get that reaction?" River moves around me, stalking closer to Aris to study him. Aris narrows his eyes.

"What are you talking about? I had no clue they were going to be here; I showed up on time, and they were here too. My father ordered me to stay and wait. I don't know what my father or Dracyl want." Aris crosses his arms. "Plus, I warned *you* to stay the fuck away from her, and you just couldn't listen. Now they have even more of a reason to suspect you both."

"Because we sat on a couch together?" I ask. "That's ridiculous, Aris, and you know it is."

"My father *is* ridiculous like that! Down to the smallest fucking detail. One touch, and that's all it takes for them to drag him out of here. Listen, I'm sorry. I know it's hard with Dracyl here; I can't even fathom, and I'm sorry there's not more I can do except play my part right now. Doing what he wants right now is the best way to get what we want in the end; we just *need* to play by the rules." He drags a hand through his hair and then down his face, exasperated.

River scoffs, shaking his head in absolute disbelief, before turning around and walking toward the door. He waits for me there, knowing that Aris is right. What more can we do but what we're told until we can find a way out? I stare at Aris for a moment, taking in the broken man with the invisible chains wrapped around his hands and ankles.

"Very well," I murmur softly, completely defeated, because it's *really* starting to make sense. I just hate that playing by the rules makes me feel so damn *weak*. I turn and follow River out, leaving Aris behind, not sparing another look at him. I can't. I want to stay mad a little while longer this time. He owes me as much since my heart is aching more than I care to admit.

"River, let's grab some fruit or a whole pie or something at the very least. We didn't eat, and my stomach's going to hate me for it later." This earns me a small smile, which I count for a victory. He rounds the corner and disappears inside the kitchen. When he comes back out, he's carrying two glorious bowls of hot pie topped with scoops of vanilla ice cream and I can't stop the moan of excitement that follows.

"This makes everything better," I declare, shoving a spoonful into my mouth as I walk toward our rooms. Another moan follows as cinnamon apples and creamy vanilla mingle with my taste buds. "Holy gods and goddesses." River chuckles, shaking his head, eating his own with the same fervor. By the time we get to our rooms, our bowls are completely clear. He takes mine, combining it with his.

"Good call on dessert for dinner," he commends me.

"I make good decisions sometimes." I shrug. A servant passes us and sees River holding the bowls, immediately taking them from him without hesitation. River thanks them before turning back to me.

"Are you okay?" he asks softly. He leans back, putting distance between us when I know he wants to do differently. I can tell the control it takes to keep off of me is taxing on him.

"I think so. I'm just going to read my book and try to sleep, I think. I'm tired and done with the day." In other words, I want to change, sneak out, and expend a shit ton of this pent-up magic before I blow someone's head off.

"Ember, you're stronger than every single person here. Me

included. Do not forget that." He looks me up and down in a way that has me curling my toes.

"Thank you for always defending me. Goodnight, River." I bite my lip before slipping into my room, shutting my door before making any bad choices that involve him and his bed.

I strip out of my dress, placing it in the laundry, before finding some loose black pants that tie at the waist and cinch at the ankle. I tuck a black tunic into them before sliding warm wool socks on and a short pair of black boots. Staying in all black will hopefully keep me cloaked in darkness and away from any possible wandering creatures that might come my way in the forest.

I grab the thick black coat, sliding my arms through before walking over to my windows. I'm on the ground floor, so there's no worrying about climbing down. I tug on the sill to see if it'll budge, and it does with a loud screech. Cringing, I shove it the rest of the way up, cold air rushing over me. Leaving the window slightly cracked open, I crouch, looking around for any patrolling guards. The last thing I need is to be caught. When the coast is clear, I take off running toward the edge of the forest.

My feet carry me faster than I've ever run before, faster than my run with Aris this morning. It's like the wind pushes me, guiding me toward where I need to go. In what feels like mere seconds, I've cleared past the field of horses, and I find myself within the darkness of the canopy of the trees. I slow, listening to the chitter of the animals in the trees, letting my eyes get used to the lighting.

The smell is almost overwhelming from the animal scat to the frozen decay. I need to venture far and deep in so no one can see or suspect anything. Moving as quickly as I can without tripping over the underbrush of dead branches and vines, I make my way toward a distant clearing. A meadow of sorts, I realize as I get closer. A small river, frozen at the edges, sits at the outskirts before the evergreen trees begin again. They're dense enough that even with my heightened vision, I can hardly see through what lies beyond, but this will do. The ground is flat, covered in small patches of snow and dead wildflowers.

I look up at the cloudy night sky, at what looks like a storm rolling in, and again, I find myself wishing I saw wings spread, flying overhead. It feels like the longer she's away, the more my soul aches, and the more it's clear that a part of me is missing and needs to be returned. It doesn't seem right that we're apart this long. I hope she'll come back before seven days, because our tether is cold and starting to pierce me, reminding me constantly that she's not there.

As if sensing that release is finally coming, my power wells up in me, pressing up against me like a prisoner would against the bars of their cell. I pull it back, reminding it that it belongs to *me* and that *I* decide how it's used. The fireplace in the dining hall was way too close of a call, and if it weren't for the servants actively dousing it in buckets of water, I'm not sure there'd be a way of explaining the sudden outage of the fire.

Opening the gateway a little, I let air flood out of me, gushing out in a dome-like shape. A laugh escapes me, the relief already so sweet. I look at one of the bundles of dead wildflowers and pause. I'm not exactly sure how my magic works; most of the time I think with a specific intent, and it usually just works the way I want it to. Raw power, no singular ability one way or another. The shadowy tendrils are a manifestation of their own. This time I get to use it all more individually.

Squatting down, I touch the base of the plants, simply willing them to grow. The dead flowers remain dead, but new buds rise in their stead, blossoming in new bundles together. White daisies, purple asters, and yellow rudbeckia grow hastily toward the moon, intertwining together.

Rising back up on my heels, I look at my hand and think about invisibility. It doesn't happen right away, but a moment later, with more intent and a clearer head, my hands disappear beneath my coat. My gasp turns into a chuckle. How *peculiar*!

I unbutton the coat, ripping my shirt out of my pants, and

sure enough, no abdomen in sight. But this proves a predicament; my clothes don't turn invisible with me. So if I were to use this, I'd need to be stark naked. I suppose that makes sense for dragons; they don't wear clothes, so invisibility wouldn't require turning anything but themselves clear. I tuck my shirt back in, buttoning the coat before willing myself to be visible, flinching a little when my skin returns. *That's going to take some getting used to.*

Overhead, thunder rumbles, and within the clouds I can see lightning start to swirl. At my fingertips, I can feel electricity pulse, almost as if my magic responds to it in the air. I raise my hand instinctively, beckoning the lightning toward me. In less time than I can prepare for, it strikes my hand, and all I can do is guide it toward the flowers I just grew, a small fire burning in its wake. I jump back, landing on my bottom as I stare at my hands and what I've just done. My right hand is burnt, the skin bubbling and crackling where the lightning struck, and I hiss softly as a raindrop falls on it. Then I watch in wonder as my palm begins to heal rapidly, becoming pink and soft again like it never happened.

That must be courtesy of Asteria. In the dragon biology book, it did say they healed incredibly fast. The only way to truly kill a dragon is to behead them or stab straight through their heart, but their hearts are protected by a layer of bone as hard as steel. So beheading them is technically easier. They can even regrow limbs and their tails, though I will not be testing that anytime soon.

With a half of a thought, the fire goes out, and the new flowers are now nothing but ash. Fire and air feel the easiest to connect to; it takes no movement to control, whereas things like the earth I have to move my hands to guide the growth, like the vines back home. I focus my attention on the river next, shifting my hands to melt the ice. The water begins to rush faster without the solid ice in the way. I try guiding a trail of water through the air, circling myself like a ribbon before weaving it in the air in a figure eight. Throwing my hands into the air, I turn it into snow, and flakes come floating down around me as if it has been snowing all along.

Cold rain follows it, the storm coming in full force. I put up my hood and create a dome of air that keeps the rain from falling on me as I begin my trek back to the castle. This is the most I've ever used my magic, and yet it feels like I've used nothing but a drop compared to the ocean that dwells within me. The release is incredible; it doesn't feel like I'm boiling alive or that I'm being stretched apart from the inside out, but this won't last long either.

I'm going to have to start learning how to do things all day long with consistent usages of my magic that can help expend some of the energy to help keep it at bay. I can't continue to allow it to take control every time I feel any kind of heightened emotion. I'll get myself caught if I haven't already. It makes me wonder if River was onto something about whether Dracyl is just a ploy to get a reaction out of me. But why? What are they looking for? Did Dracyl tell them about the rock?

The castle comes into view, and I pause at the edge of the trees, looking for any patrolling guards. When I see none, I quickly make it to my room, climbing in, miraculously remaining dry. Exhaustion quickly settles into my bones, along with the ache in my heart.

Aris is clearly hiding things from me. Pieces of information he thinks I'm better off not knowing yet because it "protects" me. And his father clearly has his fist wrapped around his throat, because Aris won't go against him, not even for me or my pride. And as much as I want Aris to stand up to his father, I know it's not that simple either. I know he's biding his time, waiting for the right moment.

I strip out of my clothes and climb into bed naked, not caring to put anything on. As I fall asleep, all I can think, all I can tell myself, is that I need to keep playing my part. Play by their rules. Stop falling into their traps, or I'm going to get River or myself killed.

CHAPTER 24

Train. Breakfast. Dance. Bathe. Read. Dinner. Read. Sneakout. Magic. Sleep. Repeat. That has been my life the last three days. I train with Aris still, and even River has joined in on the morning training sessions, though he stays to himself. However, watching him workout is something I replay in my head at night. Aris hasn't been able to do any outings into the villages due to his meetings and other commitments, so I've been confined to the castle. Madame Celine and I have spent hours together while she plays and I dance. I've even attempted to sing while she played, but it was short-lived because singing woke my magic up and I couldn't shut it down.

I've scoured the book on magic and all magic species, but there's zero mention of the Erelt people, and little more on dragons that wasn't already mentioned between the others River and I have read. We've read several others now and still, no other books have mentioned Ereltis or the Erelt. My gut is telling me that what I am has everything to do with the Erelt. I just need to know more. There were a few tidbits on magic in general that were important to note.

Signs of burnout included similar signs to what I've experienced when I lose control—overheating, boiling blood, but you begin to feel hollowed out. The well, or that box in which I keep my magic, will begin to feel depleted and empty, and it is when I keep going even when there's only drops left that I will lose my power completely for a temporary time. It can take days, if not weeks, to replenish your magic, depending on how much you wield. Some creatures hold more than others.

If I don't use my magic enough, I'd lose myself to it. This I knew, and I was starting to feel the effects already. Moments where my magic would do things on its own, times where it reacted with my emotions instead, and slipped from my self-control. Things as simple as my language—cursing in front of Zephyr or at Bleren? That was induced by my withering control from my power being so pent up inside me. Years of putting it away had finally reached its peak, even after my explosion in the field when I met Asteria.

I found that rythars and welps are indeed real and even more hideous than I imagined from the looks of their drawings. There were dozens, if not hundreds, of other heinous creatures that either still do dwell in Atravelien or have gone extinct. Some I'm very glad for their disappearance—we wouldn't have survived our journey here had they still existed. I had wondered if maybe I was something like a siren, due to the oddities of my singing. My magic tends to imbue in the melodies and only matured in my adulthood, but there were too many differences in structure and biology for me to be a siren.

River and I have played princess and guard like our lives depend on it because they very much do. We sit on different couches and walk with more than enough space between us. It's almost comical, but we're following the rules. He's caught Dracyl several times trailing us, but we don't have anything to hide, so we don't mind.

There was an incident yesterday. It was the first time I'd ever seen River kill someone. Kill someone for *me*. The first time I'd ever seen blood on his sword. He was walking me back from dinner, which Aris hadn't joined me for—the second night in a row it was just River and I. We were passing the main entrance when I heard and scented someone, but River was already assessing, already observing, and already moving closer to me. A large, burly man came rushing at us wielding his own sword, screaming,

"Filthy, treacherous Agatharean whore!" He aimed it straight for my heart, but where this man might've had the element of surprise, River had speed and agility. Quicker than I could've imagined, he pushed me back, and I obeyed. I moved out of the way, but I would not run, not even as River commanded me to get to my room. I couldn't, not as I watched River in his everyday guard uniform, fitted with brown leather straps that hold other daggers when he feels like carrying extra weapons some days. Yesterday was one of those days.

It didn't take long—not at all. It wasn't even a minute before River, so graceful in his movements, struck, knocking the sword from the man's hand and plunged his own sword straight through the man's neck. Blood sprayed onto the floor and on River as he swiftly pulled his sword right back out. The man's unseeing eyes stared forward as he dropped to his knees and then his face planted right into the white marble floor, staining it as his blood gushed into a pool of red.

River pulled out a handkerchief from his pocket, wiped the blood from his sword before he slid it back into the sheath at his hip, and stalked over to me. He had grabbed my shoulders and shook me as I stared at the dead man who had tried to take my life.

And for some reason I hadn't really cared. I hadn't felt scared as he aimed that sword toward my heart, and maybe that's because I knew River wouldn't let anything happen to me. My magic had surged, ready to defend me, and it was *then* that I felt the fear. When I felt the ability to snap the man's neck with less than half a thought. Just one mere intention, and he'd be dead by my hands, not River's. That—that is what scared me.

"Why didn't you run? Why don't you ever listen, Ember?" River had growled, and that's when I looked at him.

"I couldn't leave you," I whispered; my voice cracked, but I hadn't cried. He looked so torn, because all he wanted to do in that moment was hold me, hug me, and kiss me, and that's all I wanted too. He had let go of my shoulders as soon as more guards came running into the main entrance hall and walked over to them. Immediately, he grilled them about the lack of patrolling and tried to figure out how the man got in the first place.

It turns out the man was a civilian who had attended my welcome ball and probably felt so passionately that I shouldn't be here marrying Aris that he tried to take it upon himself to rid the kingdom of me. One of the side entrances was left unmanned, they later realized, and that's how he got in. River practically chewed the head off the Captain of the Guard. He doesn't fuck around when it comes to his princess. They promised him that they would reconcile the mistake and that I'd be safe here, but he didn't seem so sure.

Aris walked in as River was talking to the captain and didn't even look at the body as he came to me. He had cupped my face and searched my eyes in such a panicked manner as he breathed heavily, as if he'd run to me.

"I'm okay," I had assured him, placing my hand over his and rubbing my thumb over the back of his hand. It had been the closest we'd been since he'd made me feel so weak in front of his father. I'd missed him more than I cared to admit; even if we had spent our mornings training together, it wasn't the same.

"Ember, I..." He'd shut his eyes, dropping his forehead to mine. His shoulders shook, and I felt the anguish and anger rolling through him down the tether. "If River hadn't been there, you'd be dead. When they told us just minutes ago, I couldn't *bear* it. I would've scoured the heavens and hells. I would've struck deals with the gods and goddesses to get you back. I would've followed the pull you have on me to the ends of the earth just to be with you for one more moment, so that our last shared breaths were together. I'm so—" I cut him off and planted a soft kiss on his lips before I pulled away from him just so I could look into his eyes.

"No one apologizes. I'm alive. He's dead. I'm right here, Aris. Right here." I took his hand and put it over my heart to show him that it was strong and beating. "It's going to take a lot more than a silly civilian to get to me. Maybe the king will see that River is a little useful after all," I joked just as River walked over to us. Aris had smiled, though, as some of that panic melted off of him. He dropped his hand to his side as River stood beside us.

"Very funny, Ember." River rolled his eyes at me before he turned to the prince, who looked at him in a new light.

"Thank you, River." Aris bowed his head to him. Even River's eyes had widened a little.

Aris bows to no one. No one except me, that is.

"It is my honor to protect her until my very last breath. I may have had a few choice words with the captain, so if they go running to your father, perhaps you can put in a good word with him." River glanced at the captain while Aris laughed softly.

"Of course." He shoved his hands into his pockets and cleared his throat softly. "Get to your room safely; I'll see you in the morning." We bid Aris a goodnight and returned to our chambers, and that night I didn't go out and practice my magic like I usually did, because for the first time I was scared of what I was capable of.

My mornings with Aris had been brisk until last night. The word count between us had been kept to a minimum per my request, and he'd done well to respect that while I was sifting through my feelings. He's kept our training sessions almost too professional, but today I'm done with all of that. Last night cleared my head, and I could move forward for now. This is my life after all, and I was only making it more miserable. More than it had to be.

After our run, which had become longer and faster every day, we had taken a moment to watch the sunrise over the horses. Our breaths mingle visibly in the frigid air as we slow our breathing.

He hands me his waterskin silently after taking a long gulp himself. I take it gratefully, quenching my thirst.

"Did last night scare you as much as it did me?" he asks, breaking the silence first.

"Oddly enough, I don't think so. River knew something, or someone, was there the moment we entered the grand hall near the main entrance. He was hiding in the shadows of an alcove, but he sensed him. I think if you'd seen it, seen the way he switched, you'd feel the same way. There was no way that man was going to ever make it near me. Had River been near me the night Dracyl attacked me, Dracyl would be dead too. He's always there, always looking around, always assessing every room we walk into. He checks my room at night sometimes just to make sure no one is there waiting for me. I know I piss him off with my lack of self-preservation, but I don't fear for my life when I'm with him." I shove my hands under my armpits, keeping them warm.

I obviously don't tell him that I had heard and smelled the man too. Even though I technically have my magic to save me, the only time I've ever used it was against Dracyl, and even then, that was a huge mistake. It would be easier to face my death than let that secret out.

"Maybe if I spent more time with the guy, I'd understand." He chuckles softly. He guides me with a hand on the small of my back toward the entrance, noticing I'm too cold to be out here now. "I couldn't sleep. All I wanted to do was go to you and just see that you were alive. Just watch you breathe, as creepy as that sounds," he admits. I yank the door open, rubbing my hands together as we get inside and make our way toward the training room.

"Why didn't you?" I ask softly.

"I didn't want to bother you. It was late, and it didn't seem like a good idea." He starts peeling off his layers, leaving on a thin shirt and loose pants, bouncing on the balls of his feet. I follow suit, leaving me in similar attire.

"I couldn't sleep either; you could've come to just talk. You know, I'm not always trying to seduce you." I raise an eyebrow at him as I begin stretching before we start our workout. I feel his eyes watch me, even as he stretches himself.

"I beg to differ, Temptress," he purrs quietly. I laugh softly, rolling my eyes. We spend the rest of the session in a much more relaxed mood together. Gliding right back into the comfortability I've felt since the first night I met him. Now that I've got much more of the basics down, he says I should be graduating to real sparring soon.

ARIS and I spent the afternoon in several villages, riding Bedelia and his horse, Coal. River and a few other guards trail us after the incident with the outraged villager in case there are any others who may feel the same. We figured it might be good for them to see us happy together, and not just at a ball for show.

So we roamed around, stopped in shops, and talked to people in the squares. We worked with the traders in the markets and spoke to the fishers at the docks. Children ran around in their winter wear, throwing snowballs around and laughing with delight when it hit their target. Aris even got hit with one, and I couldn't help but die laughing at the bewildered look on his face when he couldn't tell where it had come from. It was an overall success and a pleasant day spent outside of the confines of the castle, which I had grown tired of. It was hard to return.

Hayden took Bedelia for me, who had taken a liking to Hayden and Hayden only. I watched as he guided her toward the stables, being extra affectionate with her after a long day of travel. River and Aris trail behind me as we walk inside, the warmth of the castle a welcome reprieve from the frigid bite outside. Aris unties my cloak and hands it to a servant, who takes it along with the rest of the coats so we can go eat.

"My father, some of his court, and Dracyl will be joining us for dinner tonight, Ember. I just received word as we arrived," Aris murmurs softly as we walk. He reaches, grabbing my hand, which I hold tightly. Glancing down, I begin to smooth out my dress and my hair. I wore a gold dress he bought for me, and though I feel lovely in it, I suddenly feel sick thinking about Dracyl eyeing me in it. Eyeing me at all. My mouth waters as nausea rolls through me. I press a hand into my stomach and take a deep breath as shakes start to rack my body. I *hate* panicking.

"Aris, does she have to?" River asks, coming to stand beside me. It takes every bit of my will not to grab his hand with my free one. Aris looks torn, looking between me and the closed door. I hate putting him in this position, so I shake my head.

"I can do it. I can; I just need a moment to gather myself. Just a moment." I let go of Aris' hand moving toward an alcove where I place my hands on my knees and focus on counting my breaths. Shutting my eyes, I focus on calming my roiling magic, tucking it into its box as I breathe. *In, two, three, four, hold. Out, two, three, four, hold.* I push it down further and further until my power is nothing but a whisper inside of me. Somewhere it can't and won't come out this evening in front of Dracyl or Bleren.

My stomach stops rolling and my heart stops racing. The tingles in my arm subside, and once I feel like I'm not a complete and utter mess, I look at the boys who watch me carefully.

"Let's go. I'm starving," I tell them, walking forward to throw the doors open myself. Aris slides into step with me, wrapping a possessive and protective arm around my waist as we walk toward the table. Most of his court is seated already, but two spots have been reserved toward the head of the table beside the king. Dracyl sits on his right side. It seems the king hasn't shown yet—he really does like his entrances.

I glance at River, who gives me a knowing nod and aims for an open spot. He has a vantage view of me, but it's far enough that it makes him uncomfortable, especially with Dracyl across from me.

Aris exchanges a look with River, something akin to *don't*

worry. I nod at River once, as if to agree, shooting a wave of comfort down the tether to soothe him. It seems to do the trick before I take my seat. Aris helps move my chair forward before sitting beside me. He slides his hand beneath the table, resting it on the inside of my thigh, gripping my leg. His thumb brushes over the material softly, but I feel it as if it were on my skin.

It's the perfect distraction. So, I focus on it—on the way his mere touch sends little zaps of electricity pulsing through me. There's a lord beside me, but he can't see anything beneath the table—we're sitting too far beneath it. Aris leans down to talk directly in my ear, murmuring against my skin.

"It's a shame this dress doesn't have a slit like the rest of them do; I'd have much easier access." His words have me biting my lip and gripping the fabric of my dress, wishing more than anything that he was right. I turn, whispering softly as I look up through my lashes.

"It is a shame, because then you'd find out I wasn't wearing anything underneath." It's not true, but he doesn't have to know that since he wants to be such a tease. His grip tightens on my leg, his fingers flexing as his hand moves upwards, just a sliver.

"Always trying to seduce me, Princess," he murmurs, our breaths mingling as we become wrapped up in each other.

"Can you blame me?" I glance at his lips, not entirely caring where we are or who's looking. This is what they wanted, right? Us in our little love bubble? Aris doesn't get to answer as the king finally enters. We all rise in unison. Aris' hand slips from my thigh, instead replacing it on my exposed back, rubbing his thumb along my spine over the scars that have been covered by my cloak and hair all day.

I clench my jaw tightly to keep from making the noise threatening to come out of my throat. Who knew a spot could be so sensitive? I practically purr beneath his touch.

Bleren, dressed in his finery, takes his seat, and we follow suit. The lords around us fall into mindless conversation about the next harvest, to upping the slave count come spring for the next harvest. This has me eyeing Aris, who gives me a look that says it's already on his list of things to change when we take the throne. Dracyl dips his head to talk to the king, and I open my ears to focus over the eating and talking, but when Dracyl notices my attention, even though I'm not watching, he leans back and faces me instead.

"How did it go in the villages?" he asks, for once no sneer in his voice.

"Quite well, everyone seemed peaceful. I think we should do it a few more times before the wedding. We might want to consider going further into the kingdom, maybe staying overnight so some areas don't feel neglected." I glance at Aris, and he nods in agreement, wiping his mouth with his napkin.

"There's still a little less than three months before the wedding, which is plenty of time to tour more of the kingdom," Aris adds. Bleren contemplates for a moment before nodding.

"Go ahead and plan it for next month; I want you back with at least a month's time for the preparations of the wedding. I hope I don't need to remind you of the importance of abstinence." He eyes both of us, and it takes every bit of my will not to roll my eyes or retort. I'm about to stab another piece of chicken with my fork when I feel it.

I feel *her.*

Every single cell in my body goes haywire, as if being set ablaze, as if the bond is setting all over again. My eyes glaze over as I grip the fork. The magic I had tucked away into the deepest and farthest parts of me surges up, dancing with joy as the missing part of our soul refills. Dracyl's head snaps up, staring at me like I've grown three heads, but I pay him no mind.

"*Ember breathe or you'll pass out,*" Asteria says from somewhere above me. I vaguely hear her crash land on the roof of the castle, the stones rumbling with her landing. Everyone looks up, thinking they've heard a rumble of thunder that's shaken the walls. I take a deep breath that I didn't realize I had begun to hold. Aris glances at me, bringing his hand back to my knee.

Of all the moments you could've chosen to return, you chose this one. While I'm surrounded? Could you have been a little more graceful with your arrival?

"Are you okay?" he asks softly.

"I think I'm going to be sick." It's not entirely a lie. I stand, pushing away from the table before rushing toward a servant near the entrance. I grab the bucket she was using to clean from her and empty my stomach contents into it. "Oh gods, I'm so sorry. I'm so sorry." I wipe my mouth, setting the bucket down, ignoring the disgusted sounds from behind me as I drop to my knees.

"You need to come to me; let me take you from here so we can settle." Her feelings come rushing through me, and the sense of urgency floods me.

How in all of the bloody hells do you expect me to get to the roof, climb onto a dragon's back, and leave unnoticed? Right fucking now? Another wave of nausea floods me, and more of my dinner fills the bucket. Aris kneels beside me, and I can hear River giving directions to a servant on what to bring to my room to take care of me before he too comes over, kneeling on my other side.

"They're pretty. No wonder you have two." I can feel her leave the roof. *"Which one is your room? I'll wait outside instead."* She circles above in the clouds, and despite the overwhelming buzzing spreading through me right now, there is nothing better than having her back. Nothing sweeter than hearing her voice, even feeling her feelings, as annoying as they are, because it means she's home.

On the west side, facing the field of horses. Which you are NOT allowed to eat. What do you mean I have two? Stop speaking in riddles; you're giving me a headache. I lean away from the bucket, feeling like nothing else could possibly come up. I wipe my mouth again, absolutely disgusted with myself and this entire predicament.

"Let's get you back to your room and clean up," Aris whispers softly. He lifts me up on one side while River lifts me by my elbow on the other. My legs wobble, completely unstable, as they lead me toward the exit and toward my room.

"Two mates. The delicious things holding you up? They're your mates. You can choose one, keep both, or neither. The choice is yours. When you have more than one, those tethers aren't set in stone; they're mendable and breakable. It doesn't happen often; the gods aren't usually so giving. They've really taken pity on you. Most of your kind only have one mate, and when they meet, that tether is set in stone the way ours is. Permanently. Soul binding to one another. Can you feel their emotions like we can feel each other?" Asteria lands somewhere outside my room, curling up like a cat while Aris and River get me inside. A pitcher of water and fresh towels have already been neatly piled atop the desk when we enter.

The energy continues to seep from me, as if Asteria's arrival is sucking everything out. My magic writhes, beating against my chest, craving to join her, to be next to her, but I can hardly move my legs. Aris shuts the door while River holds me up like I weigh nothing, and that scent calms the turmoil wrecking my body for a moment.

"Did someone put something in her food?" River asks Aris.

"I ate the same things she did, from the same servings; so did my father. Her wine was poured from the same bottle." Aris sifts through my closet, pulling out a nightgown, while River brings me toward the tub, setting me on the lip. Aris slips in, taking his place, while River grabs a washcloth, wetting it to clean my chin.

I feel theirs, but they obviously don't feel mine. I only feel theirs when it's a very heightened emotion. But gods, two mates. A dragon bond. You said my kind; I'm from Ereltis; I'm Erelt. Right? We're the only ones who form these types of bonds with you.

"I see you've done your research," she says softly, soothingly. She sends soft strokes down our own tether, and if she had hands, she'd be running them through my hair. I lean my head back against Aris' shoulder while River cleans my chest. There's nothing there, but I'm sweating now, overheating.

"She's burning up." Aris touches my forehead. "Let's get her out of this; the fabric is way too heavy; it's trapping all the heat inside." River pulls me up by my elbows while Aris unzips the back of the dress, tugging it off as it falls to my feet, exposing my naked body except for the black, lacey pair of underwear I chose this morning. Aris leans down, murmuring into my ear while holding me up gingerly.

"Liar." I chuckle softly, weakly, but I can't help it. River takes my hands as Aris guides me from behind back toward my room, nothing but the moonlight to lead us in the dark.

I was curious and had the time. I still have questions. Beads of sweat form on my brow as my breathing becomes more shallow. *Asteria, is this supposed to happen?*

"I was away too long, and when a bonded pair is separated for too long, it makes them weak. You might've felt piercing pains. Now that we are reunited, we need to settle; I need you to come to me. Our magic will essentially recharge, but we have to be touching. They need to leave, or this will get worse for both of us." I can feel her struggling the same way I am; her landing sounded harsh, and now she's just laying beside the castle, invisible no doubt, yet how she's able to use her powers while feeling like this is beyond me.

Forgoing the nightgown Aris had grabbed, they lay me down instead atop the sheets. River opens the window beside Asteria's head, letting the frigid air blow over me. I groan softly, the overheating and freezing temperature almost is too much of a mix.

"I'm going to get the doctor; cover her up," Aris says before turning.

"No," I moan, grabbing a hold of his tunic. River leans against the other side of the bed, resting his elbow on the headboard as he moves hair away that's plastered to my sweat-slicked skin. "No doctors. Let me sleep this off; I'll be fine." Aris leans on the other side, both of them looking down at me unconvinced.

"So hardheaded," River murmurs.

"So stubborn," Aris echoes.

"You know, those aren't the words I imagined you both saying when I fantasized about being naked for the both of you," I mumble. I lean up on my elbows, gathering the bit of strength I have to prove to them I'm okay to go to bed on my own. Even in my feverish, havoc-wrecked, energy-zapped state, I don't miss the way they exchange a look before looking back at me.

"Now is not the time, Ember," Asteria grumbles.

Piss off; I'm working on it. I pull my legs up, grabbing the top sheet to bring over my body. They're both so quiet, stunned to silence. Aris swallows, standing up while dragging a hand through his hair. River follows suit, clearing his throat. Aris speaks first.

"Fine, no doctors, but no training tomorrow. We'll be here in the morning to check on you. If you need anything, you ring the bells," he commands softly, and I nod, because even though I'm stubborn, I will listen to Aris telling me what to do. For the most part. River tips my chin up, and I look at him.

"Close the window when you cool down. You'll freeze in here if you don't." I nod again.

"They love to boss you around, huh?" She's joking, but her voice is distant, even though she's just on the other side of the wall. I tug on our bond, keeping her with me.

Stay awake. I don't know how to do this if you pass out on me.

"I'm trying."

"Bells and close the window. Got it. Goodnight, gentleman." I mock salute them and roll over, watching them walk toward the door. They both glance back at me once more, and I blow them a kiss for good measure, earning myself a couple of grins and rollings of the eyes. The door closes, and I wait a moment before locking it with a tendril of power. With a groan, I lift myself out of bed, grabbing the nightgown Aris pulled out and pulling it on.

My bones feel like they're grinding against one another, and my muscles feel like they've been pulled as tight as they can go. Socks. I need at least some socks before I go out there, and a cloak —where the fuck did they put my cloak?

"No clothes; they can't see you out here; three guards have already walked past me. One almost tripped on my tail," she mumbles.

You couldn't have said that before I started getting dressed? I begrudgingly shuck the nightgown off, groaning at the stiffness in my body. Hooking my fingers into the waistband of my underwear, I slide them down too, letting them drop before stumbling to the open window. Shaking uncontrollably, I ungracefully throw myself over the ledge, landing in the frozen snow with a thud. I freeze, willing myself invisible, and just like before, my body instantly turns transparent, and I no longer can see myself. Instead, I see straight through to the ground.

There's no guards for the moment, so I crawl, stifling a sob working its way up my throat. I finally hit a leathery hide, and I feel her wing lift. Blindly, I crawl beneath her wing and lean against her body, shuttering in relief as she covers me in a cocoon of her warmth. Atlas, I am with her.

I wake up the next morning to the morning chirp of a winter songbird as if it were singing directly in my ear. Wincing softly, I curl up tighter against Asteria's warm belly, covering my ears to block out the sudden onslaught of even louder sounds as I'm bombarded with the slurping of water from the troughs down the horse field. The snorts of the pigs from the barn and the bleats of the goats grow with them, and suddenly I'm afraid my eardrums are going to explode.

Asteria, make it stop. It wasn't this bad when she left; sure, everything was heightened if I focused, but it wasn't this unbearable. This is taking it to an entirely different level. She shifts beneath me, waking finally, and beautiful, blissful relief fills me as a sudden blockage goes up between me and the sound, as if she shoved invisible, magical tissues into my ears.

"While we are together, our powers and senses will be even stronger. You will have to learn how to put a damper on your abilities like I just did so that you can go about relatively normal. It doesn't mean you can't access them; they'll always be there as soon as you need them. It just makes it easier for you since you're not meant to be overwhelmed by such senses." Asteria yawns, her rancid morning breath filling the space between us. I don't dare crinkle

my nose or say anything, unsure of what her morning temperament might be like. Her stomach rumbles and her hunger floods me like a tidal wave.

How do we figure that out too? I clutch my stomach, feeling like I haven't eaten in days. Sitting up against her, I stretch as best as I can, my back aching from laying on the cold, hard ground all night. But despite that, I feel much better than I did last night. In fact, I feel *powerful.* As if my body has been remade into something invincible, something harder, faster, and stronger.

"The Elders taught me much that you and I will need to practice. The first we've already accomplished. Settling. Being away so long quite literally stretched our tether, our bond. Think about it as a literal rope; when you stretch it, it becomes loose; it loses its elasticity. So, when we were away, our bond lost its strength, causing us to become sick until we physically came together to join our power once again and restore the bond to its former state. The longer we are away from each other, the more detrimental the effects. It could be fatal." Asteria lifts her neck, stretching it out.

Did they say how long before it would be fatal? I crawl out from under her wing, back toward my window, the freezing wind biting at my skin, turning me blue by the second, though I couldn't see myself to tell. My room is no warmer when I return. My breath clouding in front of me is the reminder I didn't close it when I fell to the ground last night in my last ditch efforts to reach Asteria.

"It depends on the bonded pair and how strong they are; some can only go days; a week is pushing it for us, it seems." More hunger pains roll through me, nearly causing me to double over as my skin comes back into view. With half a thought, the fireplace is roaring with fire and the lamps are lit.

Can I visit Ereltis with you?

"They're strict on access in and out. If you're needed here, then I can't take you there without the risk of you getting stuck because of their interest in your power or identity."

I huff, disappointment rushing through me. But I have a

purpose here, and I can't abandon that for the curiosity of visiting where I come from.

"I'll feed you memories as much as I can to make up for it, my dear." I send her my appreciation in waves.

The window shuts, cutting off the onslaught of cool air and keeping the warmth in as the fire fills the room. Goosebumps spread over my arms, racing one after another until I'm covered with them. With the room finally warming up, I wave my hand to start running the water for the bath without even looking at it, without being in the same room. But sure enough, the water starts to fill the tub.

"Have you always been able to use your magic without using your hands?" The ground beneath Asteria stirs, the frozen soil crunching where her claws dig in as she rises steadily on strong arms and legs.

Not always; sometimes with earth and water I have to wave my hands or touch the ground directly, but for fire and air I just have to will it. Most things, I just think about it, feel it with intention, and it happens. Is that not how magic works? I begin sifting through my dresses, settling on the navy blue dress that Aris bought me with a deep V cut. I grab it from the wardrobe, sending a wave of air to ring the bell for Layla and Melody.

"Not your people's magic. The Erelt use their hands to coax their magic out, to direct their magic where they want it to go and how they want to shape it if their magic is elemental-based. Even the non-elemental magic users usually have to use their hands in some shape or form. To use your magic purely out of thought is unusual. Though, Ember, you are proving to be one of a kind. Dragons don't have hands, so we don't do the whole waving of the hands for the show of magic. We don't like to show off." Her wings give off a big boom as she launches herself into the air—a very not so subtle way of leaving the area. Her hunger rolls through me yet again, and I have half the mind to curse her halfway across Atravelien if she doesn't handle it right now or block me out.

Right because the big flashy scales, horns, tails, and wings aren't showing off enough. Can you do something about your hunger? And be quiet; the guards will hear you. My body just about sings from the relief the warm water brings me, my muscles finally relaxing as I slide further into the water.

"*I will do as I please. What are the guards going to do—use their toothpick swords on me hundreds of feet above them? I'm going to find something to eat; there's a delectable invasive species of wild boar—*"

Spare me the details.

"*Think of your mind as its own fortress. Then build that fortress brick by brick, stone by stone, until you have surrounded it. That's how you'll block me out.*"

You waited until now to tell me that? Instantly I envision building a wall around my mind, a protective layer to keep her out, but I also imagine a door so I can let her in and out.

"*I do as I please, Ember,*" she says again. I don't miss the satisfaction in her tone, and just like that, her wall goes up too, and with it all of her hunger pains. "*Good, I can't feel you anymore. Do you know how you made it beyond the wards? Or if one of your parents is of Erelt descent?*" A soft knock sounds at my door.

"Come in!" Layla and Melody enter, both wearing their identical black servant uniform that everyone here wears. Their soft footsteps find me in the bathroom. "Good morning, ladies," I chirp.

"Good morning; you seem to be feeling better," Melody remarks, carrying what looks like medicine on a tray in her arms.

"Much, there's definitely no need for that. I must've eaten something bad, or who knows what. But don't fuss; I'm fine. Work your magic on me, please, so I can meet Aris. We're going to visit more of the kingdom next month, and I'd like to iron out the details with him." I smile reassuringly at them, to which they exchange a look I can't read before nodding. While they work on me, I answer Asteria, letting them chatter amongst themselves.

I've lived in the castle my whole life. As far as I know, my mother and father don't have any power, so I don't think they're

Erelt. I've never detected anything from them, not that I'd know how. Could it be possible that they're still human but carry Erelt blood?

"I've never heard of that being possible for humans. You're either Erelt or a demi-child, but never just human. Plus, Erelt children have to be born within the wards to access their magic due to the way the wards are enchanted, which means you were within the wards at some point in your life." Noises become increasingly louder the further Asteria travels from me, causing the damper she placed on me to loosen. The scrape of the blade over my skin as the fine hairs of my leg are shaved off is suddenly the only thing I can hear along with Layla's heartbeat, thump, thump, thumping in my other ear. My own heart speeds up as I try to make sense of what Asteria is saying while staying calm.

How do I dampen my own abilities? I clench my fists, my nails digging crescent moons into my palms.

"*Imagine a blanket over the well inside you, as if you were tucking a baby in bed.*" Melody releases a sigh that just about blows my eardrums apart. Blanket. Blanket. I close my eyes, feigning relaxation as I envision a thick blanket encasing the box where I keep my power, and suddenly everything is soft again.

When Dracyl attacked me, I questioned him. He said he was trying to see if I 'was really the king and queen's daughter or if I was from' and then River came in and cut him off. I never figured out where he thought I was from. He poisoned me with a poison I should've been dead from in minutes, but somehow I survived, and I think this proved some theory of his. Me surviving meant something to him. My heart constricts thinking about it, as if someone is actively twisting a dagger that's been stabbed through my chest.

Layla and Melody, finally satisfied that I was hairless and that my hair was pinned in place to their liking, helped me out of the tub. Another knock comes at the door, and Melody lets out a squeak, causing Layla and I to giggle.

"That might be Aris; he said he'd come check on me," I whisper, trying to act normal with the girls.

"But you're not yet presentable, Your Highness!" Melody warns.

"Oh heavens, I wasn't going to let him in yet; we can make him wait." I shrug, sliding the dress carefully on so I don't ruin the updo Layla did. The zipper pulls the dress snug against my body. The waist hugs my curves before flowing down, whispering softly against my skin.

"We're making the prince wait?" Layla's voice rises a couple of octaves while her eyes widen.

"I'm not ready, so he has to wait; don't worry, he'll be fine." I chuckle at them, sitting at the vanity so they can finish with the cosmetics.

It means he knows you're Erelt. Erelt, live long, and heal fast, and it also means he thinks your parents aren't really your parents. How he knows that is what you need to find out. I'm sure he's doing it for the king, and I'm sure that the king has you here to keep a closer eye on you. So keep a very close wrap on those powers when you're in the public eye. I'll keep an eye on that Dracyl fellow when I can. The one with the silver hair, right? I saw him in your dreams last night. On first instinct, I start to nod, but stop myself, reminding myself to breathe instead.

Yes, the silver-headed fucker.

"Silver fucker indeed."

I'll be careful, I promise. I stare at the fire, at a complete loss. The earliest memories I can conjure are inside the castle—there's nothing beyond that. Nothing in Atravelien or inside the wards, like Asteria is saying. It doesn't make sense. If Nicholas and Eloise aren't my parents, if I wasn't born here and I was born in Ereltis, how did I end up with them? There has to be an exception somewhere, somehow. Something's off.

"Your Highness?" Melody asks tentatively. My head snaps to her, realizing I hadn't been paying attention.

"I'm sorry, my head is all over the place. What did you say?" I wrap my hands in my lap.

"We wanted to know if you're ready for the prince now."

They smile knowingly, as if I were daydreaming about him, which I imagine for my role here—that's what I should be doing. A love-sick, doe-eyed princess caught up in the charming, too good to be true, handsome prince—whose father happens to be the reason why half my kingdom is in ashes.

I take a deep breath, reminding myself that he is the mirror image of myself. That I am not who my parents are and that my parents are responsible for the destruction of just as much of his kingdom as his are of mine. That doesn't make Aris any worse of a person than it makes me.

"Yes, I'm ready. Thank you, ladies. As always, you both take my hair from rat's nest to actually princess-like, and now I look alive and awake. The people in the halls will thank you that a gaunt ghost isn't haunting them." I sketch a bow for them, causing them both to giggle.

"Oh, how you jest!" Layla chuckles, gathering her maid gown and the medicine they came with as they make their way toward the door.

"Someone's got to bring some light around here; it can be so." I trail off as Melody opens the door, revealing not the cedarwood scent I thought I'd smell but leather and smoke. My eyes trail up expensive black silk to a freshly shaved face, a sharp slanted nose, and aged, dark eyes so similar yet so angry and different from Aris'. Bleren stares down at me, contempt rolling off of him in waves, suffocating me where I stand, cementing me in place.

"Good morning, Bleren." My voice comes out small and submissive. I bow my head with a dip of my chin, not going as far as to cower, but enough to show him that he's won. I will jump when he wants me to jump. He has his princess at his beck and call.

"Good morning, Ember. I see you're feeling better. I came to check for myself that our bride-to-be wasn't coming down with anything." His voice is a deep timber, and I even find myself wanting to obey.

"Completely fine; I think it was just something I ate. It's all out of my system now. I just finished getting ready to go see your son so we could plan the trip around the kingdom that we talked about last night." Layla and Melody shift behind me, and Bleren's eyes flicker to them as if just realizing that they were there.

"Ladies, you're dismissed," he commands. They dip their heads, walking between him and I swiftly, leaving Bleren and I alone with his set of four guards a few paces behind him in the hall. Once the girls are far enough away, he closes the space between us, pushing my back into the frame of the doorway, pinching my chin between his thumb and index finger roughly. His breath fans over my face as he sneers softly enough only I can hear.

"Listen closely, dear; I'll let you parade around with my son because publicity is good. Let the kingdom see you two together and how in love you are. Share your little 'do good' capade that you think is going to make you sleep better at night, but I told you, it is my son, and my son only, that those pretty eyes are for. If you think no one's watching you, if you think I don't have eyes on you at all times, you're wrong. When—" I cut him off.

"You're wrong."

"Excuse me?" He tilts his head.

"You're telling me you have eyes on me at all times, even at night? Here? Tell me, Bleren, what do I do when I'm all alone at night in bed? Hm?" I tilt my chin up, daring to look at him in his cold, black, and loathsome eyes.

"You're playing with fire, Ember. Pull it back." The voice of reason has great timing.

He has a good way of getting under my skin.

"Your father was right; you do have a forked tongue." He smirks, as though it pleasures him to know I'm not all good. I'm not all sweet. I'm not all pleasant. "Semantics. Your room is your privacy, yes. Interrupt me again. I dare you." He pins me with a stare I don't dare match; instead, I nod.

"You touch or so much as share a knowing look with River that makes it back to me; you won't see him again, is that understood, Ember?" His grip tightens on my chin. At the sound of the threat, the blanket is ripped off the box, and my magic comes flooding out. The torches in the hall glow brighter, and the fireplace grows to a steady roar.

"Pull it back in, Ember! He's doing this to rile you up! Breathe and think about the damper again. Slow, deep breaths and tell him you understand. NOW." Her roar echoes inside my head. She's circling overhead somewhere in the clouds above the castle. I pull the magic back in the box, envisioning that blanket, smothering the flames inside me. With the damper, the torches and hearth die down to their original flickers. Everything becomes quiet and soft again.

"Yes, Bleren," I submit, clenching my jaw as I look away from him. Satisfied, he releases me.

"Good. Glad we had this little chat. You look pretty today; my son got lucky," he drawls, sounding the perfect mix between charm and authority—the opposite from the menacing scorn he was seconds ago. His eyes flicker toward my hearth for a moment before they come back to me. I wait until he finally walks away with his hands in his pockets.

"That was stupid and risky, and you have got to keep a better wrap on your emotions. You can't just let your magic out every time someone threatens people you care about," she scolds.

I don't just let my magic do anything. It does it on its own sometimes. For instance, that was all on its own.

"How long have you been storing magic inside you?" She practically halts her flight. Footsteps sound down the hall, while mint and earth fill my senses. Instantly my body starts to relax as River's door opens and Aris comes into view around the corner.

Since I was a little girl, roughly five years old. I hardly ever used it until recently—just little spurts here and there to help me with things. The last several days I've been going to a meadow to practice and let off the tension. It helps so I'm not losing so much control, but it still happens from time to time. Exhibit A.

"Good morning, Ember." River's deep, rich voice hums in my

chest. My eyes travel up to his damp curls and those swirling ocean eyes. "Was that the king I heard out here?"

"My father was here?" Aris asks before I can answer. Aris smiles at me, his sharp canines flashing with his dimples, a duo that melts me straight to my core. Gods, they took their time making these two. He's fumbling with the button of the sleeve to his white tunic, a change from his usual all-black, but it suits him. I reach forward, taking the sleeve for him and buttoning it.

"Just stopped by to make sure I was feeling better was all. He apologized that the food made me sick and said that one of the other lords in his court got sick last night too. He also made some suggestions on a couple towns for us to add to our tour." The lies roll off my tongue smoothly. Aris stares at me like I've grown four heads and seven eyes.

"He must be in a good mood today. It's about time he's shown you some good hospitality. You look like you're feeling way better; it must've been a bad cut of meat you two ate. I'm sorry, love." Aris takes my hand, brushing his lips over my knuckles before pulling me down the hall. "Let's go to my office. I have a map, and I had the servants set up breakfast for the three of us in there."

"How nice of you to think of me," River drawls from behind us. I snort, making Aris chuckle.

"Don't get used to it, brute," Aris mutters.

"They're a jolly time together."

Tell me about it.

"Using and not using your magic is going to be a lot more diffi-cult than I imagined." Asteria lands somewhere in Atravelien again; our tether taut but not unbearable. She is further now, having covered a great distance in mere minutes.

Why is that, and where are you? Aris opens the door to his office, guiding me in toward his desk with a hand on my back as we enter. River closes it, his posture stiff and tense as he looks around.

The room is much bigger than I expected. It's round, and

where walls should be, there's bookshelves built in. Windows alternate with the bookshelves, casting rays into the room. Dust particles sparkle as they hover in the air. He has a golden globe in one corner and a telescope in one window pointed toward the sky. Papers are splattered across his desk, but in the center of the room is another table at which he is now rolling out a massive map of Klyeria. Breakfast has been neatly arranged carefully on his desk behind him.

"All magic folk, dragons, Erelt, any creature born with magic in their blood, are born to use it, Ember. Not store it. It is a delicate, finicky balance we all learn. You haven't just learned control; you've learned isolation. You've caged your power. While these sessions in the meadow may help relieve some tension off the top, you have sixteen years worth of pent-up magic dwelling in your veins. How you haven't lost complete control is beyond me.

"When an Erelt tries to gather too much of their power by storing it, they usually lose their sanity and become dark magic wielders. Which is one of two ways to go dark. Their power becomes them and takes the reins, driving their motivations. There's almost no way back from that once that happens. Your kind can try to subdue them and heal what's been broken, but there's no guarantee. We're going to need to start expending larger portions of your magic. At night, you'll take rides with me further away. I'm on patrol for now, so enjoy your eye candy. If you need anything, I'll still be within reach."

You're just going to drop all of that on me and leave?! I have more questions!

"Aris just said something to you." My head snaps up from where I was staring out the window toward Atravelien, as if I could see her flying over the forest miles and miles away from here.

"Huh?" I ask, my cheeks reddening a deep shade.

"I asked where you went just now; you had this far off look." Aris chuckles, pulling me over to the breakfast table.

"Just had my head in the clouds for a moment. Thank you for

this." I take a bite into a buttery croissant, the flakes crumbling down my chest. *Heavens,* this is exactly what I needed. Silently, River hands me a cloth napkin, which I take graciously.

We spend the afternoon planning a two-week trip to travel throughout Klyeria. Where we'll stay, who we'll visit, and who we'll take with us. We spread ourselves as thin as we can across the map while still making it back in time for the final month of preparations for the wedding. The guest list, decorations, food, my dress, music, etc. There will also be a celebratory ball, a final hoorah to celebrate us one final time before the traditional ceremony takes place the next day. It seems excessive to me, but the king insists both days are tradition here. I understand now why we need the month to plan both of those festivities.

Then my fate is sealed. Peace is brokered between two warring kingdoms. The sword is put down, and the soldiers will return home. My hand in marriage to Aris is the power move that Bleren deems worthy to say enough is enough. So we will travel through the kingdom and sell our love. I won't spare a glance at River, but he'll protect my back. He'll be there at every corner, in my every shadow, his scent always mingling with mine. I'll protect him by pretending he's not tied to my very being.

I even take the time to write to my court back home, apologizing for leaving without a proper goodbye. I explain that there were circumstances that led to a quick leave, but that I missed them dearly, wishing that it didn't have to be this way. But this is necessary to save us all, and I hope one day they'll understand that. I ask how they've all been, eager to know what's been going on in their lives.

Viola, how are you and that beautiful girl of yours doing? Robert, did you ever get over that hangover from the Winter Solstice ball? Jane and Jasper, do I hear wedding bells? Daisy and Sierra, there are some dresses and jewelry I left in my room; they're yours if you want them; you'll know which ones I'm talking about. Cameron, talk to Jasper about the idea you had on harvest and taxes; your economic knowledge is incredible. Easton, I left plans for the kingdom in my desk; share them with the court when you all are ready to take over.

I let them know that I'll be gone in the next month but that I can respond until then.

Aris finds me someone who will make the journey discreetly and hand deliver it to Jasper for me, but my heart doesn't settle. Thinking of home makes the constant ache in my chest feel even worse. Jasper's goofy grin flashes through my mind; memories of us running through the halls with Chef Jean's brownies in hand plague me as I walk back to my room. I shove it back, knowing I'll never have that again. It's not worth reminiscing, no matter how much the sting of never getting to say goodbye to my best friend eats at me night after night.

CHAPTER 26

THREE WEEKS LATER

"Y*ou'll need something to wrap around your face; it'll get even colder for you where I'm taking you this time.*" Asteria is back beside the castle, and though she's invisible, I can practically see her glowing emerald eyes watching me through my window as I get ready in the nearly pitch black room. But thanks to my sharper vision, everything is easier to find. The boys bid me good night half an hour ago, and I think it's safe now to make my leave with Asteria. I find a small, black silk scarf I can tie around my nose and mouth while grabbing the knit hat Aris gave me and tugging that on.

Anything else, Your Highness? I let a shadowy tendril lift the window open, climbing out more gracefully this time before letting it shut it. My hearth flickers with a low fire so I can return to a warm room.

"*You could've brought me the spare meat from dinner,*" she grumbles, her hunger never ending.

Right, and then I could explain to the servants and cooks that the reason I was carrying arms full of meat was because my dragon outside never stops eating. Rolling my eyes, I stroll up to where I think she's kneeling. She comes into view, and my breath is stolen

348

from me. I will never get used to seeing her, even if it has been almost a month now.

Even in just the moonlight, she glistens, her scales changing different shades of green as she moves, her muscles rippling as she lowers herself further for me. Slim and serpent-like, with claws that could cut through anything like butter—she's an absolute force to be reckoned with.

"As much as I appreciate the adoration rolling off of you in waves, we have to go, Ember. Climb up." Her leg stretches out, her claws digging into the earth. It's hard getting a grip while I climb up her leg with her being so slick. Swinging over, I find the divet and sit as comfortably as I can, finding it's almost a perfect seat, as if it were made for me to sit there. The spike along her spine provides a sort of backrest, and the one in front of me, between my legs, is almost like a pommel.

Are you all designed to be ridden? I ask in wonder, realizing that where I've been sitting is almost too perfect. Before she answers, she launches into the air, not preparing me for her takeoff or when she turns invisible again. I bite down the scream that nearly escapes my throat when it looks like I'm about to fall straight through hundreds of feet down to the ground below me, but her warm body stays steady beneath mine. I squeeze my legs to a tight hold on her as she races upwards, the scarf I tied around my nose a nice barrier between me and the cutting wind ripping at my face.

Opening the box just a tad, careful to leave the blanket intact, I form an invisible shield around me, keeping the wind from slashing at my face and drying out my eyes. It comes second nature, the shield, as if putting up the barrier to keep myself safe is something I should've been doing all along. Asteria shutters a little beneath me, banking to the right as we fly over Atravelien.

From up here, I can't see where the forest starts or ends; it looks like it goes on and on for eternity. A large mountain range juts out in the distance at the eastern edge of Klyeria's borders. With the moon overhead, the mountains cast a shadow over that part of Atravelien. It's rumored that's where the nastiest of the creatures dwell. Asteria aims toward the mountains; now far enough away, she becomes visible again. My heart settles more now that I'm not staring straight through to the ground below.

"No, but dragons that are born to be bonded are born with a saddle-like genetic formation. Since bonding is so rare, no one noticed it on me, so I didn't think anything of it. Not until I started to feel your presence out there on my patrols." She starts to descend, banking toward a valley that sits between the four mountains, entering through a narrow passage between two of the peaks. Violent shivers rack my body as the wind becomes more hostile.

When did you start to feel me? Did you tell anyone? I lean forward as she nearly nosedives toward a clearing in the large field, and at the last second her wings flare back out, bringing us horizontal once more as she lands with swift grace. Despite that grace, my heart is still in my throat and my stomach's in my ass. Careful of her spikes, I slide down her leg, landing on the ground wearily.

With the mountains surrounding us, the valley is bowl-shaped. The field at the bottom lies flat and barren due to the harsh winds pushing down the mountains. There's only one entrance, and that's the passageway we entered through. Otherwise you'd have to climb or fly over the mountains themselves and the sheer size of them—well, that'd be no easy feat, not even for Asteria at those heights.

The full moon shines brightly overhead, illuminating the landscape for us. At the base of the northern mountain lies a frozen lake. Peering closer, it looks like a frozen waterfall pours from the mountain itself into the lake, and from the lake, a river snakes through the passageway into Atravelien. Asteria takes me under her wing, protecting me from the wind while we look up at the stars for a moment.

"Well, I suppose I should start by telling you how long dragons have been back. Or that we never really left—not all of us at least. As you know, we began to overpopulate. Us dragons are eager, horny creatures, and we live a long *time. So, we started to overcrowd*

Ereltis, and while your kind is crucial for us—they help birth our hatchlings—they rightfully didn't appreciate us eating their livestock.

"So we agreed to eat beyond the wards. Ereltis is big—bigger than Klyeria even, but that just shows how many of us were being born. The humans also didn't take too kindly to us eating their food either. We tried to eat the creatures in the forest instead, but we could only eat so many because most were poisonous. It was our fault, this predicament, and when the humans became successful in hunting us, we had no other choice but to leave.

"The humans had killed over a third of us. So, one third left for Holarthia, and the rest stayed in Ereltis. When the war started forty years ago, the Erelt and our Elders sent word to send dragons who had the power of invisibility. It's a rare ability, and they needed scouts for the perimeter of the wards. So I was sent with only ten other dragons, and the rest stayed. I watch the outer edges of the wards to make sure none of your soldiers breach them. Not that they can; only Erelt and magical beings can cross in and out of the borders. But on the unlikely chance, we're there to stop them from making it too far.

"Ereltis lies between both kingdoms, and the Erelt King worried that sooner or later we'd be discovered or that curious soldiers who'd read the stories would try things they shouldn't. Ereltis has found peace no other land has; peace kingdoms could only dream of. The Erelt King would do anything to protect the tranquility he's fought so fiercely for them to have.

"Which is why you don't make sense, Ember. I've asked, and no one has heard of a missing Erelt child. So you're not a long-lost daughter, but your parents aren't Erelt. Or they are and they don't have powers, which is possible because not all Erelt are born with magic. It's possible they left and brought you to Agatharea, but that seems far-fetched. All I know is that you had to have been born within the wards. I started to feel you when your powers started to mature. Your very first time using magic, you sent a wave throughout the entire forest.

"*I remember I wasn't the only one who felt it, but I knew that you belonged to me. I couldn't come to you because you weren't in Ereltis—you were in Agatharea. Magic being used outside of Ereltis is not encouraged, but you're not the first or last Erelt to leave or be banished. So it's not uncommon. Then I waited. I waited to see if you'd come to Atravelien. You'd come on the outskirts, but never close enough. When you made the trek across to Klyeria, you were right on the border of Ereltis—you felt the pull. I almost went to you then, but you weren't alone, and it would've been dangerous for you.*

"*And now here we are. Tonight I want you to grow this entire field of flowers and melt the waterfall, the lake, and the river. Then I want you to burn it all and do it again. After that, we're going to spar. I'm going to use your magic against you until you feel some semblance of exhaustion, and I don't mean physically. You'll feel it* inside *you—a heaviness. You haven't felt that yet, and I'm hoping tonight you will. We'll go all night if we have to.*" She lets me absorb everything, lets me lean into her, and lets me soak in silence for a moment.

I listen to nothing but the rushing of my own blood in my ears. Shutting my eyes, I search inward, looking in on that box where all that pent-up magic dwells, where it's covered and sleeping. I've worked so hard to keep it hidden, to keep this integral part of me isolated, caged even. To find out I was never meant to do so hurts more than I thought it would. I was supposed to grow up learning how to control it, to use it in everyday life, to *love* it— not be ashamed of it. Not cower from it. Instead, I grew up with parents who hated me and made sure my life was like living in all of the hells. With a final exhale, I open my eyes.

I only have two questions before we start today.

"*I was expecting way more.*" She snorts—actually *snorts*. "*But go on.*"

How is Ereltis so big if it lies in the small space of Atravelien between Agatharea and Klyeria? And does the continent of Holarthia have Erelt there too? Otherwise, how would your hatchlings be born?

"Really? That's what you want to know?" She asks skeptically.

I don't have the emotional capacity for anything else right now.

"It's the way the wards are enchanted. When you enter, you'll see that the space you've entered is an entirely different plane of existence. Sort of like a portal, but not quite. There are guard posts suited with Erelt guards who have a specific magic for the wards. They are the only ones who can let someone who is not Erelt in and out of the wards by opening a portion of the border for a moment. As for your second question, yes, there are Erelt on the other continent as well. That's how we knew we'd survive going over there. But we learned our lesson and have far fewer children." She lifts her wing, letting me out.

So you all don't fuck? That seems like a miserable existence for a species that lives centuries. I lift the mask back up, protecting my face from the cold, and roll my shoulders back.

"Have I ever told you that you have a filthy mouth for a princess? Dragons can still get creative without procreating." Her tail slithers suggestively, and I can't help but laugh at the onslaught of mental images she flashes for me.

I did NOT have to see that. Also, you're in my head. My head has always *been a filthy place.*

"You most certainly did need to see that. Now, field of flowers. All at once. Go." She takes a couple of steps back, giving me space I don't particularly need. The lid comes completely off, the damper staying in place on my senses while my magic fills my veins to the very brim. It warms me from within, and feeling comes back into my fingers and toes as I wiggle them in response. *"Easy does it."* Asteria warns, her claws digging into the earth behind me.

Does my magic bother you? You shuttered earlier too.

"I don't tell you this to scare you, but you are probably the most powerful thing to walk this planet in a long, long time, Ember. Your magic is a lot—even for me to handle. I'm just getting used to the feeling when you open yourself up. It's made it difficult for me to use, so I've stuck to what I know, but it's made my earth powers even more powerful. Dragons and Erelt can sense magic in each

other and other species unless they are really good at keeping it undetected, such as yourself when you store your magic away. But when you open yourself up, the power in you is like no other. It has no shape, no specificity—it just is. *It's raw and undeniable. Erelt have specific powers, one unique thing each can do, sometimes two, in rare cases three. I originally thought you just had many gifts. After our training sessions, I now know there's no end to your capabilities. Again, I find myself telling you that you're unexplainable."*

The tether between us shines with pride that flows from her in waves, filling me to the brink. There's a certain bitterness and sweetness to what she's telling me, but I appreciate it nonetheless, letting her feel all of my gratitude before turning back to the field.

I direct my magic into my hands as I kneel, planting my hands on the frozen ground. Closing my eyes, I focus very intently on an image before letting a wave flow through the field. The ground shutters before all at once, and thousands of flowers sprout, growing with quick ferocity. I can tell that what I wanted worked even just standing on the ground.

Fly up and take a look. She doesn't question me, taking a leaping takeoff above the field until she's looking down on the flowers. Throwing her head back, she lets out what can only be described as a dragon's delighted laugh. I made the flowers sprout so that they'd create a picture of her from above, or at least what I hoped would look like her. *Did I get you right?*

"You gave me a bigger butt, but I'll take it. A pity you'll be burning it later, but now we can have fun with it. Lake next." She loops upside down before landing in the same spot behind me.

The magic in me continues to pour from the box, singing with freedom as it comes out in waves instead of the trickles I'm used to. Holding my hands up toward the lake, I rotate them, and with the rotation, the ice comes undone, groans and creaks echoing off the mountains. It takes a moment to get it fully thawed since the ice is more than a foot thick, but I get it there. Suddenly, the water is splashing onto the shore. The waterfall gushes into the lake, and the river roars along against the jagged rocks. I accidentally thawed it all at once.

"Impressive. But you have to be more intentional; be more focused and specific, like you were with the flowers. If you're directing your magic to an area, a person, or a group of people, you want it to go where you want it. Not where it wants to go." She steps forward; this time I can feel her magic as she opens what I imagine is her own version of a box. A rush fills me, dancing alongside my own magic as they intertwine like old friends. Suddenly six fully grown oak trees sprout from the ground in a row. *"Walk over to one."*

I choose the fourth one and stand in front of it. A second later, the branches are moving as if they've come alive; one whacks me across the legs, sending me to the ground. Another wraps around my ankle, pulling me up to hang me above the ground, turning my entire world upside down.

ASTERIA WHAT THE FUCK? I try to pull myself up to grab the branch wrapped around my ankle with no luck.

"You have powers dummy; use them. We've been over this." She sits off to the side, perched like a cat, wearing a smile I wish I could wipe off. Shadowy tendrils flow from me instantly, and I use one to slice through the branch holding me up, sending me to the ground with a thump. Immediately another branch is reaching for me, but I'm up on my feet before it can wrap around my other ankle. A blink, and the oak in front of me is engulfed in flames.

But what I don't notice are the vines crawling up from the ground. Suddenly, my arms and legs are wrapped up, and I'm on my back. They tighten to a strong, unbreakable hold while one wraps around my neck, cutting off my air supply. With the sudden fear of my own death, all I can think of is my survival. I grab the vines around my wrist, twisting my hands to grip them, and instantly they die beneath my touch—shriveling back up into the ground. With my hands free, I take hold of the one around my neck, and that dies too. I free my feet and, with my frustration, set fire to the remaining oak trees that had now formed a circle around me, surely to beat on me had I not escaped the vines.

Stepping past the flaming trees, I set my eyes on Asteria, who cocks her head to the side as if to claim innocence. Letting the shadowy tendrils loose, they slither along the ground, covering the field between us in darkness before swallowing her in a black cloud. When I wave it away, she remains with her four limbs tied down by the tendrils. The bruises on me have already healed, but I still want to get even. Curling my hands at my side, I beckon large rocks to roll down the mountains.

"You wouldn't," she hisses.

Would I? You just choked *me. You have magic; avoid the boulders, Asteria, or get smushed.* I step back, beckoning the air to push them faster while holding down on her restraints. Asteria struggles against them before deciding to try and redirect the boulders toward me. I anticipate it though, creating divots in the ground to curve them toward her again. She chuffs angrily.

Her eyes suddenly focus on me, a predatorial glint flashing through them before her throat starts to glow. She roars, sending hot *green* flames at me across the dozens of feet that separate us. Quickly, I put my hands up to protect myself, a wall of shadows going up that deflects the fire, causing the fire to travel upwards toward the sky instead. With the shield of shadows protecting me, she gets released, and I hear her launch into the sky, the boulders whooshing past where she stood. She lets that dragon laugh out again, the mountains rumbling with her. I can't help but join her, clutching my stomach from laughing so hard.

"The fire wouldn't have burned you," she admits once we've calmed down enough, landing in front of me.

How come? A flame flickers in the center of my palm, and I focus on changing it to different colors. Blue, purple, pink, green.

"You're still wearing the shield you put up earlier. Shielding is something most, if not all, Erelt with magic can do. It can protect you from things like fire and air. It can't protect you from physical objects. It's not full-proof, but it does come in handy. I would never

mess up that pretty face of yours." She nudges me with her head, which I run my hand over. Her scales are smooth, and her horns are ribbed as they curl up.

You think I'm pretty. This causes her to huff.

"*Don't ruin the moment,*" she mumbles. I caress her jaw as an apology.

Do you have a mate? Sisters? Brothers? What are your parents like?

"*Burn the field and grow an orchard of apple trees, and I'll tell you,*" she commands.

Aye aye, captain. I release her, doing as I'm told. Turning back to the field, I let that hum fill me again, sighing in relief at the constant release. Fire comes easiest. It's the quickest connection my magic has, and in less than a breath, the entire field is ablaze in white fire, burning so rapidly that the flowers become ash floating in the wind.

"*No mate, yet. I'm still young, so there's still time to find him or her. I just worry they're back home in Holarthia. Two sisters, two brothers, and I'm the eldest of them all. My parents are loving and knowledgeable, but also stubborn and paranoid. They tried everything to get me out of coming here, but there's no denying the Elders.*"

They sound wonderful; I'd love to meet them one day, somehow, someway. I'll keep my eyes out for any eligible bachelors or bachelorettes. She snorts, rolling her eyes.

"*As if.*"

Asteria uses the wind to push the ashes away from us, sending them floating toward the mountains beside us. Pushing the magic into my fingertips, I kneel, forcing my hands into the earth, focusing on conjuring rows and rows of apple trees.

One after another, neat rows of bountiful fruit-lined trees sprout from the ground, growing tall and groaning as they come to full fruition. I stare in awe as a realization dawns on me—a realization that brings me to my knees and cracks my chest wide open.

My kingdom was burnt to ash, ridden to poverty and starvation, and were slaves to overtaxation by my parents all while I sat warm inside the castle with this ability. This ability that I buried so deeply, so profoundly, for years and years when it could've saved them. It could've saved families. *Children*. I could've kept them fed, could've provided warmth in their hearts, maybe saved some of those burning cities. And instead I sat on top of it and let them suffer, while I selfishly cried over what seems like such small problems now compared to theirs.

"Your parents' hatred and abuse of you is no small thing, Ember. You cannot blame yourself for not being able to save your entire kingdom as a child. No one can blame you for that. There is no telling what revealing your magic would have done. Do not be so harsh on yourself, my dear." Her warm breath blows over my hair as she nudges my back softly, a simple gesture to let me know she's there. I stay silent for a moment, not entirely sure I agree, but I do lean back into her nonetheless.

I will do better. Hesitation seems to roll off her, as if she still doesn't quite agree with me either, but she doesn't say anything further on the matter.

"Return the trees to the ground and refreeze the water. We need to leave this place as it was. I think we've done enough. During the day, I want you to continue to keep up the shield. When you're outside, play with the wind; it's the least suspicious thing you can do so you don't get caught. Light your own fires when you're in your room. You see where I'm going with this, don't you? You need to start doing more. We haven't done enough lately, but I think we're getting close to at least finally getting you in control."

Yes mom. She chuffs, nudging me harder. I chuckle weakly, catching myself with my hands, saving myself from face planting. Staying on the ground, I focus on pulling the trees back into the soil, absorbing them back into the earth. The scorched field still smolders in some areas, so I beckon some water from the river, smothering the burning embers of the fire. Hissing and steam fills the air, swirling around us until I'm satisfied that the water has done its job. I level the field with the same grass it had before, layering it with frozen dew to finish.

Rising to my feet, I focus on the water next, raising both arms to pull on waves of my power to freeze the river, waterfall, and lake all at once, intentionally this time. Loud cracks and groaning fill the valley as the water turns to ice, becoming still once more.

I stare at the barren land, feeling inward simultaneously. There isn't quite the exhaustion or heaviness Asteria was talking about. Instead, I'm no longer filled to the brim; the waves in me are calm and collected. They're within my control and not thrashing about, not screaming to be used and let out. The work we've done over the last few weeks has chipped at the well within me slowly but surely, allowing the turmoil to rest.

"It'll have to do for now. We'll keep working at it until it's at a more sustainable level. Let's get you back." She turns, leaning so I can climb up again. The flight back is silent but not uncomfortable. She lets me think, lets me process everything we talked about, and offers me quiet support instead. Waves of comfort are sent down our tether that soothe me into a calmer lull when we arrive. But when she hesitates from landing, even when she's invisible, I know something's wrong.

hat is it? She circles over the castle as I look straight through her to it below. I let the damper off, focusing my senses on my room specifically. My ears perk up, picking up on someone sitting, no—lying on my bed. I breathe deeply, the wind carrying his scent to me—a dirty musk. I lay the blanket back down. *Dracyl. He must be waiting for me to sneak back in so he can catch me and report it to the king.*

"*What do you want to do?*" She flies back toward the woods, landing in the shadows to cloak us.

I can make it back by foot. If I can find Aris' window and wake him, he'll help me get back in my room. He'll probably yell at me for being out, but it's my only option. I'll just tell him I was in the stables with Bedelia because I couldn't sleep, and he can tell Dracyl that we were together because we couldn't stay away or something like that. I pull up the mask, covering my mouth and nose as I survey where the guards are. Aris' room is on the opposite side of the castle from mine—all I have to do is follow our tether.

"*If it wasn't so bloody cold, I'd say just strip and go invisible, but you wouldn't be able to explain that to Aris, and you'd probably lose a toe or two. But go, go. I'll wait here until you've made it safely, and then I'll return to my post."* I slide off of her carefully, touching her cheek softly before running like the hells are chasing.

I tug on the tether, and it warms beneath my touch, borderline purring under my attention as I follow it around the corner of the castle. Two guards begin to round the following corner, walking toward me. *Fuck.* Skidding to a halt, I slam my back against the wall of an alcove. Rippling open the box, I drape myself in shadows, covering myself completely so they can't see me at all. They walk past, completely oblivious, and round the next corner. I let out the breath I was holding and keep running until I come to a harsh stop at a particular window, my gut telling—no, *pulling* me to it.

Miraculously, a candle is still lit. He's lying in his bed with his arm tucked behind his head, the other holding a book. His chest is bare, revealing sculpted muscles and a chiseled abdomen leading to a pair of black silk pajama bottoms. With no time to spare, I tap on the window softly, not wanting to spook any guards nearby. Aris' head snaps up, the book quickly shutting close. He's on his feet instantly. A dagger, from I have no idea where, is in his hand as he stalks forward to the window. It doesn't make a sound as he lifts it.

"Aris—" I'm cut off as he wraps his hand around my throat, yanking me forward. I realize that all he could probably see from inside was some random person in a mask tapping at his window. Instantly I tuck my chin down like he taught me, dropping my weight to keep him from cutting my air supply off.

"Ember?!" Immediately he lets me go, quickly sheathing the dagger into the waistband of his pants. I climb into his room quickly, closing the window behind me. "What are you doing here?" I tug the hat and mask off, running a hand through my hair to try and calm it somehow.

"I couldn't sleep, so I went for a walk and ended up in the stables with Bedelia, but when I came back to my window, Dracyl was in my bed. So, I came here. I don't want him to go back to your father making up some twisted lie that I was out doing something I wasn't, but if I show up to my room with you, he'll leave me alone." It all comes out in a panicked rush with my hands waving around and me pacing back and forth.

His room is set up identically to mine, except his decorating is much darker compared to the light decor in my room. It's meticulously clean, each book placed in a pristine manner, no clothing strewn anywhere, and I'm sure he makes his bed every morning. He takes my hands, stopping my pacing, causing me to look up at him through my lashes.

"Dracyl...is in your bed?" He speaks lethally calm, his thumbs rubbing softly over my knuckles, making me swallow.

"Yes." I bite my lip, unsure of how much of that anger is directed at me and how much is at Dracyl. He doesn't say anything as he releases me, walking toward his armoire. He takes out a pair of boots, shoving them on. I watch in wonder at the way his back muscles move, practically drooling over the way they ripple when he puts a black shirt on and then his cloak to cover it all. He turns to me, raising an eyebrow. I shrug, not bothering to hide that I was checking him out.

"Let's go," he bites. I gulp, walking hastily to his door. We make our way down the hall, a possessive hand laying on my back as his heat seeps all the way to my skin. Doing my best to act unaffected, I follow him to my room, the trek uncomfortably silent until we reach my door. The guards pay us no mind. It's just the princess and her betrothed after all; of course we'd be together this late.

Aris' fingers curl around the fabric of my coat, pulling me against him as he opens my door, slipping into that charming, seductive prince he wears so well. It's easy to follow his lead, to lean into that slightly drunken stumble into the room, to try and stifle my giggles. He's pressing a finger into my lips, quieting his maybe not-so-sober fiancé when we just happen to notice Dracyl standing near the hearth, arms crossed. Aris' entire demeanor changes, going from enraptured to shaking with anger. In less than a breath, Aris has Dracyl pinned against the wall, clutching him by the collar of his tunic.

"What the *fuck* are you doing in here?" he growls, his tone dripping with poison that'd have killed Dracyl right there and then.

"The princess wasn't in her quarters; I was simply here to question her on her whereabouts," Dracyl deadpans, as if he couldn't care less about this conversation. I glance at my bed, which has clearly been disturbed, and when I look closer, my stomach drops all the way to my toes.

To a normal person's eyesight, they may not have noticed, but to my enhanced vision, there's no missing the pair of my lace panties discarded on the bed. On them is a white sticky substance illuminated by the moonbeams through the windows. One look at Dracyl's pants, the hasty tuck of his shirt, and the unbuckled belt is all I need to confirm my worst nightmare.

I cover my mouth, afraid I'll vomit right then and there. Something in me shatters. I had tried to build myself back up since my father whipped me. Piece by piece, putting myself back together with the help of River and Aris, and now even Asteria, but somehow, this one act, and that all has come crumbling down. At the bottom it's cold, dark, and the whispers are loud. Years and years of being taught I was pathetic, worthless, and good for nothing roar back to life.

Whore, slut, filthy tramp. Lie down and open your legs. Take it like the slut you are. You'll just be a pretty face on the cover. I should've killed you a long time ago. You're a disappointment, Ember; you'll never be good enough. Nothing you do is good enough. You're too fat. This is how you make yourself throw up: take your fingers... Skip lunch. Don't eat so much. Look at Sierra; now she is a pretty girl. It's a pity you're so ugly. I fucking hate you.

"Ember... Oh Ember, please snap out of it." Suddenly Asteria's voice breaks through the onslaught of voices berating me. I realize all I've done is stare at the panties, unsure of how much time has passed. Not much, it seems, because Aris hasn't moved. Asteria

sends waves and waves of soothing comfort over me, which helps bring me somewhat to the surface. I pull myself up the rest of the way, forcing myself to be fine.

Dracyl tracks my stare at the panties and smirks, proud of his little present. My power flickers in me, nothing compared to the rampage it might've been before. I'm in control. This is good. *I'm in control. I'm okay; I'm sorry I don't know where I went just now.*

"I will incinerate him where he stands; he will never breathe again. But you're not okay, and you don't need to pretend with me." Asteria growls, her own anger seeping out into me. I reinforce the fortress around my mind, but it's just that her wrath is so powerful I can feel it wash over me from the outside.

You can't touch him, Asteria. I lean against the wall, watching as Dracyl turns back to Aris with a smug look of satisfaction.

"Why not? He can't get away with that!" Her roar fills my head, and if her roar could be heard, the entire kingdom would be cowering.

The king won't have it. It is my suffering for the greater good. Two kingdoms' peace for whatever I must endure.

"How did you know she wasn't in here to begin with? What are you smiling about?" Aris slams Dracyl against the wall, wiping that smile off his face.

"I came to ask the princess a question, and when she didn't answer, I came in to make sure she was okay. When she wasn't in her room, I decided to wait for her to ask her where she'd been on behalf of the king. To ensure she wasn't with any ill-fitted suitors." Dracyl once again makes eye contact with me over Aris' shoulder, a glint flashing through his eye. The light pouring in from the torches in the hall illuminates his face, granting me a clear view of how he looks me up and down.

"I will kill him," she declares.

We will do no such thing.

"Ember, what am I missing here? What isn't he telling me?" Aris' grip tightens, and from here I can hear his heart quicken. Even Dracyl swallows in fear, wondering if I'll out him.

"Tell him."

Why?

"Ember, tell Aris, or I will burn Dracyl. Those are your options." If it weren't for the conviction in her voice, I wouldn't listen to her, but I believe her. I believe she'd turn Dracyl to ash at first sight if I didn't tell Aris right now.

"My bed, Aris, look at my bed," I offer in defeat. I push off the wall, moving with a slight stumble to keep my act up. At the nightstand I light the oil lamp, illuminating the crumpled sheets. The underwear lies on the other side of the bed, closer to him. He turns, looking at the scene before him, dragging Dracyl with him to get a closer look.

There are no words to describe the fury that floods the tether between him and me. Dracyl anticipates the punch before I do, putting his hands up to protect his face, but even that's not fast enough to stop the blow from landing directly on his nose. A sickening crunch sounds through the room while Asteria lets out a satisfied growl. But Aris doesn't stop, and Dracyl doesn't go down without a fight.

Dracyl lands on his back, but as he goes down, he lands a punch across Aris' mouth, busting his lip. Blood blossoms, but he doesn't care, not as he finally pins Dracyl down and begins to deliver blow after blow. Try as he might, Dracyl can do nothing but try to protect himself against the wrath that is Aris. A door opens across the hall and footsteps rush in, but I'm so lost in the bloodshed, in the vengeance, that I don't pay attention to River at first. There's something about my honor being defended that has me rooted in place. He touches my shoulder, catching my attention finally. I drag my eyes away from the bloodied face of Dracyl to the bedhead of curls in front of me.

"Are you okay?" he asks in a rush, dropping his hand from my shoulder. I miss the touch instantly.

"I was out at the stables with Bedelia; when I came back to my window, he was in my bed. I went to Aris' room so Dracyl wouldn't think I was up to anything." I look up at him, and he nods, understanding what I mean. "When we got here, we pretended to just be getting me back from drinking. Aris started questioning him when I noticed... I noticed that while he was lying in my bed, he'd used a pair of my underwear to pleasure himself. Hence the bloody pulp he is now." I glance at Dracyl, who's unconscious now, but Aris hasn't slowed down. I push River to the side, moving to Aris. I know River noticed, but River seemed content to let Aris continue.

"Aris, you have to stop. You'll kill him," I murmur softly, placing my hand on his shoulder. He flinches beneath my touch, his hand cocked back to deliver yet another blow, but he hesitates, his knuckles raw and a bloody mix of Dracyl's and his own.

"He deserves to die." River's the one who speaks first, his voice nearly a growl.

"If I'm not the only one who thinks he should die, then killing him should be the right answer."

Asteria.

"How can you have mercy on him?" Aris asks, looking up at me with gutted eyes.

"I don't want your father to be angry with you," I say simply. "Have the guards collect him; the servants can change the sheets, and everything will be fine. You taught him his lesson; let us move on." I offer him my hand so he can stand; he looks at it and then me, disbelief written all over him. River scoffs softly, equally in disagreement.

He takes my hand, rising from Dracyl's unconscious, unnaturally bent body. His face is swollen, beaten to almost the same unrecognizable condition it was in the dungeons back home. It serves him right and soothes a small part of the large ache in my heart. Guards are called in, and quickly he is gathered and discarded from my room. His blood and bodily secretions are cleaned, and it's like none of it happened within minutes. People pass in and out of the room like a blur.

My hearth gets lit at some point, and someone's taken my coat, scarf, and hat for me. Aris' knuckles are wrapped, and his lip gets cleaned. Suddenly, it's just us three again. River leans against the wall beside my door, Aris against my desk, and me against my bed, playing with the mess of waves cascading down my side.

"So are you going to tell us why, yet again, you were alone?" River asks, crossing his arms. I want to roll my eyes at him, not wanting to fight this fight again when Aris answers.

"Let me handle it this time." Aris looks at River, and whatever he sees in Aris's eyes has him listening without hesitation for once. River looks at me, dipping his head in a bow.

"Goodnight, Ember. Get some rest." His eyes flicker to the bed, hot red fury flashing before he walks to his room across the hall. The tether between us pulses with rage and longing so fierce it has me following him just to close the door behind him, lest I go after him.

I know the anger isn't directed toward me; I know all he wants is to protect me and to hold me. Tonight he could do neither. Tonight, Aris will do both. I'm sure that's exactly how Aris felt when it was the other way around. I can't keep doing this to River. No matter how much he says he can take it, he deserves better than half of me. They both do. But why do I feel for them both so fiercely? Why do I burn beneath River and feel completely electrified by Aris? Why don't I want to give them up? How terrible of a person does that make me? I think I really do deserve any of the suffering that comes my way.

I lean against the wood trying to prepare myself for this argument when suddenly my body is trapped against the wall. For the third time tonight, I find myself getting choked. One of Aris' hands wraps itself around my throat while the other plants against the door as he pins my legs with his by digging his knees into my thighs.

"*Ember!*" Asteria's voice rings in my head, panicked.

I'm fine. Butt out. I shut her out completely, shutting the door that lets her peek in.

No fear comes—not an inch of it. It didn't come earlier when he grabbed my throat either because I'm not scared of Aris. He wouldn't hurt me; I've learned as much from our training, and this feels no different. If anything, and I'm sure he'd kill me if I told him this, but with his hand wrapped around my neck and his body on mine, it's a total turn-on. He's not even completely cutting off my air supply. He lowers his mouth to my ear.

"You can't walk around all alone, Ember. I know I'm training you, but you're not ready yet. You may think you are, but it's too dangerous. I could be anyone, *anyone* trying to hurt you." He applies more pressure to add to his point, and part of me has to fight from smiling up at him. "Come find me next time you can't sleep. I'm the only one who should be seen with you late at night anyway." His grip loosens just a tad, and his focus is on me and my pretty, little mouth—not my hand reaching into his waistband, drawing out the dagger from earlier.

Quickly, at a speed he can hardly detect, I duck beneath his arms, using more strength than he knows I have to shove him against the wall. The air whooshes out of him as I use my left arm to pin him across his chest, while my other hand holds the blade to the base of his neck. I press hard enough so he feels the sting of the steel, but not enough to draw blood. I can only do this because of Asteria; otherwise, before her, I had no such strength or speed. Even now, my moves are hardly as graceful as they could be. He's right; I'm not ready, but I won't admit that to him.

"I. Am. Not. Weak," I growl, staring him in the eyes. "I did not retrieve you because I thought I couldn't handle him. Not because I'm some damsel who always needs saving. He was practically *salivating* to catch me with River or someone else for that matter so he could run off and tell your father. I was saving us the headache."

"Had you stayed in your room, none of this would've happened to begin with. Ever since that villager tried to kill you, I can hardly sleep. All I have is nightmare after nightmare of you ending up on that man's sword. Sometimes it's Dracyl's, or my father's. Sometimes it's my own because I'm so fucking scared I'm going to get you killed I can't stand it—the thought of you out there alone and unsafe." His voice turns raw, soaked in pain I don't recognize. Pain rooted from a wound deeper than this.

"I'm alive, Aris. I'm here. I'm safe and well. I know how to protect myself thanks to you; it's why you're teaching me. That man *failed*." I pull the dagger from his neck, dropping my hand to my side, taking a step back to release him fully.

He stares at me, waging a battle with himself because I know he doesn't agree with me. River was there to save me, and he still doesn't think I'm well trained enough, which, he's not wrong; I still need some work. Okay, maybe a lot; I will never be some crazy good assassin. I'm strong, sure, but physical strength means nothing if I don't know how to properly fight. But, I'm not a caged animal either. I'm not a dog to be leashed or a horse to be stabled when I'm not with my handler.

"You're not weak," he repeats gently. The words settle between us quietly. He pushes off the wall, towering over me as he reaches down, prying the dagger from my fingers. I let him have it reluctantly. He uses the tip of it to tip my chin up, the cool steel causing goosebumps to spread over my shoulders. "You're strong; in fact, you're *too* strong. You're so fucking stubborn, and so godsdamn beautiful."

He flings the dagger onto the bed behind me, grabbing my face with both hands before kissing me with a ferocity he hasn't allowed himself before. Electricity zaps through my entire body, lighting up every single one of my nerve endings, sparking something inside me I hadn't known was dormant. What shattered in me stirs. Our tether warms, glowing and humming as he grips the back of my neck and holds me by the waist, opening me up with the flick of his tongue. The taste of blood makes me pause.

"Your lip! Doesn't it hurt?" I ask, pulling away. He chuckles softly, a sexy, breathy sound that has me curling my toes.

"Ember, pain is nothing compared to the pleasure your lips give me. Now kiss me, dammit."

I willingly give him anything and everything, intertwining with him with a soft moan. He groans in response, flipping us around, placing me back against the wall. His hands travel down my sides, under my thighs, to lift me up. I oblige, instinctively wrapping my legs around him. My own hands find his hair, tangling in his locks, tugging softly. He nips at my bottom lip before trailing kisses down my neck, leaning me further into the wall so his body is fully flush to mine, every hard part of him connected to me.

More, I need more. There are too many layers of clothes between us, and I need his hands in more places. He sucks on the sweet spot between my neck and shoulder, right above my collarbone, and I can't help but throw my head back. *Gods, there's nothing like him.* I squeeze my legs, desperate for friction, for anything, as he drags those sharp canines of his up the skin of my neck, biting my earlobe. It pulls another soft moan out of me, which he smothers as he brings his lips back to mine.

He pulls me off the wall, gripping me by my bottom, squeezing it hard like he's been dying to have his hands on it, but it's when he starts to walk toward my bed that everything inside me freezes. Panic sets in, gripping my heart, squeezing with all its might. I try to shake it off, act unaffected, but it's too late because he's felt it, and he's already setting me down. Breathless, I stare at the floor, unable to look at him or anything else for that matter.

"Princess, look at me," he whispers, gathering my hands in his. Embarrassed, I look up at him. Tough act over. "We'll burn it and get a new one."

"Where will I sleep?" I raise an eyebrow at him.

"It's good we stopped when we did. I'd say my room, but you're too much of a temptress. So, let's have a sleepover in the library. I used to do it all the time as a kid; the couches are really comfortable, or we can make a fort." He rubs his thumbs over my hands comfortingly, speaking in a sweet tone. I have half a mind to groan in frustration; every single part of me is on overdrive, pulsing with need for this distraction, but then, as if on cue, a yawn escapes me.

"The couches sound nice, but we'll have to make a fort in the future when we come back from our trip. Let me get changed. What about pillows and blankets?" I release his hands, traveling over to my armoire to grab a long-sleeve nightgown.

"There's some in the library already; I always have the servants keep some in there just in case. Especially now that you're here and reading all the time," he admonishes, half smiling, which gives me one dimple. I return the smile before pulling the warm sweater off. He takes a sharp breath but doesn't turn away. I didn't want him to anyway.

I kick off the boots and toe off the socks. Even going so far as to take my time rolling down the wool leggings before standing in nothing but my matching blue lace undergarments. He stuffs his hands into the pockets of those silk pajama bottoms, the black shirt stretching across his chest as he drinks me in unapologetically. Pieces of his hair have fallen onto his cheeks but he does nothing to move it as his eyes trail across my abdomen, up the slopes of my breast.

When his eyes meet mine, I don't break contact as I reach back and undo the clasp of my bra, letting it drop to the floor in front of me. The air is cool, spreading goosebumps across my chest, making my nipples harden. I swear I can see Aris' pupils dilate from here. This is cruel punishment, teasing him like this, but gods is it fun. Plus, knowing that he thought it was good we stopped definitely is a disappointment because I obviously didn't stop because his dad wants us to wait.

Putting an end to the striptease, I slide the nightgown on, which goes to my ankles. My breasts still stand at full attention, which he makes no apology for acknowledging. I slip my feet into some slippers and put on a robe for extra measure.

"There's a nightly show if you enjoyed that one." I wink at him before sauntering to the door, leading the way to the library. He's quick to follow after a few muttered curses and a second to adjust himself. I hide my smile as he catches up, slinging his arm around me and kissing the top of my head.

"Just so, so beautiful," he mutters more to himself than to me, but it warms me all the way to my toes nonetheless.

He shows me which couches are the most comfortable before retrieving pillows and blankets for us, setting everything up—insisting I can't lift a finger. I let him take care of me, even though it feels like too much. I fight off the feeling of being undeserving, but it keeps snaking its way up, settling in my chest. Peace for two kingdoms at the hands of my suffering seems fair enough. Yet here's this beautiful man, setting up makeshift beds for us so I don't have to sleep on my decimated one.

"There we go, I'll sleep right across from you. You won't be alone. Tomorrow we'll replace the other one, and then in just a couple more days we'll be out of here, far, far away from him. Okay?" He tilts my head up, rubbing his thumb over the line of my jaw.

"Okay," I whisper. He plants a soft kiss on my lips, a whisper compared to what he gave before, and it's hard not to take more than what he's giving.

"You know you're my undoing, Ember; go easy on me," he breathes against my lips.

"Then don't make it so hard on me, Aris." I brush my nose against his. He chuckles, leading me to my bed for the night, letting me lie down before putting the blanket over me. He kisses my forehead, blows out the candles, blanketing us in darkness, and settles into his own makeshift bed.

"Goodnight, beautiful," he whispers softly.

"Goodnight, handsome," I murmur. I open the doorway in my mind to check back in with Asteria. *I'm alive.*

"The tether is still in place, so I figured as much. What was he trying to accomplish?" Her tone is pissy, and I'm too tired to explain, so I replay the memory for her until he kisses me. *"It was just getting good!"*

Goodnight, Asteria.

She chuffs, annoyed. *"Goodnight, Ember."*

CHAPTER 28

ONE WEEK LATER

"Maybe you should stay here," I find myself telling River softly enough for only him to hear while we watch the servants take my bags out of my room. We're finally leaving for the first village on our tour, and it's a day's trip away in a province northeast of here.

"Why would I ever do that?" He turns and looks at me. I don't meet his gaze; instead, I continue to watch the servants bustle about as I stand there near the hearth, gathering warmth before we trek deeper into the cold. *"You won't see him again."* The king's threats echo through my mind. Ghosts of River's pain and anger days before flash through me, making me close my eyes for a moment.

"River I can't put you through—" I'm cut off by Aris popping his head into the doorway, a goofy grin plastered on his sweet face. *Wonderful timing.*

I've decided that instead of trying to have them both, letting them both go is the better thing to do. Aris and I can pretend for the masses when we're in public, but after we're married, once we're behind closed doors, he can be with whom he pleases, and River can have a normal life. River can find a wife, build a home, and maybe have children if that's what he wants. He can't have that with me if I keep stringing him along.

I don't deserve either of them.

Aris can choose his own love—not have it chosen for him. And even though he's my mate, somehow chosen for me by fate, by design, I can let him go. No matter how much I'm drawn to him, drawn to them, they're better off.

"You're wrong."

We talked about this. And are you always listening to my thoughts?

"*No,* you *talked about it, and I told you that there are ways to work through it. You're just too hard headed and so self-deprecating you can't see it. You're spiraling and taking them down with you. Your father really did a number on you, my dear. I can feel the internal wounds in you. And I only listen when you leave the door open.*" Her voice is quiet, sadder than I've heard it before. I can't find it in myself to respond; instead, I shut the door. The white, raised scars on my back flicker with ghostly pain as if they're being redelivered.

"Are we ready, folks? If we hurry and leave, we can avoid my dad. River, do you ever look happy? And please tell me you bathed; I don't want to be cooped up in the carriage with a grumpy *and* a stinky old man." Aris walks toward us.

"I did. Did you? Or did your servants have to do it for you still since you're not old enough to do it on your own yet? Poor baby has to have everyone wait on him hand and foot, right? Gods forbid he breaks a nail. Don't worry; you'll be a man one day." River crosses his arms, his sword bumping into my leg as he shifts his weight. I roll my eyes, not dignifying either of them with a response. Instead I grab the novel I checked out from Zephyr and walk out of my room, leaving them both behind.

"What did you do to her?" Aris asks River accusingly. River scoffs, walking in stride with him.

"Nothing. Nothing at all. She's been down for days. My birthday was the happiest I've seen her, but then she was right back to this yesterday. I know you had her bed replaced. But that's not going to fix what he did or how he keeps hurting her. I don't think she's been sleeping," River whispers softly, and with normal ears, I wouldn't be able to hear, but I focus with my heightened hearing, listening for Aris' response.

"I know. I just wanted her to be able to sleep in her own room." He sighs softly.

"He decimated a space that should've been safe. She had a night guard back home; maybe you should appoint one here," River says pointedly.

"I changed her locks. I only had three keys made. I was going to give you one and one to her in the carriage. She needs some semblance of independence here; a night guard outside her room is too much," Aris retorts, which I appreciate.

That does help give me some peace of mind. I haven't seen much of Dracyl since that night, and the king hasn't bothered me either. Aris wouldn't tell me what the king told him once he reported what happened. I'm not sure I want to know anymore.

"Does that mean you have the third?" River asks incredulously.

"Who else would have it?"

"Why do you need it?"

"She's going to be my wife, River. Ask yourself your dumb questions before you ask me anything." Aris shakes his head, done with his conversation with River. He goes and checks that all the carriages are ready, speaking with the head servant about the checklist of items he'd prepared.

"You're not putting me through anything. I have a job to fulfill, Ember, and I can't do that if I'm here and you're there," River says from beside me, softly enough only I can hear with only a foot of space between us. Princess and guard, nothing more. Nothing less.

"Look me in the eyes and tell me it is not hard to watch me with him. Tell me that when we parade around, selling our love to this kingdom, it will not pierce your heart that it is him and not you. That when we find an inn, and I lie with him at night and you are forced into a bed alone, you will not stare at the cold spot in the bed where my body might lay. Look at me, River, and tell me. I'll let it go if I'm wrong. But if I'm right—and I know I am—then I'd rather go unprotected than continue to hurt you." I look up at him, watching him watch Bedelia, who digs a hoof into the ground. He doesn't look at me.

He can't.

He won't.

"I'm not leaving you, Ember. But I will not lie to you either. I told you, I know the bed I chose to lie in. But if it is him you choose, all I want is your happiness, and I will always respect that." His voice is raw, and it takes everything in me to will the tears to stay back.

"I'm choosing neither, now. I'm choosing to pretend for the kingdom. It's not fair to choose one way or another. It's not like I'm going to be a real queen here. I'm just a political pawn. I planned on telling Aris tonight when we got to our first room. It's easier this way." I fiddle with my hands, staring at the ground now, watching as a tear splatters on the gravel.

"Easier for who?" It's not River who responds. I hadn't noticed he'd come up behind us, but now Aris is right behind my left shoulder. I had been too caught up in my own stupid pity to pay attention to know how much he'd heard. "Carriage, *now*. We can still avoid my father if we leave now." His tone is clipped.

I don't disobey, not wanting to see his father either. Quickly, we file into the carriage in the same order as when we arrived here. This one is roomier, with benches on both sides, so I quickly choose to sit on the side facing them both before they can argue otherwise.

There are three carriages in total: one for us, one for other guards, and one for some servants, including Layla. Melody said she gets sick on carriage rides that last too long, so she stayed behind.

Asteria will fly over us, albeit slowly, and she'll go off to hunt whenever she needs. The Elders agreed to let her leave her scout duties for the two weeks we'll be away so we don't have to worry about being too far from each other and becoming ill without one another. Where she's going to hide is another thing entirely. Invisible dragon powers are great and all, but she's still large, and I don't know how many cobblestone roads are large enough for her to be on without someone accidentally walking into her.

They all begin to move, and at the same moment I watch as the front entrance opens. Bleren walks out, but it's too late; we're too far gone. I breathe a sigh of relief that I don't have to hear another warning.

I stare out the window, unable to look at Aris or River. Exhaustion plagues me from a long night of no sleep. Nightmare after nightmare of my father and Dracyl taking turns torturing me in different ways found me every time I closed my eyes. The shadows beneath my eyes are so dark they look like bruises.

"Where is this coming from?" Aris asks, breaking the thick silence.

"You don't have to see either of your faces every time I'm with the other. I can practically feel it, the way I'm hurting you both." That's not a lie. I *do* feel it. "Letting you both go would be doing you a favor. I'll marry you, and River, you can still be my guard if that's what you want. But you can rotate with someone else and live somewhere else, build a home, and build a life with a wife. And you, Aris, you can bring whoever you want home. You can actually choose who you want to love, not have her chosen for you. I can just be the public face, and when the time comes and your father wants a baby, we can make one for him. But other than that, you don't have to see me; the castle is big enough to make sure of that." I look down at my hands folded in my lap, curls falling into my face. Asteria told me I didn't have to choose either mate.

I can set them free.

"You don't get to choose for us. Don't we have a say in this?" Aris asks softly.

"You don't get it, Ember; we don't want any of that," River says earnestly. I close my eyes, not wanting to hear this, not wanting to be convinced otherwise. I'd already made up my mind. I didn't deserve them. I don't.

"How could you want me?" I ask, my voice cracking. "Don't you want more for yourself than a woman who only has half a heart to give you? I'm too close to getting you killed, River. I don't deserve either of you." The last part comes out in a strangled whisper; more tears slide down my cheeks. I shut my eyes, trying to stop them.

"That's the thing. You don't give us each half your heart. You somehow manage to give yourself to us fully. I'll be damned if you think either of us is just going to let you go. We may fight with each other, but we don't fight over you, Ember, because the one thing we can agree on is our feelings for you. It pains me that you think that you don't deserve to be loved because you are worth so much more than you know," Aris argues, his voice firm but loving.

"I would have failed in this life if I hadn't tried loving you, despite his orders. You're worth every risk there is to take—including my life. You can choose both of us or just one, but neither of us isn't an option. It's not going to be easy, but we'll make it worth it," River promises, and I can hear it, the conviction in his voice. I nod, wiping the tears away silently, still staring into my lap.

There's no denying them, not when both tethers are beaming within me, pouring into me wave after wave the adoration and affection they're trying so dearly to convince me they feel. It washes over me head to toe, soothing the crack in my chest. It's almost overwhelming.

"Come here," Aris says quietly. I look up then, finally making eye contact with them as they watch me. Gods, they're so beautiful, I could weep. I look at the space between them, hesitating.

"Now," River commands softly. I gulp, pivoting to slide between them, my bottom sliding against their legs as I lean back.

We're all wearing thick cloaks to keep us warm in the carriage on our trek to the first village, but it's already growing too hot here with their manly body heat. Aris closes the curtains on his side, and River does the same, cloaking us in dim morning light.

"Do you understand now that everything you thought and had decided was nonsense? That you can have us both, as long as you are very, very careful? It'll be easier after the wedding once my father's attention is off of us. River and I can handle it. Right?" He looks at River over my head.

"Precisely." River nods.

"I understand that everything I thought and decided was sensible, but upon rethinking it, I have changed my mind." I crack a smile, which makes them both chuckle.

Aris dips his head, kissing me deeply for a moment, stealing my breath away. I throw my hand down, and it lands on River's knee, steadying me. He tastes like winter, his lips cold like fresh snow, but his tongue is warm like a fireplace, and I can't get enough. Before my body can recover from the currents of electricity pulsing through me when Aris pulls away, River grabs my chin, pressing his lips into mine. My body bursts into a fiery inferno as his tongue tangles with mine, pulling a soft sound from my throat. All too soon he's pulling back, looking at me with ocean eyes that have been set ablaze.

Holy heavens above and hells below. Did that really just happen? It didn't. Did it? The pulsing in my core would suggest it did, but my overactive imagination could be playing tricks on me.

"Remember that the next time you start to have doubts." Aris places a hand on my knee as he leans back, putting a foot up on the bench in front of him. River gets comfortable, taking the hand I had on his knee and intertwining our fingers.

"What if I forget? Can I get a redo?" I ask innocently.

"Don't push your luck," River warns, but the smirk on his face says otherwise. I can't help the smile that floods my face as I lay my head on Aris' shoulder, shutting my eyes. Sleep comes quickly. Peaceful, dreamless sleep—where I feel safest.

"I'm hungry."

You're always hungry. She growls, and if she were anywhere near me, I'm sure she'd snap her teeth at me. But we're a week into our trip and in the middle of the town square of a very busy city, Kora, in the very northern province of Klyeria. So she's flying high above us, invisible in the clouds.

"I'm going to hunt and find somewhere to sleep for the night. There's a forest off in the distance. I won't be too far." I can hear the flap of her wings, strong and steady, but no one else would be able to detect it.

Good, maybe that'll improve your mood. Be safe. She does the mental equivalent of sticking her forked tongue out at me and speeds off. I smother my chuckle, not wanting to look like an idiot laughing at myself as we weave through the crowd. This city has been my favorite from the moment we arrived. There's something joyous in the air, something electric I can't place my finger on, but it just feels *alive* in ways I haven't seen in others.

The streets are filled with vendors, and everyone has something to sell. Spices of all assortments fill the air, warm bread and hot cocoa drift from another, and freshly cut fish lying on ice sits in front of a man that's bartering a much too high price for his trout. When the villagers notice the royal crest on the guard's uniform, they move out of the way, bowing deeply for Aris and I. We bow our heads back, which typically shocks the absolute daylights out of them.

On more than one occasion, the guards, River included, have had to get physical with villagers who have gotten too volatile with us. Bleren's reputation has bled down to reflect on us. But that's the whole point of us going around and doing this: we want them to see our face, my face, and see that we *aren't* him.

I wander to a table where a young girl stands, no older than twelve years old, to see what she's selling. Spread on her table are watercolor paintings of animals, people, and insects. They're incredibly intricate and in a style I've never seen before, but so pristine and accurate I can't believe they're done by someone so young.

"You've done all of these? They're beautiful." I pick up a parchment painting of a fairy. The wings are that of a blue butterfly, the body is petite, rich caramel brown, and she has curly brown hair that reminds me deeply of Viola. The fairy is hovering above a pink tulip, as if she's about to go inside it for cover, and she's wearing a blue dress that looks like it's made out of flower petals. I'm suddenly hit with a wave of déjà vu that has me blinking and shaking my head to clear the fogginess. I look back at the young girl who fiddles with the beads woven into the ends of her braids. She averts her eyes, looking down sheepishly.

"My mama says I shouldn't paint things like that, but I thought the fairy was pretty. She visits me in my dreams sometimes." Her voice is sweet. The innocent kind of sweet that warms my heart and makes me forget what's going on around me for a moment. She peeks up at me, realizing who I am when she sees the guards behind me. The guys are a few tables down, not too far. She stands a little straighter, smoothing out her cloak.

"Does she have a name? Don't tell your mama I said this, but I think you should keep painting her." I wink at her, letting her know it's our little secret.

"She told me it was Sapphire. You can keep that one for free, Your Highness." She bows quickly, and I can't help but smile at her.

"My name is Ember; you can call me by my name, but as sweet as that is, I'd like to buy this one, and if it's not too much trouble, do you have your paints with you? Would you be up for painting, say, three more? Or would that be too many?" I reach into my satchel and pull out several gold coins, which could pay for anyone's entire booth, but this entire trip I've handed out as much as I could. Her eyes widen as they dash between me and my outstretched hand.

"My name is Auburn. Three is nothing! Once I painted fifteen paintings in one day. Who's first? You should go first. I have a seat; let me get set up. Oh boy, Mama is never going to believe me when I tell her this. She's sick at home, so I do this to help raise some money for food and medicine. It's not much, but it's honest work." She takes the coins, shoving them into her pockets as she hustles around her table, putting her other pieces aside to take out her paints and brushes. She pats the seat behind her table, and I oblige, pushing my curls behind my shoulders, leaving the shorter pieces to frame my face.

"Is it just you and your mama, Auburn?" I ask softly, already calculating a way to fit in a visit to her home and bring along the town's physician.

"And my baby brother, Harry. Papa is a soldier and hasn't come back yet. We're waiting for him to come home any day now since you're stopping the war. So, thank you for that. Oh! I need water." She smacks her forehead, her braids swooshing as she turns to find some.

"Hold on, I've got it." I look over to Theo, a blonde, young guard who's standing nearby. He's wearing the all-black royal guard uniform, with gold filigree on the lapels of the jacket, and at his side is his sword. But in various other places I know he has throwing knives and daggers hidden. Each guard is identical to this, including River. "Will you take this cup and fill it at the fountain in the square, please?"

He looks at the cup Auburn is holding and then at me, a smile cracking on his face. He's one of the easier-going ones, so I like to keep him near. The other is a hardass, which River likes because he won't let me get away with as much. Theo's buzz cut fades into the crowd, so I turn back to Auburn, whose face is lit with a huge smile.

"Are you always surrounded by really hot guys?" she asks dreamily, her personality really bubbling now. I smile at her, beckoning her to come next to me. She scrambles forward, leaning next to me to look where I'm looking. We both look toward Aris and River, who are talking to a merchant who happens to be selling knives and daggers. Aris throws his head back and laughs heartily, and River follows suit, holding a hand to his stomach as he cracks up at whatever joke the merchant just made. I watch, absolutely stunned, because never would I have ever thought I'd see them share a laugh together like that.

"The one with the curly hair is my personal guard, and then you know the prince is my fiancé. Does that answer your question?" I look at her sideways. She gawks very obviously, making me laugh myself.

"Consider yourself one very lucky princess." She practically drools, and I don't blame her. I glance back at the boys who are now paying for a few of those daggers and stroke the tethers—just a soft caress. They both straighten, and I stop immediately, wondering how much of it is a one-way or two-way street. Because I feel their emotions, and sometimes I send calming waves down our tethers, but I didn't think they ever really paid attention to what that might've been. What I just did might've been stupid if they can't explain what they just felt.

"Lucky indeed. And here's your water!" I smile thankfully at Theo, who simply winks at Auburn before returning to where he was standing at the end of the table. Auburn swoons for a moment before turning to her easel.

"Okay, Ember, don't move. This won't take long; you're very pretty, and pretty things don't take me long to paint," she says as a matter of fact, and I can't help but chuckle softly. "No moving!" I still my spine, looking beyond her toward Aris and River, who continue on to the next table. From beside me I hear Theo trying not to laugh at Auburn chastising me. I relax, letting my mind wander as she becomes focused and quiet.

They've bickered a lot. A lot of stupid, manly fights that often end with me telling them both to shut up or threatening to beat them. But they've also bonded in ways I hadn't imagined they would. They've had genuine conversations over pints of beer in taverns and have even managed to train in the mornings together.

I've seen a few cuts and bruises on each other, which I've been told are from sparring sessions. What I would have given to have watched those.

I would've been able to had I not gotten my menstrual cycle. I'd felt the oncoming cramps the day before we left, so I'd made sure to tell Layla and Melody to help me pack the proper items I'd needed. My cycle has always been different from other women's. I was taught to expect my cycle monthly. But mine comes every three months, and it only lasts two days. But those two days are spent in bouts of excruciating pain, heavy bleeding, and then suddenly it's over.

Asteria informed me that that's how the female Erelt always have their cycle. Unlike dragons who pop out babies whenever they want, it is difficult for the Erelt to conceive. It's a caveat to their long lifespan; therefore, their menstrual cycles are less frequent and shorter. I'm not sure what that'll mean once Bleren requests we start working on having children.

As Aris' betrothed, I'll be sharing a room with him the entire trip. Because of his insistence upon abstinence, he refuses to share a bed, insisting if we did, he'd cave, and therefore he can't risk it. Luckily for him, the rooms we've been assigned have had two beds in them, so we've slept separately. For the two days I was struggling with my cycle, he was incredibly caring. One mention of that time of month and he instantly assumed I'd be out of commission for several days. I am now in better spirits, of course.

One of those days was spent traveling, so I didn't need to put a brave face on, thankfully. The following day, I pushed through, smiling through the pain. Thanks to Asteria's healing abilities, I don't have any half-moon scars on my palms from clenching my fists so hard that my nails punctured my skin.

Things have shifted slightly between the three of us. In public, it's all about Aris and me, and there is no pretending involved. No matter what I tried to say before, I don't have to pretend what I feel for him. In private, which is usually in the carriage, River gets his share of me. Getting to hold me or brush kisses on my shoulder, neck, and lips. Doing the things that Aris gets to do when we're out. Don't get me wrong; we're not snogging in front of Aris, but he's not afraid to touch me when we're alone, or at least as alone as we'll get on this trip. Neither of them seems bothered by the other being with me anymore. I don't feel the jealousy down either tether like I used to feel.

River stays in his own room, one for the coachmen; the two other guards share, and the two servants share as well. Asteria has been the biggest issue, quite literally. There's not always a nearby forest. We've gotten too far from Atravelien for her to just fly over. It's not even that she can't make the trip—she can, but she refuses to leave my side. After Dracyl and the slip I made into whatever dark place I went—which I've tried to convince her was an accident—she just refuses. She insists that she wants to be minutes away, nothing more.

So if the inn is stone and strong enough, she's slept on top. If there's a nearby farm large enough for her to lay off to the side, she stays there. There are forests and valleys we've traveled through, so she'll travel back to those when she can. It's not ideal, but we're making do, and despite how much I insist she doesn't have to, deep down she's healing the open wound festering inside me. Thankfully, there's a forest nearby for tonight.

Like it always does, my mind wanders back to my mates. The unsettled warning I received a couple of days ago echoes in my mind again. *"If you try to save them both, you will lose both of them. There can only be one in the end,"* the fortune teller told me while holding my palms face up. We'd been walking around a traveling circus set up for the evening when we passed a black tent decorated in moons and stars.

"Your Highness," a sensual, wise voice had called out. Puzzled, I had looked at Aris curiously, who shrugged and nudged me to go in. "Just the princess," the woman had said. River and Aris hadn't been pleased but stood guard outside with Jared and Theo. I walked inside and was met with a dimly lit interior cluttered with candles, books, and crystals of all sorts littered around the tables. At the center of the tent was a beautiful woman with tan, golden skin. Her black hair was thick, long, and pulled into a braid that fell over her shoulder.

Her eyebrows were thick, and her lips plump, while a golden chain fell across her forehead as it sat pinned in her hair with a blue gem falling just between her brows. In front of her on the table was a single candle lit to brighten her features and a plain tablecloth.

"How'd you know I was out there?" I asked skeptically and had taken the seat in front of her, placing her fee on the table.

"Isn't that what I do?" she'd asked, tilting her head with a sly smile.

"Or you heard four sets of swords clinking as they walked with one soft set of footsteps." I quirked my eyebrow at her. Her smile only grew.

"I knew I'd like you." She placed her hands on the table face up. "Your hands, please. It is how I read." She wiggled her fingers for good measure. I divulged. I wasn't sure at the time how much I really believed in fortune tellers, but the night had been young, and I was curious.

I wish I had stayed away.

"What do my palms say about my future?" I asked. She shushed me as she focused, her grip iron tight as she stared into my hands, into whatever my destiny was telling her. Whatever fate she could read me. Her eyes kept dashing back and forth as if reading a book side to side, only growing more frantic as she went on and on before releasing my hands as if they'd burned her.

"You may take your money back, Your Highness; I have nothing good to offer you," she said and had begun to clean her things up, as if she was done reading for the night.

"What? What could you have possibly seen that was so bad? Please, you have to tell me," I begged, suddenly a believer. Whatever she heard in my voice had her pausing, and she had listened, had conceded because she took my hands again, and read me my fate.

I wish I had stayed ignorant like she'd warned.

"I feel a great deal of pain in you, and a great deal of power locked inside as well. Those two will come to the surface soon, and the answers you are searching for will come to light. But be wary of a mask. You have two lovers bound to you. If you try to save them both, you will lose both of them. There can only be one in the end. Fate isn't weary. It does not hesitate. It does not bow. But *you* will make kingdoms bow, Your Highness. You will experience great loss, but you will gain great peace. Only if you respect what fate has in store for you." As she finished, a haze left her eyes, as if she'd gone somewhere while she'd read to me and then returned. I nodded, thanked her for the reading, and gave her an extra gold coin before exiting her tent to stare at River and Aris.

I'd felt like my whole world had been pulled out from beneath me. There was something so strangely real about what she'd said, because how could she know any of those things? A good guess? Could she read me that well? Was I that gullible?

Asteria said that some humans were more in tune than others, so maybe she was onto something. We could take her warning into account and be wary, but Asteria also warned me not to worry too much. River and Aris asked me to tell them, but I had refused, had told them it was only meant for me. I didn't want to say it out loud anymore in fear that the more I spoke it into existence, the more it would solidify my fate.

That sucks me back to the present to see Aris tucking his hands in his pocket, talking with one of the villagers who doesn't look as happy, but Aris listens intently nonetheless, nodding vigorously before responding. River stands nearby, watching the villager's hands. His face is calculating; his entire demeanor is observing and absorbing. It's as if he's a predator waiting for his prey to mess up so he can pounce. Aris shifts, one hand coming out to gesture as he talks. That natural charm radiating off of him is enough to charm every woman in this street into his bed tonight. With River filling out his uniform better than any of the others, I find myself suddenly wishing I was alone with them both.

The villager eventually calms down, however, at whatever Aris is saying. I'm about to lift my damper so I can focus my hearing a little better when Auburn gasps softly. My eyes shift to her instantly, squinting just a tad because the sun is shining brightly on us, illuminating the deep brown tones of her skin.

"Your eyes... The sun makes them look like they're glowing! I've never seen eyes like yours before. Painting them was my favorite part. I'm almost done!" She turns back to the parchment, continuously glancing back and forth between me and her art.

"*Your eyes don't look like they're glowing; they ARE glowing! It's not even your power; you're basically the equivalent of a dragon going into heat, and worse than any dragon I've been around, get a grip. Now,*" Asteria yells into my head, nearly giving me a heart attack.

CHAPTER 29

Auburn casts me a weird look when I flinch at Asteria's sudden burst back into my psyche. She likes to come and go as she pleases, which I suppose I could do a better job of keeping the door closed, but there's a part of me that enjoys her constant company. Moments like these, however, make me want to throttle her.

What should I do? Is this more Erelt shit? I keep my chin tilted up toward the sun until I can figure out how to make the glow go away.

"It could be, or you could just be a horny bastard. Your type is complicated when it comes to procreation. I don't know everything. Just think about something terrible, like foot fungus."

Your morning breath will suffice.

"Bitch."

Love you too. I open and close my fists, emptying my head of all the fantasies and impure thoughts, instead thinking of the rancid carrion smell that wafts from her throat when she wakes, and just like that, dry spell indeed. Opening the box, I keep a blank face as I gather a wind far, far above me. Slowly, I aid the clouds to drift toward the sun quicker than they were before, and with their descent over the sun, I blink the glow out of my eyes.

At last, they return to their normal color, hot burning coals, or burnt embers of a dying fire. That's all it was, Auburn, a trick of the light. The box clicks closed inside of me, purring like a cat, happy to have been used.

I've been toying with the wind while we're outside, letting that be my main way of release and the least inconspicuous way to practice my magic without being caught. It's not always enough, but it's something.

"Finished! Aw, the sun's gone, and now your eyes aren't glowing anymore. I still captured the glow in the painting! Who's next? We'll let this dry while I paint them, and you can do more shopping or whatever princesses do." She beckons me to look, so I stand, stretching momentarily before coming beside her. The gasp I release startles her, but I can't help it. She did capture my glowing eyes, but she also captured my wanting gaze without knowing it. I don't know how she's done it, but she's managed to paint me in a way I've never seen myself; no mirror could've captured this. I grab both of her hands and look her in the eyes.

"Auburn, you're extraordinary! You have a rare talent that people would kill for. Don't ever let anyone put you down or sell you short of what you're capable of. You're capable of anything and everything. The world is at your feet. You hear me? You keep doing this. Don't stop," I say loud enough for only her ears to hear. Her lip quivers, but she nods, taking one hand away to wipe a tear that escapes.

"Yes, Your Highness," she whispers.

"Ember." I raise an eyebrow at her.

"Oh yes! Ember, right. We're on a friendly basis here," she adds quickly. Two warm presences walk up behind me, peering over my shoulder to look at the easel.

"I'm going to need you to paint that on parchment ten times bigger so I can hang that in our room at home. You've managed to paint the most gorgeous woman in the most beautiful way," Aris says, his voice a silky caress against my ear as he stares at the painting. River simply hums in agreement. It's a soft sound, one only I catch with my heightened hearing. I turn with Auburn so we can face them.

"While I agree, because you're right, that'll cost you." Auburn crosses her arms with a proud smile. I mimic her, raising my eyebrow at Aris.

"Oh, I'm prepared for whatever the cost may be. That right there is priceless." But he's not looking at the painting; he's looking at me. Auburn practically swoons beside me, and I have to elbow her to keep up her bargaining act. She clears her throat.

"Wonderful, we'll discuss prices after your paintings are done. Which of you boys wants to go next?" She looks between River and Aris, who both look at me in surprise. I shrug innocently. I wanted paintings of them too. Aris ends up going first, getting sucked into negotiations with Auburn, who starts her price at two hundred gold coins, nearly making Aris choke. River and I laugh as we walk off, perusing the other merchants while we wait.

"What were you looking at?" River asks, turning sideways to avoid two men carrying an entire pig on a spigot, causing his chest to brush my arm in the process.

"What do you mean?" I glance up at him, furrowing my eyebrows.

"While she was painting, what were you looking at? That look on your face. I know that look." There's a slight husky undertone to his voice that I don't think anyone else would pick up on, but instantly, I do.

"The both of you." I stop at a potter's table, eyeing a particularly interesting design for a pot, unsure of how a flower or plant would ever fit inside. River keeps a safe distance from me, nothing more than a guard watching over his princess. He eyes the potter, who smiles sweetly at him. He simply nods back. I almost have half the mind to knock him over the head to be nicer.

"What exactly were you thinking about?" he asks as I keep walking, his voice soft enough that only I can hear it, yet bold enough that I find myself glancing back at him. He quirks an eyebrow at me, as if silently urging me to go on.

"There are too many listening ears for me to repeat the contents within my head in those moments," I murmur back, pausing in the street as people mill about, paying us no mind.

"Bedroom eyes," he says, looking down at me. He's still several feet away; we're nothing more than two friends having a conversation.

"I beg your pardon?" I tilt my head, crossing my arms, waiting for him to explain.

"What she would've named the painting if she was six years older and knew what that look on your face actually meant," River murmurs, before turning, leading us to another table. I stumble, staring at the back of his head for a moment, stunned. This *man*. I quickly recover, gathering my cloak and dress in my hands to follow him.

"Am I that readable?" I ask once I've caught up. He glances down at me over his shoulder, a smile playing on his lips but never fully. Always so serious, my River.

"Like a book. You get a little pout in your lip when you're upset about something. A furrow in your eyebrow when something's irritating you. You have a few other tells, but I'll keep those to myself." He moves along again, frustratingly good at keeping his composure cool and collected. I groan and circle back toward Aris and Auburn to check on her progress just to see that she's done.

She's captured his signature half smile, that crooked, charming smile that reveals one dimple. For a moment I honestly contemplate leaving a guard here for her to have the rest of her life. Someone to protect her and her gift because she's *that* talented. At twelve, or at least that's what I assume she is, this is what she's capable of; imagine what a few more years will do.

"I think I understand why he wanted one ten times bigger," I whisper to her as we both look at the painting together while Aris still sits on the seat, watching us both perplexed.

"Me too," Auburn sighs softly.

"You forgot the booger hanging out of his nose," River says as he strolls up behind us, making Auburn giggle. Aris glares at him, wiping his nose on his sleeve regardless of the fact that River was obviously joking. This makes Auburn laugh even harder.

"I think it's your turn, and I shall take milady for a stroll. Auburn, we will return with those little cakes I promised you." Aris rises up behind the table. He sidesteps, glancing at the painting finally and halts midstep. "Oh, oh wow. That's incredible; you've made me look even more handsome."

"Alright, big head, move on," River grumbles. I take Aris' hand, tugging him along as Auburn places his painting beside mine to dry. He intertwines his fingers with mine, pulling me close as we head straight for the bakery.

"We need to make a detour before we go to dinner with Lord Partlet tonight." I peek up at him in hopes that he won't fight me on it.

"Where might that be?" He peers down at me as he holds the door open. Theo takes the door for him, trailing behind us silently.

"We'll also need a physician for this mission. So we'll need to find one, preferably before we return to Auburn, as I'd like to collect her and leave as quickly as possible so we don't delay ourselves any more than I already have." I bite my lip as we take our place in line. The divine smell of vanilla wafts over me, making me hum in delight.

"Go on," Aris says wearily.

"Her mother is sick, and her father is a soldier off who knows where. She sells those paintings for medicine and food. She looks like she's barely twelve, Aris," I plead.

"I suppose Lord Partlet can wait; he's not exactly pleasant." Aris cracks a knowing smile at me, the kind that lets me know I've won.

"I just want to help them as much as we can before we leave. Plus, none of your father's court is pleasant. These dinners have been abhorrent. I almost stabbed myself with a fork during Lord Harold's story about his mother's porridge recipe and how he misses 'dear mummy's milk.' I mean, the man's nearly seventy years old!" A disgusted shiver runs through me.

"Some men will always love to have their mouths on women's breasts." Aris shrugs. Theo coughs, trying to cover his laugh, but he's doing a poor job as his shoulders shake silently anyway.

"Such a dirty mouth," I mumble, shaking my head.

"You love it," he purrs.

"I'm sure your mother had a wild time trying to tame you as a child." I raise my eyebrow at him. The light in his eyes flickers, and immediately I regret having brought her up. I go to apologize, but he starts talking before I can.

"She used to chase me down the hall with a wooden spoon. She didn't even cook; she couldn't; she was terrible at it." He chuckles sadly. "She would ask the chef for one whenever I was up to something and whack my behind with it. I used to tell her when I was king that I'd banish all of the wooden spoons in the kingdom. No more spoons for her, oh no. Then she'd tell me, 'When you're king, Aris, you're going to change the world.' And I believed her. There's a small part of me that still does." We both take a step up in the line, nearing the case of a wide assortment of cakes and pastries. Sorrow drifts down our tether, making my chest ache for him. I rub my thumb over his knuckles softly.

"What did she look like?" I ask, but we have to pick out our desserts first before he can answer. I let Aris choose since he seems to know what's the best and what's not. He buys what seems like way too much, but between Auburn, Harry, and Aris, I'm sure it'll disappear quickly. He takes the bags the baker provides us, and we exit back onto the cobblestone road, walking slowly back toward her table.

"She had long, silky, straight hair, white as bone, and violet eyes. Her name was Kaya. She was beautiful. I really looked nothing like her; I obviously look a lot like my father, but I inherited a lot of her traits, like her quick wit and a weakness for sweet things." He winks at me. *Such a flirt.*

"How'd she end up with your dad then?" I ask in disbelief.

"My dad wasn't always like this, believe it or not. Back then, the law said the king had to marry royal blood. My mother was not of any royal lineage when he met her in this very city, and he was instantly drawn to her. She had a very unique appearance; between the hair and the eyes, you'd spot her a mile away. They fell for each other right away, and they fell hard. He loved her so much he changed the law for her. Nothing was going to stand in his way of marrying her and making her his queen. It was after they had me that things changed. She loved being a mother, loved being *my* mother, and I think he resented the fact that she loved someone other than him. It turned him into something else completely, someone she didn't recognize." He pauses.

At some point we'd stopped walking, instead we're standing off to the side as the city passes us by, oblivious to the fact that their future king is watching them. I haven't taken my eyes off of him, too lost in his voice, in what he's telling me. I don't dare interrupt him, letting him take his time before he continues.

"I didn't see it at first. He was so fucking sneaky about it that no one else knew but me. He never hit her face, never touched a hair on her head, but I know he wrecked her body. His anger was... It was monstrous. He'd only ever take it out on her. Even though I was the one who ruined their marriage—I was his heir. So his affections shifted. I begged him one time. Begged him to take me instead. I was Auburn's age. It was the last time I saw my mother alive.

"I remember she had smiled at me. She'd told me I was such a strong boy, her strong king. She told me one last time to banish those spoons and change the world. He'd heard her, heard those last words, and I know in my heart he killed her because of them. He told everyone she passed away in her sleep from the sickness he always told them she had. The kingdom mourned their snow queen, with the violet eyes and the penchant for cinnamon cakes from Kora's square bakery. I learned to do my father's bidding so that one day...one day, Ember, I might banish those spoons and change the world." His voice is raw, his eyes full of unshed tears he seems unwilling to let go. He looks down at me, a sad smile spreading on his face when he sees my own tears streaming down my cheeks.

He sets the bags of pastries down, which I now realize are probably full of those cinnamon cakes, and the thought pulls a tiny whimper out of me. So much about Aris starts to click into place. The incessant dedication to following his father's rules, no matter how much they hurt us. What he meant when he said he'd recognized the look on his father's face the day I'd snapped back at Bleren. He takes my face in his hands, using his thumbs to wipe the tears away.

"Aris, had I known—" He cuts me off instantly.

"No, none of that. I don't talk about her enough, and it feels good to share her with you. She would've loved you. You both have this way of making a room feel alive when you walk in. I think it's why I was so drawn to you the moment I met you." He gazes into my eyes for a moment, leaving something unsaid, something for later. I tuck it away. "Enough tears; let's go get Auburn and help her and her family." He dips his head, kissing me in a way that makes the world go silent for a moment. For a moment there's nothing but Aris.

WE NEVER MADE it to Lord Partlet's manor. We made sure to send a messenger to him, excusing our absence, explaining that we lost track of time with the villagers but that we hoped he understood the image of the crown is more important.

Auburn's mom was worse off than I had imagined.

The medicine that they could afford with the checks sent home from their father wasn't the correct kind to treat the infection crowding her lungs. I'd never heard such a horrible cough before, and it pained me thoroughly to see her in such pain. Even then, she did what every good mother does; she lit up when

Auburn came bursting through that door, lifting herself off the couch slowly to greet us despite our insisting that she stay seated.

Auburn talked a mile a minute, explaining how we'd brought food to last weeks and a physician to finally see her. The broken gratitude in her face was enough to nearly bring me to tears again, but I held it together, if not for her sake, then for Auburn's. Harry, the most adorable little toddler, no more than four, with golden eyes and a mop of curls sitting on his head, hugged his mom's leg most of the time. That is, until Aris knelt down with a box of those cinnamon cakes, and then he really came out of his shell.

Auburn's mother had already looked better, her cough soothed a touch with the correct medication finally. We paid the physician and made sure she was stocked with enough medication to cure her. But just to be sure, we left a sack of coins with her—enough that, should they run out of food or need to revisit the doctor, they'd have plenty to get what they need until she's back on her feet and their father returns.

Auburn made us promise to return tomorrow, insisting she'd actually paint the larger prints for us. We told her she didn't need to, that we'd only been joking, but she wouldn't take no for an answer. She kept the smaller parchments for reference, and we conceded. What's one more day in this beautiful city?

We mingled over those delicious cakes until it was time for us to leave, needing to actually eat something of real substance. Auburn's mother had tried to invite us to stay, offering to cook for all of us, but a group of five was too much, especially in her state. Plus, little Harry was starting to wind down from his sugar high—finally tired from his pretend swordplay with Theo, Jared, and River. Theo had disappeared into the kitchen at some point and made sandwiches for the three of them so her mother didn't have to worry about exerting herself.

I hugged each of them goodbye. Her mother thanked us profusely, and once I was able to pry Harry's arms off of me, we set out to find dinner at a local tavern in town. Eventually, we met

Layla and Kyra, who'd taken the evening to themselves, at the inn we're staying at for the night. We inform them of the revised plans of remaining in the city for one more day and give them the keys to their room. Jared and Theo follow them off to their own room shortly after, leaving us three with the inn's clerk to retrieve the remainder of our keys. This is where we run into the first issue of the trip.

"I only have one more room left. There are a few families and couples staying in the others. I can remove them, Your Highness," he offers, swallowing nervously as he glances at Aris.

"Nonsense, we'll simply move things around and make it work. We'll just take the last room then, thank you." I offer my hand for the key. The clerk sighs in relief, plopping the brass key in my palm while I exchange it for the fee of all the rooms. I can feel the hesitation rolling off of River and Aris as they follow me out of the office back onto the cobblestone road.

The rooms are lined in a row, each fashioned like an individual cabin. Almost as if someone took ten of them and glued them all together. I notice the servants', guards', and coachmen's rooms are on one end, but after glancing down at the number on the key, I see our room is the final one on the opposite end.

"I can sleep on the floor with Theo and Jared," River says, already moving toward their door.

"Wait!" I blurt in a harsh whisper. He pauses, both him and Aris looking at me. "Most rooms have had two beds thus far; I can sleep in one, and you two can share so you don't have to sleep on the floor. The guys are probably sleeping already." It's a poor excuse to keep him close, and I can tell they both see through me right away, but it was worth a try.

"I'm not sharing a bed with him, Ember," River says quietly, taking a step back toward us. It's quiet on the street. There's no one out here but us. Lamp posts are lit with flickering flames, casting warm glows over us. The same heat from earlier rises in me as I glance between the both of them.

"And you call me stubborn. Fine, but sleep on our floor then," I try instead.

"Is that really a good idea?" Aris asks, raising his eyebrow at me.

"He needs somewhere to sleep. It's not that big a deal." I cross my arms, gripping the key a little harder.

"You'd think they'd realize you're trying to get in their pants." Asteria suddenly pops in.

You've been so quiet all day and this is what you want to chime in on? I'm not trying to do that. They won't let me even if I wanted to.

"You don't try hard enough. If you did, there's no way they'd say no." As much as Asteria likes to mess around, there's something off in her voice. Something hesitant rolling off of her.

What's wrong?

"Let's talk in the morning, River just responded to you. He said you're being very 'readable' again. Whatever that means. Goodnight, Ember." Before I can argue, she shuts me out completely. I can tell she's not far; she's secluded in the same woods she was before. I just can't help but worry about what's going on with her. I tuck it away, making sure to get to the bottom of it in the morning. I look back at River, squinting my eyes at him.

"I have no idea what you mean, River." But he's already exchanging a look with Aris, who in turn is shaking his head at me, a playful glint flashing through his eyes.

"Temptress," Aris mutters. River hums in agreement as I feign innocence, walking toward our carriage to grab my night bag from inside. The boys do the same before I unlock the door, setting my things down to light the lamps I can see in the dark. The door closes softly behind me, the lock clicking in place. Aris curses a short moment later once the room is illuminated enough for us all to see.

One bed. Not two. It is big, though, bigger than any others I've seen. Bigger than even the one I have back at the castle. I'd argue that we'd be able to sleep on it more comfortably than we did when we set up tents on our journey to Klyeria through Atravelien.

"I'll head over to Theo's room to see if they have two beds," River mutters, hooking his bag over his shoulder and turning to the door.

"And if they don't? Then what? The floor? It'd be the same ordeal as here. We did this once before, and it wasn't an issue then, was it?" I untie my cloak, tossing it over the plain upholstered chair that sits beside the window. Aris is closing the curtains too, shutting out any unwanted eyes.

River studies me for a moment, his eyes roaming over the dress I wore today. The midnight fabric stands out against my skin with a heart-shaped neckline and a tight bodice that leads to a flowy, tulle skirt. The sleeves are sheer and lead up over my shoulders to a built-in collar that wraps around my throat but leaves my chest bare. I smile, satisfied, grabbing my bag instead of waiting for him to make his decision.

"I'm going to bathe. Whether you stay or not is up to you." Slinging my bag onto my arm, I walk toward the washroom.

"Save us warm water!" Aris calls after me. I snort softly, shutting the door behind me. With just a thought, the lamps become lit.

I clip up my hair and fill the tub halfway with warm water. Just enough to bathe my body but not too much that the boys won't have water for themselves. I begin using my favorite scented soaps that I asked the girls to pack for me. They even got me matching lotions that I take my time lathering onto my skin before I open my bag to see which nightgown Layla chose for tonight. She and Melody went shopping before the trip and took it upon themselves to get me an entire new set of nightwear.

Aris has just about choked every time I've gotten dressed for the night. Watching him quiver is way more satisfying than I thought it'd be. When I pull out an extremely short, fully mesh gown, my heart just about stops. They're going to *kill* me. Wicked delight floods me as I slip on a strappy pair of what could hardly be called underwear. With the sheer nightgown over it, it's as if I'm wearing nothing.

I run my hands over the straps, looking at myself in the mirror and the way the soft glow of the lamps flicker over my body. My breasts sit perky, my nipples hard and dark beneath the fabric. The way the mesh shifts across my chest already has my heart racing with how sensitive my skin is.

"Be forewarned, every night she's come out wearing a night-gown shorter, and shorter. I'm positive the girls had something to do with it." I hear Aris tell River as he gathers his things to take his own bath.

"And you're telling me you haven't..." River trails off.

"You have no idea how difficult she's making it," Aris growls. I cover my mouth to keep from laughing. He is *really* going to hate me. I place all my toiletries back into my bag once I've washed my mouth. Letting my hair cascade down my back, I open the door, not looking at them as I put my bag off to the side.

"Ember..." My name rolls off their tongue like a prayer and a curse at the same time.

CHAPTER 30

"There should be warm water left for the both of you." It's hard to hide the budding smile from my voice. A hard, throbbing need pulses down both tethers, nearly bringing me to my knees in front of them both. I allow myself to peek at them as I pull the sheets back on the bed. Neither of them has let go of a breath, not as I lift a knee onto the mattress and then the other to crawl to the middle. "Oh, do me a favor and toss me that book next to my cloak, River, please?"

I look up at him through my lashes, playing the dirtiest game I have yet. I prop myself up against the pillows, leaning against them as he brings it over me. He hands it to me but doesn't release it right away.

"You're not going to win," he says, his low, sexy voice doing more to me than he knows.

"I really have no clue what you're talking about." I pull on the book and open it. I haven't pulled the sheets over me; no, I let them look over my body and everything I've left exposed to them as I begin reading where I left off.

"I told you," Aris mutters, his voice strained before he shuts the door. River takes a seat in one of the upholstered seats facing me, his legs spread as he leans back with his hands resting on his thighs. I peek at him over the book, just to meet smoldering ocean eyes that threaten to drown me where I lie. It'd be so easy for him to just give in while we're away from everyone, away from the castle. So what is it? Male pride? Dominance? The latter makes me curl my toes and has me flickering back to my book. On their time, and only when they allow themselves to give in. I can almost hear River say, "*Good girl.*"

Soon, Aris and River are switching places. It's warmer in the room than I expected, so we don't touch the fireplace. Aris is back in his favorite silk black pajama pants, with no shirt on as he puts his things aside. When he sits, facing me finally, he runs a hand through his wet hair. I do my best not to look at him, to try and keep reading even though I've been on the same page since I've laid down. But I can't do it, so I flip over onto my stomach, pulling the pillow down so I can lay comfortably. I shut the book, setting it beside me, lifting a knee, and I swear I can hear Aris shudder from here.

It's not long before River emerges from the washroom, bare-chested and with damp curls that just about make me want to yell at them both to give up already. They take their time blowing out the lamps. Soon, they're both on either end of the bed, hesitating to lay down. River takes the book, placing it on the nightstand beside him. There's a window in the slanted ceiling providing just a sliver of light from the crescent moon in the night sky. They both let out a shaky breath before climbing in beside me, trying to do their best not to touch me but to no avail—the bed is big, but it's not *that* big.

I flip back over as they finally pull the covers up over us. My small frame fits between their large ones comfortably, and I can tell from the way my body completely relaxes near them that I won't have any problems sleeping tonight. They're both very quiet for a moment while I look up through the window in the ceiling.

"What, no goodnight kisses?" I joke softly. Aris caves first. He rolls over, using one hand to grab me by the back of my neck as he kisses me deeply. More than he usually allows himself, but I take everything he gives me, even if it's for a brief moment. I memorize the hard planes of his body as his bare skin brands itself against mine.

Every dormant part of me wakes up, coming alive in ways I never have before. Especially as River reaches over, gripping my waist with his rough hands, turning me toward him. It rips my lips from Aris, and with a possessive growl, River is kissing me—burning me from the inside out. But Aris isn't done with me, not at all. He pushes his body flush against my side, nipping at my ear, dragging his teeth against my neck before sucking on the sensitive spot just below my collarbone. I can't help the soft moans of pleasure they pull from me.

I reach back with my left hand, running it through Aris' hair, before biting River's lip, pulling on it softly. *Please, for the love of all the gods, don't stop.* I don't think I could handle it if they did. I don't know how they could now.

It's like they can read my mind because one by one, they pull away slowly, breathlessly. Detaching from me despite their obvious desire for more. I can feel how hard they both were—are. I have half a mind to reach over and touch them just to get them to come back. I don't, though; I just catch my breath.

They both do the same, lying back on their backs, dazed. Flipping onto my stomach once more, I lean over and kiss River's tan bare shoulder and then do the same to Aris' pale one on my left. I murmur goodnight to them before letting my head drop, squeezing my eyes shut to try and shut down the pulsing need in me between the three of us. I vaguely hear them whisper their goodnights before I drift off into a steamy sleep filled with fantasies about the mates beside me.

"I don't think I've ever seen anyone more perfect," Aris whispers softly. For a moment I think I'm still dreaming. Especially when from beside me River responds,

"She doesn't know it, doesn't see it, but everyone pales in comparison when they stand beside her." He drags a rough finger down the middle of my body, which is partially exposed due to the mesh nightgown having shifted in the night. It rises up above my hips and has completely let loose my right breast. I lay perfectly still, keeping my breathing as rhythmic as it was if I were still asleep, while also making sure to shut the mental door in case Asteria chose now to pop in.

"I don't know how she possibly thought I'd ever want to bring a mistress home. Why would I when I'd have her lying like this in bed every morning? Or I suppose not every morning." Even with my eyes closed, I can feel Aris glancing at River, knowing some days I'd end up in River's bed. Aris traces a finger along the strap that's still on my shoulder, sliding it off so my chest is fully exposed. The cool air brings both of my nipples to hard peaks.

"Or that I'd want to give her up to marry. My life would be empty without her in it. It was silent and void of color before her." River drags that finger back up, circling it around my breast at the same time that Aris does to the other. It draws a soft moan out of me, a raspy one, as it pulls me fully awake. My eyes fly open, and I come face to face with them as they both look down at me, leaning on one elbow on either side.

"Good morning, Princess," Aris purrs.

"Look at you, Ember," River says, pinching my nipple between his fingers. I grip the sheets between us, my hands dangerously close to both of their cocks, which I don't have to look at to know are hard. The pain and pleasure ricochet through me, causing me to squirm in place. Aris's finger trails down, tracing the top of my panties, making me arch upwards. I haven't breathed a word yet; I don't know if I even have words in me right now. I just need them to keep touching me, and I don't want to mess it up.

"Uh, uh, stay still, baby. We'll get there, I promise." Aris' wicked smile grows on his face as he continues to trace the outline of my panties, following the seam down the inner part of my thighs. I quiver as he gets so near where I'm absolutely soaked and needy, but still, he doesn't touch me there.

"We decided you've been so good that we'd concede just a tad. But you only take what we give, you understand?" River warns, his voice still in that delicious morning timbre that has me nodding eagerly.

"Yes, please, only what you give." My own voice comes out breathy as I struggle to control my breathing.

"Good, now you're about to regret wearing this to tease us," Aris murmurs in my ear before taking my thigh and spreading it open. River does the same with my other leg, and simultaneously they drag their hands from my knees inward, using their fingers to brush lightly against the fabric of my panties, still not touching me where I need them to.

They both dip their heads; Aris kisses along my jaw while River swirls his tongue around my nipple. I moan, sparks and heat exploding in me, making my magic flicker for a moment, but the box stays closed. They continue to tease me, touching me everywhere but my clit. Dragging their fingers everywhere but in me. It's almost too much—the ache, the need for them. They kiss me, my lips, my jaw, my neck, my breasts. No skin is untouched by their tongue until I'm shaking beneath them. Shaking and soaked so thoroughly, whimpering so needily that they concede, quite literally ripping my underwear off.

I'm not even sure which one ripped it. I'm too lost in ecstasy. I can't stop moving against them, moving into their touches and kisses. Can't stop pulling them in for more even though I said I wouldn't take more than I was given. When my hands brush against their hard lengths, my wrists get pinned to the bed.

"As much as I'd love for your hand to be wrapped around me

right now, this is about you, and only you." River releases my wrist to trail his hand back up my leg.

"Look at how wet you are for us, Ember. Gods, you're so beautiful," Aris marvels, his eyes wandering over my body then back to my eyes. He bows his head and kisses me, his soft hand hardly a whisper as it glides down my stomach, meeting River's at the apex of my thighs.

Finally, gloriously, they give me what I want. River slips one finger, and then two, right into me as Aris circles his index and middle fingers around my clit. The combination makes my back arch off the bed, my moans echoing off of the walls loudly. Aris swallows the sounds I'm making, his fingers moving in agonizingly slow circles.

"I'd love to make you scream right now, Ember, but you have to be quieter," Aris says against my lips, smiling down at me, and that smile could be my undoing by itself.

"Aris, I can't..." I whimper, struggling as River plunges his fingers back into me; I look at him. "River," I moan, the mix of rough and smooth fingers bringing me to the brink of insanity with pleasure.

My orgasm starts to build like a wave starting to crest, racing for the shore. With it, my core tightens as their fingers simultaneously pick up speed, and there's no staying quiet. How could I? I'm lost in the abyss of lightning and fire as every single nerve in my body roars in sweet, sweet ecstasy.

A knock on the door startles us all, edging my orgasm back from the peak. Aris immediately lifts up a bit to cover my mouth with his other hand to keep me quiet as they pick up their pace again. My eyes roll to the back of my head as my eyelids flutter shut, the wave rushing forward toward the shore again.

"Good morning, Your Highness. Is Ember ready for me? I've brought her dress for today." Layla's voice squeaks softly through the door. River bows his head to wrap his teeth around my nipple, tugging on it softly before sucking on it. He peppers kisses up my neck, kissing the hollow of my throat. All of my moans, my whimpers, and my breathless sounds are muffled by Aris' hand. I'm about to tip over the edge—I'm so close. River can feel it as my inner walls start to clench around his fingers.

"She's still bathing, Layla," Aris calls out, but he's looking down at me, watching me, completely enraptured.

"I can just come in and wait for her then," she offers.

"I'm indisposed right now; come back in fifteen minutes and we'll be ready for you, I promise," he says in a hurry, eager to watch me come undone.

"Oh! My apologies, Your Highness!" We hear her scurry off, and I think Aris is going to release my mouth, but he shakes his head at me. He knows I'll be too loud.

"Come for us, baby," Aris croons. And finally, I hit the shore —*hard*. Stars explode behind my eyes as wave after wave of my orgasm wash over me. Aris was right to keep his hand over my mouth because the damn near scream that came out of me would've been enough to alert whoever our neighbors were. They don't stop until I'm writhing beneath them, begging for them to quit.

They both release me, sucking what remains of me off of their fingers, groaning softly at the taste. They pepper me with praise as I lie there, my thighs shaking with the remnants of my climax, and to think that was just their *fingers*. Imagine what being fucked by both of them would be like. They both press a kiss into my brow before getting up and getting ready, leaving me to lie there with a hand strewn over my face to recover.

Eventually, I get up, letting the mesh nightgown fall to my feet, walking on somewhat unsteady legs into the washroom to clean myself up, wash my mouth, and tame my hair. When I exit, I lean in the doorway, looking at the both of them whilst still in no clothes. They turn and look at me, now both fully clothed and ready for the day. I crack a smile at them.

"Can we share a room the rest of the trip?" I ask before walking over to my bag, pulling on extra undergarments. "I can return the favor." River walks up behind me, kissing me on the shoulder.

"You know I'd love to, but it's too risky. We'll make sure this doesn't happen again. I'm going to step out while everyone else is still in their rooms. I'll see you for breakfast." He speaks low in my ear, and there's a small sense of sadness rolling off him, but he covers it up immediately, never staying open too long. Then he's tilting my head up to plant a soft kiss on my lips before grabbing his bag. I lift the damper momentarily to listen for any guards or the servants, but no one is out there, so I let it drop back in place. He checks behind the curtains before slipping out of the door.

Biting my lip, I turn back to Aris, because that's the first time he's truly done more than kiss me. He crosses the room in a couple of strides and takes a handful of my hair, pulling it so I'm looking up at him. I plant my hands on his chest as pure desire flares in his eyes.

"Did you two plan that?" I ask before he can say anything, too curious about how that came to be.

"No. We woke up, and the sun was streaming down on you—just you. And gods, I mean, how could we not give in just a little? How could we not touch you? Even to at least give you some relief. You won, just a little this time, but you cannot keep doing this to me, Ember. I am losing it. He's had you. He knows what it feels like to sink his cock into your perfect little pussy."

There it is, that dirty, sinful mouth.

"He knows what it's like to feel you clench around him when you climax. And for fuck's sake, Ember, he knows what that pretty, little mouth feels like wrapped around him. What you look like dragging your tongue around the tip. I've daydreamed about it. I've touched myself in the bath, in my bed, and at night fantasizing about all the unthinkable things I want to do to you. I am hanging on by a thread and watching you just now, hearing all those precious sounds you make? I almost came without a single touch from you because that's how much of an effect you have on me. So please, we are so, so close.

A month more, and then I can bury myself in you, into oblivion." He leans his forehead against mine, his voice raw and husky. Just like that, my core is pulsing all over again. I twirl the hair at the nape of his neck.

"I grew up wanting things I could never have. Things that weren't meant for a princess. The more I wanted, the more that was taken away. It kind of created a monster, the complete opposite of what they intended, honestly. Sweet, innocent, precious little Ember really gets off on the sexy, depraved, and immoral things in life. You just gave me a taste of what's to come, and I think I can be a good girl until then as long as you're promising to fulfill those unthinkable fantasies," I whisper seductively against his lips. He shudders against me, his grip growing stronger, which is answer enough.

"I promise." He kisses me long and deeply until a knock on the door breaks us apart. I smile up at him, a true beam of affection, before running into the bathroom and shutting the door and opening my mental one.

Asteria? Are you okay? I lean against the counter while Aris lets Layla in.

"*I'm fine but certainly not as good as you,*" she says suggestively. I can imagine her swishing her spiked tail.

How can you already tell?

"*You're literally radiating. Also, post-orgasm you're your most powerful. Funny, isn't it?*" I can feel her flying overhead, circling in the clouds.

You're kidding. But even as I say it, I can tell she's right; when I search inwards, just a peek inside, I'm overwhelmed by the wave of power that meets me. Holy gods and goddesses, that's a lot.

"*Told you. When we get back to the castle, we're going to have to go back to the mountains.*" There's still something in her tone that bothers me. Layla comes in, and I greet her quietly. She hands me a long-sleeve silver gown cut similarly to the navy blue one Aris bought back home. I can't wear a bra with it, so I turn around and unclasp it before slipping into the dress.

What's wrong? What happened?

"I don't want you to be mad."

I can't be mad at you.

"You can heal, Ember. Not just yourself, but you can heal others. I was going to tell you, but I knew you'd try to heal her mother. You can't; it's simply too risky. But I didn't want to hide it from you either."

You were that worried I'd be mad at you for not telling me? I can feel the guilt radiating off of her.

"That and I need to return to Holarthia once more to talk to the Elders. They have questions about you. When I requested leave from my post from my commander, he put in the request, which went through the chain of command. Ultimately, it was approved on the condition that I return to Holarthia to answer to the Elders once more." This is what makes my heart sink.

How long will you be gone? Not another week, Asteria; that was too long.

"Ember, are you okay? You look pale," Layla asks. She's just set down a warm pair of white boots for me to put on beneath the dress. Slipping on some socks first, I take the boots to put them on before following her back into the room to grab my cloak and my book so we can leave.

"Oh, I'm fine. I was just thinking about how we'll be going home soon, is all," I lie smoothly.

"Don't worry, we still have some time before then to enjoy," she assures me before heading toward her carriage.

"No, only a couple of days this time. No more than three since we know more will result in us having to settle. It'll only take me a day to fly to Holarthia if I only stop to eat and drink once."

Please don't hurt yourself. It nearly makes me sick to my stomach with worry just thinking about her overexerting herself.

"Your concern is sweet, Ember, but I'll be fine. You can dote on me when I come back."

Why didn't you tell me sooner?

"Because of how worried you are right now."

You sound like Aris.

"Perhaps he has a point in some of his reasons." That makes my mouth taste sour. I sit silently between the boys, fiddling with the book in my hands. *"Spit it out."*

The whole not telling me things because I'm somehow too fragile is getting really old, really quick. It's one thing for my soon-to-be husband to do it. It's another for my bonded dragon to do it too.

"I was trying to let you enjoy your trip," she argues weakly. *"When you love someone, you'd do anything not to hurt that person. Every time I thought about telling you, you were having too good of a time. Then that lady went and read your fortune—or misfortune. You know how much I hate the thought of leaving you. You know that. Especially with that fucker back at the castle. I don't think you're fragile, Ember. But put yourself in any of our shoes with what you've been through, and you'd avoid sharing any semblance of bad news with you too."* The last part of what she says has me puzzled for a moment. It makes me wonder exactly how bad what Aris is hiding from me still is. He claims he's doing it in the name of protecting me—that when the time is right, he'll tell me.

I understand and appreciate that sentiment, but I want you to promise right now there will be no more hiding anything between the both of us. No matter how small or unimportant it may seem. You're the other half of my soul, Asteria. Were I to look in the mirror, I'd see you in the reflection. You're eternally mine, and I'm infinitely yours, down to the very fiber of our last breath. There is nothing, absolutely nothing, that stands between you and me.

"When did you get so poetic?"

I'll kill you.

"For as long as my heart beats, Ember, I am yours. I won't hide anything from you, no matter the circumstances. You have my word, you stubborn, fierce girl. Do you know why I really think you're named Ember?" The coachman makes his way toward Auburn's house; we have plans to take them for breakfast after retrieving the paintings and then setting out for the next town.

Why's that?

"Not because of your eyes, but because you are like the dying

embers of a flame; you are the last flicker to hold on, the last fight to keep the warmth. You are the final piece of hope, Ember. That is who you are."

Now who's the poetic one? But before she can respond, both she and I smell *it* at the same time. She flies ahead of us toward the smoke we just smelt. Dread fills me as something doesn't feel right. I lean over River and shove the curtain open, but we can't see anything yet. We're nowhere near anything—Asteria and I can smell too far in advance.

"What's wrong?" River asks, taking my hand that's still gripping the curtain and moving it down into his lap to hold it.

"Something doesn't feel right. Can we ask the coachman to stop? Let me take Bedelia," I ask Aris, pleading in my voice. Bedelia is attached to the servant's carriage with Coal; if I can unhook her, we can get there quicker.

"What do you mean? We'll be there in twenty or so minutes," Aris counters, cocking his head to the side, confused.

"Ember, the house has been burnt. They're still putting the flames out." Absolute devastation floods our tether, and I know whatever she's seeing is terrible.

"Aris, *please.*" I don't even wait for an answer from him; I'm already climbing over his lap, pushing the carriage door open, and jumping out of it while it's still moving. The ground is uneven where I land, making me stumble before I catch myself. The coachman behind us yanks on the reins of Coal and Bedelia, halting their trot. Bedelia neighs, as if sensing my panic. I run to her and begin unhooking her from the carriage.

There are shouts all around me; Aris and River are already out of the carriage, and the coachman is perplexed and angry. Theo and Jared are unsure of what to do as they wait for instruction from Aris, who walks right up to me.

"Ember, what are you *doing?*" He grabs my arm to face him. I exhale harshly and look beyond him to the plume of smoke that's visible now that we're outside of the carriages.

"Look." I point before returning to what I was doing, finally getting her free. Aris curses under his breath, River doing the same; instantly he runs to undo the horse of our carriage while Aris undoes Coal. I don't wait for them. I place my hands on Bedelia's back, hoisting myself up until I can swing my leg over and grab the reins that remain on her.

She takes off at lightning speed, sensing the need to not waste any more time. It's as if the wind itself carries her, pushing at her hooves to move her faster and faster. She cuts the time in half, delivering me to my worst nightmare. I slide off of her, running almost as fast as she did toward the house that I had just been in last night. The house that had that beautiful baby boy and the young painter who painted fairies. The house that was now nothing more than a few wooden boards and dying embers.

CHAPTER 31

Numb pain washes over me as I take in the scene before me. Any and every townsperson that could be here is here, passing buckets of water to slow the fire. An officer notices me walking toward the home and tries to put his arm out.

"I'm sorry you can't go near there; we're investigating," he commands.

"I'm Princess Ember. What happened here?" I use my rank for the first time to get the information I need. He pales hearing who I am and seeing that I'm here witnessing this.

"Did you by chance help the young girl who lived here?" he asks. *Lived.* My stomach recoils.

"Easy, Ember. We don't know anything yet. Maybe they got out. I'm looking right now," she says soothingly. I focus on breathing, focusing on hoping she's right.

"I did; Auburn is her name. We came here to bring her mother a physician."

"We caught one of what we think may have been a group of thieves who followed Auburn and you all back here after seeing you give her money in the square. They waited until you left to attack. He says there were two others, but they got away before we got here. The one we have is injured. The little boy confirmed the story as well." The relief that fills me is a sweet bliss I've never known.

"And the girl?" I ask, begging all gods and all goddesses above and below that she's alive.

"Alive and unscathed. The mother is the only one who didn't make it. She saved the kids by holding off the group and getting them to run. I'm sorry, Your Highness. It's a real tragedy, and rest assured we will find them. The children are over there." He points to the side where two huddled figures are beneath a blanket, rocking side to side. From here I can see several bundles of parchment paper, and a strangled sob finally breaks through me.

I run toward them as Aris and River finally arrive at the scene. I fall to my knees in front of them, and at first I don't think Auburn understands it's me. She looks up, a sort of haze in her eyes as she rocks her sleeping brother, and then that haze clears. Tears replace them, as if she hadn't cried until this very moment. As if she hadn't let herself cry because of Harry.

Sobs start to rack her fragile body, and instantly Aris is beside me. He takes Harry from her arms, and I take her into mine, letting her cry into my chest. Her wails echo through the yard, and everyone pauses, looking over because the child is finally crying, finally showing an emotion other than shock. Quickly they go back to cleaning the debris, shifting through what might be salvageable and what isn't.

"My aunt lives two towns away. We just have to figure out how to get there." She lifts her head, hiccuping, her sweet voice cracking. "They didn't take what you gave us. Mama made us run with it. I took my paintings, and we *ran*, but it's not enough to buy a house. Papa won't have a house to come home to. How will he know where we are?" Another sob shakes her.

"Oh, what a sweet, sweet soul."

"When we send the royal decree to stop the war once our marriage is official, I will personally make sure that your father makes it home to you, Auburn. Because a home isn't a place, it's really the people who we call home. We will make sure you get to your aunts safely. We are so, so sorry that those terrible people did this to you," Aris says, sitting on the ground with a still sleeping Harry. Harry's curls are damp with sweat, and there's soot staining his clothes and forehead.

"What if they come back because you're helping me again?" she whispers, fear dripping from her so heavily I can smell it.

"*Don't you* dare *blame yourself, Ember,*" Asteria warns. But the guilt has already made a home in my chest.

"They won't do that. You know why? Because the whole town is helping you, and if they did something else, they'd face the wrath of an entire city," Aris answers, glancing at me.

"He's right. They won't try again. But I am so sorry, Auburn. Your mama is a warrior," I whisper into the top of her head, pulling her close again. She hugs me, sniffling, and we stay like that for a while. River helps the officers, immediately jumping in with their investigation of the only thief who's in a carriage off the road.

The well within me feels volcanic. Fury and rage fester and boil, and all the carefully crafted control I'd mastered starts to wither. The lid starts to crumble, the damper starts to melt, and all I can feel is my power's wrath. All I yearn for is vengeance for the girl in my arms and the innocence stripped off of her. Clouds roll in with fervor they didn't have before.

"*Easy, Ember.*"

This will put the fire out quicker; those embers keep bringing the flames back to life. The irony isn't lost on me.

"Let's get them under some cover," I murmur to Aris. He looks at me perplexed; it doesn't look like it's going to rain just yet, but he listens nonetheless. We move to an empty carriage where he lies Harry on the bench, and Auburn sits, placing her paintings down.

"I saved yours. I never got to do the big ones I was planning to do, but you can still have the ones I did yesterday." She pulls them out of the pile along with the blue fairy I had forgotten to take.

"I'll paint you again one day; I'm sure of it," she says confidently, her voice still so raspy from crying.

"You will, when we're king and queen, we'll call you to the castle and you'll paint our portrait to be hung in the royal hall with all of the other kings and queens before us. You'll go down in history with the other famous painters," Aris declares, and this cracks a smile from her.

Her smile drives my power further, making the thunder boom loudly. A couple of surprised shouts ring out from behind where Aris and I stand facing the kids. Shortly after, rain begins to pour in large droplets. It doesn't take long to soak the ground completely, making us look like we've dunked ourselves in the lake with our clothes on. But it puts the fire out, which brings cheers and shouts of victory from the crowd.

I don't stop the rain for a while yet; the release is too good, and my anger is so thorough that I don't know that I *can* stop even if I wanted to. Eventually, River comes over to us, and I hear him tell Aris that they've put together a carriage and chaperone from the local orphanage to accompany them to their aunt's over the next couple of days. They'll have secure lodging at the orphanage with food and clothes until they're set to make the two day journey to Linel, the town she lives in.

I refuse to leave their side. Not to change, not to eat, not even when it's time to take them to the orphanage after they've been fed lunch by a villager who begins bringing meals for everyone who worked tirelessly to put the fire out. No, I sit in that carriage with Auburn and hold her hand when she wants it held. Harry lays in my lap after he eats and plays with the flaps of my cloak even though they're still wet. He tells me he likes it better than the burning; that water is friendlier, and my beating heart cracks further.

A coachman takes us to the orphanage, and when we arrive outside a tall building that resembles a schoolhouse, the three of us pause and stare at it. It's white, a bright white as if someone has recently painted it, with a tall pointed ceiling that points straight toward the skies that are still crying the tears that I refuse to let go.

The windows are large, meant to let the sunshine in on the children while they learn and play, waiting for someone to come and take them away. It's only a couple of days that they'll spend here, just until they go to be with their family—family that will help them heal. Their father will be home soon, and they will grieve together. I promise it to myself. I make the gods swear upon it.

"We'll go inside when you're ready," I tell them quietly, rubbing Harry's back softly. I cleaned the soot off his cheeks earlier, revealing the baby-smooth, dark skin beneath, and I even tried to comb through his curls to tame them as much as I could. I only succeeded a little bit. Auburn looks up at me, those beads in her hair clinking softly.

"He'll find us?" she asks one more time.

"He'll find you," I assure her, rubbing my thumb over her hand, which seems so small now.

"Do you think they'll have paint inside?" She glances back at the building, assessing it, tears wobbling in those too young and too pained eyes.

"I'll make sure they do. You keep painting, Auburn. Never stop. Paint her. Even when it hurts. It will heal you more than you know, and it will help you to remember her. So he will always remember what his mama looked like." I look down at Harry, who's all too quiet for a little boy his age. He should be bouncing around the carriage, and I should be trying to corral him into a seat. Yet, he just continues to trace shapes into the fabric of my cloak, content to stay there for as long as I'll let him. Forever, Harry, if I had it my way.

"Why were you so nice to me, Ember? To us? Out of all the people selling things on the street?" She doesn't face me when she asks, and her voice is little more than a whisper.

"Your table was the first thing I'd seen of heart, soul, and passion. Not only were you a twelve-year-old girl—" She cuts me off.

"Eleven. My birthday is in three months. But a close guess." There's a slight warmth there, just slight.

"Eleven going on seventeen, I swear. But you had the most fascinating way of painting. Most painters I know paint realistically. You paint…like you pulled the inner essence right out of you, dipped your paintbrush in, and used it on the parchment. I think you were put in my path and I was put in yours by fate, a tricky, funky thing I have a love-hate relationship with. I wanted to help in any way I could, because people like you, Auburn, need to know that there are people that believe in them. I believe in you. That glow in you is something special. Show Harry how to shine." She peeks at me, those tears finally falling.

"You used some big words like essence, but I think I get the gist." She laughs softly, throwing her arms around my neck as quiet sobs fill the carriage once more. Harry even rises, leaning against me as well as I wrap my arms around the both of them. Pain flares in my chest, and as a result, rain pelts the top of the roof as it comes down harder, making it hard to see outside when I glance out the window. "I think I'm ready to go in, but we're going to get soaked," she says once she's calmed down again, pulling back to wipe her face.

"Give it a second; I think it'll calm down soon. It always gets heavy to lighten up," I assure her again. Taking deep breaths to ease the ache, I loosen the constant wave of power I've poured into the storm, bringing it to a soft drizzle over the span of a couple of minutes to make it a little more believable.

"While I'm glad you've found a release, using your emotions to drive your power is not ideal," she warns.

Causing two children to lose their mother isn't ideal either, I snap. She stays quiet, not caring to receive more of my internal wrath.

Auburn opens the door for us, tucking the paintings that are her own under her cloak—leaving mine behind in the carriage. I gather Harry in my arms, who lays his head on my shoulder, tucking his face into my neck. He breathes in deeply.

"You smell like flowers and honey," he says as a matter of fact.

"Thank you, it's the bath soap I use." I look down at him curiously.

"I want to smell like flowers and honey," he whispers, like it's our secret.

"I'll see if I can send you the same soap via a messenger," I whisper back to him. He nods, content with this. We reach the door where Auburn's already waiting inside. She looks behind me as I hear footsteps sound on the gravel walkway.

"We wanted to say goodbye before we left," Aris says, and without having to turn around, I can hear the sad smile on his face.

"Maybe one last sword fight?" River offers softly to Harry, but he doesn't nod, and my beating heart becomes stone, its final beat forming in hard rock as Harry burrows further into my neck. Still I face forward, unable to look River or Aris in the eye. They did nothing wrong. I just can't face them with all of the shame I'm feeling. Asteria's disagreement rolls through me, enough that I shut the door completely.

"That's okay, buddy. We'll duel again someday. We'll need to see if you can defeat three knights all at once again. Keep practicing; you'll be the finest warrior in the land," River tells him, standing directly behind me as he speaks to Harry.

I can feel River's body heat seeping into me, warming me through layers of soaked clothes that have frozen me to the bone so thoroughly I've gone numb. I just didn't care. Harry nods slowly, the only thing he offers, but River takes it. Aris comes and pats him on the back softly, recognizing his lack of room for goodbyes.

Instead, both of them shift to Auburn, who sheepishly looks down at her shoes. She's placed her paintings on a table in the entrance hallway, no longer keeping them below her cloak. Aris glances at the paintings, and she tracks his gaze.

"Yours are in the carriage; don't worry." She smiles softly, bashfully. She wipes her cheeks again, wiping away the remnants of her tears and wails, staying tough for them. "Thank you, Prince Aris, for stopping this war, bringing my dad home, and for bringing Ember around." She looks at me with a light I don't deserve, but in this moment I'm reminded of the single line that makes all of it worth it. Two kingdoms' peace for whatever I must endure. And endure for her I shall.

"It is my honor to serve you, Auburn, the both of you. We won't forget you; in fact, like I promised, I will be making sure your father comes home to you. And you'll be in our castle before you know it." He gives her one of my favorite smiles, the kind that offers both dimples and is kind and soft. She nods eagerly, overcome with emotion again, and runs into his open arms, hugging him tightly. Then she's switching, hugging River with the same might that makes even River stumble a step back. But then he's kneeling, hugging her back, murmuring something to her I don't listen to—allowing them their own secrets.

Finally, she looks at me, and that lip quivers once more, but the tears don't shed. I kneel with Harry, who plants his feet on the floor, finally extracting his arms from around my neck. He holds my face in his small hands, staring at me with big golden eyes.

"The fairies say they miss you. It's time to go home. Don't forget my soap. I love you." But it sounds more like 'wove' with his soft toddler accent still sticking through.

He pats my cheek softly before going and taking the hand of the woman who organized their stay here. He puzzles me to my core, rooting me in my place. I glance at Auburn, who said they'd visited her at night. I figured she'd just seen pictures of fairies in books and recreated them. It must be a four-year-old conjecture. Nothing more than a wild imagination. Fairies are real, sure. I have a dragon, so why wouldn't they be? But why would fairies be all the way out here visiting children? I add it to the list of questions I need to ask Asteria.

Auburn steps to where I'm still kneeling, still taken aback by

Harry. I rise, taking both of her hands in mine. We're silent for a beat, and for a moment I wonder how often the gods do this. How often do they create intentional pathways set to cross one way or another? How much of our lives is designed by fate, and how much of it is our doing? I pull her close, wrapping my arms around her shoulders, because despite the answer and despite what my presence in her life may have caused, she's made an impression on me I'll cherish forever.

"Can't. Breathe," she wheezes playfully. I release her, chuckling softly, and she smiles up at me. "I'll see you again, Ember. Aris still owes me two hundred gold coins." She winks before turning to the woman who smiles kindly at her.

I watch their small frames disappear down the hall. The numbness in my body spreads through my mind until I can breathe normally. I close the lid on the box, releasing the storm. My heart remains encased in stone, desperately wanting to beat but to no avail. Finally, once they've disappeared completely, I make my way outside. A cold, brisk breeze whips across my face, blowing damp curls awry.

"Ember," Aris calls softly from behind me. I pause, not turning, not looking, simply waiting—staring forward at the street that begins to fill with people once again now that the cold rain has lifted. "Ember, please," he begs. The gravel crunches as he takes the spot in front of me, swallowing my vision. I come face to face with his chest. He's so tall, I forget how much he towers over me when I'm not wearing heels. Slowly, I look up. The gray clouds over him make him look so stark. His gold-flecked onyx eyes, hair that's darker than the midnight sky, pale skin—it's all so vivid.

"She was going to die anyway," he says blatantly. It feels like a slap across the face, and I can't help but flinch, but he doesn't lighten up. "The physician pulled me aside and told me because he didn't want to let you down. Her infection had spread too far and too severely. The medication would have given her more time, but she would have died, Ember. Without that medication she would've been dead in weeks. You cannot change what was destined to happen.

"You can play the what-if game all day. It is a *tragedy* what happened, and justice will be served. But I will be damned if you think I'm going to let you punish yourself as if you're the cause of her death when the perpetrators are out there—the real ones who deserve slow and painful punishment. You gave that mama a good night with her children. A night where she could move and engage with them. You gave those children hope and peace in their grieving. You showed kindness where no royalty, no monarchy, and no authority ever had before.

"So I dare you, Ember, I dare you to look me in the eyes and tell me you're the cause. Because I can see it all over you. You're soaked to the bone. You haven't eaten. You wouldn't look at us because you're *ashamed.* My love, what a heart you have to feel so deeply, so profoundly, for those children that you take on the responsibility so thoughtlessly. It is not your fault. Do you hear me? It is not your fault. Say it." He takes my hands in his, reminding me just how cold I am with his warmth, which feels scalding to the touch. Searching my eyes, he waits. The stone around my heart cracks.

I look at River, who's standing off to the side with his arms crossed over his chest. The rain has weighed down his wavy hair, pushing it down further into his eyes. Those brooding, stormy eyes. He looks so severe right now. Aris is saying everything that needs to be said in the way that I need to hear it because Aris has that way with words. River does too, but in fewer words. He says so much more in just looks and his body language. I've read him for a little less than a year when he did nothing but ignore me. I know which stance means what.

This right now, this one means he's angry. Angry with me. Because he doesn't like when I do this to myself. He doesn't like it when I don't take care of myself. Ever the guard. Ever my protector. I can feel it down our tether now too, but even more than that, he's angry I'd ever feel like this in the first place.

"It's not my fault," I murmur weakly, losing eye contact.

"Look me in the eye, dammit, and believe it," Aris demands. My eyes flicker back to him as his grip tightens. I close my eyes, trying to fight myself. The stone starts to crumble, the beating heart breaking through as the rock falls away. I can't change fate. The gods make sure of that.

However unfair it may be.

"It's not my fault," I say, looking him in the eye with conviction.

"You are good, Ember." He kisses my brow. "We've prepared the carriages again and put together a meal for the road. We can make it to the next town by nightfall if you'd like to finish the tour, but we can also go home. The choice is completely yours," he offers. This choice. Mine to make.

"Let's finish it. We can't give up on the rest of the kingdom. Let's keep going." I look at River, who relaxes a little but not much. He won't until I've changed and I've eaten. Then he'll feel better. I nod, understanding, and he gives me a curt nod back.

I follow them back to the carriage where a fresh cloak and warm clothes have been left. They let me change before they join me inside. We eat silently, watching Kora pass by as the coachman leads us out of the large, bustling city. The fish, spices, and warm bread fill my nose, and I memorize the distinct smell that makes this place itself, tucking it away to call on later. I think about the girl with the beads in her hair and the boy who wants to smell like honey and flowers and lean my head back against the seat.

This city, where beauty and tragedy collided in one fell swoop.

CHAPTER 32

ONE MONTH LATER

The month comes and goes in a haze of days that blend together until I couldn't recognize when one day began and one ended. They all looked the same when we returned. A small office that looks over the field of horses was assigned to me while I helped plan the details of our upcoming wedding and the celebratory ball that happens the day before.

Servants, chefs, musicians, dancers, and so many more have come in and out of my office day in and day out to iron out detail after detail down to the smallest of the smallest for each day. The king has had request after request, and I have fulfilled every single one with a pleasant smile. I'm supposed to wear white both days, but the seamstress and I agreed that for the celebratory ball I'll be wearing a red gown instead. A last nod to Agatharea before my life is completely given to Klyeria. It was her idea—the first words she'd said to me since she started making my dresses.

Aris' birthday came and went. Bleren insisted on a party despite his son's protests, and if I thought I knew debauchery, I didn't until his father was in charge of handling the details. All of the lords were there; in fact, there were more gentlemen in attendance than women. "An intimate gathering. Nothing too big, don't worry," Bleren had assured.

Aris had warned me I shouldn't come, and I hadn't understood. Had been too curious and too stubborn to stay in my room.When the half-naked women dressed in black linen draped across their bodies sauntered into the room, suddenly it all made sense. Especially when a singular seat was placed in the center of the room and Aris was dragged away from beside me. One apologetic look and I was gone, not bothering to stay while those girls had their moment with him. River had stayed behind, doing his due diligence with Bleren and not running after his princess to see if she was okay.

Hypocritical. I know. They share, but I can't. We have to play by Bleren's rules, and if he wants his son to have fun, get drunk, and fool around with women in front of a room full of other men, so be it. I just couldn't stick around to watch it happen. I left his gift on his bed instead, the same way I left River his present after we'd snuck out into town for dinner months ago to celebrate his birthday in January.

I'd taken notice of the type of books Aris liked to read and found one in a shop he hadn't yet. I took my time annotating notes for him so he could see my thoughts along the way. He's a prince, so buying him something extravagant seemed silly. For River, I got Asteria to bring me a dragon tooth from one of the baby dragons in her commander's den in Ereltis. I carved a hole into the thick part of it and wove a leather strap through it to create a necklace. An homage to our time researching dragons together. He joked that it looked real; little does he know that it is.

They were both over the moon for their gifts when they discovered them. I'd felt like they were too small, but they both acted as if I'd given them a castle. Those moments are the brightest amongst the rest. Anything to block out the blasted warning that never ceases to chant and whisper at all times of the day. *There can only be one in the end.*

Most days I'm haunted by memories. I'm plagued by nightmares that follow me even when I'm awake. That golden-eyed little boy and vivacious young painter live in the forefront of my mind. The plume of smoke reaching for the sky flashes every time I close my eyes. So I've channeled it every time Asteria takes me to the mountains, draining myself further and further. We've pushed myself to my absolute limits, finally finding where burnout might actually start to occur.

But not only did that happen after an entire week of us going night after night, but it took nonstop magic use each time, draining me to my very bones. To say I'm walking these halls as the living dead is an understatement. However, not having to worry about controlling my magic on top of handling my mental strife is sweet relief when my well is near empty during the day and replenished by night. I sleep a few hours in the morning and repeat the day. I don't care to close my eyes anyway; that's when all the dark things berate me.

Asteria dotes on me. She helps me channel my magic through my own control and not through my emotions. She soothes me and makes me laugh when it counts. She's a hovering mother hen that I wave off other times.

She returned after three days, just like she said she would. The Elders wanted to know more about my childhood, which she didn't have answers for. She told them what she knew, which was nothing concrete. They also wanted to know more about my magic, to which she confided that I did indeed have multiple gifts, but she didn't tell them how many that actually meant—letting them assume that I had the typical two, maybe three. She's protective, overly so, even if that means from her own Elders and their unknown motives. Other than that, they didn't have much else to ask, so she returned as fast as she could.

The final ache in my chest is missing home. Jasper, Jane, and Viola have been on my mind most of all. My whole court, in fact, and what the future of my kingdom will be. They responded to my letter.

No wedding bells just yet, but keep listening, they told me. Viola and her future missus are moving to her province into her manor. Easton found my plans and took them with him for safekeeping. The girls took the rest of the dresses and jewelry and even sent me some of theirs in return as a thank you. Cameron and Jasper are already meeting about how to change the course of what our fathers have done to the economy of the kingdom.

And yes, Ember, Robert got over that hangover, but there's more in his future he promised. My tears stained the letters they've sent since then as I've reread them dozens of times, almost as if I can hear their voices talking over one another, reading it to me themselves.

They have always existed in the corners of my mind, lurking nightly as the ache of missing home became more prominent the more time passed. I'd always thought I'd want to leave it and all the pain it's caused me.

Now that I have?

All I crave is to be back there, even if it's to endure a snobby look from Robert one more time or hear Easton crack one of his witty jokes. I want to dance with Jasper again and watch Viola draw us from the corner of the room. I want to listen to Daisy's sweet singing voice and make amends with Sierra because it was never fair that she and I were compared our whole lives—pinned against one another.

I'd been separated from my court, told that I couldn't grow up the way they did because I was going to be queen, and queens didn't act like they did. When I was pulled away from the group, they'd never thought of the power dynamic until that point. Never worried about me being their queen and having a say until I started being treated differently than they were. Jasper never cared; he kept treating me the same, and Viola was the most indifferent of the rest, but the wall had been planted. I really, *really* hated that wall. Recently, it felt like that wall was coming down. Like we could actually rule together as one—until the rug had been ripped out from beneath me.

Aris and River have been extremely attentive. The latter has rubbed the knots out of my neck when it's just us in my office for a brief moment. The former murmurs sweet encouragement to me during our training sessions every morning, trying to build up my broken spirit. There are some days when memories of both of their hands from *that* morning play, and I can almost feel them over me like a phantom touch. It's those moments when the haze isn't so foggy. Because those moments remind me that they're both here now, alive and well, and fate hasn't taken either of them away.

Currently, I've just finished handwriting name placement tags for hundreds of guests for both days. With the door locked, I used my shadowy tendrils to write at least ten tags at once, working smarter, not harder, this time around. I lean my head against the smooth, cherry wood polish of the desk and close my eyes. Maybe I can squeeze in a nap before I need to do anything else.

That thought is sorely interrupted as a polite knock I've come to know as Melody's sounds at the door. I rise, smoothing out the black dress I chose today. A simple long-sleeve, off-the-shoulder dress that's form-fitting until my hips, where it flows out in midnight chiffon. I've paired it with black flats and kept my hair natural and down. Asteria joked that I looked ready for a funeral. I told her if she kept joking, it'd be hers. Then she reminded me that it would be ours, and I shut up. Opening the door, I spot both Melody and Layla smiling pleasantly.

"Hello ladies, what might I do for you?" I ask softly, leaning in the doorway. "Wait, is it lunchtime already? I told Aris I'd have a picnic with him since it's unseasonably warm, and I may have lost track of time; you know how I can be." Layla grabs my hands, pausing me mid-spiral.

"No, Ember, you haven't missed lunch. There's just a package that has arrived that you must sign for at the main entrance. It's very large; I believe it is the food parcel, so the kitchen might start some preparations since we are a week away. The prince and king are in a meeting, so you're the only one left to receive it." A soft smile floods her youthful features. Melody peeks at River, who's stood outside my office for the better part of the morning. It's often too risky for him to be alone with me inside, so he stands guard, the way one should. It pains me more than I can admit, but Melody's infatuation with River is much too relatable.

"Wonderful, let's go sign for it, shall we?" I glance at River with a smile I haven't had in days. Something melts in his eyes, like a glacier dissipating in the ocean. He falls into step with me as the girls lead the way. There's a bounce in their step, one I don't normally see, but it's refreshing. Maybe the aura of marriage in the air gets everyone happy one way or another. River's arm brushes mine softly, his only way of telling me he's there with me. His only way of telling me that he'd be kissing me right then and there if he could. I dip my head, hiding another smile as we near the huge front doors.

I can hear horses trot in place outside, at least four of them, and a ruckus of chatter. It throws me for a loop for a moment, and I look at Melody and Layla, who only smile at me until I drop the damper a little more and realize—it's a chatter I recognize. Chatter I grew up listening to, and when the doors open, my heart stops and my legs threaten to give out from beneath me. Layla and Melody step to the side, revealing my favorite lopsided grin standing at the bottom of the steps.

With a mind of their own, my feet begin running, tears streaming down my face and into the wind as I fly down the stairs right into his open arms, nearly taking us to the ground. He laughs into the top of my head, his own voice thick and full of emotion as he holds onto me just as tight as I am him. His hand wraps around the back of my head and the other all the way around my back, and I breathe in the scent of home. The scent of my best friend, the twin flame that I never got to say goodbye to.

I can't control the inconsolable sobs as I clutch onto him, afraid if I let go he might disappear, as if this is some sick joke my mind conjured up. Jasper rubs my back, gripping my neck just a little harder, almost like he's reassuring me he's here and not going anywhere.

"I'm here. We're here," he says softly, and hearing his voice has me pulling back to look into those green eyes. He's got more facial hair now. It seems like he's growing out a small beard, which suits him—makes him look older. His hair is the same curly brown, just rolled out of bed, but sort of put myself together it's always been. Jasper makes it work for him every time. Suddenly, I pull out of his arms, and I'm grabbing Viola next, and she's laughing as I squeeze her and breathe her in.

It's not enough, even as I hold her and take her jasmine scent in, letting her bouncy curls get in my face. Jane giggles when I get to her; her sweet, joyful laugh is enough to ignite the fire in me that I thought went out completely. The tears don't stop as I go down the line taking them each into my arms, kissing each and every one of their faces.

"Nuh uh, you'll get boogers on my coat, and I just bought this. It's *real* fur." Robert backs away as I finally get to him. I wipe my nose, even though I know I don't have any, and I launch myself onto him anyway, hanging on like a monkey on a tree. Then they're all laughing, and the sound, oh *gods,* that sound. Robert concedes, hugging me briefly before setting me down, chuckling himself. I take a couple of steps back and take them all in at once, noticing their luggage behind them.

"Who's responsible for this surprise?" I put my hands on my hips. I'm vaguely aware as Aris comes and joins River behind me at the top of the stairs. To my utter astonishment, Jane raises her hand meekly.

"That would be me. He'll deny it, but he was absolutely *moping* around the castle. It was an incredibly dreary sight. So, I reached out to the prince to see if we could score invitations to the wedding. Instead, we got invitations for an entire week's stay to be with you *and* the wedding. Seems like he's not the only one who needed it." She smiles fondly at Jasper and then me.

"I was planning a visit with Willow, but Jane beat me to it. Plus, this is way better. Look at this place. No wonder Nicholas was still at war; he was probably jealous that Bleren had style." Viola looks the castle up and down appreciatively. She always had a penchant for decor and fashion. Her eyes land on Aris behind me, and her body bristles some. As if on cue, the rest of my court looks at him, and I'm sure my greeting makes it look as if I've had a terrible time here.

"*It hasn't been all sunshine and rainbows,*" Asteria grumbles. She's perched on top of the castle, invisible of course, on a flat top of one of the towers. "*I am glad to see you happy, Ember.*" Emotion is thick in her usually sarcastic and sultry voice, making my heart squeeze harder than it already was.

I've always been okay, Asteria. You need not worry so much.

"*That's what you always say.*" She sticks her tongue out at me; at least she does the mental equivalent before I turn to Aris, who's walked down the steps to greet my court.

Jane has leaned into Jasper's side, who's wrapped an arm around her waist. Seeing her outside of the castle and amongst them is a pleasant surprise, but I'm glad they let her go with. She deserves reprieve from that place. Easton looks down his nose at Aris while Cameron crosses his arms. Daisy and Sierra try their best to look angry when really they're just swooning. Viola just seems skeptical, as if she doesn't know what to think of any of this.

"I hope your trip wasn't too uncomfortable. I am honored to have you here, and more importantly, I am happy to see Ember lit up again." Aris looks down at me, and the draw of his gaze is too powerful not to meet. There's so much unsaid there, but there's also a promise to speak later. I nod, stepping closer to him before turning back to the curious stares now looking at us.

"If it weren't for Cameron farting the entire way here, we might've had a good time," Jasper mumbles. Cameron's freckled cheeks and neck turn bright red.

"You know milk hurts my stomach, and Chef Jean served us creamy porridge for breakfast before we left. What was I supposed to do? Turn him down?" He puts his hands up.

"Yes!" The guys groan in unison. The girls snicker, shaking their heads.

"Daisy had to stop to pee eight times in just four hours. We told her to stop drinking from her waterskin so much, but she wouldn't listen," Sierra says next, shaking her curly blond hair at Daisy, who squints angrily at her.

"Hydrating helps keep those nasty spots off your back," Daisy retorts.

"Okay, okay, you all have spent way too much time cooped up together. And you must be hungry, so let's get you settled in some rooms, and then we'll have lunch in the gardens where there's plenty of fresh air to stave off any flatulence," I suggest, smiling at them. One glance at Cameron and a middle finger is being thrown my way. Gods, it's so good to have them here.

Servants quickly grab their luggage while they follow Aris and I inside. River falls behind me, and I hear him fall into conversation with Jasper behind me.

"How's she been?" Jasper asks quietly, letting Jane walk with Viola instead.

"There are good days and there are bad days," Rivers responds softly, offering the truth in a vague manner. "When Aris told me you were all coming, I knew it was exactly what she needed; I was only mad I hadn't thought of it myself. Smart girl you have."

"It's not the same without her. She was the spark. The last bit of hope. There's been uprising after uprising without her up to take the throne. Even naming me as the next heir wouldn't do anything to heal what Nicholas and Eloise have broken. Whatever you do, you can't let her find out about it. You have to let her think we have Agatharea under control. We're going to figure it out. I'm already working on a plan to overthrow them. I just want this week to be about making her happy," Jasper whispers softly, so softly that I wish I had heard him wrong. I wish I had put the damper back down and ignored their conversation as we showed everyone to their rooms, which are all in the same hall as mine to keep them close to me.

The whole point of this is to broker peace, but what does that mean if my kingdom won't rest? No more war, but no more queen who promised a better future either. I ball my hand into a fist to stay calm. I have to accept what I can't control. Agatharea is no longer mine; it is theirs, and I trust them to do what it takes to restore our kingdom.

"As much as I would have agreed with you before, I've learned my lesson time and time again with her. Keeping her in the dark is worse than you think. You all can talk to her; I'm sure she'll have ideas." River's silk, deep voice fills my ears, warming me up as we pause in front of a room for Jane and Jasper. I turn around with Aris and Jane, looking at River and Jasper with a smile that shows I have no idea what they were talking about.

"Alright, you two, the servants make a mean conceivement blockage cocktail you can drink every—" Jane shoves her hand over my mouth, her eyes wide and cheeks bright red. I laugh against her hands, which are riddled with calluses from all the scrubbing and washing she does. I stick my tongue out, which causes her to squeal, pulling her hand away. "I'm just down the hall if you need anything. Melody and Layla will escort you all to the gardens in about thirty minutes for lunch." I reach out and squeeze Jasper's hand, needing to feel that he's real one more time before I let him get settled in his room.

WE'RE all laid out in the library, strewn about, staring at the ceiling, absolutely stuffed to the heavens. My head is in Aris' lap, while Viola's is in mine as we lie on pillows and blankets. Sierra's in Cameron's lap, which is a new development I hadn't heard of and would've never guessed. Jasper is on the floor with Jane, and River is lying on the couch, while Easton and Robert are passing a bottle of wine back and forth. Daisy lies on her belly on a blanket that's been spread out, her head on her arms as her eyes drift close, her beautiful blonde hair falling all around her.

The silence is comfortable, a change from all the chatter and discussion we had while we were eating just moments before. The fireplace feels nice as it spreads over my skin, warming the prickles of cold that spread with the cool draft that blows through the library. We're all in our sleepwear, and it's peaceful. In fact, it almost makes me want to weep all over again. My fingers mindlessly find their way back to Viola, touching her shoulder softly to ensure she's there. She touches my hand, grabbing ahold of it as if reassuring me she is.

"I wish you could come back with us," she finds herself saying. And from the way she sounds, I'm not entirely sure she means to say it aloud. We're all bottles deep into Aris' wine collection; our bottle dangles from her other hand, half empty.

"I do too," I say softly. Jasper, who's right at my feet and keeps poking them, looks at me with solemn green eyes.

"The kingdom is angry with your parents for selling you off. They want their princess back. Their queen." He flicks my big toe. Jane sits up, tucking a piece of dark, short hair behind her ear. Jasper flips onto his stomach, using his elbows to scoot closer to me. It's such a boyish maneuver—such a Jasper thing to do.

"Which one of you has my father named heir?" I ask, looking from Jasper to the rest of the men. All eyes go back to Jasper, as I expected. As I knew but had to ask.

The word father tastes bitter on my tongue. The more that Asteria and I have gone back and forth on it, the more it hasn't made sense. Especially as we throw in what Dracyl had to say. My parents had a hard time conceiving after me. They always tried for a boy but were never successful. We've theorized that perhaps I was a surrogate and they didn't know where I actually came from.

"It was the first thing he did when he got back. He told us you were never coming back, that you'd never be queen, and that I was the new heir to the throne. I'm not exactly thrilled about it." He looks less than pleased. Jasper was already upset he had to act like a lord, let alone a king. Gods forbid he has to tuck in his shirt properly.

"I could do it if you abdicate," Cameron offers, gesturing with the bottle.

"You, who couldn't tell Chef you wouldn't eat his porridge, would be king?" Robert deadpans.

"My dietary issues are much different than tax law and foreign trade," Cameron counters, though his words are slurred.

"You're not one to talk, mister 'Don't step on my boots; you'll ruin the suede!' I'm not sure you're what Agatharea needs either," Easton says, rolling his eyes. Daisy giggles with her eyes still shut. I could listen to them bicker like this all night. Aris absentmindedly traces the line of my collarbone to my shoulder and then back again. I glance over at River, who seems just as amused as I do. He meets my gaze, watching me with Aris, heat rising in those ocean eyes. I look away before anyone can notice what all three of us are surely thinking.

"I haven't abdicated," Jasper reminds them. "I don't plan to, seeing as we're going to do this as a team effort. Now, I'm much too buzzed off this excellent wine to be talking about such a dreary subject. A little birdy informed me earlier that Ember finally sang for the kingdom, and I think it's only fair she sings for us. So as my first royal decree, I declare that, um, fuck, how do you word this shit?" We all laugh, and I lift myself off of Aris, jostling Viola in the process, who groans in protest.

"To my defense, I have no idea what changed. I couldn't then, and suddenly I can now. Must be some weird maturing of the vocal cord thing." I shrug.

Actually, I've been meaning to ask if that's another Erelt thing I didn't know about. I jab at Asteria, who's out on a night patrol.

"What thing? I wasn't listening. Had to report some Klyerian soldiers poking around at the Ereltis border." She sounds like she's further away tonight, further than she usually is, which means she's actually *in* Ereltis. When she's there, she always sounds faint, and I can't see what she sees anymore because of how heavily enchanted they've warded the kingdom.

Why couldn't anyone hear me sing when I was a child, but now as an adult they can?

"Erelt and sirens are similar in that some of them are born with

the power of persuasion through their voice—their singing voice. So to stave off any children persuading their parents to do whatever they want growing up, or just being out of control in general, families with that power give their children an elixir that's enchanted to keep their singing voices from being heard until they've reached adulthood as a precaution. Even if the child doesn't develop that power. But if they do develop it, they can learn to control whether they're using it with their power or for pure entertainment. So be intentional when you sing. You must've been given the elixir if that particular power runs in your family. It only works as long as you're singing; if you stop, then they stop whatever you're asking them to do. Some people can fight it off too if they try hard enough." I listen intently to Asteria while finding a spot to stand and then clearing my throat, acting like I'm thinking of what to sing.

The Erelt keep getting more complicated and stranger every day.

"You sure do. If only you could visit," she says before she goes quiet again. I look over at the curious eyes that are watching me and shake my head.

"I have no clue what to sing." I purse my lips, glancing around. "And I don't have an accompaniment. Looks like you're out of luck, Your Majesty." I mock a bow for Jasper, going to take a seat on the couch beside River when Jasper puts a hand up to stop me, rising up.

"Uh, uh, do you remember when you were eight years old and you came crying—"

"Do you really have to—" My eyes widen, knowing exactly where he's going with this.

"Because you wanted to sing the duet with me, not Sierra. Sorry, Sierra, but eight-year-old you did *not* cut it for Ember, apparently—"

"I'm going to kill—" I'm ready to choke him. Sierra takes a sip of wine, raising an eyebrow at me; I glance at her apologetically.

"You tried so hard to get me to hear you, but I couldn't. So, Sierra stayed. A bit out of tune, but hey, she tried. All you wanted was to sing with your best friend, and you couldn't. You cried for weeks, Ember. So come on. Sing with me." He reaches his hand out to me, and when I take it, he pulls me and my heartstrings with him, reminding me why he's always been my best friend to begin with.

"I was this close to kicking you out of the castle," I mumble to him as I take the spot beside him; he only smiles, those goofy dimples making up for it all. "For the record, Sierra, it had nothing to do with your vocal talent and everything to do with the fact that I just wanted to fit in with you guys. In fact, I spent a lot of my adolescent years trying to figure out how to look like you because of how beautiful I thought you were." I wrap my arms around my middle, smiling at her sheepishly.

"I never hated you," she says softly. And that's all that needs to be said. I nod at her, understanding passing between us.

"Shall we?" Jasper says.

CHAPTER 33

We finally settle on a song, and I let him take the lead as I'm still so rusty. Now that I understand how connected my singing and power are, I can focus on disconnecting them. When I tried singing with Madame Celine, I was still filled with so much magic it was too difficult to wrangle it in—to keep it from intertwining. Even the first time I did it at the welcome ball, the entire crowd felt it at first until I pulled it back inside. At least now I know.

Jasper hums the first note before he starts, his smooth baritone voice filling the library so impressively I almost forget to enter when it's my turn. I'd memorized so many of the songs they'd learned over the years, having snuck in on some of their lessons whenever I could. He's dressed in some navy blue, soft pajama pants and a matching soft, short-sleeved shirt. Jane is ogling him with no shame, and with the blush creeping up her neck, I'm hoping we'll find out just how soundproof these rooms are.

With my well emptier than usual from all my constant use, it's not hard to keep it from intertwining with my singing, though I do feel the pull. It reminds me of how I usually feel when I play cello, how electric and magnetic the room feels with me. Two particular sets of eyes bore into me, setting fire and electrifying my skin where I stand. I'm only wearing a black nightgown, the thin straps baring my shoulders, and the hem falling just above my knees. All of the girls are wearing the same thing in various different colors, and the guys don't look much different from each other either. Save for Aris in his favorite silk bottoms.

My hair falls over my shoulders, protecting the scars on my back. I arch an eyebrow at them both as our duet comes to an end, our voices ringing in perfect harmony. I'm only met with a sly smirk and another knowing look that drags up the length of my legs. Soft applause pulls me away, making me look back at Jasper with a huge smile.

"You're telling me you were holding *that* out on us?" He looks at me in disbelief.

"I'm going to need you to come back and sing me to sleep every night," Daisy says sweetly.

"You're telling me you weren't already asleep?" Sierra asks, her head now in the crook of Cameron's shoulder, while his hand holds her legs up against him.

"I'm just enjoying the ambiance with my eyes closed," Daisy mumbles. Jasper walks up behind me, putting his hands on my shoulders to shake me the way he always has before I can stop him, and then suddenly it's all too late. His thumbs brush over the raised skin—the white scars that litter my destroyed back. One touch and his grip tightens before I can pull out of it.

"Jasper, no—" I yank forward, frantic and panicked. I look at River and Aris, who understand immediately and hop up, coming to my side. But it's too late; Jasper's already pushed my hair aside and seen what he's needed to. Aris pulls me into his side, letting my hair cover my back again, and suddenly I feel so stupid for not covering up more. I'd just wanted to have a normal night. At this point, everyone in the castle has seen them. Gods, the rest of this kingdom could see the scars Agatharea left me, and I wouldn't care.

But this? Jasper? My court? It's different. I never wanted them to see me as anything less than what they already did. Glancing around, I can already see the curious and confused looks. Jane watches Jasper from the floor, concern written across her face as he stands before me. I face him finally, trying not to feel ashamed, but the red heat of embarrassment rushes to my cheeks and up my neck.

"Who?" His voice is more broken and guttural than I've ever heard it before.

"Jasper, please," I whimper, my shaking voice a crying plea.

"Who did that to you?" he asks again, a borderline growl in his voice, his hands flexing at his sides. I swallow the lump forming in my throat and look around again. He looks to Aris beside me and then River, scrutiny and judgment lying so heavily in his gaze that the words come tumbling out of my mouth.

"My father," I whisper, defeated. "The night before we left."

"Show them," he commands, and it's the last thing I expect. My eyes go wide, and I feel River and Aris tense from beside me.

"You can't make her do that." River's the first to speak in my silent shock, but Jasper doesn't back down. He doesn't take his eyes off of me, his stare burning deep into the things I've laid hidden.

"Show. Them." He emphasizes each word. "Because they wouldn't believe me."

"You told them?" I furrow my eyebrows, not understanding. "Why would you do that?"

"Because they wouldn't agree to my plan." He glares at them over my head.

"Because what you spoke of was treason!" Easton shouts, rising from his seat. Everyone begins to rise or at least sit up straighter. Daisy stands, leaning against the lip of a table.

"You were asking too much, Jasper," Viola says softly.

"The king and queen are harsh and greedy, sure, but what you tried to accuse them of? We would've seen it, and we didn't," Cameron says, equally as quiet, still sitting with Sierra, whose eyes look sadly upon me as if she's not so sure, and she's the only one.

"We know they locked you away and were hard on you, but you were supposed to be the queen, so of course you had to go through that. But hit her? Come on, Jasper. And then to propose what you did?" Robert scoffs, as if the isolated treatment I went through in my childhood was rational and just. Jasper shoots him a look that has him shutting him up.

"What plan are they talking about, Jasper?" I pull his attention back to me.

"Show them, and I'll tell you, because then maybe they'll understand how awful Nicholas and Eloise really are. They'll understand I wasn't lying." His voice breaks again at the end, and if it weren't for that, if it weren't for the conviction in which he spoke, I wouldn't do it. I don't think I could. Not like this. But the light that's flickered out of my favorite pair of green eyes has me stepping out of Aris' side. A rough hand catches my wrist, making me turn.

"You don't have to; they should believe you by your word." River's anger burns into me.

"He wouldn't make me do this if it wasn't important, River. I'm still repairing the rift between me and them," I tell him quietly. Aris shakes his head silently, not agreeing, but he knows I'm going to do it anyway. They know I bare my scars on my own terms, but this is a worthy exception.

Stepping out of River's hold and into the center, I find myself under the intense stare of my former court. Skepticism is written all over them, and how could I blame them? My father never left evidence on my face, and if he did, there was always an excuse. Suddenly, the tether between Aris and me grows stark with agony, and I know that if I looked at him, he'd be drawing the same conclusions. For a brief moment, I realize he's seeing his mother, not me, as I turn, the flames of the fire casting light on my back. I wish I could soothe that permanent ache in his soul.

The silence that fills my head is deafening as I sweep my hair over my shoulder, revealing the low dip of the nightgown. The cool air brushes over the ruined skin, and for a brief moment no one says anything as I let my long, wavy hair settle along my back, covering the scars once more.

"It is for most that seeing is believing. I am sorry, my dear, that you had to do that." Asteria's voice is soft and soothing, and I almost sigh in relief upon hearing her.

I just hope it's worth it. I turn around and look at them, and between the looks of horror and disgust, I find myself not able to control the quiver in my lip. Robert, who's turned pale, turns quickly, running off to a nearby trash bin placed by a servant, and vomits into it. Sierra sniffles while Cameron stares at the floor, almost looking ashamed. It's Viola who speaks first.

"It wasn't a book." She sounds angry. Angry with herself.

"No, it wasn't." I shake my head, walking back to River and Aris for comfort. Instinctively, Aris wraps an arm around my waist. River stands close beside me on my other side, his warmth seeping in. Discreetly, his knuckles brush against my skin, and momentarily I'm filled with a bit of strength from them both.

"It happened the night you left," Jasper repeats. "That's why you never said bye? Those were the circumstances?" He looks at Aris, struggling with his words and anger.

"I couldn't..." I closed my eyes, unsure of how to explain that night. "I barely made it to my room. By the time they cleaned me up, all I wanted was sleep. Then we left so early in the morning, and I just figured I'd be back in a month." I try not to look at Aris, but now they all are.

"But he knew you weren't coming back. The whole time." Jasper's anger is so palpable I could grab it from the air around us. "You let her go without letting her say goodbye."

"How was I supposed to know what he was going to do to her?" Aris counters.

"That's beside the matter. She was expecting to come back. I never got to say goodbye, godsdamn it! She was never coming back." Jasper's eyes flicker back to me, completely broken, and when Jane had said he was "moping," I hadn't realized what level that had been.

"Jasper..." I remove myself from Aris. "What were you planning?" Because now I can see it—I can see it in his eyes. My sweet, silly, beastly best friend is suddenly so haunted, and I don't know how I hadn't seen it until now.

"To kill him." He looks away. "Poison him somehow so it looked natural so he'd be gone and taken care of. Your mother's a pushover. I don't care what happens to her, but all we need is him out of the way, and we can make some real changes. We could avenge your name. Gods, Ember, had I known what he did to you, I would've already done it." He runs a hand over his face, wiping away a stray tear. I look at the rest of them, who now seem so grave compared to the joyous group they were just moments ago. It's hard not to feel like that's all my fault yet again.

"And that's where they drew the line," I say softly, understanding finally.

"We didn't know, Ember," Daisy says, hiccuping. "Why didn't you tell us?"

"Well, you're my court, but we weren't close like that. Not yet. Like Robert said, I was going to be queen, and I just had to bear it until then. There was nothing anyone could do to stop it. He's the king. Do not feel guilt now. I am not angry with any of you. Think about what this week will hold for the first time in four decades. *Peace*. Soldiers will return to their homes, to real beds, and their children. No more villages burnt to ashes. No more death ceremonies with scrolls so long and agonizing it makes you wonder how we keep losing that many people. I may not be Queen of Agatharea, but my marriage to Aris will do some good.

"It's a start. We have to start somewhere. Though I'm sure Aris and River would join you in a heartbeat to kill my father, I would never ask that of any of you. But there have to be laws buried deep in the tombs of our libraries that could help figure out how to overthrow him. Do your research first; gather the support of your parents, because the key to it is turning his own court against him. Do it for our people. I am okay here. Please, *please* let us have a fun week. Don't worry about politics. Let me just enjoy the fact that you're actually here, living and breathing in front of me right now." I smile at them, and it's a real and bright smile.

Robert has come back and is now sitting and nodding. I look at Jane, who's been incredibly still and the most difficult to read, but her eyes are trained on Jasper, who looks torn between his emotions. Viola's looking at me with so much turmoil in her eyes. She's smart; she always has been, and I think there's a part of her that's angry she missed it. And I think there's an even bigger part of her that's angrier she denied Jasper. Easton still has a contemplative look. I tilt my head at him, as if asking what's on his mind.

"I have an idea, but it can wait until after the wedding," he answers quietly. I nod appreciatively.

"I'm so sorry you had to go through that, Ember," Sierra says, her voice thick with her own tears. "You didn't deserve that—any of it. I'm sorry we didn't believe you, either. I don't think we wanted to." There's a certain peace that fills my chest at her words.

"Thank you, Sierra. I just wish I had more time with you all as my court to really build a future together." A sad smile touches her lips, and she nods. "Let's call it a night. You all can sleep in actual beds tonight and for as long as you'd like. Then we'll see where the day takes us. I'm just about done with wedding planning, so I should be able to slip away and be a ruckus with you all."

Jasper, who's been so quiet, finally moves toward me as everyone stands, gathering themselves and whatever garbage to place into the bin. I faintly hear Daisy make a gagging noise when she passes by it, and Easton laughs at her weak stomach when it comes to other people's bodily fluids.

Goodnights are murmured until Jane, Viola, and Jasper are the only ones left with us. Viola comes toward me, and I remove myself from Aris' arms to step into hers. She holds me for a long while, her jasmine scent soothing the ache that had started the moment Jasper grabbed my shoulders.

"Long live the queen," she whispers into my ear. Those tears come back in full force, and I hold her tighter. "You will always be mine, Ember. We will rule in your honor." She pulls back, holding me by the shoulders to look into my eyes.

"There's no one else I trust more than you all in this room right now." I look at her, then Jane and Jasper. I don't have to look at River and Aris because they know I'm talking about them too. "I know you will make the people of Agatharea proud." I grab Jane next, holding her small frame close. She holds me back tentatively, then, realizing I'm not going to break, she tightens her grip.

"And you, Jane. When you marry Jasper, you'll be queen. And think of what that means. You can give the people a *voice*. Their queen will understand them in ways no queen before them has. Not even me. They'll love you, and Viola can teach you everything there is to know about royalty. It's a bunch of snobbery if you ask Jasper, and he's not wrong, but you'll do just fine." I kiss the top of her head before pulling away to see her smiling face.

"I only wish to make you proud," she says. "I hope that with us both being queens, we can still send each other books."

"Oh absolutely, that reminds me I have one you should read while you're here." I wink at her, letting her know which kind it is. She giggles before turning to Jasper.

"I'll wait for you in our room. Viola, want to walk together?" Viola nods, and they both go, arms linked together. The fire crackles, filling the silence after the leave.

I wish I could tell what Jasper was thinking, what he was feeling. Some light flickers back in those eyes as I come to stand in front of him, taking his hands. I can see the weight as if it were physically sitting on his shoulders, weighing him down.

"He sold you. Like you were nothing," he whispers, looking down at me.

"Peace for two kingdoms, Jasper," I remind him.

"What peace do you have?" He searches my eyes.

"They give me solace." I nod to River and Aris, and he looks in their direction. They're both standing with their arms crossed, both still unhappy with what he made me do. And yet, they've remained so quiet, letting me do what I needed to and say what I wanted.

"So there's no chance I can sneak you home?" There's a faint glimmer of hope in his eyes.

"I promised a little girl her dad was coming home to her—there's no chance." His offer to bring me home does pierce my heart, though, because for a whisper of a moment, I contemplate it.

The answer remains no.

"Ember, I'm so—" I cut him off right away.

"Absolutely not. I'll shove your head in the garbage bin if you apologize. Come on, it's getting late, and I'm getting cold. By royal decree, I do declare that my best friend remains thy silly self and makes me laugh until my belly hurts the rest of this week. Do you accept the terms and conditions?" I raise my eyebrow at him.

"Spoken like a true queen. I am at your service, Your Majesty." He lets go of my hands to sketch a bow for me.

Laughing softly, I follow him out, Aris and River falling in step behind us. I bid him goodnight before he slips into his room, saluting me before he shuts the door. When we make it to my room, both Aris and River walk right in. I don't bother hiding my frustrated sigh as I shut the door behind me.

"What?" I ask, crossing my arms while Aris lights a couple of candles, illuminating the room in a warm glow.

Aris faces me, letting that cool mask he wears around everyone else drop, and beneath it lies cool anger. "You have to stop doing that." It's one of the first things he's said to me all night.

"Doing what?" I furrow my eyebrows.

"Making yourself suffer for the sake of others," River answers. They stand side by side, and I almost want to groan out of frustration again because when they join up against me, it's impossible to win an argument with them.

"That was necessary," I mumble, looking away because there's still just a slight bit of wine running through me, and they both look so good it's distracting me from holding my ground.

"It wasn't. I know you love Jasper, for whatever reasons you may have, but he shouldn't have made you do that. You're too stubborn to see that," River says, and the pull of his voice is too much not to look.

"Seeing is believing, and it did the job. Why is that such an issue?" Asteria was right.

"That's bullshit, Ember," Aris growls. "You could've convinced them with words. You could've told them a small part of your story. You didn't have to stand there like a zoo animal and expose yourself. But you don't *listen* to us. We both knew there was no use in trying to convince you otherwise."

"You don't know them." But even as I say it, I know it's not true. I just don't want to admit they're right. I know it was unnecessary, and deep down I hated it, but if it meant spurring them in the right direction, then so be it. Whatever I must endure.

"I know them enough," River retorts, and he does. He's spent enough time around them.

"How is this any different than the shit Bleren makes me do?" I gesture with my hand, sweeping across the room.

"Because those people are supposed to care about you, and they won't kill you if you don't listen." Aris takes a deep, frustrated breath. I open my mouth and then close it.

Anger, burning and hot, bubbles in my chest, swirling in the well within me. If steam could come out of my ears, I'm sure it would. I turn away from them and toward the windows, staring at the reflection the candles create. They watch me quietly, but I'm much too riled up to talk anymore. I did what I had to, and I'll continue to do whatever it takes to make sure these kingdoms know tranquility. No matter what it takes, no matter what I have to go through.

"Get out," I find myself saying. I hear both of them bristle as I close my eyes, not wanting to see them in the reflection of the window.

"Ember, please," River says softly.

"Look at us." Aris takes a step forward.

"I said, get out. Now." I make my voice more firm, almost believing it myself even though I know I'm acting a fool. Still, they both hesitate. Slowly, one by one, they walk to my door.

"We only want what's best for you," Aris murmurs.

I can feel River watching me as if his eyes were my own. His tether practically tugs me to look at him, but I remain where I am. "We don't want to watch you suffer." Then the door clicks behind them.

With half a thought, the candles go out and the door becomes locked. I climb into bed, bringing the blanket up to my chin as I curl up on my side. I close my mental door, knowing that Asteria is and will side with them, and I just don't want to hear it from her either. As I fall asleep, I try not to think of their faces as I turned around. Or of Jasper and the brokenness I'd left him with.

I try not to think of any of it.

CHAPTER 34

The week goes by quickly. At first, it was strained. Aris and River showed up inside my room the very next morning using their key to get in, and despite my best efforts, I couldn't stay angry. I was the one in the wrong, and I agreed to at least try to be a little more self-preservative.

Everyone else kept glancing at me like I was going to implode, or they'd be very delicate with me as if I were porcelain. It wasn't until I took them into town to a local tavern and got absolutely drunk with them that everything settled back to normal. Aris didn't join us that night; he was preoccupied with meetings with his father and their court. River, of course, did go, but he did not drink.

I did learn that it takes a considerable amount for Erelt to get drunk due to their fast healing abilities. So whilst everyone was belligerent, I was pleasantly buzzed and only slightly incoherent. Simple enough for River to get me back in one piece. That didn't stop me from seeing if I could seduce him into bed that night.

Despite making him very hard, very quickly, with my suddenly very dirty mouth, he refused. It was still too dangerous for us as much as he wanted to, and trust me, he wanted to. He did kiss me though. That he couldn't refuse and that almost got him, especially since my hands roamed on their own accord. But one growl later and he'd detached himself from me, bidding me a goodnight.

Today is the celebratory ball, and I'm still in bed dreading the moment anyone knows I'm awake. I had a really long night with Asteria, practicing as much as we could before I had to call it quits and get some rest. Sixteen years worth of stuffing my magic way, way down, and I'm finally, finally finding relief. I no longer feel like my skin is stretching against its will. Or if I get upset that the lid is going to fly open at any moment. My well runs so deep, and I am more powerful than I ever could've imagined. But all the extra that I'd shoved so far down has finally been burnt off from our work throughout the night. So, I'm reading and soaking in the last bits of peace before my impending doom knocks on the door.

"You like to read a lot of romance," she says, not really as a question.

And?

"Is that how you learned to fuck?" She snorts, and I can imagine her swishing her tail.

That's precisely how I learned. Are you still a virgin? Or how do dragons learn? Is there a dragon sex talk during the pivotal dragon teenage years?

"I'm not a virgin. I winged it but also had a vague idea from conversations with friends. Dragons don't do the whole sex talk now. They just tell you not to, so we don't overpopulate again." I can feel her rolling her eyes, as if dragons would ever actually abstain.

Who'd you lose it to? I close my book, rolling over onto my stomach, closing my eyes, preparing for mental images. She flashes a memory of a tall, muscular black dragon. A wicked-looking fellow with red eyes and a smirk.

"His name is Mont. He was very good in the sack, but that was it. His sister, Locia—" Another flash of an image. A silver dragon, blue eyes, and a sleek, shimmering body. She had long, curling horns the color of fresh snow. *"She was even better. I actually*

really liked her and almost thought we could be mates until she actually found hers, and it wasn't me. But she was good while it lasted." There's a part of me that's sad she hasn't found a mate yet, but I'm also excited to be a part of her escapades.

You went from sibling to sibling?

"They didn't care. We're not trivial like humans or Erelt," she says as a matter of fact. I snort out loud. I'm about to answer when that damning knock comes and my cocoon of safety and warmth is busted. But it's not the soft knock I expected from Melody or Layla. It's abrupt, and the shuffling and shushing in the hallway are too much for my liking, so I drop the damper and listen.

"Shut up, you buffoon; she'll hear you," Robert whispers, to whom I have no clue.

"She probably already has with your loud mouth," Easton counters. *Ah.* I rush and throw on my robe to cover my naked body before hurriedly washing my mouth. Raking my hands through my hair to try and calm it somewhat, I open the door like I had no idea they were all out here waiting for me.

Every single one of them, including Aris and River, is wearing a silly hat made of paper decorated in paint. It's a tradition we started when we were children on each other's birthdays. We'd make these ridiculous hats and wear them in celebration for their entire day. Viola and Jane are holding a cake together; the top is decorated with intricate green frosting and candles that have already begun to melt. Jasper's the first to hastily start singing happy birthday from the top of his lungs before the others join in harmoniously.

I can't help but laugh as they push forward through the door, forcing me back into the room as they pile in. It shuts behind them as the final note is sung and held out on a dramatically long note while they wait for me to make a wish and blow out the candles. Closing my eyes, I wish for the only thing I can think of: *I wish that we'll have many more days like this* and then blow the small fires out.

"A good wish, my dear." Her voice hums through me with pride and joy for a moment until she turns contemplative.

Soft cheers fill the room before the cake is taken to my desk to be cut and served for breakfast. This is way better than I was expecting to start the day off. I'd honestly completely forgotten what today was or that the ball fell on my birthday at all. It all had come together so quickly I'd lost track and hadn't realized. I didn't think they'd pay attention either. As if reading my mind, Jasper finds me and says,

"You didn't think I'd forget, did you?" He grabs my shoulders and shakes them before I turn to look at him and his cheesy face.

"No, but I sure did," I admit, shaking my head. "Got too wrapped up in everything. It completely slipped my mind."

"Is it really your birthday?" Asteria asks.

No, the cake and singing were all pretend. I roll my eyes internally.

"Do you feel...different at all?"

Not at all, why? I turn toward the window, looking out toward the field, past it toward the forest beyond. She's out there, somewhere.

"Erelt are typically strongest on their birthdays and on solstices. Something to do with the cycles, I'm not sure of the exact reasoning behind it. I'm not trying to pull you down, but I don't think today is your actual birthday," she says sadly, and for whatever reason, deep down I know she's right, and somehow, I think I've always known. My birthday has always felt weirdly off.

There's a day late in the fall that I wake up feeling somewhat how she described. I never paid attention to it, but now that she's said it, it does happen every year. It's never been to the extent this past solstice has been, but then again, this Winter Solstice was completely different from any other I've experienced.

Maybe I'm not even turning twenty-one. Someone touches my shoulder, pulling me out of my head with a startle. The cedar-wood scent calms me a moment later, and I relax into his touch, right into his back, as he wraps his arms around me with a piece of cake to offer.

"For the birthday girl," he says, kissing the top of my head. I lean my head back, looking up at him upside down with a smile.

"Why, thank you." I take the cake happily and take a bite. "Cake for breakfast is just what I needed to start this day off." The morning sun reflects off the dew in the grass, illuminating them like thousands of sparkles amongst the blades. My court makes themselves comfortable around my room, some sitting on the floor to eat, others leaning against the wall.

"When you're done, will you open your gifts?" Daisy asks. I peek over to her, my mouth full of cake and eyes wide. I swallow hastily.

"Gifts?" I groan, not exactly thrilled. She nods with her chin to the pile they've made against the wall beside the door. "You guys..."

"You guys, nothing; it's your birthday, Em. We weren't allowed to do this before," Jasper says, setting his now empty plate down on the desk. Huffing in resignation, I finish my cake, enjoying every last bite before piling my plate on top of his. They've pulled the desk chair over so I can sit and open them one by one.

Between Sierra and Daisy, I now have a complete set of my own cosmetics and a few new pieces of jewelry to add to my collection. From Jane, two new romance books. Viola drew a picture of me from the Winter Solstice and also bought me a short green dress that reminds me of the dress she wore to Marbs the night we all went out. Robert and Cameron both picked out perfumes, which I'm told were approved by the girls. They do smell really good, so I do love them. Easton really took a liking to Bedelia, so he had some riding boots made as well as more comfortable clothing for me to ride in.

Jasper got his hands on a book of sheet music from a coveted composer and is responsible for bringing my cello back in one piece so I can play while I'm here. River had gotten into contact with Auburn and Harry's aunt and was able to get a letter from Auburn to me that included several paintings of other fairies. He'd used the address from which I sent Harry the soap that I promised him. I'd also sent money to help support her with two new mouths to feed. I hadn't had the heart to reach out to Auburn or Harry yet, but he finally did, and reading her words in her voice nearly brought me to tears.

Finally, Aris kneels in front of me, blocking my view of everyone as he places a small box in my lap. It's velvet and rectangular—big enough to fit a necklace in it. I look up at him as he covers my hands with his, his own shaking slightly as if he's nervous to give me what it is.

"There's an explanation, but only for your ears." He squeezes my hands, and I nod understandingly.

I open the box and gasp softly. It's a gold necklace; the chain is spun and twists intricately until it meets a red ruby that looks like it's almost glowing. The ruby is shaped like a diamond, and on the right and left corners of each point sits a trio of bright, shimmering diamonds. It's stunning and unlike any piece I've ever owned before. It'll go perfectly with my dress for tonight.

"It's beautiful," I whisper in awe. "I can't wait to hear the story." Because I know it's not just something he found at the shop. No, this means something to him. He doesn't say anything; he only plants a soft kiss on my lips before rising back up and joining everyone. I can't help the blush that makes its way up my neck, especially when Viola raises an eyebrow at me and Daisy and Sierra swoon for me.

"Thank you, everyone. I can't express enough how absolutely grateful I am for all of you. Just having you here this weekend has been..." A lump forms in my throat, cutting me off as tears well in my eyes. My gaze shoots to Jasper, who nods knowingly, probably understanding more than any of them how the gift of their presence was more than enough.

"You've gotten so mushy," Robert says.

"Rightfully so," Easton remarks.

"You could learn a thing or two," Daisy points out.

"We're glad to be here," Viola says, her smile imprinting on my heart. I commit it to memory—every last one of them, as if I weren't going to see them ever again. Sniffling, I stand and start pulling them into hugs again against their protests.

"Shut up and let me love you," I mumble. Jasper holds me for a long while, his hand clutching the back of my neck as we hold each other close. My tears stain his shirt, but he doesn't say anything, not as his own fall into my hair. *You've always had me, and you always will.* It echoes through my mind, his words to me the moment I was scared I'd lose him before. In this moment I know I *will* always have him, my best friend, no matter what separates us. When I move to Robert, he throws his hands up.

"But the boogers," Robert groans.

"You'll miss my boogers when you get back." I stick my tongue out at him, and this time he doesn't fight me off.

THE DRESS IS MAGNIFICENT. The seamstress has truly outdone herself, and to go the extra mile, she's duplicated it in white on the off chance that the king throws a fit and I have to change. But for the entrance, for the statement I want to make— it's absolutely perfect.

The thin straps lead to a deep red wine bodice covered in flowery vines that spill into the waist and flow down the hips before disappearing into mounds and mounds of tulle. She's cut two slits so when I walk, both legs slip out, and on one leg she's wrapped a matching red garter to be visible. The chest dips into a somewhat low v, sinking to my sternum, and the back is open until the bottom of my waist. An ode to Agatharea, my kingdom in color. Both the good and the bad on display.

The girls took their time with the hot tool they heated up using the heat from the fire to create softer, more organized waves in my hair. The necklace Aris gave me goes perfectly with the dress, as I expected, lying right in the crook of my collarbones. Later in the day, while I was finalizing preparations in the ballroom, he found me and explained that it was his mother's. In fact, it was the last thing he owned of hers, and he wanted me to have it. His exact words having been,

"I knew from the moment I met you that I was yours, and this is the last way I can show you, Ember, that no matter what you see or what you hear, my heart belongs to you." I melted, completely and thoroughly, and I'm still not sure I've recovered.

Melody and Layla also used the new cosmetics that Daisy and Sierra got me, and it's suffice to say I've never felt as beautiful as I do right now. The girls left a few moments ago, and now I'm just waiting for River and Aris to join me so we can be announced. The king asked that it be masquerade themed, which I found odd for a wedding celebration, but I went with it. It gave us girls a reason to go shopping, and we found adequate masks for us and all of the boys to wear tonight.

All of the girls also bought new dresses for today and tomorrow, so everyone is excited to be dressed to the nines tonight. I bid my court goodbye a few hours ago to get ready and told them I'd meet them inside at the ball once things were already up and going. I spray some of the perfume Cameron got me while waiting for the guys to arrive.

"I can smell you from here; I think that's enough."

Buzz off; it's got to last. You wouldn't know a thing about smelling good. I set the bottle down as a knock comes at my door. Cedarwood and mint waft toward me, and the scent is a heady mix that makes my toes curl.

"You're so rude."

You started it. Now, allow me some privacy for all the dirty things I'm about to think when I open this door and lay eyes on these two.

"You're no fun! I never get to stay." And with that I shut the mental door and open the real one. I don't think any of us are

prepared to see each other, not with the silence that follows as I drink them in. River is dressed in the Klyerian royal guard uniform for special events like this. Black pants, a black tunic with the golden crest of the kingdom sewn into the breast pocket. But it's tailored to fit him like an absolute glove. Every seam seems to hug every muscle of his arms and chest before it's tucked into his pants where his sword is strapped to. His facial hair is trimmed nice and neat, and his curls are still a little damp. The golden hue of his skin and the blue of his eyes seem to stand out so much more against the black. He looks really godsdamn good in it.

Then there's Aris, who always wears all black, and though that hasn't changed, it's the severity in which he looks that nearly brings me to my knees. His tunic is unbuttoned at the top, revealing a sliver of his smooth, chiseled chest. The seams are lined with gold, making it shimmer as he moves. The sleeves are already rolled up, revealing his strong, veiny forearms. It's tucked into a pair of black pants and a belt to tie it all together. There are no words. Not a single one, as I ogle shamelessly—as they do the same.

When I meet Aris' eyes, I find anger. He pushes in past me, effectively turning the heat into frustration.

River steps in, closing the door behind him, and I hear the lock slide into place. He leans against the door, watching Aris as I turn and do the same. I can hear him swallow and take a few deep breaths before he faces me head-on, standing by the windows. He's staring at my dress, and it dawns on me that it's the color. I take a step forward toward him, placing myself between him and River with my back to River.

"One. Rule," he says, still not looking at me.

"It's a fucking dress, Aris. We're getting married tomorrow, and I have a beautiful white dress to wear then. He's demanded hundreds of things; do you really think he's going to remember something as minuscule as what color I need to wear today?" I cross my arms, hating that we're back to this stupid argument yet again. He takes a step forward toward me, and I take one back.

"Why test him at all? What's the point?" He takes another step, and I concede back again.

"My court is here, and this is the final day I have as a true Agatharean before that is ripped away from me. This is all I have to offer as tribute." I tip my chin up, but this isn't the right answer because he takes yet another angry step, and I find myself backed right into River. His hands find my waist, the tips of his fingers digging into my hips as he steadies me against his chest, holding me close as I face off with Aris.

"I can't even begin to explain how bad of an idea that is, Ember. As valiant and beautiful as I think that is. It's also risky and stupid, and he'd have your head in an *instant* if he knew that's what you were doing. Why can't you just listen?" A few more steps from Aris and he'll be right in front of me.

"She was raised to be a fucking queen. The whole idea is that they bow down to *her*, not the other way around," River says, his chest vibrating against my back. I can feel his heart beating against me, and I can't help but lean further into him when his grip tightens on my hips, molding me perfectly against him. Aris is so wrapped up in his anger he hasn't realized how he's backed me up. I struggle to keep my bravado up with River's fingers causing my body to instantly go haywire.

"He bows to no one, and he'll be damned if he lets her make a fool of him. Your whole thing is her safety; you should care more about this," Aris argues.

"I also care about the fact that we keep driving her into the ground in order to keep her safe. When is that going to stop? When do you step out from being daddy's puppet and start putting her first?" River counters. Aris finally closes the distance between us, staring River down over my head.

"That's enough. We're arguing about a dress. About the fucking color. If you feel so strongly that he'll hurt me over it, then take it off me." I tip my head up, leaning it against River's chest so I can look Aris in the eye. His eyes flare, and I can see it— I can see the precariously slipping self-control he works so hard to hold on to. I've stayed away this month. With the exception of my drunken night, I hadn't made any advances on either of them. I'd been so wrapped up in my head to really think about what my body and heart wanted from them.

"This one looks so good though," River mumbles in my ear.

"I have the same exact one in white." I smirk. "A backup for this exact moment. I just thought I'd actually make it to the dance floor before someone made me change."

"You had a white one the whole time." Aris' jaw clenches as he looks down at me, his eyes roaming over my lips, down the slopes of my breasts, which are rising and falling quicker and quicker.

"I'm not dense. I know your father. I just want what I want, Aris. I wanted some sense of control." I watch as his gaze falls to where River has a hold on me, to where my hands lay over River's.

"I can give you control, Ember. Just not in the way you need it. Not yet. It's not safe for you against him." Aris' eyes finally come back up to mine, heat igniting every inch of my skin from what lies in his gaze.

"What exactly are you offering?" I search his eyes for an answer, my heart thrashing so quickly it almost hurts.

"Unzip it." The words aren't directed at me, but to River, who surprisingly listens without protest. His hands leave my hips, finding the zipper at the bottom of my back and tugging it down in one smooth motion.

I watch wordlessly as Aris takes the straps and calmly pushes them off my shoulders, pulling the dress down until it pools at my feet, and I'm standing in front of them in nothing but red lace underwear. He takes the dress as I step out of it and my heels and throws it to the side, not looking to see where it lands, not taking his eyes off the skin in front of him. The hunger there is so stark, so needy my own knees quiver. River's hands come back, holding me up and against him, the hard length of his own member pressing against me.

"I'm at your mercy. You've won. I don't know if I'm more angry that I had to take you out of the dress...or because you looked so damn good in it." Aris leans forward, taking my head in his hands. "Or because you're so stubborn that you went and put it on in the first place. Because if you hadn't, I wouldn't have lost. I was a goner the moment you opened that door." And with that he slams his lips into mine, and stars explode behind my eyes. His tongue mingles with mine, pulling sounds from my throat. All too soon those lips are traveling down my neck and rough hands are traveling up my chest.

Aris drops to his knees in front of me while River's lips kiss down my jaw to the spot below my ear where he sucks, making me moan both at the sensation and at the sight before me. This isn't happening. It can't be real. Yet, those are Aris' fingers hooking into the waistband of my panties and yanking them off.

"Are you sure?" I ask breathlessly. I'm not entirely sure myself how I have the means to form coherent words, but I ask none-theless because it's the least I can do for having pushed him this far.

"It's too late, Princess. You're all I've wanted since you walked through those doors at the Winter Solstice ball. All I've seen when I closed my eyes to go to bed. All I've tasted since that night at the inn." He looks up at me, and gods, I have never been so turned on than in this moment with River behind me and Aris on his knees in front of me.

"Be a good girl and let him have you," River says low in my ear, his rough hands grabbing both breasts. I don't have to be told twice before I'm throwing one leg over Aris' shoulder, and he's leaning forward to dine like a starved man. River's hand comes across my mouth to silence my moans. "That's it, baby," he says, his voice enough to talk me straight to orgasm.

Aris' tongue is the smooth heavens against my aching, throb-bing bud. He grabs my thighs, pulling me forward as he eats me out like he's never eaten before. I'm already so close to climaxing, and he's only just begun. One of my hands finds its way into his hair while the other travels behind me, stroking the hard length of

River, desperate to please him. River's groan of pleasure sounding in my ear nearly sends me over the edge.

River continues to play with my nipples while Aris slips a finger into me, and I just about lose it when he starts to pump it in time with his tongue. All at once, everything in me roars to life, sending me flying off the cliff into a sea of ecstasy that seems never-ending. I sag against River as I climax and practically scream against his hand, which he clamps harder against my lips.

"Ember," he warns, but there's no use. If someone hears me, they'll hear me. We'll deal with the consequences later. Aris doesn't stop until I'm practically squirming away from him, breathless and dazed. His lips are red and glazed, and I want to lick them up. But I turn instead to River and kiss him. His hand snakes behind my neck, pulling me close as Aris appears at my back this time and peppers my shoulders with kisses.

I work on pulling River's shirt out of his pants, needing their clothes off. *Now.* He unhooks his sword, letting it drop to the side before pulling his shirt off. I can hear Aris doing the same before a bare chest is at my back, and he's kissing my neck while I'm kissing River again.

I'm burning, and I'm being electrified all at once, and it's a glorious mixture that I never want to stop feeling—that I never want to give up. It dawns on me at this moment that I don't ever want to choose. They both bring me to life. How could I possibly give that up? I've somehow fallen in love with them both at the same time, and there's no going back now. No matter how many rules I'm breaking. Why else would fate lead me here?

I reach down to stroke them both, and I'm met with breathless groans. There are still too many layers of clothes between us, and I can't take it, so I push off of River, making Aris take a step back. It allows for me to drop to my knees and start working on Aris' belt buckle.

"Yours too," I tell River. He hesitates until I look up at him through my lashes, and then he obliges, ready to do anything his princess tells him. Aris watches me, barely breathing, as I finally pull his pants and briefs down to release his cock. Gods, it is glorious. Long, slender, and throbbing already. I can't wait to get my mouth on it, and I don't think he can either.

Once their pants are out of their way, I take them both in my hands, and they hiss. Fuck, I've *dreamed* of this moment—getting to pleasure them both. I take Aris in my mouth first because it's only fair seeing as he's never had my mouth around him before.

"Oh gods, Ember," he growls. And those are the exact words I fantasized he'd say.

CHAPTER 35

I pump River slowly while taking my time with Aris, running my tongue from his base up to the tip before taking River in my mouth. River's soft moan only makes me ache more for them. I could do this forever if they wanted. Aris stops the motion of my hand by catching my wrist, and I stop the bob of my head, coming off of River's cock with a soft popping sound.

"Come here," Aris commands, and gods, the tone of his voice is like nothing I've ever heard from him. They help me up onto my feet, guiding me toward my bed, and a rush of excitement fills me. River slaps my ass softly, and I laugh as I climb up, turning to face them as I settle on my knees, my hair falling over my shoulders.

"Bend over," River tells me. I obey, doing as I'm told in the center of the bed as Aris comes behind me and River comes atop the bed with me. "Look at how pretty you are for us, Ember." He moves my hair to one side, grabbing ahold of it in one hand. I look up at him, holding eye contact as I wrap my mouth around his tip, sucking softly before taking him fully down my throat. His mouth opens as he watches me, his breaths ragged.

Aris takes my hips, his fingers digging into the soft tissue of my ass as he aligns himself at my entrance. I'm already moaning on River's cock in anticipation, dripping with the need to be filled by him. There's nothing that could've prepared me for the sensation of feeling Aris in me for the first time. *Nothing*. When he brings himself to the hilt, coating himself fully in all my desire, it's like I'm no longer in my body anymore.

"Oh, sweet goddess, Ember. You can't be real." Aris' disbelief is palpable as I have him fully enraptured—heart, body, and soul. I can feel it through the tether as it pulses into me.

I once said that I would ruin myself for River. But I realize now that all along my fate would lead me to be ruined by them both. Complete and utter destruction. There's no coming back from this. From them. My life exists in terms of before, during, and hopefully never after them.

He brings himself out again before slamming back in, and that sends me forward onto River. It takes us into a rhythm, a melodious, indescribable rhythm made for the three of us. The tethers in me connecting their souls to mine glow and throb with passion I've never known before. Aris drives harder, hitting the exact spot I need him to, and another orgasm crests and crashes. I rise up off of River, my back colliding with Aris' chest as pleasure floods every nerve ending I have.

"Fuck, Ember, you feel so fucking good. So much better than I ever could've imagined," Aris says into my ear, nipping at it. Before I know it, I'm being turned around, and River is grabbing my legs to pull my ass against him. Before he inserts himself, I feel him lean down and take a taste for himself.

"Gods, it's been too long," he murmurs, lapping me up until I'm quivering and pleading for him to fuck me.

"Please, River," I beg, propping myself on my elbows so I can focus on Aris.

"Since you asked so nicely." His tongue drags up, and he bites the flesh of my bottom before using my arousal to coat his cock.

My moans echo off the wall, unable to silence myself or any

effect they're having on me. I take the moment to run my tongue around the tip of Aris' before wrapping my lips around him. He says my name like a curse and a prayer. Like he's trying his best to hold off and enjoy everything I'm giving him all at once.

River fills me, and fire fills my veins, burning me from the inside out. For a moment, I feel like I need to blink it out of my eyes. Aris' eyes widen for a moment when we make eye contact again, and I'm worried that maybe my eyes are glowing again. But the heat in them dissipates, and Aris tangles his hands in my hair, shoving his cock further down my throat. Any concerns are quickly thrown out as I focus on nothing but the feeling of being fucked by the both of them.

It's filthy. It's raw and the least queen-like thing I could ever be caught doing, and yet I am so profoundly happy that I couldn't care even if Bleren himself walked in right now. River reaches down between my legs using two fingers to rub my clit while fucking me at such a perfect pace I could cry real tears at the pleasure coursing through my body. Another climax starts to build in my core, and my hands clutch the sheets as the world crumbles away.

Both of them lose themselves in me, taking what they need as the three of us find release within seconds of each other. Aris finishes down my throat, and I swallow every last drop of his sweet release, licking and moaning as we finish. River spills over my back, and the way he growls my name has me committing it to memory so I can play it on repeat forever.

Just like before, he cleans me up before I crawl to the middle of the bed, flopping down to recover for a moment. My eyes are closed, but I can hear them shuffle around, putting at least half their clothing back on.

"Lay with me for a moment," I whisper. They both listen. Aris lies on my left, while River lies on my right. So I turn and lay my head on Aris' chest and let my legs drape over River's hips. River puts his hand over my legs, caressing them softly while Aris traces my collarbones like he did several days ago. They both have just their briefs on.

"You're extraordinary," Aris says, a sort of daze to his tone.

"I am lucky enough to have found not one, but two great loves in this life." My eyes drift close, not from sleepiness but from contentment that lays over me like a blanket.

"But who's better?" Aris asks.

"It's okay; you can let him down easy," River drawls.

"It's not a competition," I grumble.

"Nor would it be a fair one since I haven't gone solo," Aris points out.

"You're both insufferable." I roll my eyes.

"Ah, but you love it." River strokes a hand up my leg. My heart pings, and suddenly it's quiet. I know they're waiting. Wanting. Holding their breath. Even I am. I close my eyes again, looking inward at those two soul-binding tethers. My mates. My choice. Bound to me by fate. But I fell for them both, and now I don't want to choose. I won't choose.

"I do. I love you. I love you both. Is that wretched of me? My soul is pulled in two different directions, and yet I find I want to follow them both. That isn't the way the world is meant to work. I know it is not. But did that not feel...right? If not for a moment, did it not feel aligned? Aris, you electrify me, and River, you burn me, and together you make me come alive in ways I thought were impossible. You've both put pieces back together time and time again, and now you hold my heart. And I understand if—" I'm cut off because they already know where I'm going with it, because they know me. They know how I am.

"Ember," River chastises.

"We've been over this," Aris murmurs.

"But how long can you—" I try again.

"Baby," River says softly.

"I love you," Aris says finally. And the words make my heart roar. "We're two stubborn fucks unwilling to give up on you. If I can have you for the rest of my life, then I'll put up with the brute."

"And I love you. You know that I plan to protect you until the day I die. If having you until that day means putting up with his spoiled ass, then so be it," River says, his voice thick with emotion.

Tears begin to spill out of the corners of my eyes. I'm lying here, my body and soul bare to them, and somehow they're loving every bit of me, internal, external scars, and all. I fight to prove to myself that I deserve it even when such a large part of me is saying I don't. I quietly shut those voices up and soak in the moment for what it is.

"Those better be happy tears." Aris gently wipes them away using the pad of his thumb.

"They're I love you so much I can't contain myself tears." Which is the partial truth. They both laugh softly when a knock comes at my door, one I recognize immediately as Melody.

"Your Highness? Is everything okay? They're waiting to announce you all," she calls through the door.

"I'm okay! I had a dress malfunction, but I'll be out in a few. You don't have to wait around; I'll be fine!" I call out, panic spreading through my chest.

"Are you sure?" she asks.

"Positive!" I chirp, rolling off of both of them. Melody's footsteps sound down the hall. Quickly I find another pair of panties and then pull out the identical white dress.

"Are you sure she can't wear the red one?" River asks Aris while they get dressed again.

"If we want a smooth night, then no. As much as I loved it and wished she could, it's better if she didn't. For her safety and her courts'," he says sadly, and I truly believe he thinks his father would do something drastic if I wore it, so I leave the white dress on.

Once some simple white heels are on, I find my way to the

mirror and chuckle softly at the mess they made of me and quickly get to work. Using the cosmetics I watched the girls use, I touch up the areas that came off, and before I know it, it's like nothing ever happened. Just a couple of hand rakes through my hair and I look just like I did before the girls left. We never added lip stain in fear that there'd be too much red, but now that I'm wearing white, I add some anyway. When I exit, the guys both stop messing with their clothes and stare at me.

"Do I still look thoroughly fucked?" I touch the necklace at the base of my throat.

"Sadly, no. But you look absolutely beautiful." Aris devours me with his gaze from where he stands.

"Breathtaking. Truly." River drinks me in like he's never seen me before.

"You two clean up quite nicely yourselves. Too handsome, one might say," I joke. I grab my mask and open both my mental and physical doors. "Shall we?" They chuckle and follow me out.

"You dirty, dirty girl." Asteria swishes that tail of hers.

I regret nothing.

"Now, the Crown Prince Aris Blackwood and his betrothed, Princess Ember Canmore!" The announcer's voice booms through the grand ballroom, echoing off the arched ceilings decorated in big bouquets of hung flowers that look like they've been dipped in black and gold. The chandeliers sparkle with dangling crystals that cast rays of prism light all over the room from the brightly lit candles. The ballroom is bigger than any room I've ever set foot in, and filling it with decor was a lengthy process.

River slinks in behind us, sticking to the shadows unnoticed as deafening applause fills the room at our arrival. No one seems to bat an eye at our timely untimeliness, as Jasper would put it.

But the anger from Bleren indicates that he's the *only* one. Go figure.

We're escorted to our table, which is oh so lovingly beside his father and his court for dinner. Thankfully, Aris sits in between Bleren and I while River sits on my left. The safety of having them both beside me softens the fact that we're anywhere near Bleren and Dracyl, who sits on the other side of Bleren. He's wearing a silver tunic fitted with black pants that bring out his oddly gray eyes and make his blonde hair look icier today.

Before I sit, he locks eyes with me, and it's the first time I've looked him in the eyes since he defiled my bed. I don't look away, not giving him the satisfaction of cowering beneath him. This only seems to spur him on, a spark igniting in that scornful gaze of his. Something passes over his face, a look, like he knows something. It's unsettling, and a sudden chill runs over me, raising goosebumps across my body. Shivering, I quickly take my seat, ripping my eyes from his as I face forward, leaning into Aris for his warmth.

"Cold, Princess?" He rubs a hand on my thigh, trying to spark some heat back into me.

"Aren't you? It's freezing in here." My teeth begin to chatter as the temperature plummets further. There must be a draft getting in somewhere.

"I'm perfectly fine. Here, drink; it'll warm you up," he murmurs in my ear, his breath a soft caress as he reaches over to grab my chalice of wine for me. I grab it, whispering my thanks as the announcer continues to announce other lords and ladies. River glances at me with worried eyes, unable to express anything now that we're here.

I scrunch my nose at him, my mask shifting with the movement. It's my latest signal to him that I'm okay. It doesn't always do the trick, but it does for now. The wine settles in my stomach, spreading slowly into my veins, but it's not enough to settle my vibrating body that can't seem to stay still as the chill settles into my bones.

Why is it so damn cold in here? I pop open the lid of the well within me, allowing a small lick of flames to caress me from the inside, warming my skin against whatever cold front is waging war against me.

"*Is everything okay there?*" Asteria's voice is far and muffled. She's back in Ereltis reporting to her commander.

Just frigid, but I'm using that trick you taught me. Everything okay there?

"*Just more pesky soldiers. They're poking around more and more lately. We don't understand why. We send some creatures their way to disperse them every time they set up camp, but they always return. They're gone for now.*" Confusion wraps both of our minds, rendering us silent as we contemplate what Bleren might be up to. I shut the lid when I feel sufficiently warm, the cold not so biting anymore as it melts away, having given up its fight somehow.

I realize I haven't paid attention to a word that's been said nor the fact that food has been served, too dazed by the cold, the warmth, and the growing concern of what Bleren is trying to accomplish, if anything, when it comes to Ereltis. The war is no more, so what does Ereltis have to do with anything? Is it even Ereltis he's after? Why else would he be directly at the border?

Mindlessly, I pick at the food, scanning the crowd for my court, but with all the masked faces, it's hard to decipher who is who. Especially considering there are close to three hundred in attendance tonight. Still, I look for Jasper's put-together head of disheveled hair and Viola's beautiful curls. To no avail do I spot them. Anxiety builds and builds, finding release by bouncing my left knee up and down relentlessly.

River's knuckles caress the outside of my leg through the slit, seeking to soothe the seemingly silly fear he's sensing in me. I glance at him, a look of appreciation and something more shining in my eyes before quickly looking away again. Where are they? *Where are they?*

"Not hungry?" Aris interrupts my thoughts, making me jump.

"You'd think I would be after that." I look up at him through my lashes, and his eyes darken. "I was just looking for my court. It's hard to spot them in a crowd like that."

It's hard not to feel like a fool for worrying so quickly. It's such an easy explanation, really, and I'm sure as soon as this feast is over, they'll rush over to me. We'll drink ourselves silly into the night, and I'll be properly hungover for my wedding tomorrow. Our wedding. *Fuck. Gods. Shit.*

This stupid, silly heart refuses to listen to logic, because right now, it's whispering that they're gone. Gone for good. Never coming back. Of course it was too good to be true. Come on, Ember. Why would anything ever be so sweet and simple for you?

Gods, why doesn't it ever shut up?

"Ember?" Oh. Right. Aris was talking.

"I'm sorry, I did it again." I shake my head as if shaking out those thoughts, shaking out the distractions.

"It's okay, love," Aris says, softly, much too softly, much more caring than I deserve. "I just said as soon as we're done, we'll help you find them."

"Jasper has a weird knack for finding you like some sort of magnet, so I'm sure it won't be long before his annoying ass comes meandering over," River grumbles. Giggles tumble out of me.

"What do you have against Jasper?"

"He's so...jolly." River shivers, as if repulsed.

"You...don't like how happy he is?" He can't be serious. My smile grows larger as his grimace grows grimmer. Aris and I both angle our bodies toward him as he crosses his arms across his broad chest, clearly uncomfortable.

"Well, not exactly." He pauses. "Actually, precisely." He leaves it at that. Not one for many words, but when it comes to River, he never needs many. I read so much more in him and his body, in his eyes and the soul beneath that I don't always need his words to tell me everything. There's so much locked away, and I can't help but wonder what lies deep beneath the surface. In due time, I'll let him reveal that on his own.

"Such a brute at heart," Aris mutters. A snort escapes me as River's fingers twitch toward the throwing knife tucked into one of the holsters strapped across his chest on a leather band.

"Behave," I warn, and they both straighten up. We finish dinner quickly, eager to get this night along, and thankfully it seems the king is as well. He doesn't bother us, and I'm surprised, considering this is our celebration ball, and I figured we'd get some sort of warning to put on a good show or I don't know. *Something.* But other than the pointed angry stare for our couple of minutes of tardiness—okay, perhaps more than a couple of minutes—we get nothing.

His drab conversation with Dracyl is nothing more than political nonsense, and when it turns to the women in the room, I let my damper fall, not caring to eavesdrop any longer. Though as I peek over at them, I'm met with Dracyl's icy stare again, and another shiver wracks my body. I get the odd feeling he knew I was listening, but I know I'm just being paranoid.

"Lords and Ladies, citizens of Klyeria, my son and his beautiful, soon-to-be bride, I am so happy to have you all here to celebrate a final night before we join their hands in marriage. Through them we make our kingdom stronger. We make Klyeria better than it ever was before. We will put this war behind us and take a step forward toward a brighter future, one that holds opportunities you'd never thought possible. Possibilities you couldn't dream of. And we owe that all to our dear Ember. So, please. Raise your glass and join me in a toast to the princess. To Ember!"

The king's words ring out so loudly, so distinctly across the hall, and cheers echo back at us as the clinks of hundreds of chalices follow his toast. He holds my gaze as he brings his glass to his lips. A storm of rage and loathing is so hostile in his eyes that I almost look away.

I raise my glass to him, taking a tentative sip of my wine, but it goes down bitterly. There's something about what he's saying that's sending more warning bells off, especially with his serpentine smile. But no one else seems to notice. Aris smiles at me brightly, leaning forward so closely his nose brushes mine, and suddenly the noise of the room melts away.

"We're going to change their world, Ember," he whispers against my lips.

"Do you really think we can pull this off?" I tilt my head up to look into his eyes, searching the depths of the star-flecked sky that stares back at me.

"Don't you?" There's a stark hope in his voice that pierces my heart, pierces the doubt that's taken root in my chest since I've set foot here.

"I think we can do anything once we get him out of here," I murmur softly. He absorbs those words, capturing my lips with his in a swift kiss that leaves me reeling for more. But the announcer is calling us to the dance floor for the first dance. Before I get up, I press a hand into River's knee, squeezing softly before pushing up, and I don't miss the glint in his eyes before being tugged away by Aris.

I scan the crowd as we walk to the center, searching for familiar faces or half faces of my court. Still no goofy grins or dimples. No bouncy curls. No immaculately done blonde updos or bright ginger heads. Not the ones that matter, anyway.

They're gone.

They're gone.

They're gone.

"Ember." My name is spoken like a caress. Adoring. Patient and kind. Pulling me out of the depths of my panic. "We'll find them, I promise." Smooth fingers tip my chin up reassuringly, while others trail down the groove of my spine, settling on the small of my back. It grounds me in the way I need grounding.

Swallowing, I nod. Not capable of words right now as the panic has wrapped its hands around my throat. Logically, I know they're around here somewhere. Illogically, something much worse has happened. Even more illogically, they've gone home without saying goodbye.

Letting my body go on autopilot and allowing Aris to take the lead against a beautiful yet simple melody, we fall into a graceful dance. It's so easy with him. It always has been. Almost infuriatingly so. I let him lure me into my enemy's lair. Let him right into my heart and soul because when I look at him, I see *me*. It's terrifying having fallen in love with the boy I grew up knowing as my enemy my whole life—hating him with every fiber of my being only to meet him and have that change instantly.

Asteria? I know she's far away, but I just want to feel her presence. I just want to feel her for a moment while we dance, while I search, while I process what tonight really means under the scrutiny of the king.

"*I'm here, Ember.*" Her presence fills me like a hearth being lit on the coldest winter night. I don't let it hinder my focus with Aris as we near the end of the melody.

I think something is seriously wrong here tonight. It's hard not to feel like a coward with the fear wrapping around me like a snake wrapping around its prey.

"*I'm not close enough to sense anything, my dear, but follow your gut. You're smart, and you're strong. Focus and stay alert. I'm coming to you.*" My stomach drops, and I falter with Aris, who swiftly makes it seem purposeful, dropping me into a dip before spinning me into a complicated move that I follow with ease.

No! Stay there.

"*Absolutely not. If you're in danger, then I'm coming to you.*"

My gut says you need to stay there. You just said to listen to it.

"*Why would I do that?*"

Because you're safer there.

"*No, why would I listen to you?*"

You insufferable beast. If Bleren ever finds out about you, you put your entire species at risk of being hunted again. Stay. Fucking. Put.

The melody ends, and Aris dips me once more, looking down at me with a peculiar look on his face. I scrunch my nose at him until he puts us back on steady feet and kisses my forehead. With our love on display, the civilians eat it up, grabbing at the tangible adoration filling the air.

They waste no time flooding the dancefloor when the band picks up in rhythm, playing hastily and joyfully. I take that as my cue to escape and start searching faces and bodies more closely, not caring how closely I need to get to people just to make sure I'm not missing them. Frantically, I scour through the crowd, leaving Aris behind in my haste to find the cause of my aching heart.

"He hasn't found out about me yet. We've been careful, Ember. You'll find them. It's a big crowd; they're in there somewhere. Deep breaths." She sends wave after wave of soothing caresses over my mind, which do little to calm the storm raging in my chest. I'm trying. Really I am, but until I set sight on those green eyes, I will not rest in this godsforsaken castle.

Suddenly, I've reached the other end of the hall, and still none of my court has appeared. They would've come to me by now. We agreed to it. I turn around and bump into a familiar hard chest. River grabs my hands, looking down at me with turmoil-filled eyes.

"I haven't found them either." He hates admitting it, feeling as though he's let me down somehow.

"Maybe they're playing a prank. One I'll surely kill them for. There has to be an explanation. Perhaps they're piss drunk in the gardens or..." I trail off, removing myself from River and his calming hands when I see Aris shouldering his way toward us, his black mask doing nothing to hide the intense beauty of his face. "Anything?"

"Not a single one of them." His concern is palpable, and his concern makes everything in my chest start to fester.

"Aris, what is your father up to? What is it that you never told me?" I try to keep my voice even. Even as I look over his shoulder at the scrutinizing pair of eyes watching me.

"Ember, we can't do this. Not here. Not now." I don't have to look at him to see the begging in his eyes. I yet again find myself in the familiar position with River standing at my back and me arguing with Aris in front of me. Dragging my eyes away from Bleren's, I settle them on Aris.

"My court is missing, and they wouldn't leave me. So I will ask again. What is your father up to?"

CHAPTER 36

"He still wants the land between us." Aris doesn't look me in the eye as he speaks. "And for reasons I still don't understand. He thinks you're the key to securing that land, hence our marriage. There's something about your lineage that he thinks he knows that Nicholas and Eloise don't. Or they did know, and they still bartered you away, but I don't think he's right. He won't tell me the details. So don't ask." He runs a hand over his mouth, letting out a frustrated sigh.

"And you thought you couldn't tell me this, why?" *Stay calm, Ember. Punching your fiancé in the throat isn't ladylike.* But I'm not the only one angry because a frustrated growl comes from behind me as River takes a step around me.

"You—" River grits, but I cut him off before he can rip Aris' head off.

"Let him explain," I snap, at my wits' end. River huffs, quieting reluctantly.

"Because I thought you'd leave if you knew he was still scheming after the one thing this bloody war is over. And if you left—" He cuts himself off. As if the thought itself is so painful he can't even speak it. The agony is so stark in his eyes, and with

479

them being the only thing I can see with the mask, it nearly tears me apart. Damn this bleeding thing in my chest.

"Gods, Ember, I am *hollow* without you. Yes, I want to save our kingdoms, but that means nothing to me, *nothing* if you're not here with me. Until you, I would've done anything for this kingdom. Anything. But if I had to choose between them and you? I'd choose you. Every. Single. Time. I know what kind of man that makes me, but I'd do it. I'd let the world burn for you. For what good am I without you there reminding me to behave?" He cracks a smile, and I can't help the way my lungs heave for breaths that don't seem to come.

"My father is the means to an end. A timeline. I don't know what he's up to. We'll figure it out and counteract. We just need to get married first so we have real power. We are nothing right now in the eyes of our laws. Until you say 'I do' tomorrow, we can do nothing against him. Nothing legal, at least if we do not want to commit blatant treason and simply slaughter him. And trust me, I've thought of every possible way to do it. So, I didn't tell you because I wanted to do this the right way. So I could try and be somewhat of a decent man."

All I can do is stare for a moment. If it weren't for the tether between us, there'd be no way to know that what he was telling me, what he was feeling, was the truth. But what pulses between us is so pure it can't be mistaken for anything other than what he confesses. I don't know if his love terrifies, excites me, or if perhaps I understand. *If you try to save them both, you will lose both of them. There can only be one in the end.* I think I'd let the world burn to save them both in the end.

He's after Ereltis, Asteria. He must think he can use me to get in, but how could he know I have powers? My stomach's in knots just thinking about what Bleren would do if he had access to that kingdom. Asteria has described such great peace and tranquility there. He'd disrupt hundreds of years of undisturbed life.

"I don't think he does, and that's the issue he's trying to solve.

That is the danger you are in, my dear. Lock it down tight. If he never sees it, then he can't use you."

"I cannot do this if you are not honest with me. I told you that. You may be scared to lose me, but I have lost *everything*, Aris. My kingdom. My family. All I have left are you both. So give me the chance to make those decisions, however terrifying for you they may be, for myself. Let me see what hostile court I am walking into. This changes so much more than you know, but for now I just want to find my court before they leave. If they haven't already." I glance around, searching the masked faces again, hoping I missed them somehow in the swarm of people, and yet —nothing.

Aris looks like he has more to say, more to argue on his behalf, like keeping things from me was for my benefit and his. But he shuts his mouth and wordlessly follows me through the crowd as I search and search and search, calling out their names relentlessly. River's hand occasionally finds mine, a constant, wordless form of telling me he's there with me. His anger with Aris is tangible, but he keeps it contained for my sake.

Hours. Hours go by. And each minute. Each second that I don't see those dimples, the knife in my chest twists and twists and twists. Bleren watches from the dais with Dracyl seated comfortably beside him. There's something in his eyes, in his serpentine smile, that turns my heart to stone. Somehow I know, and I think I knew from the moment I realized they weren't in here—that he is responsible for this.

But I won't stop. I won't. We decide to search outside of the ballroom. We search the gardens. The library. Their rooms. Nothing. Nothing. Nothing.

"*Keep going, Ember. I'm with you.*" Her frustration rolls through me. I know she wants to be here, but with Bleren increasingly on my tail, I don't need him on hers.

"Let's try the ballroom once more. We can take the masks off now. Perhaps that might help." River drags a hand down the small of my back, never straying away from the ruined skin there. I nod silently, following them both. Aris takes my hand, and I'm grateful despite my anger with him because I'm only capable of so much. Only capable of focusing on my court. On my favorite colors. Greens, reds, blondes, browns. On curls and dimples. On laughs and giggles.

River opens the door, and I'm so wrapped up in those colors. So lost in that crooked smile that I didn't notice how silent it had gotten. The roar of three hundred people dwindles down to the rush of blood in my ears as I take in the scene before me.

I blink.

Blink again.

Before I can do or think anything, a sword slides from its sheath, followed by a grunt and a murmur of words I don't catch. That's River's sword, but River's not holding it. Aris is.

Against River's neck.

Onyx eyes flecked in gold meet mine in a pleading look. A look that begs understanding. A look that tells me to play along. To *listen.*

Eight people kneel at the bottom of the dais, facing me. Eight. My court. My friends. My family. They stare at me with wide terrified eyes—eyes that almost bring me to my knees, but I don't give Bleren the satisfaction. Not while Aris drags River to stand beside them all.

Behind each and every one of them stands a guard that holds a long, sharp dagger to their precious throats, ready to kill at a moment's notice. My fingers flex at my side as I'm left alone in the center.

I can't feel anymore. It hurts so much that everything's gone numb. The roaring in my head is so loud I can't hear anything else. I can't see anything except the piercing green eyes ringed with bruises. *Bruises.* My stomach rolls as I take in the cuts; the smell of blood hits me like a tidal wave, and fire fills my veins like anger I've never known.

"Bring out our final guests," Bleren orders.

My head whips toward the doors opposite me as two guards

usher in Nicholas and Eloise. Their wrists are bound, but otherwise they're seemingly unharmed. Red tinges my vision as seats are brought for them to sit in. *Seats.*

"I can no longer sit by and watch this."

I will not say it again, Asteria. If you show up, you will reveal that dragons are back in existence. If he's trying to use me, I will be damned before he uses you too. I will only allow you as close as the edge of the forest, and that is it. Unless I am about to die, you stay put. Now let me concentrate.

She doesn't argue with me any further even though I know she wants to. I look back to my court, trying to communicate that I'll get them out of this somehow. Somehow. Even if it means my blood is spilled. Jane stares blankly ahead, seemingly in shock. Daisy hiccups, something she does when she's cried a lot. Viola stares at the floor with anger and fear mixed all in one. Easton clenches and unclenches his jaw, ready at any moment to strike. Robert is pale and shaking. Cameron keeps glancing at Sierra, who's looking at me with hope. It crushes me, and I dip my chin at her. *I will get you out.*

Then there's my Jasper. My sweet, golden-hearted best friend, who's more limp than the rest of them, and from here I can hear his ragged breaths—more labored than they should be. He put up more of a fight than any of them, and I don't know whether that makes me more proud or more brokenhearted. His green eyes beg me to run. To go. To leave before it's too late. Except they also know I'd never do that.

Finally, I shift to River, who struggles against Aris' grip, but with the sword pressed against the pulsing vein of his neck, there's not much he can do but submit. Rage like I've never seen brims beneath his skin, vibrating with vengeance-seeking release.

With all of my loved ones, save my parents, secured to Bleren's liking, he rises finally. He clasps his hands together, taking a deep breath before smiling at me. Dracyl joins him at his side, almost as his protector with the way he never strays too far from him.

"At last, your search is over." He sweeps an arm over their

heads. I rip the blasted mask from my face, letting it slide from my fingers. "You almost spoiled the night and everything I had planned too. It would've been a shame if I had to end their lives too early." Bleren looks down at my court with insincere pity, making my heart thrash like a wild animal in its cage. The well within me, only a quarter full from all our work this week, roars to life at the sight of all our loved ones in danger. The ache to protect is so harsh I almost take a step forward.

"Control, Ember. This is what he wants. Listen before you act. Let's find a way through." Her voice of reason tamps down the sudden lurch in power.

"What do you want, Bleren?" I stare at him. "Can't we settle whatever this is without them?"

"I thought we could, dear, but you haven't the slightest care in the world for yourself. So I need them to ensure I get what I need. But before we get there, I'd like for Nicholas to tell us a little story." Bleren gestures to the guard standing behind my father. The guard taps my father on the shoulder with an armored hand, and Nicholas has half the decency to look somewhat scared as he glances up.

"What do you mean, Bleren?" His voice comes out much more even than I expect. Much stronger and with a bite.

"Your Majesty," Bleren corrects. "Tell Ember her origin story. How she came to Agatharea." He sits back on his throne, crossing an ankle over his knee as he leans back. He's clad in gold, the crown atop his head glinting in the light, a heavy reminder of the power he holds here.

"Your Majesty," Nicholas grits. "I don't understand what you mean. You want us to tell her the story of her birth?" He twists to look at Bleren over his shoulder, staring him down. Bleren doesn't say a word. Instead, he waves another hand to another guard, who steps forward and places his own sharp dagger against Eloise's neck. This spurs my father into action, turning him forward to face me with more disdain than he's ever held before. The scars on my back begin to burn like they're being delivered all over again.

"Twenty-two years ago we sent a group of soldiers along the border of Ereltis, a kingdom of magic warded off between Agatharea and Klyeria that lies in Atravelien. The mission was led by Kain Silvius." A sharp intake of breath interrupts his story for a moment. A breath from River, who's staring at Nicholas with wide eyes. Silvius. That's River's surname. Which means Kain was... Oh gods, that mission was led by his father. Nicholas carries on like it means nothing, but I know he said it on purpose.

"We were always looking for weak points in the wards that protect the kingdom. We wanted to share their power. That's all we ever wanted. Our people starve. They freeze. They endure illness. But Ereltis? They have magic that could help us, and yet they refuse. But bloody Klyeria wanted the same thing, so the war came as we fought for a way in to claim power to help our kingdoms. Ereltis is greedy. Selfish. They kept their power to themselves." He shakes his head, disgusted they'd do such a thing when he can't see that the reason his kingdom suffers in the first place is at *his* hands.

"Kain was a brilliant leader. His instincts were unmatched. It's a pity they weren't passed down." He glances at River.

"Don't talk about him like that." The lethal venom in my voice is enough for my father to look back at me. "Get to the fucking point."

His eyes narrow on me, wandering over me in a way that makes me feel small. "What have you turned into? His Majesty really did me a favor by taking you off my hands."

Grunts sound to the right and left as Jasper and River struggle against the people who hold them, practically snarling at my father. My fingers twitch at my side, begging to release the magic inside me that could so easily snap the necks of those who restrain them. My eyes flicker to Aris, whose blank stare reveals nothing as he restrains River. The sight of him holding River sends confusing waves of agony through me, so I look away. Play the part.

"Things were quiet like they always are. They couldn't get

through no matter what they tried. Then suddenly there's a little girl, no more than two, maybe three, giggling through those wards. Kain said you were chasing a fairy, which led you right to us. Thankfully, you liked Kain, so you went with him when he asked if you wanted to go on a little adventure to see more fairies." Nicholas pauses, running a tired hand over his exasperated face.

"You were supposed to be our ticket in. We had a precious child—their precious child. A baby girl of all things. Surely they'd answer us now, right? So, we left letters demanding that they let us enter in exchange for your return. We wanted access to their kingdom, to their power, and to their magic. We left them right where you appeared—right where we figured they'd come looking for you. The letters disappeared, but they were never answered. Days went by. Months. Then it had been a year since you first came to us, and we had to answer for the fact that we had a child running around the castle walls." Eloise goes still beside him, glancing toward my court with a certain fear in her eyes, a fear of the truth finally coming out. Whatever it is.

"We'd already had a daughter around your age. Same complexion. Dark hair. Not the same eyes, but children's eyes change colors sometimes, and that could be easily explained. If Ereltis wasn't going to come back for you, then we were going to keep you. Your power would be of great use to us one day. We could use you when we were ready to breach their wards and wreak havoc upon them for abandoning you. They chose their peace over you. Instead of rescuing you, they chose their kingdom over a child.

"You think I'm the cruel one? We took you in. We gave up our daughter and made *you* the heir to the throne. No one batted an eye when we changed our 'daughter's' name two years into her life because we're the king and queen. We do as we please. But then, your powers never came. We waited and waited for a sight of it. To feel it in the castle. For anything. But nothing. What an absolute waste of breath and space you were. We gave up *everything* for you to receive nothing in the end. Absolutely nothing. I hated you every second you were there. Every day you woke up was another day I was reminded of how much you'd caused my failure."

The last bits of whatever pieces of me that were still standing, still put together, finally crumble. The dust is blown away, and in the end there's nothing left. I don't want to believe him. And yet, it all makes so much sense finally. I can feel Asteria moving closer, her heart pounding in rhythm with mine as if the breaking of my soul is breaking hers as well.

"Ember I've never heard a whisper of a child going missing from the wards. They could be wrong."

This doesn't feel wrong. We both know I'm right.

"I've given enough. Bleren believes that there's something more to you, and I don't think he's right, but I don't care anymore. So I bartered you away. No more war. No more Ember. It was a win-win for me. Getting rid of the powerless bitch that took everything from me is something I should've done a long time ago. There is no way into Ereltis, Your Majesty. Your fight is futile." Eloise reaches over with bound hands and lays them over his own. They stare at my court again, and this time I realize it's not my court they're looking at. It's *Jane.*

It hits me then. It hits me so hard I actually falter a step. The dark, short, wavy hair that matches my father's. Her green eyes that mirror his. She's almost a complete and utter replica of him, and I can't, for the life of me, understand how I never saw it before. Suddenly, her sweet, innocent face morphs into something much more sinister. She stands, and the guard lets her. They let her walk beside Bleren, who smiles adoringly at her.

"Thank you, my dear, for your help in acquiring them all here today. With all your help thus far." Bleren tilts his head at me, and I start shaking my head.

No. No. No. No. No. No. No. Not her. Please. Gods. The ache in my chest gets unbearably sharper. The betrayal turns everything in me into ice. Burning ice that freezes me in place as I do nothing but stare at her, hardly breathing.

"Why?" I whisper.

"Because you never understood nor appreciated what you had. You had what I was supposed to, and you still bitched and moaned about it. Poor little Ember, she gets to be queen; she has food, and dresses, and riches, and jewels. She has servants, and baths, and whatever it is she desires. Oh, Daddy hits her? Boo fucking hoo. At least you had him. They couldn't look at me. Acknowledge me. Love me. I was nothing to them the moment you stepped foot in that castle. So, I did whatever I had to in order to get you back out. That all started by helping Dracyl find you at Marbs." Her smile is like nothing it's ever been before.

Jasper has managed to turn and stare at her. I'm sure the heartbreak he's feeling is killing him. It's killing me. The tethers in me only add to the ache as their emotions fill me, their anger and trepidation pulsing down relentlessly, but I can't look at them, or I think I'll start falling apart.

"Jane I... I never took any of that for granted. I—" She cuts me off, raising a hand to shut me up.

"I don't want to hear it. I really don't. Go on, Bleren. Tell her the rest." Jane walks down toward Eloise, kneeling beside her to take her hand. In some odd way, it doesn't seem she blames them. She only blames me, and maybe I am to blame, and maybe I did take it for granted.

"Don't you dare. Don't you dare listen to these fools. I will not let them take you down with them, Ember. Lift that chin. Now." I do as I'm told, lifting it as Bleren continues.

"You're wrong, Nicholas. This fight isn't futile. You just didn't know how to fight it properly. See, you've beaten Ember down so thoroughly that she has no regard for herself. There's no will to protect herself. You whipped her, right? See, normally, their magic has a sense of self-preservation. But dear Ember here has a bit of self-hatred so deep, thanks to you, that she refuses to use it. Even when we sent Dracyl to attack her, it wasn't until the very last moment before he defiled her that her magic took over and protected her. Still, that wasn't enough for me.

"It wasn't enough to prove that she was truly what you said

she was. Even with her surviving the poison. When we brought her here, we thought maybe riling her up would do the trick, and boy, she has a temper, a beautiful one at that. There were a few moments, odd moments, where the fires would act accordingly with that temper of hers. Yet still, that wasn't enough to say that it was her." As Bleren speaks, he moves down the dais, walking to stand behind Jasper. He takes the dagger from the guard and takes his place instead.

All thoughts empty from my head as the lid is blown straight off and magic fills every crevice of my body. I don't let it out, but it's right there. Right on the surface. Ready. Dracyl's eyes light up, almost in delight, as he skims over me.

"Atta girl," he purrs, standing beside the king still. Ever his protector. I furrow my eyebrows, gritting my teeth to keep my magic contained. Bleren glances at Dracyl and then smiles knowingly at me.

"Ah, see, Nicholas. What you failed to realize, and what we eventually figured out, is that though Ember will never protect herself, she *will* protect the ones she loves, and that is when her power is provoked the most. Dracyl here sensed it for the first time when River was threatened, and that is when we knew. So, I continued to test that theory.

"I sent those thieves into the house of that little girl. I was hoping you'd get there sooner and do something more... dramatic. But you didn't arrive quickly enough. Though I hear the storm came quickly and out of nowhere. Yet, still, how could I prove that was you?" He tilts the dagger up, and I whimper. Jasper looks at me with no fear. The only thing there that shines is his love.

As if kneeling there at the brink of death for me is something he'd do so willingly. As if this was thoughtless for him. I'm shaking my head at him, begging him, and still he only looks at me adoringly.

"So, you've pushed me to use more drastic measures. Before you are eight of the people you care about. I will slaughter each and every one of them if you do not show me what you are capable of. Starting here with your beloved friend. If you do as I say, then I will let them go. You will come with me, and we will find our way into Ereltis to take the power I seek. I have an army of nearly fifty thousand ready at my disposal and more after that. That kingdom doesn't care about you, Ember. So you should not care about them. If you try anything against me or any of the guards, Dracyl will kill you and your court." There's a violent promise in his words, and I know I can't risk going after him if I were to release my power against anyone holding a dagger right now.

Aris leans down to speak in River's ear, talking so softly no one notices. But I do, and my ears pick up on it.

"I won't hurt you. If he orders me to, I'd sooner drive this sword through my own heart than kill the man she loves. If he does, I'll let you go. You take her and run. I'll deal with him." He leans back with the same blank face, and I continue to stare at Bleren like I didn't hear anything.

Asteria. I have to.

"I know, dear. I know, but he still won't get in. You can't drag people that aren't Erelt in with you. It won't work."

Then it's a good thing he doesn't know that.

"Ember, please, you don't have to do this. Don't make yourself his puppet. Don't lower yourself more than you already have," Jasper pleads, his voice ragged and breathless from hardly being able to speak with the blade against his skin.

He'd rather die than let me hand myself over. Two people who love each other to their demise.

"Jasper. You sweet, silly boy. I love you." I take a step back, letting the magic seep past my skin finally, releasing sweet relief. As I release it in the form of shadows billowing from my fingertips, dragging along the floor toward my court, I look them in the eye, begging them not to be afraid. Their gasps don't come from fear but pure shock. Everyone, but Jasper, seems to be surprised by my abilities.

I let the tendrils caress their cheeks; one combs through the curl at River's ear before another pokes Robert's nose. From where I stand, I can feel them relax, even with blades held against their lifelines. As the power of the shadows makes its way around, grabbing the crown off Bleren's head and placing it on Aris' instead, I let a flame come alive in my palm.

"Impossible," Nicholas spits out.

"You're blind if you didn't see what was right in front of you," Jasper mutters.

"You knew?" I ask, daring another step toward them. There's still so much space separating us, but the closer I can get, the better chance I have to do *something*. The flame in my hand grows hotter and brighter before changing into a floating orb of water. Bleren whistles impressed.

"The day you saved me, I vowed to keep it a secret. What you did could've cost you, and I knew I'd never let them get a hold of you like that." Jasper holds my gaze.

He knew. All this time he knew, and he never faltered in his love. Never treated me any different. *Nythiem, I beg you again, please do not take him.*

"I hate to interrupt whatever this is, but what else can you do?" Bleren asks, watching the display of changing elements in my hand. I allow a breeze to intentionally blow through everyone; murmurs of amazement start to come from even the guards.

It's Dracyl's icy, rageful glare that has me on guard still. Suddenly, my feet are encased in ice, and I'm frozen where I stand. I've never had to sense someone else's power before, so I don't know how to see how much he holds.

Is that him? I can feel Asteria atop the castle now, unable to abide by my orders.

"It is; he does well to isolate his magic, which is why I've never sensed him before. His magic is dark, Ember. It's no wonder he's outside of Ereltis. Please be careful."

And you stay put.

With half a thought, I melt the ice at my feet, rolling my

ankles to shake out the frigid cold that bit into my skin. I glare back at Dracyl.

"How are you *doing* that?" he growls.

"What do you mean?" I smile at him, creating a storm cloud above his head that begins to rain solely on him. But when he waves his hands and pushes them forward to throw icy daggers my way, all I can do is throw up a wall of shadows that stop them in their tracks.

Lowering the wall to look at him once more, I let the cloud dissipate. The well within me drains even further.

"How do you have so many elements? So many aspects of power?" He looks over me in disbelief. It's the first time Dracyl has ever looked at me with something more than sexual hunger. No, this is something akin to awe and jealousy.

"I don't know. This is what I have." I leave it at that, not admitting that my magic goes beyond the elements and shadows I've shown them today. I don't explain that it's raw power, capable of taking on any form I want it to.

"This is excellent. Incredible, really. You are exactly what I need to get inside and rip them to shreds. Good work, dear." Bleren nods approvingly. "See, I couldn't allow you to marry my son if you didn't have everything I needed you to have now, could I?"

He looks to Aris, who swallows, nodding at his father with a certain loyalty that can't be denied.

"Of course, Father. She is a marvel with all that power. Surely we can put the swords to rest?" Aris' voice is strong, that of a prince who will be king one day.

But Bleren has other ideas. He looks at me, tilting his head again.

"You've had such a hard time listening." My heart begins to beat rapidly, thrashing. The shadows come billowing out from my fingers, poised to strike, but the message in Jasper's eyes makes me pause. *You've always had me, and you always will. I will follow you.* It shines there, so stark, so loud. I nod at him, mouthing the words "I love you" before looking back to Bleren, unsure of what he's going to do—or what he's going to order of his guards, who still stand perfectly still with the rest of my court.

"You think I don't know you fucked him? In my own castle?" Bleren's voice is so dark, so full of malice, that I can't help the tremor that begins to shake my body. I search for a way to end him, but Dracyl's hands are poised and ready, and the dagger at Jasper's neck is already drawing a thin line of blood. The scent alone makes my knees quiver.

"Bleren, please, I beg of you." I hate the weakness in my voice, but submitting to him is the only way through this. *Gods, what have I done?*

"I fear it's too late to beg. I just hope this teaches you a lesson to never disobey me again. Going forward, I need you to listen to my every command." Without hesitation, Bleren drags the dagger across the neck of my best friend. Of my lifeline. Of the boy who wiped boogers on my dress and stood up for me when it mattered.

In the last seconds before the life blinks out of my favorite pair of green eyes, he gives me a sad, crooked smile. One that flashes the dimples that will haunt my dreams until the day I die, and then he's gone.

Jasper's gone.

CHAPTER 37

I can't hear anything—not a single thing beyond my own screams as I watch his blood stain the marble. Someone's whimper tears me away from his body now lying on the floor, unseeing, unmoving.

I don't wait another moment. The magic within me seeks vengeance with renewed hatred like no other. In less than half a thought, the necks of each guard holding my court are snapped in half by the shadows billowing from my fingers, staining them blacker than the night sky.

In my haste to avenge the beautiful boy bleeding at my feet, Aris has released River to lunge for his father. River follows him, both aiming for the king. But Dracyl is faster than that, and before I can shoot out anything—fire, shadows, rock—he has flung another icy dagger at River this time, and it pierces his side. Dracyl only hits Aris in the head with a club of ice, rendering him unconscious within seconds of taking River down, moving so swiftly I can hardly track him. *Gods, this can't be happening.*

"I can help."

I will not jeopardize you too. Let me concentrate, please, I beg her. I beg her with everything in me to stay where she is. Not just for her safety, but for the lives of all the others she'd put in peril because of me. There will be no more blood spilled on my behalf.

"River!" Ghostly pain echoes in my own side, through my ribs, deathly close to puncturing my lung. But nothing has actually hurt me. I realize through the tether that I am feeling River's pain. I throw a wall of air at Dracyl, knocking him back several feet before running toward my court and River.

But this blasted dress is slowing me down. With fire, I burn the bottom half off, leaving it hanging at the top of my knees so I can move without hesitation. And while I'm at it, I kick off my heels, leaving me barefoot but at least in control of my body.

Jane spurs into action, untying her parents, but they don't make it far. Not as more guards show up at the entrance behind us.

"End them! Seize the girl, but *end* them!" Bleren bellows. I don't turn to watch as swords are unsheathed and driven through their hearts. But I hear it. I hear the moment the blade enters their skin, and the woman I thought was my mother screams for her life. I hear his heart stop, the one I thought he never had. And I wait for grief to hit me, but nothing comes.

Nothing.

It's already taken root in my chest the moment I saw the blade swipe against *his* neck.

Bleren is being shielded by a wall of ice so thick it'd take forever to melt through. It's buying enough time for guards to surround him and drag him out. I know if I kill him, Dracyl will kill everyone in front of me, and I don't have enough power to save them all anymore. Not against him. I only have enough to do what I'm about to do. They rush toward me, some stopping to stare at Jasper.

"There's not much time. Please, you need to listen to me. You are the only hope left for Agatharea. Viola, you're the next in line. Take the throne. All of you, take that kingdom by storm and bring it back to life. Take the horses in the field and go home. Don't stop until you get there. Don't look back. Don't come back for me. I love you all more than you know, and I am so sorry I couldn't do more." I don't give them time to respond. I only look each of them in their beautiful faces, before holding my hand out and blowing a hole into the wall.

The entire castle shakes with the severity of the blast, but it does the job, leading right to the field to get what they need. They don't hesitate. They only look back once before running as fast as they can into the inky black night, and I stop watching.

"I'll watch them. I've already taken care of the guards outside. The ground magically swallowed them whole. I am far enough away that Dracyl wouldn't be able to sense my power." Asteria's voice is quiet, and I know that this is killing her as much as it is me. Because this would be over in an instant if she was down here. Endure, endure, endure.

I walk forward toward River, staring at the icy dagger that somehow won't melt when I'm being frozen in place again. And not only that, but my skin becomes laden with frost, the cold sinking all the way to my bones. I'm stuck in place as more guards run in and toward me, ready to strike.

"No! I need her alive!" Bleren commands. "Bring her to me when you're done." He directs it to Dracyl, as if Dracyl will beat me. That wall of ice follows the king out as Dracyl turns to me with a smile that twists my stomach.

I let fire fill my veins again, melting me from the inside out before beckoning the pieces of stone from the blast I caused, aiming them at the guards who have come to join him. Quickly, they're unconscious or buried beneath rubble.

That's not how I wanted to use it. With the door blocked off from allowing any more guards in, I have little chance left.

Aris stirs, but they don't notice. He makes eye contact with me, and with begging eyes, I look at River.

Please.

Please take him.

I can save you both if you both leave *now*.

He seems to understand. And he hates it. He hates that in this moment he loves me enough to leave me. He loves me enough to save River so I don't have to watch another person I love die.

With the last drops of magic, I cover the room in darkness, shadowing it in the night. River's grunt fills my ears as Aris drags him away, and I don't lift that darkness until I'm sure Aris has taken him into that dark field.

Dracyl curses heavily as his vision is taken from him.

"You can't control me. My power cannot be contained." I walk toward him, letting my voice get close. I can see him, but he can't see me. Dracyl turns in my direction, his hands moving to make more sharp ice. The well within me quivers, nearing burnout, but I push on, leaving us in the void.

"Ember, you have to stop."

I can't. Not yet.

"I will destroy you," I promise as I walk toward the clearing of the wall. I don't have enough power in me to take on Dracyl. If I lift the darkness, he'd kill me despite the king's orders. I'm sure of it. I have to use this as my chance to leave now. I get to the edge when a thought slams into me so painfully I almost scream.

Using my last moments to escape, I run to Jasper's body. A sob breaks through my chest at the sight I can see even in the darkness. Dracyl is flinging dagger after dagger toward where he thinks I am. He's getting closer and closer, but the shadows are still too much for him.

With the last bit of strength given to me from Asteria and the adrenaline coursing through me, I groan as I lift his body. He's so heavy, and I would've joked with him about how many brownies he's been eating, and he would've poked me and told me only as many as I have. I only make it a few steps before my knees buckle.

I'm crying uncontrollably now because I *need* to take him with me. I can't leave him here. But he's too heavy; my power is burning me from the inside out now, and Asteria's strength is fleeting. I'm not strong enough for this on my own.

"I'm right outside, Ember. You just have to make it to the hole. I can't use my magic this close to him, or he'll know I'm here. Come

dear, let us be rid of this place." I sob in relief, laying him on the ground instead, carefully dragging him from beneath his arms. His head leans against my torso, and like this I can't see the slice in his throat.

I'm so sorry.

My sweet, silly boy.

Just help me carry you a little further.

But as if the gods were against me, one of Dracyl's icy daggers finally finds the side of my thigh, tearing at the muscle. Pain sears through me, washing down my leg, and the shadows begin to flicker.

No.

NO.

I will not let them have you.

I push past the burning soaring through my well, past the agony in my thigh, past the strain in my muscles, and scream as I take those last steps. The room sinks into shadows so dark they spill beyond, wrapping around the castle.

I drop to my knees with his body, cradling him against me in front of her.

Take him, please. We have to take him.

"*I'll hold him in my claws carefully; climb on and release your-self. We'll find your mates, and I'll take you to Ereltis, where it's safe, and a healer will save River, for I cannot heal the type of wound he has; I am not familiar with human anatomy. Now you don't ever have to come back to this place, so it won't matter if the Erelt Royals keep you there.*" I climb onto her back, wincing against my wound that isn't healing like it should because my magic isn't full. In fact, as soon as she gathers Jasper's body and she's airborne, my magic's just—gone.

"*You pushed it too far, Ember. It will come back; there's just no telling with the kind of power you have how long it'll take. It could be a day. A week. It could be a month. Your well is so big, so deep, that kind of replenishment is unheard of. It comes back all at once, so we'll have to be prepared. We might even have to keep you sepa-*

rated from others until it comes back. Replenishment can be unpre-dictable in its return."

Okay. Words elude me as I peer below us, searching for a familiar black horse that might have two bodies atop it. Ahead of us I can see a fast-paced shadow moving swiftly in the trees.

Coal! There!

Asteria swoops down, finding a clearing twenty yards ahead of them to set me down. She stays with Jasper's body, protecting him as if he were her own. She even allows herself to be visible, because where we're going they're going to have to know eventually.

"Here! I'm here!" I scream. The sound of pounding hooves against the earth nears until Coal rears up, nearly dropping Aris and River, who's lying against Aris' chest, still unconscious. The bleeding has slowed, but he's lost so much that he needs to see a healer now or it'll be too late.

Aris drops down, leaving River carefully leaning atop Coal's head before running to me, gathering me in his arms. There's a part of me that wants him and a part of me that recoils. So, I pull away and try to ignore the flash of hurt over his face.

"Are you okay?" He searches me frantically, his eyes wild with fear. The gash on his head is thick with blood already clotting, which is a good sign. The moon is bright, shining down on our dirty faces laden with tears and sweat.

"Only a gash on my leg. I need you not to ask questions right now. I need you not to protest. I just need you to follow. That's my dragon; her name is Asteria. She will eat you if you hurt me. She just told me to tell you that even though this is not the time nor the place. We are going to Ereltis for a healer. Can you follow us while we're in the sky?" Aris stares at Asteria over my head, in shock, awe, and fear.

"I love when they look at me like that." She swishes her tail, happy to be appreciated and feared all in one.

"Y-yes. Yes, I can. You're going to ride her?" He looks back at me bewildered.

"Yes. Come, we have no more time." I turn back, mounting

her as best as I can with my injured leg, and he gets back on Coal with River, holding him against his body safely.

Asteria has to fly slowly for Coal to keep up, but we're at the border quickly. Quicker than I thought. I've been so close to home this entire time, and until recently, I didn't know it. I don't dwell on it. I can't. There's no time or room in my pain to process everything else I've learned tonight.

"We can't take Jasper inside, Ember. We have to bury him out here," she says solemnly. I sigh softly, a lump forming in my throat again. Dismounting takes some time before I come to his body, a body that's become cold without life to take hold of the boy I once knew, the boy I still love.

"Can you form a grave?" I look up at her. We look around and suddenly spot a willow tree near a small creek. "Right there, underneath."

I'm vaguely aware that Aris dismounts Coal. But I can't pay attention to him as the ground shifts into a perfect rectangle, six feet deep.

Six feet to lay to rest the soul of whom would've been the best king of them all.

I want more time to lay with his body. To say goodbye. But River's dying, and I can't lose them both. So I kneel and kiss his forehead, whispering a goodbye that's only meant for Jasper. A goodbye no one else listens to. One that goes up into the heavens with him.

Asteria lowers his body into the ground and allows the soil to shift back over him, growing a border of flowers to mark his grave. In the tree, she engraves his name, permanently marking this as his resting place.

"Long Live The King
Jasper Wellington
Sweet, Silly Boy"

Sobs wrack my body again, and I promise him I'll be back.

Aris takes my hand, and I let him because if I don't, I won't go. He pulls me toward the presumed Ereltis border, and I can feel it. Even without my magic to answer its call, I can feel it pulling at my skin as if the essence it's made out of is the same as I am.

"*You and I will have to enter and plead with the guards to grant their entry.*" I nod and turn to Aris.

"You have to stay here. We need to ask for permission for you and River. Once we get that, we'll come for you. Stay with him." Aris nods, going to kiss my hand, but I pull it away before he can, moving with Asteria to step through the wards.

They press against me for a moment before sliding over me like gloss. The air on the other side is sweet, losing that sickening scent Atravelien always carries. My eyes take a moment to adjust, but when they do, my breath is stolen from me.

The night sky looks as if powder was blown onto it; the stars are strewn across it so heavily it's almost too bright to be considered nighttime. It's so green and so vibrant here. The forest we've stepped into is wet and much more humid, with vines and larger leaves strewn about. The forest has a clear path that leads straight down into a village that's lit with lamps. Lamps that have floating orbs of light within them.

"Oy! You there! State your business." The guard, who I would've expected to have been dressed in metal armor, is instead dressed in loose linen shorts and a tight shirt cut off at the shoulders. It's significantly warmer here, as if winter isn't in effect right now. He looks young, maybe a couple of years older than I am. He spoke with an accent, one I can't place my finger on, and I probably shouldn't expect to. He's got long black hair pulled into a bun atop his head, and he's very tan, as if every day is spent in the sun. Asteria steps in and speaks for me. Dragons are very respected around here.

"*We are bonded. She has two mates, one of whom is severely wounded and needs immediate entry.*" I don't know why I expected anything less, but her lips move as she speaks out loud, allowing for the guard to hear her. She keeps it simple, not giving away too much. There's so much yet to unravel. I'm not sure how anyone here is going to take my true identity yet. Even so, admitting I have *two mates* out loud seems ridiculous. Improper. But he doesn't bat an eye.

"Why don't they just come in?" He tilts his head, confused.

"They're human." I look at him with pleading eyes. "Please, he's dying, and he doesn't have much time left. He needs someone *now.*"

He looks apprehensive, confused even, as if Erelt mating with humans is unheard of. Except, my name is Ember, and apparently everything I do is unheard of. But then he's staring at me, staring deeply into my eyes as if in a trance before shaking his head like he's seen a ghost. He looks back to Asteria when she growls angrily.

"*You will be responsible for the death of her mate if you don't let him in right now. You know what the law is.*" Asteria's tone is undeniable, and the glow of her throat means she's seconds away from burning this man to a crisp. No one fucks with her girl.

"Okay! Okay," he mutters what sounds like a few curses in a language I've never heard before as he walks toward the warded border. He moves his hands in a circular motion as he mutters incoherently, but as he does, a hole in the ward begins to form.

Aris' eyes practically pop out of his head as he takes in the scene before him. But he spurs into action quickly, nudging Coal through the ward. The horse huffs nervously but bravely moves through. River groans, moving to rip the icy dagger out that *still* hasn't melted.

"No!" I run forward, stopping him from doing so. Thankfully, he falls unconscious again, his back slumping against Aris, but the wound begins to bleed again with fervor from the agitation.

The wards close, Atravelean disappearing with it, and with it the grave beyond.

"There's a healer just at the bottom of the hill in a yellow house, the best we have. Go." The guard nods at me, and I throw my arms around him, hugging him. He must not get many hugs because his body goes stiff before patting my shoulder awkwardly.

We waste no time. Asteria collects River, keeping him more steady in her claws than bouncing on Coal while I ride atop her back. Aris meets us at the bottom as we find the house the guard described.

The gravity of the situation begins to choke me as Aris helps the middle-aged woman lay River on her table.

He can't.

Gods, he can't.

How much more are you going to take from me?

How much more must I endure?

The fortune teller's words echo so loudly in my head that there can only be one in the end. But surely, this isn't the end. Not yet. Not so soon. River takes a breath, a shallow breath that nearly tears me in two. I grip his hand, wishing I could heal him myself. Wishing I hadn't expended all that magic during the week.

Aris stands in the corner, blood splattered all over him. A mixture of his own and River's surely. Maybe even Jasper's when it sprayed and he lunged for his father. He's staring at his hands, which are shaking, and there's a part of me that wants to console him and another that isn't sure I can go near him just yet. Because when I look at him right now, all I can see is his father.

All I can see is the look on Bleren's face as he *delighted* in taking Jasper's life. So I look away. Hating myself more than I ever have before.

I'm so focused on River that I don't notice when another figure walks into the room. Aris doesn't move either, but when the healer sighs in relief and says,

"Grandma, good you're awake. This... This isn't good. I'll need your insight on it." Well, that gets my attention. I look up, and I must be hallucinating.

At this point the pain of this night must be messing with my head because that's not Olga standing in front of me. Here. In Ereltis.

Except it is.

And she's staring at me.

"You know her? She's been outside of the wards to see you?"

Seems like it. But I never knew that. I thought she was homeless.

"Who are these folk?" she asks, and her warm voice floats over me. It's too much. It's all too much.

"They just need our help, Gran. We'll ask questions later." The healer looks between me and Olga. I've looked away because she obviously doesn't want her to know we know each other, and I have nothing left in me but what's left to focus on saving River.

"What's wrong with the dagger?" I bring the attention back to him.

"This dagger is imbued with dark magic." The woman's voice itself is healing. I feel as though she could look upon a wound and it would heal beneath her gaze. The skin where the dagger is protruding is black, as if it is frostbitten.

Except it's not. The veins are inky, stemming out like branches as if infected by the ice itself, which has also started to turn black, fading into the blue ice.

"What does that mean then?" I look down at his face, his brutally beautiful face that I've fallen so irrevocably in love with, and move a wet lock to the side, trailing the finger down his cheek. *River, I still have so much to say to you.*

"Save those words, Ember; he has to hear them. He will hear them." She's so sure, and even here in the safety and peace of Ereltis, she sits outside, guarding the entrance, perched like a cat.

"It means this is going to be harder than you think. It's going to take longer and many sessions to weed this magic out of his system, but it's not impossible." The healer's eyes are a soft shade of brown, much like her skin, and her hair, which is braided like Auburn's, swishes at her hips. She's every bit of a healer. Through and through. My mate's life is in her hands, and I know in my heart she can do it. I have no doubts when I look at her.

But the tether between River and me is weakening. So, I tug. I tug and tug and tug. Stay, River. Please, stay. Come back to me.

I don't know when I started to cry, but the fear that had been choking me finally lets loose the dam, and I can't stop the rush that follows.

I look down at River again, at his unconscious, bleeding body, and choke back another sob. He takes another rasping breath, but it's a breath nonetheless. He's alive, and I'm going to keep it that way. I don't give a damn what the gods and goddesses have planned for me. I don't give a fuck what our fate was *supposed* to be. I look the healer in the eyes, pleading with everything I have left in me.

"Save him."

EPILOGUE

ARIS

Gods, he is one heavy bastard. Coal gallops at a steady pace beneath us, his muscles working at a tireless pace through Atravelien. He avoids roots and branches, moving with grace no horse I've ever seen capable of. It's as if he was blessed by the gods themselves.

So it doesn't take much for me to hold River against my body, and the reins in my other hand. The dagger, if I can even call it that, is sticking out of his right side, and it should have melted by now.

For fuck's sake, magic ice?

What an absolute shitshow, and I suppose I should've known. All the signs, all the pieces were right there in front of me, but when your every thought is occupied by something else. *Someone* else. It's hard to see things for what they are.

Deep down, I'd known what and who she was, and that meant I'd known my father was right all along.

Gods, I'm a bloody fool.

The sun doesn't make eyes glow like that. That day when Madame Celine played for us, I'd watch how affected Ember was, and the music had struck a chord so deep in her that power came to the surface.

Those beautiful eyes of hers flared to life, bright as a burning flame, flickering like the fire in a hearth. I'd thought the sun was playing tricks on me. I convinced myself that's what it was, but then Auburn painted those same eyes again, and I knew. I *knew.*

Ember had power beyond my wildest dreams.

Power that went beyond making me kneel before her.

Magic that thrums in her veins, and it made sense. The day she walked into the ballroom on the Winter Solstice, she electrified the entire room. I shuddered. Me. Who normally bows for *no one*—was ready to crawl on my hands and knees for her right then and there. I felt her all the way to my bones, and I knew then that she was like no other woman I'd ever met before.

Seeing what she was capable of tonight was…incredible. It was terrifying and thrilling. But I know that she's broken. The things she saw. The things she had to do.

I pause Coal for a moment. River groans against me, and the sound constricts my chest. Godsdamn you, you stupid brute. If it weren't for you, I could go back to her, but she'd never forgive me. At this point, even if I do save you, I don't know if she'd forgive me then either.

We might've been able to avoid so much of today had I been honest with her.

Had I not let the fear of losing another woman I love get in the way.

Digging my heel into Coal, he takes off again only to kick up on his hind legs, nearly dropping River and I. I hold on with all the strength I can muster in my legs and arms, hoping I don't pop the dagger out of him in the process.

When my eyes adjust, I don't believe what I'm seeing. That can't be right.

That's not a fucking dragon.

But that is my girl, and she's screaming,

"Here! I'm here!" That's her. She's running toward me. I lean River onto Coal's head, letting his arms drop on either side to balance him before dismounting to bolt toward her.

Instantly, I'm gathering her in my arms, breathing in her sweet honey scent that even now, covered in blood, tears, and sweat, is still there wrapping around me like a blanket. She's whole, and she's alive. She's here.

Gods, please don't let this be a joke. Please. I beg of you. I know what I have done. I know what consequences I may face, but please let her be real.

Then she's pulling away all too soon, not looking at me, and the crack in my chest nearly drops me to my knees. *This is my damnation.* I can hear the gods whisper it into my ear. *Look at how you've broken her.*

"Are you okay?" It's all I can ask as I look at her, searching for any fatal wounds she might be hiding. I don't see any—except for a slice on her thigh.

"Only a gash on my leg. I need you not to ask questions right now. I need you not to protest. I just need you to follow. That's my dragon; her name is Asteria. She will eat you if you hurt me. She just told me to tell you that even though this is not the time nor the place. We are going to Ereltis for a healer. Can you follow us while we're in the sky?" Her voice sounds void of any emotion. As if right now it's just one foot in front of the other. Otherwise she'll crumble. I look at the dragon I thought was my imagination, gulping loudly.

"Y-yes. Yes, I can. You're going to ride her?" My girl...is on the back of a dragon? Who in all of the hells is she?

"Yes. Come, we have no more time." And then she's off, mounting the huge, green, serpentine beast. I have hardly any time to watch in adoration before I'm getting back on Coal.

It isn't until I look up, watching them fly, that I realize a body is hanging from the claws of the dragon, Asteria.

Oh gods.

She...

Oh *Ember*.

She managed to take his body with her.

When they land at what I guess is the border of this place,

Ereltis, she looks as if she's talking with Asteria again. There's a far-off look in her eyes, and suddenly it clicks. All of the times when she'd fall into herself, when she would go somewhere else for a moment, I just thought she was lost in thought.

This whole time she must've been conversing with her dragon. When Ember asks quietly, "Can you form a grave?" I almost lose it. I watch as Asteria moves toward a willow tree, and somehow, the earth begins to move, forming a perfect grave before she retrieves Jasper's body. She lays him inside it carefully before shifting the soil back over, and that's when I come off Coal.

Ember doesn't pay me any attention, and I stay back, letting her take her time.

She doesn't need me right now.

That thought alone is enough to kill me.

When Asteria engraves his name into the tree, she *loses* it. And gods, the sound of her cries—it tears me apart. My beautiful girl. Just as sweet and just as silly as her best friend, the twin to her flame, is breaking, and I don't know how to fix it.

I can't fix it.

I can't bring him back.

River's shallow breaths bring me back to the present. So I take her hand, pulling her toward me because if we don't go, she'll lose him too, and we can't let that happen. She's lost enough. She lets me lead her away, lets me hold her hand a little while longer, and I soak it in.

The skin of her hands burns into mine, and I relish the millions of tiny electric zaps that flood from her into me. If this is the last time she lets me touch her, then I want to commit it to memory. I want to dream about it every night until the day I die, and even then take it to the hells with me because I know my soul is too stained to see the heavens.

"You have to stay here. We need to ask for permission for you and River. Once we get that, we'll come for you. Stay with him." She's still not looking at me, but I nod nonetheless. I risk trying to kiss the knuckles of her hand, but she pulls it away before I get the chance.

True damnation.

I mount Coal with River again, pulling him against me once more. He's begun to heat up, and the labor in which he exerts to breathe is not a good sign.

"Listen, brute. You have to live. One of us has to be here to love her. One of us has to be around to help her put those pieces back together or just be there as she puts them together herself. So you can't die because it has to be you. I think we always knew it was going to be you. They always fall for the silent, brooding ones," I mutter the last part, shaking the hair out of my eyes. He only groans softly, not an indication that he understood or is even conscious. But he has to fight. He has to.

Soon enough, there's a hole being formed in the middle of Atravelien. On the other side is, I assume, the guard, even though he looks nothing like one, and Ember. Asteria huffs, an indication for me to hurry.

So we do. We get him into the healer's house, and it's all a blur. All I can do is stand to the side and watch as Ember stands beside River, looking down at him with eyes she never had for me. She's murmuring things to him. Telling him he needs to live. To fight.

I can't help but stare at the blood on my hands. The blood I may have helped spill, even if I didn't want it. *I didn't want this.* They begin to shake, and I can't stop it. I can't stop because there's something off about this place from the moment I crossed that border.

Something in me stirs, stretching like a cat waking up from a nap, opening one eye before closing it again. The shaking becomes worse, and it's like I can't breathe from the sensation swirling in me.

Then suddenly, it stops and feels like it locks back up—like it was never there.

Whatever it is, and whatever it was, must be from the adrenaline of everything going on. Shaking my head, I try to clear away the haze that filled me only moments ago. I focus on River's body and on Ember, who seems so depleted, and I realize she hasn't used a lick of that power she showed us. She looks at the healer with all the conviction, all the determination, and says,

"Save him."

ACKNOWLEDGMENTS

First and foremost, I'd like to thank my husband, Caleb, for being such a gentle and sweet listener as I wrote this. It took me years and you listened to every single crazy idea I had. You're hardly a reader and yet you took the time to read this chapter by chapter just to support me. I can't explain enough how much it means to me that you've been a part of this. You've endlessly supported me, not blinking an eye when I'd ask about the cost of things to publish this because you believed in me so thoroughly. Thank you, my love.

Thank you to my friend and editor, Friday Gervais, for editing this in the capacity you did. I couldn't have made this body of work the way it is without you. I can't wait to see you out there in the world editing more books because any author would be extremely lucky to have you looking through their work.

To Ellen H., TheAuthorAtelier, the wonderful artist who created my covers, I can not thank you enough. They turned out so beautiful and I'm so happy to share your work with the world. You took my vision and made it a masterpiece. I'm so excited to put this out there.

Thank you to Nicole Strojek and Fotini Anastopoulos, you both have been incredible whenever I asked for advice, ideas, and your thoughts on anything related to this book. Especially you, Nicole, for having read any part of this before I was done, just so I can hear your thoughts from a reader's perspective.

To my book club, you girls have been so ever-loving supportive since I told you all about this. I can't express enough gratitude to you all. I can't wait to read this as part of our book club and hear all of your thoughts.

To Anna Grigg and Erika Cuevas, you both are such a light in my life. From letting me read to you, to letting me yap non-stop, you both have been so steadfast in your support. I am so beyond grateful.

To the rest of my friends and family, thank you, thank you, thank you. Simply put, I wouldn't be where I am if it weren't for your support and constant hype. Whether it was simply following my social media pages, listening to me rant about the book, or even buying it, you all have been so incredibly kind and uplifting.

And finally, thank you to any and all of my readers. Whether you're a friend, a family member, or a newcomer, I am so beyond excited to have shared this with you and can not wait to get the next book out to you guys. I hope you enjoyed reading about these characters and this world as much as I loved creating them.

I'll see you all in Ereltis soon enough.

ABOUT THE AUTHOR

YETSIRA KATSION is a first time author, but before that she grew up in the suburbs of Chicago, and spent a lot of her time with her nose stuck in a book. Tucked in the stacks of a library, she found her home in other worlds created by her favorite authors. Yetsira has a full time job and still manages to spend most of her time reading, writing, or watching movies. She's married to her wonderful and supportive husband, Caleb Katsion, and she's the mother to their adorable, chill, and sassy cat, Dobby. (Don't worry, they gave her a sock—she is free.)

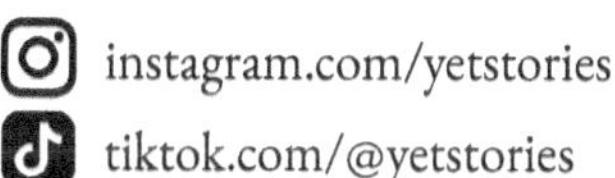

9 79899 1995313